St. Martin's Paperbacks Titles
by Barbara Pierce

COURTING THE COUNTESS

TEMPTING THE HEIRESS

WICKED
UNDER
The COVERS

BARBARA PIERCE

ST. MARTIN'S PAPERBACKS

This is a work of fiction. All of the characters, organizations and events portrayed in this novel are either products of the author's imagination or are used fictitiously.

WICKED UNDER THE COVERS

Copyright © 2006 by Barbara Pierce.

Cover photo © Shirley Green

ISBN: 0-312-34821-5
EAN: 9780312-34821-2

Printed in the United States of America

St. Martin's Paperbacks edition / July 2006

St. Martin's Paperbacks are published by St. Martin's Press, 175 Fifth Avenue, New York, NY 10010.

10 9 8 7 6 5 4 3 2

For Todd—
My partner in mischief

Love and scandal are the best sweeteners of tea.
—Henry Fielding, *Lady Matchless in Love in Several Masques*
Act 4, Scene 11 (1728)

WICKED
UNDER
The COVERS

I

Middlesex, England—March 1807

L ady Fayre Eloisa Carlisle was ruined.

The notion did not exactly strike terror in Fayre's besotted heart. Not while her body still thrummed from the lingering aftereffects of arduous lovemaking she had experienced in the arms of her lover an hour earlier. If someone had told her three months ago that she was destined to meet a gentleman who would seduce her away from her world of protocol and decorum, she would have boldly called that person a liar.

With her eyes still closed, she expelled a soft sigh of contentment, thinking of the man who slept beside her. Fayre had never experienced such a visceral reaction to a man. Lord Thatcher Standish was simply extraordinary. At five and twenty, he represented both beauty and good breeding. A veritable tower of masculinity when compared to her smaller stature, Lord Standish, with his straight, dark blond locks, soulful brown eyes, and subtle wit, had caused quite a curious buzz with the unmarried ladies of the *ton*. He was the Marquess of Pennefeather's second son, but this had not diminished his popularity with the royal court. His circle of roguish friends and amusements was vastly different from Fayre's staid sphere. It was not surprising they had not encountered each other last season. *Our chance meeting at Brighton three months ago has sealed your fate, my lord,* Fayre thought with a trace of smugness. It was later that Lord Standish had confessed that he had fallen in love with her from afar as he had observed her chatting with one of the Prince of Wales's cousins. Too familiar with ambitious suitors, Fayre had initially dismissed his favorable opinion as false flattery.

However, Lord Standish had been determined to prove himself honorable in her eyes. An evening had not passed when she could not pick his handsome face out of the crowd, those soulful eyes focused wholly on her. To her delight, he composed poetry praising her beauty, the warmth of her smile. One night before she retired, he had surprised her by appearing outside her window and serenading her with touching songs of unrequited love.

He sent her gifts. Hothouse flowers had arrived by the basket each afternoon and also small tokens of affection such as handkerchiefs with her initials stitched on them and perfume that reminded Fayre of a meadow covered in wild flowers. No gentleman had ever pursued her with such earnest and romantic fervor.

Fayre had been charmed by his devotion.

Smiling at her memories, Fayre rolled onto her back and her hand reached for the man who occupied her pleasant thoughts. Her eyes snapped open when her hand connected with the cool surface of a pillow. Bewildered, she sat up and searched the room.

She was alone. Where had he gone?

Lord Standish had boldly expressed a desire to sleep in her arms throughout the night. Everything had been arranged in advance. They had both accepted Lord and Lady Mewe's invitation to join the festivities at their country house specifically for their tryst. The party at Mewe Manor had been vastly appealing, because Fayre knew her family had chosen not to attend. This was a matter of discretion, rather than fear of what her father, the Duke of Solitea, might do to Lord Standish if he had learned she had taken him as her lover. If one considered the countless affairs both he and her mother engaged in, they might, in fact, heartily approve that she had finally begun acting like a true Carlisle.

Where had he gone?

Fayre pondered the question while she quickly dressed. Lord Standish had been so pleased they had managed this time together. They still had hours before the servants would begin their early morning tasks. Considering the risks they had taken, she could not imagine why he had not remained to enjoy the benefits.

The predawn air was frigid so Fayre picked up her shawl and wrapped it around her shoulders. She did not take a candle, trusting she could make the quick trip down the hall to Lord Standish's bedchamber without breaking her toe on a stick of furniture. Fayre was dressed only in her nightclothes; however, she had no intention of encountering anyone but her lover. The very least she could do, if he was determined to keep her honor intact by leaving early, was to tuck him into his bed and kiss him sweetly on the lips. If he wanted more, Fayre thought wickedly, she was willing to grant it.

Slowly opening her door, she winced at the mournful groan the hinges made. She froze, hoping the sound had not alerted anyone. Perhaps she should make a casual remark to the viscountess at breakfast that her staff had been neglectful of their duties. No one could possibly conduct a discreet affair with a house filled with squeaky doors. Fayre held her breath and listened. The task was almost impossible with her heart pounding and her jangling nerves. Perhaps she did not possess the Carlisle spirit after all.

The notion brought her up short. Just because she appreciated rules and had actually paid attention to the lessons she was taught, unlike her brother Tem, it did not mean she lacked spirit! Fayre was eighteen and enlightened in the ways of the jaded *ton*. She could walk down a dark passageway to her lover's bedchamber without inducing a fit of vapors.

Drawing in a determined breath, she jerked the door open. Surprisingly, the action made little sound. Encouraged, she walked through the door. Using the wall as her guide, Fayre headed for Lord Standish's chamber. She mentally counted off the doors as she shuffled past them. The situation would turn rather awkward if she knocked on the wrong door. She was sweating despite the cold air, but she viewed the entire affair as an exciting adventure.

Or she had, until she heard the sound of someone

fumbling with a doorknob. Eyes wide, Fayre almost knocked over a table in her haste to press herself closer to the wall. She managed to keep the table upright, but her right knee collided with one of the table legs. Muttering an oath and clutching the injured knee, she gaped in horror as the door opened and a sliver of candlelight illuminated a section of the passageway. Fayre hobbled behind the long, narrow rectangular table and crouched down. She prayed it would conceal her. To her dismay, even in the darkness her nightgown seemed to glow. She cursed herself for wearing a white gown. What had she been thinking? There was nothing stealthy about the color white! Her mind raced with possible explanations of why she was walking in the middle of the night half dressed and without the benefit of a candle. *Sleepwalking.* The word surfaced from the chaos in her head. Yes, she was walking in her sleep, she reasoned frantically as she watched the shadow on the floor shift and expand. It made perfect sense. She only wished it were true.

Her breath caught in her throat as a man stepped through the doorway. Good grief, it was Lord Standish. The relief she experienced was a watershed. What providence that it was the man she sought! Fayre started to rise from her crouched position, pleased that he was returning to her bedchamber. She opened her mouth to call out to him, but hesitated. Perhaps it was a trick of the light, but his expression seemed menacing as he glanced down the hall. Fayre held her breath and crouched lower.

Lord Standish peered at the darkness cloaking her, and sniffed the air like an animal. He then raised his left arm and sniffed. Had he left her to bathe? Feeling a rising sense of alarm, Fayre wondered if she was the one who was odorous? She tugged on the bodice of her nightgown and tentatively sniffed. There was nothing offensive about the garment. Relieved, she smoothed the fabric back in place. From his furtive glances at the dark passageway, Fayre assumed the candle was blinding him from seeing beyond the small circle of dim light it created. Once he was satisfied with his scent and the passageway, Lord Standish gave one final glance in her direction before heading off in the opposite direction.

Fayre's eyes narrowed at this unexpected development. Using the surface of the table for support, she stiffly stood up. If he was not returning to her bedchamber, where the devil was he going at this hour, or more importantly, to whom?

The Carlisle clan had been called many things. However, no one had ever accused them of being cowardly. Fayre was no exception. She waited until enough distance would muffle her footsteps, and then she followed her lover. The candle Lord Standish carried benefited her twofold. Not only did it allow her to keep track of the errant Lord Standish at a discreet distance, his light also revealed hidden obstacles, making her progress less treacherous.

Fayre followed him down two floors and through a part of the large house she had not visited in the light of day. Or had she? This house was so confusing in the dark. They both jumped, visibly startled by the roaring laughter that abruptly boomed from behind one of the closed doors to what Fayre assumed was the music room. It appeared not everyone had sought their beds for the night. Lord Standish seemed equally perplexed by this discovery. He stared at the door, listening to the conversation within for a few minutes before continuing through a side door.

The next corridor was so narrow Fayre assumed it was used by the servants and not the family. It was also messy. She barely avoided tripping over several canvas-covered chairs that had been stacked on top of each other. She could not fathom where Lord Standish was going. He seemed to know his way and now only rarely checked behind him to see if anyone was observing him. At times, she thought she could hear him whistling faintly.

The narrow passage opened to a long gallery. Fayre slipped behind one of the huge marble pillars that lined the gallery, accenting the full-length portraits of Lord Mewe's ancestors. Lord Standish sauntered down the long gallery without gazing at the pictures and turned left. At Arianrod, the Duke of Solitea's country estate, their gallery had no exit at the end. It was possible the viscount's gallery was designed in the same manner. Cautiously, Fayre moved silently from pillar to pillar, hoping she would not come face-to-face with Lord Standish should he circle around without her knowledge.

Fayre noticed the light that had been her wavering beacon had stilled. Lord Standish had reached his destination. As she moved closer, she heard the soft murmur of voices. Fayre ignored the sickening dread bubbling in her stomach and peered around the left corner. It took merely a glimpse to confirm her suspicions. Biting her lower lip, she retreated slowly until she was hidden behind one of the pillars framing the entrance to the small alcove. Fayre doubted that Lord Standish had seen her. He was too busy devouring the woman he had pushed against the wall.

"There is time for this later, Thatcher. What of the girl?" the woman asked when Lord Standish moved to her neck.

"I left her blissfully snoring in her bed."

Forgetting herself for just one second, Fayre's lips parted as if to challenge the fiend's outrageous lie. *By God, I do not snore!* She clapped her hand over her mouth, finding it ludicrous that she was fretting over a tiny insult when the duplicitous fraud was breaking her heart.

The woman pushed him away. "The deed is done?"

Frustrated by her resistance, Lord Standish expelled a harsh breath. He braced his hand against the wall above the woman's right shoulder. "Yes. Lady Fayre Carlisle surrendered her virginity with the carelessness of a Covent Garden whore." He grabbed her breast with his other hand and squeezed. "I did my part, Othilia. Now I want my reward."

Part? Reward? Fayre had forgotten that she had her hand clamped over her mouth until she felt the warm splash of tears on her hand. Carefully, she lowered her hand. Her fingers curled and unfurled at her side, betraying her agitation. She risked another peek.

"Seducing the little paragon of virtue is only the first act of our little drama." The woman panted, and tilted her head back so he could feast on her succulent mouth. She evaded his next foray and wickedly smiled. "Oh, how I wish I could have arranged for Solitea to come upon you just as you deflowered his precious daughter. His devastation might have kept me smiling for years."

The man Fayre had believed she had fallen in love with snorted with laughter. "Though not very practical, my love, when the duke gelds me." He ground his pelvis against her. "I know you would miss my rod almost as much as I." The woman pulled his face to her breasts, while his hand curled possessively over her rounded hip.

Fayre pressed her cheek against the chilled marble and silently wept. Her slender frame shook with repressed grief. She was so distracted by Lord Standish's betrayal, it had taken her several minutes before she recalled the woman's name. Othilia, he had called her. She only knew of one lady who bore the first name Othilia, and that was Lady Hipgrave.

She was also her father's mistress.

Or had been. Fayre rubbed her brow, feeling the stirrings of a headache. She would be the first to admit that she had stopped paying attention to her sire's current companions years ago.

"Not here," the countess huskily murmured, though she was hardly discouraging him. "We might be discovered."

"That did not stop us from enjoying Mewe's conservatory last evening." He had been steadily working his hand down to the hem of her skirt. A good portion of her leg was exposed.

"We have plans to make, Thatcher," Lady Hipgrave explained, widening her legs slightly to accommodate his exploring hand. "Despoiling the little virgin was just the prelude. Now the *ton* must learn what naughty games the Carlisle chit has been playing in your bed."

Standish stopped nibbling on the woman's shoulder. Lifting his head, he said, "Is that necessary? As it stands, her brother will be issuing challenges every time I step out of my house."

Fayre ground her teeth at the countess's trill of laughter. Wiping her eyes with her fingers, she hugged the marble pillar and listened.

"Not likely. Lord Temmes is almost as depraved as his father with regard to his liaisons. It would be rather hypocritical of him to accuse a gentleman of debauchery when he has seduced his fair share of innocents."

Lord Standish shook his head, unconvinced. "Not when that innocent is his sister," he countered.

"Darling, there is no such creature as an innocent Carlisle," Lady Hipgrave purred. "Lady Fayre's downfall was sadly inevitable. I should know. His Grace has shared my bed off and on for eight years."

The countess had only been twenty when Fayre's father had seduced her. Even if Lady Hipgrave had been a virgin when she climbed into the duke's bed, no one could ever convince Fayre that she had not been there willingly. Fayre knew enough about the young countess to form an unflattering opinion of her character. There had been rumors when she was younger that she had been the Prince of Wales's mistress first. How she had gained the duke's attentions was a favorite tale of the gossips. Fayre had heard several versions. One version ended with the prince growing bored with her and discarding her for another. The countess, in retaliation, had set her sights on the duke as a means of slighting the heir to the throne. Another version was more dramatic. It pitted both gentlemen against each other for the lady's affections. If one believed the gossip, there had been a very public argument, the details of which varied with each storyteller. In the end, she had chosen the duke over the Prince of Wales.

Even eight years ago, at the tender age of ten and tucked away with her governess at Arianrod, Fayre had heard the servants talk about her father and his beautiful mistress. The lady's machinations had even roused her mother's ire, Fayre recalled, and she knew of no other woman who was more tolerant of her husband's infidelities.

For generations the Carlisle males had been notorious for two things: their illicit love affairs and their equally dramatic deaths. With the exception of her father, Fayre could not think of one male ancestor who had inherited the title who had not died before his fortieth birthday. As a child, she had worried about what the servants had referred to as the Solitea curse. Nevertheless, her father had lived past his fortieth birthday and beyond. Considering his choice in mistresses, Fayre decided this feat was nothing short of a miracle.

The sound of Lord Standish's voice brought Fayre back to the present.

"I regret telling you about Jinny and Solitea. You think of nothing else these days," he complained.

"Even if you had not told me that the duke had invited that bitch to his bed, someone else would have been pleased to share the good news with me." Lady Hipgrave stroked his face in a soothing gesture.

There was a wealth of bitterness in the countess's voice. Fayre might have sympathized if the lady had not maliciously sent one of her lovers to Fayre as an emissary of revenge for her father's misdeeds. Fayre wrapped her arms around herself in a comforting gesture. Everything Lord Standish had said to her was a lie. Their courtship had never been about love. He had never felt anything for her. Fayre faced the truth unflinchingly, letting the pain wash through her. She needed to be using her head, not mourning the loss of an illusion.

Fayre suspected she knew this Jinny of whom Lord Standish spoke, though she knew the woman as Lady Talemon. Four years younger than Lady Hipgrave, the ambitious young lady had married her earl when she was sixteen. She had buried him when she was nineteen. The widow had grieved for her husband and then gone on to make the most of her title and money. She moved within the high echelon of the *ton*, spending her time dallying with the royal princes and their friends. Her beauty and liaisons had garnered her many enemies, including Lady Hipgrave.

It must have galled the countess when the Duke of Solitea had chosen a younger, prettier rival as his latest companion. A predator in the truest sense, the countess had attacked who she had perceived was the weakest Carlisle. Fayre wiped away the tears she could not will away. Oh, she could not fault Lady Hipgrave for viewing her as a means to hurt the duke. However, the lady had underestimated her prey. Fayre was far from helpless and she was liable to strike back if provoked.

There was no doubt she had stepped beyond feeling provoked. She felt murderous. Unlike her family, she had never permitted herself to be caught up in the illusion of love. It was that fact alone that had made Lord Standish unique. The feelings she had felt for him now shamed her. She could not decide who she despised more, the two people who were trying to ruin her, or herself for allowing them to do so.

"It must be public," Lady Hipgrave murmured.

Lord Standish swore aloud. "My God, woman, you are fondling my balls in front of Mewe's ugly ancestors. How public must it be before you let me have you?"

"Not us," the countess protested with a laugh. "The Carlisle chit. When you cast her aside, I want you to do it in front of witnesses. I suppose the young fool fancies herself in love with you?"

"Completely." His firm assurance was a knife in Fayre's heart. He shoved the countess's skirt higher. "There are few women who can resist my, ah, charms."

There was an unspoken challenge in the countess's eyes. "Except me."

"Oh, I think I have something here that will persuade

you, sweet Othilia." Lord Standish had his back to Fayre, but there was little doubt of his intentions.

Lady Hipgrave squirmed in his arms in an effort to hold him off. "In public, Thatcher."

"Yes, in public. I promise. Now let me have you," he entreated.

"I want her devastated. She will be both mocked and pitied by the *ton* for her fall from grace. I will settle for nothing less."

"Lady Fayre's tears will taste of wormwood," he vowed, kissing her harshly on the mouth. "She will embrace sorrow as a lover, and take no other man to her bed for the rest of her life."

"Is there no limit to your arrogance?" the countess marveled with approval twinkling in her eyes.

"Absolutely none. Permit me to demonstrate." Lord Standish shoved the countess against the wall. She made a startled sound, which turned into a moan as he thrust into her.

Fayre watched the rutting couple dispassionately. The coldness of the night seeped into her bones. She told herself to slip away quietly while they were preoccupied. Confronting the pair served no purpose, and in her present state, she was likely to do or say something she might later regret.

Leave.

It was a sensible notion. Unfortunately, she was not feeling particularly sensible at the moment.

Fayre used the marble pillar for support as she walked out into the open. "You make the most unusual sounds when you are in the throes of passion, my lord. It reminds me of a boar rooting for scraps of garbage in the filthy muck. Do you not agree, Lady Hipgrave?"

"Damn me!" Lord Standish exclaimed, glancing at Fayre in genuine disbelief. He was completely undone by her sudden appearance. "W-what the hell are you doing?" He jerked himself out of the countess and tried to stuff his turgid member back into his breeches.

"I beg your pardon for interrupting. My ears are weary from listening to the pair of you drone on and on." Fayre admired the blasé inflection she managed, while she felt raw and bleeding inside. There was simply nothing she could do about either her tear-ravaged face, or the tremor in her hands. "Regardless, I have been rude for interrupting. Please carry on, my lord. I know from personal experience your ardor is regrettably brief."

Lady Hipgrave pulled her bodice up, covering her exposed breasts. "I have noticed this lamentable problem as well, Lady Fayre," she said, shaking out her wrinkled skirt so that it covered her legs. The countess ignored her lover's protest. "Still, a beautiful man like Thatcher has other uses."

"Like sending him to seduce an innocent woman who has done nothing to you."

The older woman did not even bother to feign ignorance. "You should be grateful I chose our Lord Standish to be your first lover. There are others who match his beauty, but are not . . . shall we say, as gentle."

Fayre glared at Lord Standish, wishing she could not recall that he had been indeed a tender lover. But he had claimed her innocence and it had been nothing more than a task for him, like writing a letter or currying his favorite stallion. "There is a name for gentlemen like you."

Once he had buttoned the falls on his breeches, Lord Standish turned to face her. His dark-blond hair was in damp disarray and there was a slight coloring on his cheek. Fayre suspected it had more to do with her interrupting his labors than shame.

"And what is it, my lady? Disreputable rake? Liar?" he defiantly taunted.

She stepped closer into the light and searched his face. Fayre wanted desperately to see some tiny sign that he regretted the part he had played in hurting her. She shook her head, saddened that all she saw was outraged arrogance. "No, my lord. Lady Hipgrave's trull."

The pinkish hue on his cheeks darkened at her insult. The corner of his mouth twitched. "You are the one who behaved no better than a doxy, Lady Fayre. Though considering who your mother is, I expected no less. Or should I say, I expected more."

The composure she had managed snapped its tenuous tether. Blinded by fury, she struck him across the face. The impact had him staggering into Lady Hipgrave. "Leave my family out of this!"

The countess shoved Lord Standish away. "Oh, I fear I cannot comply, my dear girl. It will spoil my fun."

Fayre's hands curled into fists. The voluptuous Lady Hipgrave was six inches taller and outweighed her by several stone. Her disadvantage was not going to stop her from bloodying the woman's pouting lower lip. Fayre took a menacing step toward the countess.

From behind someone seized her roughly by the shoulder. She whirled and snarled at the offending hand.

"Ho, what do we have here?" her host, Lord Mewe, demanded in a cheerfully slurring voice. He was not alone. The five gentlemen and three women standing behind him gaped in undisguised fascination at the scene they had interrupted.

Lord Standish glared at all of them, the imprint of

Fayre's hand burning on his left cheek. "Mewe, I thought you passed out hours ago," he said, visibly struggling to appear nonchalant.

"Balderdash! I never pass out. Besides, you supposedly retired hours ago so how would you know?" The viscount gave Standish an exaggerated wink. "Taking 'em on in pairs, are we now?"

Fayre deliberately took a deep breath and tried to slow down her breathing. She pulled her shawl tighter, suddenly aware of her half-dressed state. "My lord, this is very awkward."

"Calm yourself, child." Lord Mewe patted her shoulder and withdrew his hand. "You are among friends. There is no need for explanations."

"But my lord, I feel I must. I—" Fayre's confidence wavered as she glimpsed Lady Hipgrave's expression. The woman did not seem bothered that their host and several guests had stumbled across them. In fact, the countess's eyes gleamed with merriment. One would have thought the woman had been granted her fondest wish.

Perhaps she had.

"What we must do is retire," the countess finished Fayre's sentence. "I for one am exhausted." Her inflection hinted at a double meaning to her innocuous words. Several of the gentlemen behind Lord Mewe chuckled behind their closed fists.

Fayre shifted her gaze from one guest to the next, confirming her worst fears, for their faces were as easy to read as the *Morning Post*. They had put the vilest twist on what had occurred between the threesome. If any of them had doubts, she was certain Lady Hipgrave and Lord Standish would serve up enough half-truths to confirm their suspicions. By breakfast everyone in the household would know she was involved in some sordid affair with Lord Standish and her father's ex-mistress. Fayre despaired, worrying that the gossip would reach London before she managed the journey by coach.

Fayre cleared her throat, and gave her host an appealing glance. "I suppose you would not believe I have a problem with sleepwalking."

Everyone roared with laughter.

Oh, God.

She was ruined!

2

"What are you doing here?"

The question was not directed at Maccus Knight Brawley. Even so, he lowered the newspaper he held out in front of him and lifted his brow at the young lady who had inspired the anger infused within the older woman's whispered query.

In truth, he had lost interest in the paper the instant *she* had entered the restaurant dressed in a crisp dark-blue spencer worn over a cambric walking dress with lace ruff. Her face lacked artifice and had a youthful glow. He doubted she had celebrated her twentieth birthday, while twenty-seven had passed for him. When she had entered the restaurant, a shaft of sunlight had haloed her slender figure as she searched the room for her companion. Maccus had never considered himself poetic in the slightest. Nevertheless, if someone had asked him to describe her in that moment, he would have said that she reminded him of spring. She wore sunlight like other ladies donned a cloak. His mystery lady was too far away to ascertain the color of her eyes; however, her hair was an unusual color. It was cinnamon in hue, and yet possessed an inner fire he could not put words to. Tiny corkscrew ringlets framed her face and, like most of the ladies present, she had the majority of her tresses tucked away within a cottage bonnet. He would have offered her anything just to see her remove her bonnet. A hunger he had never felt before rose within him. The intensity of it astounded him. He crushed a section of the newspaper in his hand when her eyes betrayed her delight at spotting her companion. Maccus hoped she did not belong to another man. He wanted the petite, celestial creature for himself.

Smiling at someone beyond his left shoulder, she passed his table leaving her scent drifting on the air. He closed his eyes and the image of a meadow blooming with vibrant color came to mind. How his friends and business associates would have collapsed in a fit of laughter if he had voiced his musings aloud. Maccus was determined to learn the lady's name. He considered it fortuitous that her companion was seated within earshot.

"You have no business parading about town as if—"

"As if what, Mama?" the younger woman demanded in a pleasant, albeit exasperated tone.

Maccus shifted and glanced over his shoulder. Seeing them together, he noted a slight resemblance between mother and daughter. They shared the same nose, and tilted their chins in the same haughty manner. Both women put aside their argument when a waiter approached them. The mystery lady in the blue spencer politely declined all offers the waiter suggested and sent him away. The man passed by his table with a silly grin on his face. Maccus sympathized with the waiter. He might have worn a similar smitten expression if she had deigned to speak with him.

The younger woman held up a silencing hand. "Have a care as to how you answer that question," she warned, continuing the argument the waiter had interrupted. "Otherwise our conversation will be repeated at every ball this evening."

The older woman sagged in her chair, conceding defeat. "Oh, Fayre, my darling daughter, you are correct. I do not know what has come over me of late. Ever since—"

"Not now, Mama," Fayre said, cutting off her mother's words. As if sensing his interest, her gaze shifted and unexpectedly focused directly on Maccus. The impact of that intelligent perusal left him breathless. With a dismissive sniff, her attention switched back to her mother. "Papa has returned. He desires a word with all of us. I thought it best that I be the one who searched for you."

"Your father never thinks these matters through. He should have locked you in your room and sent your brother out to find me."

"When I left, my brother had not arrived at the town house. Besides, I was not certain if I would find you alone or . . ." She shrugged daintily, not bothering to finish her thought.

Her mother brought her gloved hand up to her face and

gasped. There was latent humor and a hint of mischief in her expression when she said, "Oh . . . Oh, I see."

Maccus clearly did not. Something unspoken had passed between the two ladies.

"Quite right," the daughter said crisply. "Appreciate the fact I occasionally do possess some sense. Come along, Mama. We can face Papa together."

Maccus discreetly observed the two women leave. Intriguing. His mystery lady possessed a few secrets. Even more fascinating was that he had not been the only patron observing the exchange between mother and daughter. After the ladies had departed, the chatter in the room escalated to a noticeable degree.

Secrets.

Maccus had a few of his own. He also had an abundant curiosity and natural talent for ferreting out what others preferred to keep buried. Setting aside his newspaper, he clasped his hands together. Her name was Fayre. Money would gain him her entire name before he paid his bill. Learning more about the lady's private business would take a little longer. It did not matter how long it took. He was a patient man.

An image of her face appeared in his mind. He wondered if she had ever allowed a lover to remove the pins from her hair, had permitted him to slip his hands through that thick, fragrant bounty of cinnamon and savor its silkiness against his heated flesh. Maccus felt his cock harden in response.

He growled in frustration at his lack of control. His desires in the past had been merely goals he attained through careful planning and ruthless execution when he had the advantage.

He did not allow them to govern him.
Until now.

Fayre had not tarried at Mewe Manor. The thought of enduring breakfast, of sitting at the same table with Lord Standish and Lady Hipgrave—she shivered in reaction. Two hours after the dreadful encounter in the alcove, she had departed the manor.

It was on the journey back to Arianrod that she permitted herself to grieve. She could not recall much about the journey. By the time she had arrived at the family's estate, Fayre had dried her tears and a comfortable numbness had eased her pain. To her immense relief, her family had already settled in London. Perhaps it had been cowardly, but she remained at Arianrod for ten days. She used the healing solitude to reflect on her encounters with Lord Standish and the words they had exchanged.

By the time she could see London on the horizon Fayre was prepared to face the gossips. What strengthened her resolve was the fact that she knew she would have the support of her family. Above all others, they would certainly understand how she had gotten herself into this unfortunate predicament.

Her family had not understood.

It was also her humble opinion that they were extremely hypocritical when one added up the sum total of their failed love affairs. In light of her father's temper, she wisely kept her opinion to herself.

"Bloody hell!" her father roared for the hundredth time. He had not been rational since he had learned of her involvement with the Marquess of Pennefeather's second son. "Standish, of all gentlemen. How could you have chosen such a bounder as a lover?"

He chose me, Papa, she forlornly thought. Fayre had concluded during her time at Arianrod not to reveal all the sordid details she had learned from Lady Hipgrave and Lord Standish. The countess had succeeded in hurting her and there was nothing she could do to change the fact she had loved unwisely. She could, however, shield her father from learning that his careless dismissal of his lover had triggered her current predicament. Fayre loved him too dearly to cause him pain. As long as she remained silent, she was denying Lady Hipgrave her coup de grâce. She took comfort in that small triumph over the vindictive woman.

"Answer me!"

Fayre was sitting sideways on the sofa with her head facedown against her bent arm. She wearily raised her head and blinked. "The three of you have been ranting and issuing threats for hours, Papa. I doubt you have heard a single word I have said."

"I will listen to you when you stop spouting nonsense," her father countered, his fury battering her like a surging sea in a storm. "Tell me that Standish took you against your will. I promise, the man will not live to see another dawn."

It was a pleasant thought. Especially since the love she had felt for Lord Standish had withered in the face of adversity. Betrayal and revenge tended to dampen a lady's ardor. "For your sake, I wish I could make such a confession. To my utter regret, I went to him willingly."

"I will call him out," her brother said, having spent the past hour in brooding silence with his arms crossed against his torso.

Fayre was finding his incessant staring annoying. His given name was Fayne, but he was also the Marquess of Temmes. To family and close friends, he was simply Tem. They resembled each other in looks; both had inherited the unusual reddish-brown hair and handsomeness from their Carlisle ancestors. Beyond sharing a few physical traits, she and her brother had nothing in common. As a child she had tried not to become too attached to him. After all, she had reasoned, if the Solitea curse were real, he was destined to die tragically young.

"No, Tem, you cannot call him out. I was willing. I was also a fool. Leave Standish alone," Fayre snapped at her brother.

Her brother pushed away from the wall and moved closer to their father. At twenty-three, he matched their sire in height, but he had the muscled leanness of youth. He had also inherited the Carlisle appetite for sport. Tem's favorite wore silk and muslin. Fayre realized even his frown was identical to their father's. She found both of them extremely intimidating.

"You love him," Tem said flatly. His expression plainly revealed her folly was beyond his comprehension. "Have you heard the lies he is spreading about you throughout London?"

She laughed bitterly. Fayre had heard the rumors. Letters from numerous acquaintances had begun arriving days before her arrival in London. The missives varied in tone from curious to smug. There were several individuals in particular who seemed to take pleasure in sharing the viscount's version of events. "No, brother, I do not love Lord Standish. Nor do I care what tales he tells."

"Well, you should," her father said. His face was a mottled unflattering red. "He has made a mockery of the

Carlisle name, daughter. For that alone I should rip your great-grandfather's sword down from its mounting on the wall and pierce the bastard's heart!" He tilted his head and gave her a pitying glance. "I thought you were cut of different cloth, my dear girl. Better than the rest of us. When Standish has finished ruining your good name with his outlandish tales, you will just be another cautionary tale for every green miss enjoying her first season."

Fayre chewed on her lip, hurt by her father's bluntness. "And here I thought you would be pleased that I was carrying on in the spirit of the Carlisle tradition," she muttered waspishly.

Tem closed his eyes and shook his head in dismay at her audacity. A strangling sound gurgled in her father's throat and Fayre straightened from her slouched martyred position, truly concerned about his health.

Her mother inadvertently spared her from her father's explosive wrath. Much to Fayre's disgust her mother had spent most of the family interrogation weeping.

"We must accept that our Fayre is ruined in the eyes of polite society," the duchess said, her voice wobbling as she dabbed at her eyes with a handkerchief. "This is hardly the time for recriminations. We need to be thinking of her future."

Fayre frowned. Her mother said the word *future* as she would the phrase *sentenced to death*.

"What future?" the duke demanded. "I can think of a dozen respectable gentlemen who would not take her now!"

"And I can think of a dozen not-so-respectable who would, now that Standish has had her," Tem murmured lazily.

The duchess gasped. It was not his observation that

shocked her mother, but rather that Tem had spoken so boldly in front of the one Carlisle who was once considered respectable. The hypocrites were genuinely *disappointed* in her. Fayre glared at her brother. She liked him much better when he was brooding—and silent. "You are not helping matters, *Fayne*," she said, deliberately using the whimsical name that matched her own just to annoy him. If he uttered another word, she vowed she would pick up Great-grandfather's sword herself.

"Carlisle, my love, is there nothing we can do to stanch the damage Standish has done?" her mother asked, hiccupping into her handkerchief.

"She could marry the bastard."

Fayre's fingers curled into claws and scraped against the fabric of the sofa. "No, I will not marry the bastard. Nor am I retiring to Arianrod, Mama," she said, anticipating her next suggestion.

"I hear Italy is rather pleasant this time of year," her mother said, unwilling to give up her notion of exile.

She rubbed her temple. The calm Fayre had tried to maintain was deteriorating with her growing frustration. "For how long? A season? A year? The next fifty years?"

Her father slammed his fist several times down on the table beside her. A vase and several porcelain creatures jumped with the thundering impact of his heavy fist. The tiny treasures shattered one by one as they hopped over the edge and struck the floor. "I will kill him for seducing you," her father growled, finally regaining his speech. It was a shame his reasoning had cracked along with the fragile gewgaws.

Her mother sniffed into her handkerchief. "I had such high ambitions for you, my daughter. However, Fayre, your stubbornness leaves us with only one option. We marry you off as quickly as we can. Mayhap to an older gentleman from the north; someone who does not keep up with town news?"

She grimaced at the hope in her mother's voice. Tem, curse him, baldly laughed. "Mama, you have overlooked one other choice," Fayre said with icy determination. "I can remain in London for the season."

3

"And how did your mother and father react to your announcement that you planned to remain in town for the duration of the season?"

Fayre gave her friend Miss Callie Mableward a mischievous grin. Four days had passed since she had told her family that she refused to retire to the country. Her mother had not spoken a word to her since their argument. Tem had disappeared almost immediately. She considered his absence a blessing. Two days had gone by since she had last seen her father. Fayre assumed the duke was off dallying with his latest mistress. If that particular lady was Lady Talemon, then she hoped Lady Hipgrave was gnashing her teeth with frustration. By the time Callie's invitation to ride with her at Hyde Park had arrived, Fayre had been eager to escape the solitude of the town house.

Fayre expelled a weary sigh. "Oh, you know how stubborn I can be when I have my mind set on something. What could they say?"

Callie pursed her lips in contemplation. "Your family is not speaking to you."

Fayre's lips parted in surprise. "How did you know?"

Callie sighed. "Lord Temmes told me."

She lifted her brow, astounded by her brother's gall. "Tem told you? How is this possible? I have not seen my brother since the night the three of them tried to ship me off to Italy for the rest of my life."

Her friend fidgeted, clearly uncomfortable with the subject. "Do not be angry, Fayre. For all his faults, I believe he is genuinely concerned about you."

Fayre clutched Callie's hand and squeezed her fingers encouragingly. "Tell me everything about your visit with my brother."

He could not believe his luck, Maccus thought as the two women passed them in the opposite direction. Then again, he was a man who fashioned his own luck. It was no mere chance he rode his horse each afternoon through Hyde Park. He had been searching for a certain lady, one who he knew possessed hair the color of cinnamon fire. As he had predicted, he had gained the mysterious Fayre's full name before he had departed the restaurant where he had first seen her bathed in sunlight. Lady Fayre Carlisle. She was the Duke of Solitea's daughter. He chuckled softly. His goals had definitely become loftier since he had settled in London.

Maccus subtly maneuvered his gelding closer to his riding companion this afternoon. Lewth Prettejohn, Viscount Yemant, had the dubious honor of being the first acquaintance Maccus had established in the new life he had made for himself in London. The viscount was contemplative in temperament, lacking the boisterous excess of many of his peers. This did not mean his company was soporific. Indeed, the man possessed a cultivated intelligence that Maccus privately envied. Their connection had been unplanned. Maccus had been sitting in a coffeehouse two months earlier, reading his newspaper and blatantly listening to the heated discussion about the impact of a recent trade tariff. While others pounded their fists and shouted their opinions to the group, it was Lord Yemant's calm, authoritative voice that held sway.

Impressed, Maccus later struck up a conversation with the gentleman. They discovered that afternoon that they shared similar opinions on several subjects and a tentative friendship was formed. The following week, the young lord invited Maccus to join him at the coffeehouse. Yemant did not speak much about his personal life, and Maccus felt no inclination to pry; at least, not so transparently. Life had taught him never to underestimate a man, no matter how expensive his tailor or how tutored his intellect.

It took a few discreet inquiries to learn that Lord Yemant's refined circumstances were fairly recent. The title had originally passed on to the gentleman's uncle. His father had been the third son to the unlucky Prettejohns. The young viscount had already lost his sire and one uncle, when the previous Lord Yemant fell down a flight of stairs and died from his injuries. Maccus had wondered, albeit briefly, if his successor had had a hand in his uncle's death. He dismissed the sinister notion almost immediately. Young Yemant tended to be fanciful in his theories, but he was a scholar at heart, not a cold-blooded murderer.

Nodding vaguely behind him, Maccus asked, "By chance did you notice the carriage we just passed?"

Lord Yemant adjusted his hat out of habit, and glanced back at the equipage that had caught his companion's interest. He grinned slightly as he straightened. "A fine carriage, indeed, Brawley," he drawled. "Thinking about investing in one?"

"And here I credited you with some passable wit, Yemant," Maccus replied dryly, knowing his friend was poking at him. "I was referring to the fancy muslin garnishing it; specifically, the one holding the blue parasol."

The viscount chuckled. "I admire your aspirations, not to mention your refined taste, my friend. Though I wager the Duke of Solitea's daughter would bristle at being described as fancy muslin."

"Solitea, you say? I have heard a few amusing tales about that clan," Maccus admitted casually.

"Just a few? If you decide to remain in town, the gossips will fill your ears about the Dukes of Solitea."

"The dukedom is rather old, I take it?"

"Unlike many of the gentlemen who have inherited the title," Yemant quipped. "The males of the clan have a tangled, albeit reckless history."

He glanced back at the carriage, but the growing distance made the ladies indistinguishable. "And what of the Solitea women?"

"Most are just as wild and excessive as the men. So-litea's daughter, Lady Fayre, seemed the rare exception, at least until recently," the viscount said, his brow furrowing. "The debacle with Standish has tainted her good standing with the *ton,* or so it appears, depending on whose side you support."

"I am not familiar with Standish, though I assume Lady Fayre is? Intimately." To Maccus's surprise, the rud-diness of Yemant's cheeks deepened at the bald statement.

"I prefer not to besmirch the poor lady further by adding to the speculation making the rounds," the other man said tersely. "Whatever her sins, she is suffering both publicly and privately for them."

Maccus quirked his brow questioningly at the vis-count's vehement defense. He wondered if Lady Fayre knew Yemant was halfway in love with her. The realiza-tion irked him for some undefined reason.

"For a scholar, you assume the mantle of knight with ease." Coming to a private decision, he maneuvered his horse so that Yemant was forced to halt. "Introduce me to the lady who is worthy of your virtuous devotion."

Before the Lord Yemant could sputter out his polite re-fusal, Maccus had them reversing their direction and the horses closing the distance between him and his beautiful quarry.

Slow-moving shadows of dappled sunlight moved across Fayre and Callie's skirts from the tree branches over-head as the carriage bumped and rattled through the park. It had turned out to be a charming afternoon. The park was brimming with carriages and strolling pedestrians. If Fayre had not been so blinded by her brother's interference, she might have noticed the knowing looks and whispers her presence in the park had incited.

"The Solitea heirs rarely live to see gray in their hair. Whether he perishes by my hand now or is taken later by fate is of little consequence," she said, pondering her dark thoughts aloud.

"Fayre, you are being unreasonable," Callie muttered, exasperated by her companion's churlish behavior.

Fayre pouted. "That is due to the fact that I am not feeling particularly reasonable."

What she truly wanted was to stand up and scream out her frustration. The carriage approaching them quelled any irrational actions. Years of practiced etiquette forced her to smile at the two ladies. She recognized the ladies, but did not know them personally. They stared at her boldly and neither returned her silent greeting. The muscles in her cheeks tightened painfully as she watched the young woman on the right turn to her companion and whisper into the older woman's ear. As the two carriages passed each other, Fayre heard the words *Standish* and *ruined*. Even the sound of their rattling carriage could not dim their tittering. They were probably eager to share the news with their friends that foolish Lady Fayre had dared to show her face in public.

Fayre felt her face prickle with the heat of humiliation. The need to lash out at her accusers and the curious put a fine edge to her temper so she redirected it at the person least likely to cause her more trouble—her brother. "I still cannot believe Tem called on you with the intention of bribing you to spend the afternoon with me."

"Naturally, I refused the bribe," her friend swiftly replied, attempting to diffuse Fayre's outrage. "I am here merely as your friend, Fayre. Despite the stir your liaison with Lord Standish has created, I would not be surprised if you have other supporters."

"My brother still had no right to pull you into our current family spectacle like this, Callie," Fayre said flatly, unwilling to allow the tiny fact that her friend's support was genuine and not procured with Solitea gold appease her. "He has spent a large portion of his life ignoring me in pursuit of pleasure. I cannot fathom why he would suddenly change his ways."

Callie reached out for Fayre's hand and clasped it. Fayre blinked at the surprising strength of her friend's dainty fingers. Callie's eyes, a warm chocolate hue, were earnest and direct when their gazes met. "In spite of his feckless ways, perhaps Lord Temmes could not ignore his sister's pain."

Fayre dismissed the suggestion with a soft unladylike snort, ignoring the quick twist of pain in her chest. It would have been so simple to succumb to the misery she refused to reveal to anyone, including her family. Nevertheless, this was her private burden to bear and it would not do to falter. "Pain? That is a tad dramatic, do you not think? Standish has bruised my pride, nothing more. I find his lies extremely irksome. Tem's inference merely lends credence to Standish's boorish tales."

Callie gave her a doubtful glance. "If you say so."

Fayre shifted her attention away from Callie. Her friend was too polite to speak it aloud but her pitying expression called her a liar. She lifted her chin as she watched yet another pedestrian point at their carriage. Willing the sting of tears away, she vowed privately to herself that she could cry out her fury and pain later when there was no one to see her resolve crumble.

"Good day, ladies. It is an enchanting afternoon for a

carriage ride. Might I and my companion ride beside you for a time?"

Fayre inclined her head, acknowledging the man's greeting. Although tears were blurring her vision, preventing her from seeing the two gentlemen clearly, she recognized the distinct voice of Lord Yemant. He and his male companion kept pace with their carriage so she saw no reason to order her coachman to halt. If she were lucky, the gentlemen might become bored and ride onward.

"Yes, indeed, a remarkable afternoon," Lord Yemant said cheerfully, echoing his earlier statement. "I vow we have encountered a third of the *ton* on this dusty rut alone."

The flirtatious ladies of the *ton* called him "Pretty John," a witty play on his family name. His elegant features complemented his nickname. His face was long and his chin ended in a rounded point. There was intelligence in his blue eyes and a hint of a smile that made the observer long for it to fully bloom. She knew firsthand how engaging he could be when he let down his guard. His hair was a medium brown that reminded her of tea. The cut was short and fashionable.

Fayre had encountered him on several occasions. Each time, the viscount had been an unerringly polite dance partner and had possessed a reserve that bordered on endearingly shy. She also could not fathom why he would approach her so publicly. "I agree with your assessment, my lord. The afternoon has been most agreeable." A pity she could not say the same for her life. "It has been some time since we last saw each other. I trust you are well?"

"Indeed, my lady. Like you and your companion, my friend and I could not resist taking advantage of such a pleasant day."

Realizing she was behaving rudely, she introduced

Callie to the gentlemen. Wary that her eyes bore evidence
of tears, Fayre had yet to allow her gaze to settle directly
on Lord Yemant or his friend. Feigning interest in their
surroundings, she listened to Lord Yemant's rambling account of his day. His nervousness was unexpectedly
draining, and Fayre felt the need to think of a polite excuse to dismiss them.

A discreet cough from the viscount's companion had
the gentleman wincing. "Forgive me, I have been remiss,
ladies. Lady Fayre and Miss Mableward, may I present
Mr. Maccus Brawley."

As Lord Yemant finished his introduction, Fayre was
beginning to feel like herself again—until she focused her
attention on Mr. Brawley. She sucked in her breath, startled to discover that his assessing gaze was fixed on her.
Callie, oblivious to their silent appraisal of each other,
was saying something to Lord Yemant. Fayre barely paid
attention to her friend's cheerful chatter. If Fayre had not
been still suffering over the betrayal of Standish and his
mistress, she might have conceded that Mr. Maccus Brawley was a dangerously handsome gentleman.

Although the cut of his coat was as fashionable as the
viscount's, the man reminded her of a buccaneer. His hair
was straight and the color of jet. Strands of hair spiked
from beneath his hat, some of the longer lengths around
his face brushed his high cheekbones, adding a roguish
flair. Unlike Lord Yemant, Mr. Brawley defied current
fashion by keeping the hair at his back longer. It was tied
in a neat queue. Fayre's gaze drifted back to his face. His
skin was darker than his companion's. The limited
amount of flesh exposed made it impossible to determine
whether or not the sun had tanned him or he could claim

Mediterranean blood. There was an exotic beauty to his features, emphasized by a slim moustache outlining his full lips and a shadow of stubble on his chin. *Does the man not have a dependable valet?* she wondered, and then mentally chastised herself for her curiosity. Fayre usually viewed facial hair on a gentleman as repellant. For some reason, she thought it seemed fitting on Mr. Brawley.

Horrified by the perilous admission—was she not in enough trouble because she had fallen for a handsome scoundrel?—Fayre decided that she definitely needed to shift her attentions elsewhere. Breaking away from his compelling gray eyes rimmed with dark blue, her gaze glided down to his right shoulder. Mr. Brawley had very strong shoulders that had nothing to do with his excellent tailor. Her admiring gaze had a will of its own as her attention moved leisurely from his chest, to his narrowed waist, around the curve of his muscled buttock, and down to his well-defined calf. Fayre resisted the urge to shiver. Mr. Brawley had a fine, laudable physique. In truth, she could not think of another man who wore his clothes as well.

"Lady Fayre," the man she had been boldly staring at said in a low, husky drawl. "I think you and I were fated to meet."

Fayre parted her lips, stunned by his outrageous statement. What sharp reprimand she intended froze in her throat. It was his eyes. Framed by dark eyebrows and long lashes, his gray eyes captured and entranced her.

Noticing the effect he was having on her, Mr. Maccus Brawley shifted slightly on his saddle and responded with a slow, provocative wink.

Fayre's green eyes narrowed at his arrogance. He might

look like a pirate, but he was the devil to a woman with a wounded heart.

M accus almost laughed aloud at Lady Fayre's reaction. When they first caught up with her carriage, she had not glanced in his direction once as she spoke to Yemant. When she had finally deigned to notice him, the impact of her wide, startled green eyes was like a punch to his chest. From his distant observations, he had thought she was an appealing creature. Now, feeling her gaze on his face like a silken caress, he reconsidered and decided that she was the most extraordinarily stunning woman he had ever encountered. He was looking forward to their impending partnership. All he had to do was charm her into agreeing. The manner in which she had admired him so appreciatively left little doubt that he would gain her consent to his offer this very afternoon.

"It would do you credit not to overestimate our brief acquaintance, Mr. Brawley," Lady Fayre said, eerily responding to his thoughts. He realized his error with her next words. "Your scheme was ill-fated before you even approached our carriage."

Callie gasped at her friend's rudeness. "Fayre!"

Lord Yemant looked distinctly uncomfortable. "I am certain Mr. Brawley meant no insult, my lady. Please accept our apologies."

Maccus shot the viscount an irritated glance. "When it is warranted, I can make my own apologies, Yemant." Perhaps he needed to reassess his approach with Solitea's daughter. He was used to women who sighed and melted at lingering stares and arrogant declarations. Lady Fayre was gripping her parasol as if she intended to strike him with it.

"I grow weary of sitting," Lady Fayre said, addressing her companion. "If you do not object, Miss Mableward, I would prefer to return to the house."

"Of course," Callie hastily agreed. The quick, shy glance she sent Yemant betrayed her desire to remain and continue her conversation with the viscount.

Maccus was not above using this realization to his advantage. He called out to the coachman, ordering him to halt the carriage. Ignoring Yemant's bewildered expression and Lady Fayre's countermand, Maccus reined in his horse next to the carriage and dismounted. He secured his horse to the carriage.

Lady Fayre rose unsteadily to her feet, preparing to reprimand both her coachman and Maccus. She seemed torn as to whom to take on first. Maccus settled the matter for her by opening the carriage door.

"What do you think you are doing, Mr. Brawley?" she furiously demanded.

"Being a gentleman by assisting a lady in distress." Maccus seized her hand. Lady Fayre was too upset to think of appearances. She pulled her hand out of his and then wiped her gloved hand on her skirt. The telling action fired Maccus's temper. She shrieked when he wrapped his hands around her slender waist and hauled her out of the carriage.

"Release me this instant!" she said, her body vibrating with suppressed anger. She kicked him the second he set her on her feet.

"My God, Brawley! Are you insane? You cannot manhandle a female you have taken a fancy to!" Yemant exclaimed, dismounting from his horse. "And in the park of all places!"

"Fayre, are you hurt?" Callie asked, sliding closer to

the open carriage door. Uncertain of her part, she glanced helplessly at the viscount for guidance.

Lady Fayre was not flustered like her friend. The lady knew what she wanted. She wanted to make him suffer. "No." Lady Fayre glared at Maccus.

If she kicked him again, Maccus planned to do more than put his hands on her. A part of him welcomed her defiance. However, business came first. "Yemant, calm yourself. There is no need to rush to the lady's defense. She has admitted that she is unhurt. I was simply a tad overzealous fulfilling Lady Fayre's desire for an escort while she walked."

Her face suffused with color, clashing with her fiery tresses. "I made no such request!" Standing rigidly, she searched the area with her luminous green gaze to see if anyone had noticed them. Unfortunately, the lovely afternoon had lured many people outdoors.

"Many consider shyness the stamp of a refined lady." Maccus fought back the urge to laugh. Nothing he had seen in the duke's daughter indicated that she was a timid creature. Nevertheless, if she challenged his remark, she was admitting that she was not a proper lady. "Now, my lady, you are among friends. There is no need to deny your discomfort and I am eager to provide a respectful escort while Miss Mableward and Lord Yemant continue their conversation." He bent his mouth closer to her ear and whispered, "If you vilify me, Yemant will be forced to challenge me. He is too good a man to permit me to sully a lady's honor. Can your reputation withstand yet another public assault?"

Her friend, gripping the side of the carriage, said with insincere enthusiasm, "I could join you if you like?" She glanced longingly at Lord Yemant. The viscount was unaware of her devoted gaze because he was still frowning at Maccus. Lady Fayre, however, had noticed.

Accepting that there was no graceful way out of the situation, short of creating a public spectacle, she said, "No, Callie, there is no need to bother. Remain with Lord Yemant. I will accept Mr. Brawley's generous offer to accompany me. It appears I need a walk. We shall not be long."

Miss Mableward handed Lady Fayre her parasol. "Take however long you need. Pray do not hurry on my account."

Lord Yemant was still unhappy with Maccus's high-handed tactics. He was an honorable gentleman, and would never forgive himself if Lady Fayre suffered in Maccus's care because of his faulty judgment.

Maccus extended his bent arm to her in mocking courtesy. Her green eyes were ablaze as she raised her chin a notch and walked past him. "Come along, Mr. Brawley, before I am overwhelmed by my distress," she said, deliberately returning his own words to him.

The air quivered with the anticipation of battle.

Maccus bowed to Miss Mableward and gave a brief nod in Yemant's direction before strolling after Lady Fayre. His eye was on the woman wearing the blue velvet spencer over a white cambric dress. He rarely allowed his pleasures to interfere with his business goals. However, Maccus suspected the lady he was pursuing would tempt him into breaking his own rules.

Fayre crossed the open field toward a copse of trees, putting as much distance as she could from the carriage. Mr. Brawley had something to say to her and she preferred he said it without the benefit of an audience. She shuddered, thinking about her confrontation with Lord Standish and Lady Hipgrave. No, she definitely did not want to play out her life again in front of the masses.

She sensed him before he touched her on the sleeve. The sensation reminded her of being jolted by one of those French static electric machines. Fayre abruptly halted. "Mr. Brawley, unhand me. Heavens, your manners are atrocious! A gentleman never touches a lady unless invited to do so," she said.

Mr. Brawley did not release her. He moved in front of her, preventing her from escaping. Fayre glanced past him, but no one seemed to be overtly paying attention to them. Still, that did not mean they were not being watched. Turning her face up to his, she did not trust the gleam in his gray eyes.

"In my experience, a lady walking alone is sending out all sorts of interesting invitations," he said, definitely intrigued with the notion.

Smug, lecherous wretch, she thought. He had deliberately maneuvered her away from her friend. Any curiosity she had about this gentleman or his motives was slowly evaporating with her patience. Her lips formed into a dangerous smile that usually had most gentlemen stepping back.

"Play nice, my lady," Mr. Brawley chided. "Remember our audience. Besides, when a lady takes a bite out of me, I prefer a more private setting." His gaze focused on her mouth.

It was disturbing to have him looking at her so intensely. There was a dark brooding sensuality about him that beckoned to her, but she intended to resist his thrall. She had let her heart rule her choices and had paid dearly for her foolishness. "Who are you? Really? Lord Yemant is a respectable gentleman. I cannot imagine why he would associate with a man such as you."

He did not take offense at her snide remark. Instead he asked, "And what kind of man am I, sweet Lady Fayre?"

"Someone from the criminal class, I would wager." Her eyes narrowed, recalling her first impression of him. "Or a pirate, perhaps."

Mr. Brawley grinned. "Beautiful and intelligent." He shook his head, enjoying a private joke. "And a commendable imagination. I knew the first time I saw you that you were the one I sought."

Fayre's forehead furrowed. Bewildered, she carefully said, "The first time? Sir, we just met. You must have confused me with another lady." A sense of relief washed over her with the knowledge that his attentions were misdirected.

His expression was enigmatic as he lightly stroked her cheek. "Fate is never so simple or so kind, my lady," he said casually. "Come, let us continue our walk." He threaded her hand through his arm and with a friendly pat pulled her along.

Uncertain how to proceed, she strolled with him in silence. Mr. Brawley treated her as if they were acquainted; however, she could not recall encountering him at the countless balls and house parties she had attended over the years. She would have definitely remembered him. He was a gentleman who left a distinct impression on a lady. Fayre was used to people approaching her and claiming an informal connection to her and her family. Their false sincerity usually unmasked them. Mr. Brawley was not claiming that he knew her family. He claimed he knew *her*. His gray eyes glittered down at her mockingly as if he knew all her secrets, even the ones she dared not tell her family.

He was beginning to frighten her.

She could despise him simply for that alone. Fayre was not a sniveling coward. She had stood up to Standish while her heart lay shattered at their feet. Mr. Brawley with his teasing gray eyes was nothing in comparison. "No more subterfuge, sir, or I will leave you now and return to my carriage. Do I know you, Mr. Brawley?"

He gave her a considering look and then shrugged carelessly. "No. Not in the manner I led you to believe." As they approached a low-hanging branch pregnant with fragrant white blooms, he raised it high so she could pass under it. "But I will."

Such arrogance! "I am not really interested in knowing you, sir."

"Oh, I am aware of what you think of me, Lady Fayre. That lovely face of yours is rather transparent at times," he said, laughing.

"Then you should also realize that you are wasting your time. Your charming disposition might be appealing for some ladies, but I am unmoved by it."

"You tempt me to stop and prove you wrong." He sighed. "Regretfully, we will have to savor that delightful challenge later," Mr. Brawley said, giving her a sly wink. "Just a short delay, I promise, my lady. There is something about being in your presence that saps my immeasurable patience. All I intend to do this afternoon is propose a business offer."

One minute he was promising to kiss her, the next he wanted to discuss business. She had never encountered a gentleman who left her so bemused—and slightly insulted. "A business venture, Mr. Brawley? If you desire to do business with my family, I suggest that you contact our solicitor. Those affairs do not concern me."

He stilled her by tightening his grip on her arm. "I have no need of your family or your solicitor. What I want is you."

His outlandish statement gave her a fluttery feeling in her stomach. She absently placed her hand on her abdomen. Fayre cleared her dry throat. "Well, sir, you cannot have me."

"Is that what you told Standish after you caught him with his mistress?" he mildly asked, watching her face.

Fayre was not prone to violence. She had never struck a man in the face before Standish, though the man had richly deserved the slap and much more. Mr. Brawley's calculated query had her fingers itching for him to be her second. She closed her hand into a fist and kept it rigidly at her side.

"Well, done, my lady. Your control is remarkable. I am impressed." He softly applauded.

"What do you know about Standish? Did he send you to me?" she asked, horrified to think that Standish and Lady Hipgrave were still several steps ahead of her. God, she was a fool! She turned and her eyes scanned the field of picnickers and strolling pedestrians, looking for the quickest path to her carriage.

He did not try to stop her from reversing their direction and crossing the field. Her long skirts hindered her pace, so he caught up to her easily. "Standish did not send me to you. I tend after my own interests. Meddling in other people's problems is generally boring unless I have something to gain in the bargain."

"I have nothing to offer you, Mr. Brawley."

"I disagree."

His cocksure demeanor was insufferable. Exasperated, she demanded, "What do you want from me?"

"A bargain between us, Lady Fayre; one that benefits us both."

A soft sound of disbelief caught in her throat. "Your generosity overwhelms me, sir. Unfortunately, I will have to decline."

Mr. Brawley's handsome face lost some of its lazy charm as his jaw tightened. "You have not even heard my proposal."

"Even if I had, I would still reject it." She squinted against the sun, wishing the carriage were closer.

"Revenge." He reached out and steadied her when she stumbled. "You desire it. You do not strike me as a lady who sits idle while Standish and his lover make you the laughingstock of the season. I could help you gain your revenge over them."

She hesitated for a moment. Mr. Brawley's knowledge of her affair with Lord Standish seemed to extend beyond the circulating rumors. A flash of hot shame whipped through her, followed by righteous anger that a complete stranger knew something so intimate about her. She needed no one's assistance, especially not that of a rude, arrogant pirate! "No."

Irritation flashed in his eyes. He was not a gentleman used to rejection. "The park was a poor choice to approach you, I see that now."

"It matters not—"

He cut her off with a gesture. "No, do not refuse me. You will have an ally, Fayre. Think over what I offer you. We can meet later." He scowled at a passing couple. "Someplace with fewer people."

"And Mr. Brawley, what do you want from me if I decide to accept your gracious offer?"

"I need a lady of distinction." He dismissed the confession with a shake of his hand as if he had said too much. "We can talk about the details later. Just think about how I might help you." He saw the doubt in her expression. "Despite your first impression of me, I can promise you that what I want from you is not criminal."

As they approached the carriage, she risked a glance in his direction. How had he guessed that she intended to pay Standish and Lady Hipgrave back for their humiliation? Not even her family or friends suspected. At what price could she gain his cooperation or his silence? She dared not contemplate what a gentleman like Mr. Brawley wanted from her. Most likely she did not want to know. "I doubt I will change my mind on this."

She left him standing in the field and walked alone the remaining distance to her friends with a cheerful smile pasted on her face.

Maccus watched Lord Yemant help Lady Fayre into the carriage. Once she settled in her seat, she cast a quick wary glance his way. Lady Fayre stared at him as if she were trying to decide if he was a forbidden temptation or the devil himself. Maccus could have told her that he was both.

4

Eight days had passed since Mr. Brawley had dragged her away from her friend and made his outrageous offer. She did not need his assistance with Standish and Lady Hipgrave. The couple was her problem. She would deal with them eventually. For now, she was determined to enjoy London. Sitting at her dressing table, Fayre tilted her head to the side and admired the image staring back at her.

"Amelie, as always you have done magnificent work," she said, pleased by how her maid had swept up her waist-length hair and twisted it into a complicated arrangement of braids and disheveled curls.

"Hair like yours makes my work easy enough," the maid said cheerfully, making minute adjustments to her handiwork. "I once worked for an older lady who had hair thin as my granddad. Now, she was always wanting fancy curls in her hair but they just wouldn't take. All that crimping had me fretting that she would be bald by season's end."

Fayre laughed, wondering how many employers Amelie had served before she had been hired into the Solitea household. She could not be older than sixteen. "So was your mistress bald by the end of the season?"

"Looked like a freshly hatched chick, I tell you. It was turbans and plumes for her the following season," Amelie said, stepping away to retrieve the jewelry case on the table.

The vibrant hue of Fayre's hair needed little adornment; however, Fayre had a weakness for jewelry that her father seemed happy to indulge. This evening Amelie had looped gold roping around the braiding at the back, providing a brilliant accent for the thick cascade of curls. Fayre turned away from the mirror, giving her maid the opportunity to place a small tiara made of emeralds, diamonds, and tiny pearls on her head.

"You look like a queen, my lady."

"Heaven forbid," Fayre muttered, taking the tiara's matching choker out of the case. She had no aspirations to marry into the royal family. "I will finish up here, Amelie. Why do you not go down to the kitchen and have your supper?"

"Are you sure, my lady? I don't mind staying."

Amelie was so young and eager to please her. She was a joy in comparison to her predecessor. Fayre had not shed any tears over her former maid's departure. The woman

had been a weary, morose creature who had a nasty habit
of stabbing errant pins into Fayre's tender flesh at each
opportunity. Fayre gave Amelie a slight smile. "You have
done all the work. All I have to do is accept the compli-
ments. Go on, and enjoy the rest of your evening."

Her smile faded at the sound of the door closing behind Amelie. Fayre picked out the pair of gold armlets
from the leather jewelry case and slipped them on to her
upper arms. She stood and smoothed out the wrinkles in
her skirt. A glimpse of her face had her leaning into the
mirror for a closer look. Fayre pinched her cheeks,
adding to their natural coloring. The hint of fear in her
green eyes shamed her.

"You can do this, Fayre," she said to her image, thinking of the evening ahead of her. The stares and snide
comments cut into her spirit more than she was willing to
admit. "You are too strong to let Standish and his haughty
whore win."

Fayre whirled away from the mirror, prepared to battle
the *ton*.

"A re you certain?" Maccus poured his visitor a generous
glass of brandy and handed it to him. He poured
nothing for himself. His father had demonstrated in his
tender years how spirits weakened a man. Long ago Maccus had vowed not to touch the stuff.

"You pay me too well, Brawley, not to strive for accu-
racy," Mr. Cabot Dossett said dryly. "It took some effort,
but I located and spoke to a relative of the man you hired
me to find."

Fierce elation surged through Maccus. "I want to meet
him."

"No promises, but if the price is to his liking, he might be willing to meet with you." Dossett swallowed a healthy portion of his brandy.

Lady Fayre had been entirely too close to the truth that afternoon in the park when she accused him of being a member of the criminal class. How would she react if she knew Maccus had once made a lucrative living as a smuggler? He rarely spoke of his former life, but he had been good at his trade. So good that his enemies had ambushed him and his crew one night on a lone stretch of beach, and left him for dead.

"I realize I am just the hired help, but we also share a common history. Are you sure you want to go digging in the past?" his friend asked, bringing Maccus back to the present.

Dossett was a good man. Their friendship extended into their youth when they were too green and poor to refuse the sort of jobs that were likely to get a man hanged if he was caught. Though they had taken different paths, by some miracle both of them had pulled themselves out of the muck. Dossett worked as a Bow Street runner now. He was discreet, thorough, and always willing to do favors for an old friend.

"I am just seeking answers to some old questions," Maccus replied evenly. "I have no intention of risking what I have built here in London."

Although he had told Fayre the truth when he said that he required her assistance in gaining entrée into the polished world of the *ton,* he needed no one's help in making him rich. Maccus was already rich, and his business prospects were improving with each passing year. While some people were gifted in the arts, he had an uncanny talent for making risky ventures pay off. Playing at the

Exchange had seemed a sensible choice for a man like him to channel his luck and intelligence.

Dossett gave him a considering look. "I cannot talk you out of this?"

"No, so let us focus on something more interesting." Dossett could set up the meeting, but his friend had no part to play after Maccus had gained the information he sought. "Speaking of more pleasurable subjects, what are Lady Fayre Carlisle's plans for this evening?"

Accepting that he could not alter Maccus's plotted course, Dossett idly crossed his ankles and concentrated on new business. "I spoke to one of the servants personally. The family will be attending the theater this evening."

Satisfaction gleamed in Maccus's expression. For more than a week, Lady Fayre had remained out of reach. He had promised to give her time to consider his offer, but his patience waned with each passing day of silence. While he focused on the demands of his business interests, Lady Fayre lingered in his mind. By hiring Dossett, he was aware of her activities since they had parted. If she was troubled by the talk stirred up by Standish, she was hiding it well. Maccus could tick off on his fingers the various balls, lectures, and card parties she had attended. It was a world of breeding and privilege she lived in, and Maccus, like most people, was not invited to participate. His money could buy his way in, but it did not make him one of them. With Lady Fayre's cooperation he intended to change all that.

"Should I have someone follow the family this evening?" Dossett asked, interrupting Maccus's silent musings.

"No. The information you have provided is adequate for my needs. I will contact you if I require your services again," Maccus assured him.

"Forgive me for prying again, Mac, but I'm curious. The Duke of Solitea is not a man to be trifled with. If he learns of your interest in his family—"

"He won't," Maccus snapped. "Besides, I am not interested in His Grace." Now, trifling with the daughter was a different matter.

"I recognize that look in your eyes, Mac. It means trouble."

"You are mistaken, Cabot. I live the life of an honest man these days. Each night when I lay my head upon my pillow, I sleep the virtuous sleep of the angels."

"See that you keep doing so." Grimacing at his tone, his friend set down his glass of brandy. Dossett leaned forward and rested his elbows on his legs. He met Maccus's gaze unflinchingly. "Look, you and I have come a long way since the cold, wet nights of fleeing riding officers; a time when a few pints of beer and some food to fill our bellies was more important than the plate on which it was served."

"Are we reminiscing about the good ol' days, Cabot, or does this lecture have a point?" Maccus asked, settling back into his chair to get comfortable.

"Right. Direct. It was one of the things I like about you." Dossett stood and retrieved his hat from the table. "You have shed the old ways and have made something of yourself, Mac. Just don't fool yourself into thinking that your new life isn't filled with dangers. The villains in the world you are poking your ambitious fingers into might wear clean linen and have silver buckles on their shoes; nevertheless, they can still aim a pistol at your blackguard heart or pierce your spleen with a cutlass."

"You worry too much, Cabot. Silver buckles do not gain my trust. Hell, I trust no one," Maccus admitted, eyeing his friend speculatively, "not even you. I live a quieter life now. All I want is to conduct a little business and, mayhap, find some sweet-smelling vixen who could entertain me in her bed."

Dossett remained unconvinced. No one ever claimed he was a dim-witted man. "And Solitea's daughter?"

"Alas, business." If, however, Lady Fayre could not fight her attraction to him and ended up in his bed, Maccus was magnanimous and willing to indulge her. "Lord Yemant introduced us."

"If I have overstepped the bounds of our friendship, please accept my sincere apologies. My authority in London is limited, Mac. If you make enemies here, there is little I can do to save you," Dossett warned.

"I will not require rescuing," Maccus replied lightly, though his friend's concern touched him. The man was probably the only one he knew who thought his hide was worth saving. "I shall be the consummate gentleman." He gave Dossett a beatific smile.

Dossett nodded and headed for the door. "Then I will say no more about it." Pausing at the threshold, he added, "I forgot to mention. Trevor is also in London. Word from a few of my sources is that he is searching for you. I leave it up to you how easily you want to be found." He touched the brim of his hat. "Until later, my friend."

Silently efficient, his manservant, Hobbs, appeared in the doorway and escorted Dossett to the front hall.

Alone, Maccus stared down at his hands in contemplation. So Trevor was in town. Maccus wearily scrubbed his face with his right hand. He had not seen his half brother in five years. He somehow doubted Trevor's unexpected arrival was precipitated by a longing to renew family ties.

More likely the boy had trouble at his heels, and he was leading the past straight to Maccus's door.

"Very well, sister mine," Tem said into her ear as he led Fayre away from their mother.

If Her Grace was aware of their departure, she gave no sign of it as she chatted with a longtime friend. He bowed his head, giving two sisters an engaging grin. The young ladies giggled as Fayre and Tem passed them.

"We are alone, or as much as one can be in public. What has you so stirred up this evening? You fidgeted in your seat the entire way to the theater."

Fayre discreetly searched the lobby for familiar faces. "Nothing."

Tem snorted. "Rot! The merciless kicks you delivered to my shins and calves on the drive here have left me mottled with bruises."

"Stop acting like an infant," she scolded, content to follow her brother's lead through the perilous path of patrons. Some looked bored, others curious, and a few others Fayre would have categorized as malicious. She refused to show weakness to any of them. Cocking her head playfully, she said, "You deserve worse for your mischief. Besides, I was simply gaining your attention."

"You have it now, though a polite cough would have sufficed," Tem muttered irritably. Recalling her accusation, he added, "Worse? For what? I have done nothing."

"You called on Miss Mableward on my behalf."

"Oh. Right." Having no defense for his actions, he attacked. "Silly chit was supposed to keep silent about that part."

Fayre's eyes flared with her temper. "What did you expect? Callie is my friend. We share secrets, not keep them from each other."

Tem frowned. "I expected the amiable Miss Mableward to keep her bloody mouth shut about our business. What does a man have to do when sharing confidences with a woman? Swear a blood oath?"

It was just like Tem to blame Callie and women in general for his error. "No, Fayne, just stop sticking your nose into my concerns."

"Fayne," he growled. "I despise that asinine name. What the devil was Mother thinking when she chose it?"

"She was thinking you were trying to change the subject," Fayre replied sweetly. "And you are failing miserably, brother."

"Good God, Fayre, this is hardly the moment to discuss the family's dirty laundry."

Fayre sighed. "Agreed. But this nasty business is mine to handle, Tem. Having you meddle makes me feel—" She looked away, floundering for the proper word.

Rapidly losing his patience, her brother pressed, "Feel what? That you are not alone? That you are loved by your family?"

She felt the sting of tears. "No, Tem. Shame," Fayre softly confessed, unable to say more. She was certain a grand majority of the *ton* thought she ought to feel ashamed for allowing Standish to seduce her. They were bound to be disappointed. She felt no shame for loving Standish; only that he had been unworthy and she had been too blinded by her feelings to see the truth.

Taken aback by the sheen of tears glistening in her green gaze, Tem dragged her to the nearest corner and used his body to shield her from view of the curious. "Here now," he crooned, pressing a handkerchief into her hands. "There will be none of that in my presence."

Tem seemed so unsettled Fayre discovered she could laugh after all. "Oh, brother, you should see your face." The urge to cry faded with her laughter. She dabbed at the corner of her eyes out of habit, rather than of necessity. "If I had known I could strike terror in your heart just by turning on the waterworks, I would have done this years ago."

"I have no doubt, you red-haired imp," he mused, pressing a soft kiss to her forehead. "It is just that you cry so rarely. For that alone, I want to hunt Standish down and murder him with my bare hands."

"A woman's tears are a ludicrous reason to kill a man." She stuffed the handkerchief into her reticule. "Just keep your promise and leave Standish alone."

"Why the tether, Fayre?" he asked, his frustration evident in his eyes. "The man betrayed you. You said that you felt shame. What is wrong with you, girl? Are you not angry? Where is your spirit? Do you not want revenge?"

"Of course," she hissed, the calm façade she wore eroded. "Standish will pay for his treachery."

"When?"

Fayre remained silent.

Tem swore under his breath. "Despite what he has done, you still love the bastard. Is that why you are protecting him?"

"No! I do not love Standish. What feelings I had for him died that night when I discovered him with Lady Hipgrave. You just are not in possession of all the details."

"Then talk to me, Fayre. If you are too softhearted to strike down your lover, then use me as your sword of vengeance." He gripped both her hands. "Take me into your gentle hands, point me in Standish's direction, and I will smite him in half."

"A tempting offer, Tem. Honestly." She took his left hand and raised it to her cheek. "I would not risk your life for revenge. Standish thinks he has gotten away unpunished—"

"He has," Tem said bluntly.

"Only for the moment," she countered, irritated to have the truth waved in her face. "Good fortune has a way of reversing itself."

Tem released her hands and crossed his arms over his chest. He gave her a considering stare. "What are you up to, dear sister?"

"Nothing that concerns you," Fayre said, smiling. "Now if you want to assist me, I do have a small task for you. I need you to obtain some information for me."

"Regarding?"

Fayre took a deep breath. She could not believe she was even considering the rogue's bargain. "A particular gentleman. His name is Maccus Brawley."

M accus braced his hands on the railing as he quietly observed the activity down below. His lofty perch had its limitations, however; it did provide him with a first-rate view of the theater's front entrance. He recognized Lady Fayre before he had glimpsed her face. She had entered the lobby with her mother and a young gentleman that Maccus hoped for the lady's sake was a male relative. His grip tightened on the wooden railing as he watched the man place a proprietary hand on her arm. They strolled off, away from the duchess, sharing confidences, no doubt. If Lady Fayre was seeking a replacement for Lord Standish, she would have to delay her quest for pleasure. Maccus's plans for her did not include him fighting off a jealous lover. The couple's change in direction revealed the man's profile. A glint of the rich cinnamon hue at his ears solved the mystery of Lady Fayre's escort. The gentleman was obviously her brother, Lord Temmes. Maccus felt the tension in his shoulders ease with this revelation.

He stepped away from the railing and began searching for his theater box. Brothers tended to be adequate watchdogs for their younger sisters. No gentleman would approach Lady Fayre while she was under the viscount's protection. This slightly hindered Maccus's plans, as well, though he was not discouraged. He counted on Lady Fayre's independent nature to place her directly into his eager hands.

"We have lingered too long, Fayre," Tem said, placing his hand on her back. "Let us collect Mother and hasten on to the box, else our ears will be pealing with her discontent at missing the beginning of the play."

"None of the plays make any sense to her. Mama spends most of the play gossiping with her friends or watching the goings-on in the other boxes." Fayre did not mention that her mother also flirted outrageously with the gentlemen in the nearby boxes, too much to heed the minor dramatics below. "If you—" Her mind blanked as she glimpsed a familiar face in the distance. *No!* Craning her head, she wished the gentleman would turn her way so she could get a better look at him.

Tem had his back to the crowd. With an indulgent smile on his lips at what he perceived as her being scatterbrained, he asked, "If I what?"

Several people blocked her view as they crossed between her and the gentleman. The path cleared momentarily and her worst fears were confirmed. *Standish.* She had managed to avoid the man so far. Why had he chosen to attend the theater this evening? He usually preferred spending his evenings at his clubs.

"What did you say?" Fayre asked her brother, too distracted to pay attention. She felt the color drain from her face. Good heavens! What was she going to do if her brother noticed Lord Standish? Tem was likely to throttle the man in a lobby filled with witnesses.

Tem was scowling at her. "Are you all right? You look too pale for my liking."

Fayre deliberately concentrated on her brother. "What a horrible thing to say to a lady. Is this how you court your admirers? If so, it is no small wonder you are still unwed."

"I do just fine with the ladies, Miss Impertinent, not that it is any of your concern."

"I could care less," she said blithely as they looked for their mother. "I was just thinking of the Solitea curse and all. With so little time, it would be prudent to seek out a lady soon and beget your heir."

"You have a hell of a lot of nerve to accuse me of lack of tact," Tem grumbled.

He was too irritated with her to notice when she stepped forward to subtly block his view of Standish. Fayre did not release the breath she was holding until she saw her mother.

"Oh, there you are, my darlings!" their mother said,

fluttering with nervous energy. "Have you been enjoying yourselves? You can tell me all about it later. We must get along to our box. We do not want to miss a minute of the play. Lady Ranney was just telling me how marvelous it is."

Fayre climbed the staircase, following behind Tem and their mother. She could not resist turning back and searching the throng for Standish. Her gaze immediately clashed with his insolent stare. Fayre broke the connection and focused on climbing the stairs without stumbling. Standish knew she was here. He had purposely placed himself in her path, hoping there would be a scene. She was pleased that she had thwarted him. One thing was certain. Lord Standish was far from finished with her.

Despite the short notice, Lord Yemant had not disappointed Maccus. The box the viscount had secured gave them an advantageous view of the stage. Although, Yemant had explained, the true entertainment transpired in the multitude of boxes. Many of the refined spectators used the theater to be seen and elevate their status in polite society. It was a place where a gentleman could hunt for a prospective bride or secure a new mistress. Maccus scanned the immense auditorium, which was filled to capacity, with new respect. His former life had given him little opportunity to explore the gentler arts. He noted that the box one level down and to the left was occupied with four very attractive ladies. Their dresses and jewels marked them as ladies of quality. Maccus observed as two gentlemen entered their box and introductions were made.

"Lovely, are they not?" Yemant said, noticing his friend's interest.

The fragile blonde at the end looked as if she were formed from spun sugar. "Indeed. Are they sisters?"

His friend appeared amused by the question. "I believe so. What does it matter? If you have the blunt, any or all of them can be yours."

"Are you serious?" Maccus asked, glancing at Yemant for confirmation. "They are a family of courtesans?" Most of the prostitutes he had encountered over the years could have comfortably lived out their lives on the proceeds from just one of the dresses and its complementing jewelry. "They look like duchesses."

"And likely treated better. Those ladies have more influence than you or I could ever hope to attain," the viscount said wryly.

"Speak only for yourself," Maccus retorted. Admiring the delectable sisters as they conducted their business in front of the majority of the *ton*, he tried to envision one of them in his bed. Regretfully, none of the enticing beauties appealed to him. Once he might have claimed that his ideal woman was a pale blonde with eyes the color of a robin's egg. His tastes had changed, Maccus ruefully admitted to himself. The hair he envisioned splayed across his sheets was rich cinnamon and the face staring up at him in mindless passion possessed dark green eyes.

The vision was so clear it visibly unsettled him.

Lord Yemant leaned closer, not wanting the others in their box to overhear him. "If you wish, we could pay our respects to the ladies."

Maccus raised his brows. "Is there no one in London with whom you are not acquainted?"

The viscount grinned, looking slightly abashed by

Maccus's admiration. "These ladies are the sort no gentleman ever admits to knowing. In my case, however, it happens to be the truth. I thought that after the incident in the park, I should introduce you to ladies who do not mind loutish handling in public."

A subtle heat rose in Maccus's face. "My handling of Lady Fayre was not loutish, as you so indelicately put it. The lady found me charming."

"The *lady* kicked you in the shins," Yemant said blandly. "You are fortunate she recovered her composure quickly, else she would have flattened your thick skull with her parasol."

"I like a spirited woman," Maccus said, his searching gaze passing over the courtesans. One tier up and to the right, he found the lady he was seeking. "Besides, I would not be sitting here watching you ogle costly courtesans if Lady Fayre were not expecting me." It was not exactly a lie. If the lady had learned anything about Maccus during their brief exchange, it should have been that he was not easily discouraged. She should be expecting him to approach her again.

Flabbergasted, Yemant choked. "The devil you say! I was *not* ogling the courtesans!" Maccus looked blandly at his friend, wondering if lack of experience with women was the reason for the man's discomfort. It was apparent to Maccus that Yemant *liked* looking at women even if he loathed admitting it. His reaction was damned peculiar from Maccus's point of view. The older woman next to the viscount, noticing his distress, leaned over and thumped on his back. Red-faced, he mumbled his gratitude to the helpful woman.

Maccus saw his chance when Lady Fayre rose from her seat and disappeared through the curtains. He also stood. "Ogling is safer than owning. Those soiled doves will beggar you, Yemant. I'll wager this kind lady"—he nodded to the matron who had assisted the viscount during his coughing fit—"knows a sweet miss or two who will keep you honorable."

The matron eyed Lord Yemant speculatively.

"Damn you, Maccus Brawley! Come back here."

Maccus grinned at the hoarse curse the viscount hurled at him. Dashing through the curtains, he raced down the passageway hoping to cross paths with a certain lady.

Desperately needing a respite, Fayre quietly left the theater box. She had whispered to her mother that she was excusing herself for private reasons and one glance at her daughter's pinched mouth and bloodless face had her mother consenting. Tem, slouched in his seat, had made an effort to join her, but Fayre placed her hand on his shoulder, stilling his actions.

She wanted to be alone. Unfortunately, there was no such thing as solitude in a public place. Even with the commencement of the play, there were people milling about in the passageways. Two ladies smiled faintly as she passed by them. Fayre would have preferred descending the staircase down to the lobby, where freedom awaited just beyond the double doors. Instead she headed for one of the large private saloons.

This evening was a debacle. Her nerves were as taut as harpsichord strings with the knowledge that Tem and Standish had come within a hairsbreadth of each other. To make matters worse, she discovered in a matter of seconds after being seated that Lady Hipgrave was also present in the theater. The countess was seated to the left with two boxes separating them. Their proximity gave Fayre the luxury of not having to look directly into Lady Hipgrave's mocking face. Nevertheless, Fayre had to endure the odious woman's laughter occasionally, which even the din within the auditorium could not mask.

Fayre could not bear it. She had known her decision to remain in London would frequently place her directly in the path of Standish and Lady Hipgrave. It was a minor miracle that they had not encountered each other sooner. Regardless, she had not been prepared for her visceral reaction to seeing them again. Bile burned the back of her throat as the smell of overripe humanity and acrid smoke offended her senses. Entering the saloon, she opened her fan with a practiced flick of her wrist, savoring the cooler air of the room. Tall, arched windows banked the opposite wall of the large rectangular room. Shakily, Fayre walked to the nearest chair and sank into it. Closing her eyes, she stirred the air in front of her face. Wearily, she wondered how long she would have to pay for her supposed sins.

"Forgive me for saying so, my dear," Lady Hipgrave said, her voice full of indulgent humor. "But that greenish tinge in your cheeks positively ruins your average looks."

Fayre snapped her fan shut. The countess's presence was like a brisk slap in the face. Shaking off her melancholy, Fayre hardened her green eyes contemptuously at the lady's companions. "Still playing to an audience, Countess? If you take the stairs down and follow the passage to the left, you might find the masses more appreciative." She wanted to get up from her chair and quit the room. Frustratingly, the countess had positioned herself directly in front of Fayre. She would have to shove the woman to clear the way, which was probably what the spiteful witch intended.

"Witty," Lady Hipgrave said, her tone implying the opposite. "We have missed you of late."

"Odd, since I never left. Mayhap it is simply a matter of looking up, Lady Hipgrave," Fayre replied, implying that her family moved in loftier social circles. The countess's lips thinned to a line at the insult.

"Has the Duke joined you this evening? I would be remiss if I did not pay my respects."

The woman was delusional if she thought Fayre was going to allow her near the duke or the rest of the family. "Do not trouble yourself. I believe other . . . interests keep him occupied of late, so any disrespect on your part is of little concern to him." Lady Hipgrave's face reddened. "Oh, dear, did I speak out of turn? Perhaps you should send one of your companions for some lemonade. Now you are the one who looks a little green."

Ignoring the woman's proximity, Fayre stood. She was relieved when Lady Hipgrave took several steps back. "Though I have enjoyed our little chat, you will have to excuse me. My family is anticipating my return."

"How disappointing that Lord Standish could not join us this time," Lady Hipgrave called out to her as Fayre retreated. "When I see him, shall I give him your love?"

A footman opened the door. Fayre abruptly halted at the threshold and bravely faced her tormentor. "I value mine too highly to offer it to the royal court's whore. Give him yours instead." Not waiting for a response, Fayre turned sharply on her heel and left the saloon.

5

Maccus caught Lady Fayre in his arms as she ran out of the saloon. Had he not held her tightly against his chest, she would have sunk boneless to her knees. "Steady now. On your feet, lady. You delivered your salvo with fire and guts. This is no place to show weakness," he snapped, deciding the last thing she needed was coddling.

"I feel sick," she mumbled, as she leaned into him for support. She managed to remain on her feet.

"Are you carrying Standish's child?"

She stiffened at the question. "No! I have been spared a permanent connection to that blackguard." Her face whitened as another thought occurred to her. "Good heavens, do you think my dear friends inside are asking themselves the same question?"

"It is a logical question," he replied, relieved she was not pregnant and telling himself that his reaction was for her benefit. "It would be a vicious twist to the sordid tale, don't you agree?"

Lost in her thoughts, she did not bother answering, not that he really needed confirmation regarding her former companion's character. He checked both directions of the passageway, trying to figure out the quickest route to the lobby. "Come along. We'll get you some air to clear your head."

Lady Fayre refused to move. "I have been gone too long. My family—"

Right. He did not want her family interfering at an inopportune moment. "You." Maccus grabbed a passing footman by the arm. "I need you to deliver a message to the lady's family." He told the footman where to find Lady Fayre's family and provided a brief message explaining her absence. The servant hurried off.

Lady Fayre stepped back from him. Her color was better and the temper Maccus expected was back in her eyes. "How did you know where to find my family?"

"Simple enough. I saw you sitting with them." He preferred having her lean against him, but he would settle for her hand on his arm. Maccus suspected she would rebuke an unspoken invitation to touch him so he took up her hand himself and placed it on his arm. "I suggest we do not linger, my lady. The countess and her cohorts are likely to appear in the passage at any moment and it would be a shame to ruin your spectacular exit."

"You were eavesdropping?" she said, aghast.

"I was searching for you," he corrected. "The eaves-dropping was incidental." It had also been informative.

Maccus managed to get her down to the lobby without further argument. She balked as he nudged her through the lobby's door and into the street.

"We cannot go outdoors."

"I see no guards barring our way."

"No, it is unseemly."

Maccus followed the direction of her concerned gaze, and blinked at the passionate display just beyond the flickering light of the lanterns. "Oh, I don't know," he said, cocking his head to see where the lady had put her other questing hand. "I'm game if you are, but it might get a trifle awkward if your mother and brother find us."

Through gritted teeth, she said, "That was not an invitation, you madman."

"Oh, really? A pity." Maccus contrived to appear disappointed, but her reaction to his baiting was too delightful. Instead, he ended up laughing. "Let us walk then. By the by, did I mention how lovely you look this evening?" Maccus asked, following the long line of waiting coaches. He sincerely meant the praise. Lady Fayre was a mouthwatering morsel. She wore a white round-train dress with double puffed sleeves. A green military-style sash made of cobweb muslin was draped over her right shoulder. The front revealed a teasing hint of bosom, but he particularly liked the low-cut back. Compared to Lady Fayre, the blond courtesans he had admired earlier were plain and uninspiring.

"I am not walking London's dark streets with you, Mr. Brawley. We will attract every thief in the vicinity and I, for one, do not want to end this horrendous evening with a knife at my throat," she said, attempting to pull him back toward the theater.

Belatedly, Maccus realized the woman had in her hair a small fortune in jewels. "You do rather shine like a beacon for every creature of the shadows," he said, glowering at how even her white dress glowed. "I suppose you have a cloak inside."

She was pleased he finally understood the dangers of their situation. "Yes, I do, and that is where I should be. So let us return—"

"No need. We have reached our destination." Maccus gave the coachman a salute as the man jumped down from his perch and opened the door for them. "G' evening, George. We will be driving Lady Fayre home." She gaped at him as he casually rattled off the directions to her residence.

The coachman's gaze roamed appreciatively over her. A little too appreciatively for Maccus's taste. He stared unblinkingly at his servant until the man shrugged sheepishly.

"Uh, very good, sir," the man mumbled.

Lady Fayre shook her head and stepped backward. "I cannot go with you!"

"The footman has already told your family that you have left for home," he reminded her. Maccus took her hand and helped her into the coach. "It will seem odd if you are not there when they arrive home."

"You promise to take me home. Forthwith, and no mischief?"

The compartment of the coach was too dim to see her face distinctly, but the suspicion was evident in her soft voice. He leaned past her, calculatingly bringing his face inches from hers. Without shifting his gaze from her face, he adjusted the lantern to make it brighter.

"There, that's better, now," he said huskily.

Lady Fayre swallowed visibly. "Better?"

"To seal our bargain."

Fayre tensed, expecting Mr. Brawley to kiss her. He surprised her by settling back into his seat opposite hers. The coach rolled forward and she reached for the sides to keep from sliding.

"I have not agreed to any bargain, Mr. Brawley."

"You will," he assured with a confidence that made her jaw ache. "You have enemies, my lady, and they will not disappear just because you wish it. The minor verbal tussle with Lady Hipgrave is proof enough of that."

"How did you know—" She broke off with a shake of her head. He seemed to know a lot about her business. Fayre put that concern aside for the moment. "Suppose I agree to your assistance. What do you want in exchange?"

Despite the lantern, his face still dwelled in the shadows. Only those light gray eyes of his gleamed at her with unspoken amusement. "And if I demanded your soul?"

Fayre had never considered herself superstitious, and yet his nonchalant query left her speechless for a few seconds. Sitting with him in the shadowed confines of his coach, she could almost believe he was serious. "It would confirm my first impression of you, Mr. Brawley."

"Pray, do not spare me," he taunted.

"That you, sir, are no gentleman. Your mockery of my pain is mean-spirited and indicative of a flawed disposition." If she had any sense, she should demand that he halt the coach and allow her to disembark. She would take her chances with the thieves.

"You are correct," he said quietly, his lips twisting into a parody of a smile. "At least in part. I am no gentleman. That is where I require your assistance."

He was leaning negligently against the right wall of the coach, studying her over the bridge he had made with his fingers. His expression was intensely expectant.

"I—I do not understand what you want from me," she said, her voice sounding faint to her ears.

"Entrance to your world, Lady Fayre," he replied, parting his hands in an encompassing gesture. "You are the key."

His statement, while flattering, was wholly erroneous. "You have the wrong person, Mr. Brawley. There are others better suited for this task," she argued, shifting away from the glare of the lantern so she could see his face. "A gentleman? Perhaps Lord Yemant?"

"No," he said flatly. "Yemant has his own part, but his position in polite society is relatively new. He cannot assist me like you, Fayre."

He spoke her name like an incantation. Mr. Brawley gently took up her hand and rubbed his thumb across her wrist. "I have not given you permission to address me thus. Even then, it is highly improper," she said breathlessly, marveling at how nicely formed his hands were.

"See? You are already instructing me," Mr. Brawley said, drawing her to his side. "I need someone to educate me on the intricacies of your gilded world and open doors for me. I knew when I first saw you that you were my fate."

He seemed so confident that their alliance would benefit them both. Lost in thought, she glanced down at their clasped hands. Mr. Brawley had said at their introduction that they had been fated to meet. Had it been fate or had he purposely sought her out? "You met me before—before the park."

"You are a clever lady. Aye, I saw you once before. Though you were too busy arguing with your mother to notice."

Fayre nodded slowly, recalling the afternoon she had gone searching for her mother. "Naturally, you asked people about me." She doubted he had difficulty finding people who were willing to tell him the gossip being bandied about town regarding her and Standish.

"Once I learned your name, it was simple enough to find out what I needed to know about you."

There was more to it, she suspected. He dressed as though he had the means to pay people to pry into her private life. "Ah, I see." She closed her eyes. The clarity of his reasoning was sickeningly apparent. "It was not enough to have someone with connections and education, was it, Mr. Brawley? You needed someone who had slipped from grace; someone who—" Fayre cleared her throat quietly. "Me."

He made a disgruntled sound. "Oh, for God's sake, stop looking at me as if I were the one who bedded you and then told half of London. I am the one who is offering to help you out of your mess or at the very least help you gain a measure of revenge on your vile seducer."

"He did not precisely seduce me. I went to his bed willingly. I thought I loved him, you know," she said sadly.

"Spare me the details," he said curtly, snapping her out of her slide into melancholy. "You are not the first innocent to be swayed into bed by a handsome face and patent lies."

She bristled at his brutish honesty. "I am not mourning my loss of my maidenhead, you dolt. Lord Standish stole something more precious." Fayre had lost a part of herself with his betrayal. Her miscalculation of Standish's true motives and character had her questioning all her decisions. She despised the man for it. "I do not expect you to understand."

"Why not? Because I am a man, hence I am just another vile seducer?"

He leaned back, glaring at her like an outraged fallen angel. She could easily see him seducing young innocents. "I meant no disrespect. Being a man, you cannot understand my feelings, that is all I meant."

Mr. Brawley stared at her, his eyes silently judging her. Fayre fidgeted under his scrutiny. Finally, he said, "Trust. You have lost faith in yourself; in your ability to sift the truth from the lies."

She blinked in surprise at his insightfulness. "Yes. So you can see my quandary about you, Mr. Brawley."

"What do your instincts tell you?"

Fayre laughed. "Oh, my instincts tell me not to trust you, sir."

Maccus was still smiling when he entered his town house, the Lady Fayre's words resounding in his head. It was a sad situation that a lady's distrust made her all the more appealing. There were too many stupid chits with fair faces residing in London in Maccus's opinion. Arguing with the stubborn Lady Fayre had lightened his mood immensely.

"Ev'ning, sir," his manservant, Hobbs, said, greeting him at the front door. "Good hunting, I take it?"

Maccus had no doubt that Lady Fayre would not approve of Hobbs as head of his household. Much like himself, the servant was rough around the edges. The man's forthright manner had cost him countless positions in the past. Neither did his appearance engender the quiet confidence one expected in his staff.

At fifty, Hobbs's lanky length was stooped and his wiry gray hair seemed to be always escaping its queue. It gave him an unkempt, lazy appearance to the observer, although it was misleading. The manservant earned every shilling he was paid.

When the man had appeared on Maccus's doorstep a year earlier looking for employment, he had hired Hobbs literally off the street. Maccus knew the man's manners were too brash for polite society and the references he had presented were highly questionable. Still, Maccus recognized the ambition in the man's belligerent gaze. The civilized world was cruel to usurpers and Maccus saw a kindred spirit in the older gentleman. Hobbs was grateful for what he perceived as a chance to improve his station in life and worked hard so his employer would never regret his decision.

"Aye, I found the Lady Fayre." Dossett's information had always been reliable. "Even took the lady home."

"Go on with ye," Hobbs said in disbelief.

"The lady needed an errant knight, a service I was quite willing to provide." Predicting that Lady Fayre expected him to take advantage of her vulnerability, Maccus had remained until the end a gentleman. It had been a difficult task. Having her sit beside him in the confines of the enclosed coach and inhaling her subtle womanly scent had given him several wicked thoughts; the foremost had been the irresistible urge to kiss the lady senseless. He might have let his less refined instincts kick in had gaining her consent not been so important.

Hobbs folded Maccus's black cloak over his arm and followed him into the library. "And what did the young missus say when ye told 'er the price of an ar'nt knight these days?"

"Like most women would, she balked at the offer. She doesn't trust me, Hobbs," Maccus said, smiling.

The manservant hoarsely chuckled. "This one's got something under her bonnet, eh?"

"And a sharp tongue to match." Maccus wondered if she was as candidly opinionated with the gentlemen of the *ton,* or if he was an exception. "She's made enemies and she is outmatched. If she didn't realize it before, I think her experience at the theater convinced her."

"Those th'aters can get rough and are no place for a gentle lady."

"How right you are." Who would have guessed those pretty gilded private boxes above the masses held their own dangers? "Well, she now has us to look after her." It was obvious her family was not seeing to her safety. He had gotten close to Lady Fayre and had slipped her away from her family without raising an alarm. If he had an ounce of honor, he should have dragged the lady back to her family and scolded them for their carelessness. If he felt a twinge of guilt for using a young woman, he ruthlessly squelched it. For the Soliteas' negligence was indeed a boon.

Fayre did not see her brother again until the following afternoon. While she had been enjoying a walk through the gardens, she had caught sight of him near the stables. She glanced back at the house, realizing the timing could not be any better. Her father was out of the house and her mother had refused to join her for a walk because of a slight headache. She dashed down the stone path toward the stables, hoping to talk to Tem before he rode off.

Tem had crouched down and was sliding his hand over one of the horse's fetlocks. He lifted his head and squinted in her direction. "I thought you were paying calls today?"

Fayre's smile dimmed as she realized someone was keeping him informed of her activities. "I will later. I was waiting for you."

"I thought you might." Her brother rose and rubbed his horse affectionately on the rump. Ordering one of the grooms to see to his horse, he joined her. "Walk with me. Are we alone?"

"Yes, Mama is resting in her room. Papa had appointments so we will not see him until the evening," she said, trying to match his pace and finding it impossible. "Good grief, Tem, I am not your horse. Slow down. My legs are getting tangled in the folds of my skirt. I am likely to pitch forward onto my face at any moment."

Tem stopped and gave her the opportunity to close the gap between them. His expression was grim as he held out his hand. "I could not have described your actions these past months more succinctly."

Fayre stumbled, and used his offered hand to steady herself. "A bit harsh, do you not think? If you came to lecture me on my folly, Tem, I have other tasks I can attend to."

"Well, someone needs to look after you. If the duke were aware you were associating with a gentleman like Maccus Brawley, he would put you on the first ship out of port. I for one think a switch to your backside is in order."

Her brother had a look in his eyes that warned her he

was very tempted to follow through on his threat. "For knowing a man's name? Oh my, what wickedness," she mocked, batting her eyelashes at him. "Lock me in my room and serve me broth and stale bread."

He grabbed her by the arm and shook her. "I am not jesting, Fayre. Maccus Brawley is no one to trifle with. Keep away from him."

"Lord Yemant considers him trustworthy and a friend. Otherwise, why would he bother introducing him to Callie and me?"

"When was this?" Tem demanded.

"The day you decided to interfere in my life by persuading Callie to entertain me in the park. So if you want to blame someone for the introduction, blame yourself," she muttered, leaning down and breaking off a stem of blooming currant. She brought the sprig of tiny red flowers up to her nose and inhaled.

"Why are you interested in this man, Fayre?"

If she told him the truth, her family would lock her in her room until she came to her senses. "I was just curious. Lord Yemant mentioned that Mr. Brawley was relatively new to town."

"Is he? In truth, I could find out little about the man, but my instincts tell me that London is not new to Mr. Brawley. The fortune he has accrued, nevertheless, is. He is becoming something of a legend for those who dabble on the 'change. This recently acquired wealth has allowed him to afford the town house that he recently purchased and new friends like Yemant."

"That is hardly criminal, Tem. He is not the first who has bought his way into polite society."

"Perhaps not, but Brawley is canny and ambitious. Marrying into an established family is a logical next step."

She was well acquainted with fortune hunters. "It is a step many impoverished gentlemen of the *ton* have taken," Fayre dryly reminded her brother. "If Mr. Brawley finds an excuse to drop to his knees in my presence, I promise I will flee the room before he utters a single word."

"There are other ways of securing your consent, you naïve little fool!" Tem shouted in a burst of anger. "Seducing you might bring him closer to his goal!"

Fayre stared mutely at her brother, her mind blanking to blessed numbness. It was a pity the pain caused by Tem's words returned seconds later. "Like Standish," she said, her voice quaking with hurt. "I was dim-witted enough to fall for one man's lies, so naturally, when another rogue comes along I will believe him, as well." She pushed away from him and blindly walked off.

Tem went after her. He was not a cruel man, and his face was riddled with guilt at causing his beloved sister pain. "You are not dim-witted, Fayre. I think you were lonely when Standish came along. For a while, you were so dazzled by the notion of being in love with him that you did not see beyond his pretty face and lies."

"How wonderful! Not only was I dim-witted, I was also desperate." She switched directions, trying to avoid her brother's hands. "Do me a favor, Tem. Stop trying to explain away my lapse into idiocy."

"About Brawley—" Tem began.

"Forget Mr. Brawley," she said, cutting him off. "I regret even bringing up his name. The brief conversation we had kindled my curiosity and I just wanted to learn more about the gentleman. So set aside your concerns. The man is not plotting to marry into the family."

Tem was too stubborn to let his suspicions fade with her calm assurances. "He wants something from you."

It grated to hear her brother echoing her private reservations about accepting any bargain with Mr. Brawley. Fayre knew what the man wanted. He wanted *her*. She felt her body instinctively responding as he watched her through those hungry, possessive gray eyes. Maccus Brawley was planning to stake his claim on her.

Fayre gave her brother a brilliant smile. "Then he shall be disappointed."

6

This was ridiculous. Setting up accidental meetings with Lord Standish had been less complicated than planning a single encounter with a gentleman she had no intention of indulging in a love affair with. It was a genuine challenge to meet someone in public without revealing your intentions to the observers. Once she worked out the logistics, perhaps she should offer her services to the crown.

The argument she had with her brother had not discouraged her from her decision to accept Mr. Brawley's bargain. The arrogant man had been correct. She needed his assistance if she wanted to beat Lady Hipgrave at her own game. The price he demanded for his help seemed inconsequential since she had been born to the life of privilege and etiquette he so obviously coveted. If he wanted entrée into her world, she would be his guide through the murky waters of polite society.

Fayre had her coachman drive her to Pall Mall. Earlier she had sent Mr. Brawley a message to meet her at the Shakespeare Gallery. The British Institution had purchased the property for their art exhibitions. It had been the goal of the institution to form a school for young painters. The proceeds from the gallery and the yearly subscriptions funded the small school. She had supported the institution's efforts since its opening in January 1806. If her family were still watching her activities, they would not think it odd that she had paid a visit to the gallery before it closed for the summer.

"You are highly unpredictable, Lady Fayre," Mr. Brawley murmured behind her. "When I received your message proposing the location of our meeting, I was anticipating a less public setting."

Fayre studied the painting before her. The painter had copied Rembrandt's *The Sacrifice of Abraham*. It was a fair representation, although the artist had failed to match the chiaroscuro effect of the original painting. "Any less public than Solitea's daughter knocking on your front door?" she asked, finally glancing back at him, her brow arching questioningly.

"Ah, not exactly discreet."

Mr. Brawley had purchased a town house in one of the older yet respectable squares. Someone was bound to recognize the Solitea crest. "There are ways around such matters, of course."

"Naturally," he agreed, standing so close she felt his warm breath on her ear. "How fortunate we are to have your vast experience to call upon in a crisis."

He was baiting her again. The man seemed to enjoy provoking her anger. "Not so vast, Mr. Brawley. Just sensible."

"There is a lesson to be learned here, I am sure." He stared at the painting that had captured her attention. He shook his head, obviously unimpressed with the picture. "Though I doubt it has anything to do with art. I am a simple man, my lady. For clarity's sake, why do you not speak plainly?"

There was nothing simple about the gentleman. "Very well, sir." Two gentlemen joined them to admire the Rembrandt. Fayre and Mr. Brawley strolled nonchalantly to the next painting to continue their conversation in private. "I have agreed to your bargain. Do not, however, mistake my agreement for trust. I am not some foolish chit you can hoodwink with a charming smile while you delve into deeper play behind my back. If you overstep your bounds, sir, I shall cut you dead the next time we meet and you can consign your generous assistance to perdition."

Mr. Brawley sighed. "Standish struck a devastating blow, didn't he?"

Fayre tried to focus on the copy of Vandyke's *Cupid and Psyche* in front of her, but the turmoil welling in her breast was too distracting. "My feelings about Lord Standish are not a subject I wish to discuss with you."

Her forbidding tone did not discourage him in the least. "Then maybe I am asking the wrong question. What I really want to know is how long do you intend to make us pay?"

Fayre was so puzzled by his question, she gave up on the pretense of studying the picture and met his level gaze. "Us? Pay? I do not know what you speak of."

"I am referring to every gent who comes along after Standish. How long will you punish every one of us for the bastard's sins? If you want blood, shouldn't you be concentrating on taking slices out of his hide instead of mine?"

"I *am*," she said angrily, ashamed that he saw her behavior in such a distasteful light.

"With *my* help," he growled back. "Do not forget that part." He cocked his head, noticing the people wandering nearby. A student to the right of them had set up her easel and was preparing to paint. No one seemed interested in their argument.

"That still remains to be seen, Mr. Brawley," she said sweetly.

He curled his arm around her waist. His grip was neither tender nor playful. "We are finished here. I let you have things your way, now it is my turn."

He masterfully escorted her through the arched doorway and through the next. There was no way she could escape his firm embrace without drawing notice. "Release me! I cannot leave now. I intended to purchase one of these pictures before the exhibit closes."

"I have faith you will recover from the crushing disappointment," he said, stepping out into the street. The arm around her waist slid free and caught her wrist. Grunting in satisfaction, he tugged her to the left toward a hackney.

"Wait! I have my own carriage here. Mr. Brawley, where are we going?"

He nodded to the coachman as he bustled her into the carriage. "Someplace of my choosing, my lady. I appreciate your efforts to enlighten me by letting me stare at a few dozen pictures until my sight glazes over. Sadly, I am a lost cause in this idle pastime. I don't think I'm fashioned to be a patron of the fine arts."

"I cannot remain here too long."

This was the fourth comment Lady Fayre had uttered on the subject in the past thirty minutes, and frankly, Maccus was feeling the lady was not truly appreciative of his grand gesture. It was a rare occasion for him to open his private life to anyone. Inspiration had struck as he had bundled the protesting lady into the nearest hired coach. The anticipation of showing Lady Fayre his house increased as they had drawn closer. It should not have mattered what his companion thought of his recent purchase. Regardless, his nerves were agonizingly stretched beyond their limits while he waited for her to praise or condemn his choice.

"If our time together is so limited, I suggest we do not fritter it away on art exhibitions," Maccus said mildly.

Lady Fayre sent him a quick, nervous smile. "You really have no interest in art?" She reverently stroked the bronze arm of the gladiator displayed in the front hall.

He froze, riveted by the gentle manner in which she touched each piece of statuary she encountered. It was oddly sensual, although he doubted she was aware of her actions. He had never been more envious of a chunk of metal in his life. "None. So you will be wasting your time convincing me otherwise," he said tersely, in an attempt to conceal his discomfort.

"Oh, I shall not bother. Nevertheless, I daresay the art I have glimpsed in this hall alone calls you a liar, Mr. Brawley."

He took her elbow and guided her to the drawing room. "The house and contents were sold to me in its entirety. I have not owned the property long, and have yet to alter the previous owner's influence."

"I am curious how you managed to purchase this house. I was not even aware it had been placed on the auction block."

Crossing his arms, Maccus leaned against the mantel. Intrigued, he asked, "Prying into my finances, Lady Fayre?"

"Not in the least," she denied swiftly. "It is just that my mother's family was acquainted with the previous owner, Lady Chute. I recall, as a small child, chasing after the pair of small dogs she was partial to up and down the horseshoe-shaped stairs."

Maccus could envision a petite, fiery long-haired imp squealing with glee as she dashed after a pair of old dogs that probably wanted to be left alone. "I was given to understand that Lady Chute has been dead for five years."

"Yes, she had a weak heart and it finally gave out," Lady Fayre said, her voice rich with regret. Instead of sitting, she went to the window. "We were residing at our country estate and did not attend the funeral. I never met the heir."

"Neither did I. I heard he was a bit of an eccentric who preferred living on the coast. A friend contacted me when he learned the nephew was discreetly making inquiries about selling the house."

"Why the secrecy? Lady Chute was an avid collector of objets d'art, which in themselves must be of considerable value. Age has not diminished the grandeur of the house, even if the façade is bland in comparison to some of the new architecture. I know several families that would have bought the house for its pastoral window views alone."

She was studying the view as she spoke. He liked the graceful lines of her profile. Lady Fayre complemented the old-fashioned interior of the elegant drawing room. Pushing off from the mantel and stalking her from behind, Maccus realized he liked having her in his house. "Are you begrudging me my good fortune, my lady?" He stroked the indentation at the back of her neck.

To his delight, she shivered and glared at him, her green faerie eyes sparking. "Do not be silly. I thought the nephew's actions odd, that is all."

He placed his hand on the window casement, effectively caging her. "My friend Dossett explained that several members of Lady Chute's family were not pleased with the meager amounts settled on them. One of the cousins had an acute affection for gambling and considerable losses to show for his efforts. There was pressure from the elders for the nephew to add to the various settlements, but he was reluctant to part with his inheritance. Since he did not want the house, it seemed sensible to sell it before one of his scheming relatives began stripping it of its valuable contents."

"Ah, I see." Suddenly realizing her predicament, Lady Fayre tried to step away, but she was trapped. "Mr. Brawley," she began, probably wondering when she had lost the upper hand.

"My given name is Maccus. You will not go to perdition for using it. In fact, I insist," he said, staring at her lips, marveling at their fullness. He was aware that willful ladies, even the noble kind, had a tendency to bite.

"You have asked for my guidance," she protested, her forehead furrowing in frustration.

"In some instances, instinct prevails over your rules. Permit me to demonstrate," Maccus said, just wanting a small taste.

With two fingers he tipped her face upward and lowered his mouth to hers. Her full lips were rigid, already forming the numerous reasons why they should not be kissing. He jerked his mouth away. "Say my name, Fayre."

She squeezed her eyes shut and shook her head. "This is not right."

"Not the way you are doing it. Standish must have been a lousy lover," he said, despising the unknown man for touching her.

Her mouth parted in shock at his crudeness and he ruthlessly took advantage. Sealing his mouth over hers, his hands moved from the window casement to her slender shoulders. Not satisfied with the tiny taste he had originally wanted, he groaned and pulled back. His fingers tightened on her shoulders. "Who are you kissing, Fayre?"

She had placed one hand on his chest. The other delicately brushed over her slightly swollen lower lip. "You." Knowing he expected more, she added, "Maccus. But I still do not think—"

Painfully aroused, he silenced her with a quick, hard kiss. "Good. Let's see how long I can keep you in that condition."

"Two and twenty minutes," Fayre murmured, still befuddled by her encounter with Mr. Maccus Brawley six hours later. The man had kissed her senseless. Worse still, she had liked it.

"Fayre, what is wrong with you?" Callie whispered, dragging her back to the present. They had attended Lord and Lady Pindar's ball this evening together with her friend's mother acting as their chaperone. "You have been staring at Mr. Lesterfeld so intently his face is as red as strawberries in the summer."

She should have slapped Mr. Brawley when he first put his hands on her. Instead she had melted against him the instant his tongue had playfully stroked hers. "I am in trouble, Callie."

Becoming alarmed, her friend pushed her toward the balcony. "Come along. You obviously need fresh air to clear your head."

The ballroom was overflowing with guests, but Callie was determined. Within minutes the cool evening air was bathing Fayre's face. She moved away from the doors, preferring the shadows.

"You owe me for saving you," Callie said, leaning against the stone wall. "Mr. Lesterfeld was on the verge of breaking under your passionate stare. A few minutes more and he would have been begging you to marry him."

Perplexed by her friend's glee, Fayre asked, "Lesterfeld? What does Mr. Lesterfeld have to do with this?"

Callie choked on her laughter. "Goodness, it is worse that I thought. Poor Mr. Lesterfeld. Done in by stargazing. God save him if you ever look him straight in the eye."

"Oh no," Fayre groaned, dreading that she had inadvertently encouraged the bashful gentleman fifteen years her senior. He had quietly buried one wife and was seeking a replacement. "I had not even noticed." This was what happened when you spent the afternoon kissing an inappropriate gentleman. "Maccus Brawley is to blame."

Callie turned to face her, the humor of Fayre's predicament still dancing in her warm brown eyes. "Maccus Brawley. You mean the gentleman we met in the park

with Lord Yemant? What does he have to do with poor
Mr. Lesterfeld?"

A cross town, Maccus had tracked Lord Standish to
one of London's seedier gaming hells, aptly named,
Moirai's Lust. The establishment welcomed anyone
willing to risk his fortune on a turn of a card or the faithless dice. Often, young noblemen drunk on their self-
importance and the belief that they would live forever
found their way to the dangerous alley. When their luck
failed them at the tables, there were several brothels in
the vicinity willing to lighten their purses before they fell
drunkenly into their beds.

The stench in the alley reminded him of his childhood—
of the narrow dingy streets packed with years of dirt,
sewage, and rotting garbage. It was a place where no one
grew old because disease, hunger, and violence claimed
the ones who were fortunate enough to live beyond infancy. Few individuals found their way out of the crooked
maze of dead-end streets. Maccus had survived. It was
nothing he boasted about. Rather, he wished he could
wipe the images and foul odors from his mind.

He entered the gaming hell, dodging two fighting men
and the three who were sweeping the combatants into the
street. The hell consisted of a large main room with private saloons that could be had for a price. A woman observing a game of whist looked up and smiled as he
approached.

"Good evening, handsome," she purred, appreciating
what she saw and likely calculating his wealth. If she was
a prostitute, she was a well-paid one. The quality of the

green dress clinging to her curvaceous figure rivaled what was worn in most ballrooms. "In the mood for games?"

Maccus shook his head ruefully. The dark-haired temptress might have appealed to him a few weeks earlier, but not this evening. A certain lady with hair of cinnamon fire was haunting him. He could still taste her on his lips; her scent made him hunger for more, like a tantalizing spice.

"I am looking for Xavier," he shouted over the din of voices.

The brunette accepted his rejection genially. "And would he want to be found by you, handsome?"

"Maccus Brawley. And yes, Xavier tolerates my presence," he replied, his voice infused with charm.

Inclining her head, she said, "Try one of the back tables. There was an uproar earlier over a woman." She rolled her eyes in disdain at the idiocy of men. "Knives were drawn. Xavier is soothing the delicate feelings of his noble patrons."

"You have my gratitude." Maccus bowed over her extended hand. "And who are you?"

The smile she bestowed on him had his stomach clenching. She reminded him of a sleek black cat toying with a little mouse with her sharp, lethal claws. "It is not who I am that is of importance, Mr. Brawley. What you might find more fascinating is who I can be for you— perhaps, later, when your commitments have waned." She sauntered by him, letting her supple body brush against his.

"Are you a diviner?" he asked as she passed.

"No, handsome. Your face gave you away. I have seen that look countless times, and only a woman could put such a prickly mix of perplexity and annoyance on an intelligent man's face. Best wishes on the hunt."

"I must have your oath that you will not tell a soul," Fayre insisted, thinking what her brother might do to Mr. Brawley if he learned of their meeting.

Callie sobered, realizing Fayre was not jesting. "Of course you have it. On my honor," she promised. "What is troubling you? Is it Standish again?"

"No," Fayre said, wrinkling her face at the thought of the loathsome man. "Not Standish. It is Mr. Brawley."

"Are you letting his rudeness at the park bother you?" Callie asked, visibly relieved Fayre's upset was something she could address. "Lord Yemant was very apologetic about his friend, though if you are seeking a kind word from that gentleman I believe he will leave you wanting."

Leave her wanting. He had certainly done that! "I have seen him since the park; this afternoon, in fact. We both attended the same art exhibition," she admitted, already regretting her reckless confession. Mr. Brawley had not sworn her to secrecy about their bargain, though she was positive he did not want her attempt at polishing him to be common knowledge among the *ton*.

Callie squealed in excitement and seized both Fayre's hands. "Was this a planned meeting?" she asked eagerly. "Oh, what am I thinking? You despised Mr. Brawley almost immediately. I was worried you were planning to bash his head in with your parasol."

Fayre winced, conceding that the thought of denting Mr. Brawley's hard skull had occurred to her more than once. "I did not despise him exactly. His arrogance offended me. After Lord Standish, I have had my fill of gentlemen who believe every lady they encounter should yield to their dictates."

"Good grief, Fayre, this reminds me of that romantic novel we were reading to each other last autumn. How did it go . . . 'so sparks their indignation, slowly it fans into the flames of love,'" Callie quoted excitedly. "It sounds like the gentleman is courting you."

Fayre could just imagine Mr. Brawley's cynical response to such an outlandish suggestion. There was no romance involved in a bargain. "One kiss does not amount to a courtship."

"He kissed you!"

"Hush, keep your voice down," Fayre said, checking around them to see if they had been overheard. "There are enough rumors being bandied about regarding my close friendship with Lord Standish and Lady Hipgrave. We do not need to add Mr. Brawley to the unsavory broth of innuendos."

The quiet reminder of Fayre's current state of disgrace dimmed Callie's natural vibrancy. "Perhaps your Mr. Brawley is a sign that despite Lord Standish's slanderous efforts, most of polite society is sympathetic to your unfortunate plight."

Callie's view of her fellow man was too optimistic for her not to be disappointed one day. "According to my mother, sympathy rarely extends beyond the morning room. The only reason I have not been publicly shunned this season is due to my family's considerable influence. Still, it has not prevented the daring from sniping at me."

Only this morning, her mother was upset with her because Lady Winthrope had omitted Fayre's name on the invitation to next week's card party. The royal princesses were expected and the marchioness was being highly

selective in choosing her guests. Fayre had shrugged off
the slight, not particularly caring if she attended the card
party. The duchess, however, viewed it as a personal slap
in the face and an indication of the severity of her daughter's disgrace. Fayre had left the morning room before her
mother could suggest once again that Fayre should retire
to Arianrod.

"And what of Mr. Brawley?"

Fayre rubbed her head. "An aberration. I cannot think
of one reason why he kissed me." *Or why I liked it.* "Curiosity, I suppose."

Callie pursed her lips, glancing at her slyly. "He is a
handsome gentleman."

It was no reason to kiss a man. Fayre recalled how
Lord Standish had held her protectively in his arms and
declared his enduring love. She then thought of Mr.
Brawley and his effortless charm as he proposed his mu-
tually beneficial bargain. "Those are the worst kind."

Xavier was not at the back tables as the raven-haired
temptress had predicted. Maccus located him in one
of the private saloons. He stood in the doorway with three
other onlookers as Xavier seized one of his patrons by the
front of his coat, lifted the man off his feet and slammed
him against the wall. The struggling man never had a
chance. Xavier was a blond giant and built like a black-
smith. He also had fury on his side. Maccus winced in
sympathy as the proprietor drove his fist into the unlucky
man's gut.

"I run a fair establishment. The next time you accuse
the bank of cheating, you'll lose more than a hundred
pounds," Xavier said, setting the man back on his feet and

sh...
ba...
cur...
who...
the l...
he sp...

Rea...
wandere...
and kept...
ders to th...
them, Xav...
my door an...

"I leave t...
business of c...
head at the kn...
told you were s... feelings in the back."

Xavier snort... Not likely. I don't care how fancy a gent's coat is cut. No one accuses me of cheating."

There was enough deadly sincerity in the man's expression to convince Maccus that no one crossed Xavier, and if they were foolish enough to try, it was a mistake they lived to regret.

"I haven't seen you around for some time. What brings you to my door?" Xavier asked, setting a chair on its legs. He beckoned for Maccus to sit.

Maccus refused. He walked around to the other side of the overturned table and grabbed hold of it. It was heavier than it looked, but no match for two strong men. "I've come to collect on an old debt. I need a favor."

The announcement did not seem to surprise or disturb his companion. "It took you long enough," Xavier said nonchalantly. "What do you need?"

There was no hesitation in the proprietor's tone. No

no paid his debts. door and beckoned
nt for a few minutes until
arching for. "Are you familiar

s cronies are new patrons to Moirai's
gold and stupidity make them welcome,"
, his disgust for anyone who did not respect
's books evident. "Why?"

So the gents have had a run of bad luck?" Maccus
asked, watching the brunette he had spoken to earlier
saunter over to Standish's table.

"Some."

Standish had lost interest in the cards in his hands.
Maccus smiled slightly as the woman dodged the viscount's groping hand with practiced efficiency. "Some
have wretched luck every time they sit at a gaming table.
I want his pockets bled dry, Xavier."

The proprietor had seen the interaction between the
woman and Standish and he did not seemed too pleased
with the nobleman, either. "How long?"

"Until he is no longer welcome at your tables." His
meaning was clear. If Standish was reckless enough to
throw away his fortune, then Xavier should take it.

Xavier heaved a heavy sigh. "Consider the debt paid,
my friend. It is regrettable, but I see a dark cloud of mis-
fortune settling above Lord Standish. Many in his unfa-
vorable predicament never recover."

The dark cloud had settled over Standish the moment
Maccus had learned the viscount had seduced Lady
Fayre, although he did not speak his thoughts aloud. His
gaze returned to Standish. The man had left the table and
was in pursuit of the woman. Xavier had noticed, too, and

from his forbidding expression the proprietor was going to relish emptying Standish's purse.

"I have been meaning to ask. Who is the temptress in green?"

Maccus did not believe it was possible, but his friend looked grimmer. "Moirai in the flesh. Standish isn't the only man here bedeviled by ill fortune."

7

"Is nothing sacred, woman?" Maccus bellowed, warily staring at the razor in Fayre's hand.

They were circling around each other in the kitchen. She had managed to pay three calls to Mr. Brawley's house since she had confessed the kiss to Callie in the Pindars' garden. Each time she saw him, anticipation coiled in her stomach in expectation of him pulling her into a rough embrace and thoroughly ravishing her mouth.

"Honestly," Fayre said, placing her hand on her hip as she shook the blade at him. "You are acting as if I intend to castrate you."

Exasperatingly, with regard to his behavior, Mr. Brawley had been a perfect gentleman. He appeared sincere when he had asked for her assistance. It had taken several afternoons to scrutinize his wardrobe and offer suggestions, not that she could fault his conservative selections. Hobbs, she discovered, was an unusual choice for a gentleman's manservant. The man did not have the temperament one expected for a personal servant, but it was obvious Mr. Brawley and Hobbs had a private understanding, if not affection for each other. Fayre had given Hobbs the name of her brother's tailor and the address of a reputable haberdashery in Piccadilly. She also planned on introducing the man to her father's valet since he was willing to improve and his skills reflected on his master.

"Some men might view your actions as such," Mr. Brawley retorted, glaring at his manservant. "Hobbs, you are not much help just sitting there cackling like an old hag. Do something!"

Mr. Brawley had been amazingly cooperative until she had suggested the services of a barber to remove his unfashionable moustache. He flatly refused. If she wanted him shaved, he had told her, she was going to have to do it herself. Perhaps he thought such a personal task would deter her from her goal. Ha! He had underestimated her because she intended to triumph.

"I confess that you look rather dashing with a moustache, Mr. Brawley, but it must go. No fashionable gentleman wears them these days. Since you mulishly refuse to visit a barber, I am forced to attend the matter myself." Fayre signaled the manservant with a nod. "Hobbs, if you please," she said, her tone ringing with authority.

It was clear that Hobbs's former experience with polite society had been disastrous. His insolence seemed second nature, despite his master's numerous warnings, but Fayre privately thought the older man was warming to her. He confirmed her suspicions by hopping up from his perch and grabbing Mr. Brawley from behind.

"I never expected you to turn traitor, Hobbs. Consider yourself on the streets!" Mr. Brawley grumbled, halfheartedly resisting the manservant as he dragged him backward to the stool the servant had abandoned earlier.

"Cease blustering." Hobbs dumped him onto the stool and held him in place. He tugged hard on Mr. Brawley's queue to tip his head back. "When you asked for polish, that means from boots to face. Let the lady see to 'er task."

Fayre bit back a smile. Mr. Brawley had the look of a sullen child. He was not fighting to get off the stool, but he was not surrendering gracefully. "Shall we have Hobbs bring you some lavender to calm your nerves?"

His gray eyes raked over her contemptuously. "My nerves are just fine!"

"Oh dear, I have insulted you," she said in a manner that revealed she was not sorry at all. "Perhaps something stronger? A glass of brandy?" she asked, teasing him.

"I never touch the stuff. It rots a man's mind and loosens his tongue. So do your worst, miss," he dared, his lean body taut with outrage.

She blinked at his vehement rejection of a simple glass of brandy. There was a story there, Fayre mused, but he was too angry with her to explain his odd reaction. "Such sterling faith in my abilities," she mockingly lamented. "I confess, I do not have the spirit for this business if shaving off whiskers means Hobbs has to bash your skull in with one of the cook's best copper pots to gain your cooperation."

Fayre pivoted on her heel as if to leave.

"Wait."

Naturally, she had no intention of leaving, but his soft command gave her a measure of control over the enigmatic Mr. Brawley, which she eagerly seized.

Slowly turning back toward him, she politely inquired, "Yes?"

He glared up at her, defiant. "Do you truly know how to wield a razor?"

Fayre drew herself up to full height. "You might be surprised, but I can do a number of mundane tasks amazingly well." She did not bother mentioning that two summers earlier when one of her male cousins broke his arm while hunting at Arianrod, she had taken up the chore of shaving him daily. "Besides, the notion of holding a blade to your throat is vastly appealing."

Mr. Brawley braced his hands on his thighs and laughed heartily. "I'm certain it is." He motioned her closer. "You can't do a decent job of it clear across the room."

She picked up the small bowl on the table before she joined him. Within the bowl was a shaving paste she had mixed herself containing soap, honey, ambergris, and oil of bergamot. She had asked her father's valet for the recipe. She set the razor down and picked up the shaving brush. Dipping it into a cup of tepid water, she swirled the thick bristles into the paste.

Rolling his eyes up at Hobbs, Mr. Brawley said, "Restraints won't be necessary, Fayre. I promise to behave."

Belatedly, she noticed Hobbs had not released his master's shoulders. "You have done a fine job keeping your master in line, Hobbs. Since I have his promise he will cooperate, you can go about your duties."

Hobbs tugged on a front lock of his hair. "Aye, milady. Just holler if you need me," he said, and left the kitchen.

Mr. Brawley groaned. "Fayre . . . Fayre . . . you are corrupting my staff."

"I have told you countless times that it is not proper to call me by my given name," she scolded, but in truth she liked the way he said her name. "And I am not corrupting anyone. Hobbs was just being respectful."

"Hobbs is surly and disrespectful to everyone," Mr. Brawley said, tilting his face up to give her better access. "One smile from you and he is doing your bidding."

Fayre brushed the shaving paste across the line of his jaw. "Not likely," she scoffed, dipping the brush back into the bowl.

"You are never going to get this done if you don't move in closer." Mr. Brawley wrapped his hands around her hips and pulled her closer so that she was positioned between his legs. She jolted when her leg brushed against his inner thigh.

The weakness settling in her limbs made her feel like a silly goose. She was just shaving the man, for heaven's sake, not making love to him. Setting down the bowl of shaving paste, she refused to allow the intimacy of the act of shaving him affect her. Fayre finished slathering the paste over the lower half of his face. They had a bargain between them. Nothing else.

Fayre dropped the brush into the cup of water and reached for the razor. Hobbs had sharpened the edge, so if she faltered at her task she was likely to give him a scar or cut his throat.

"Be gentle," he said calmly as if reading her thoughts. He tilted his head back and closed his eyes.

Biting her lower lip, she concentrated on her task. Delicately placing the blade to his skin, she delivered the first stroke. The bared flesh across his jaw was free of blood, much to her relief. Rinsing the razor, she continued.

"I have never been shaved by a woman," Mr. Brawley mused, his left hand caressing her hip. "It is a pleasurable experience I hope to repeat."

His lingering touch was a lightning stroke to her womb. Fayre rested her wrist on his shoulder to keep her hand from trembling. "You will not think it is pleasurable if I accidentally slice off your nose. Hold still!" she ordered, trying to shake off the feelings churning inside of her. "I will have no more mischief from you, Mr. Brawley."

"Maccus," he corrected dreamily. "Your tongue will not blacken and wither if you utter my name aloud. Grant me this boon, and I will grant yours—and more."

The fine arch of her left eyebrow lifted questioningly at his husky promise. *And more.* Such a promise covered quite a large ambiguous field of unspoken desires.

"Maccus, then," she conceded, unwilling to battle him while her nerves were frayed by her task and his proximity. With tiny strokes she removed the small moustache he had favored and then began to work on the underside of his jaw.

"I like to hear my name come from your lips, Fayre," he admitted while she washed the shaving paste and hair stubble from the razor. "Your voice softens when you say it, and there is a slight hesitation I think is endearingly sweet."

She did not speak thusly! Only a woman falling in lo— No, she was not that harebrained. He was exaggerating to keep her off balance. She brusquely turned his head to the side and then up. It only took two strokes and she was finished. "You are mistaken, Maccus," she said, deliberately using his name to prove her point. "The softness and hesitancy you hear is simply outrage regarding your arrogance."

"I have embarrassed you."

Fayre slapped down the razor. "No." She picked up a towel Hobbs had soaking in a bowl of warm water and wrung it out. Maccus Brawley and his arrogance had succeeded where she had failed in dousing the awareness she seemed to feel in his presence. Using the towel, she wiped away the remaining traces of the shaving paste.

"Enough! I'd rather keep my skin." He took the towel from her hand and tossed it back into the bowl. "Do you approve?"

Fayre tried to step back, but Maccus was quicker. He grabbed a fistful of her skirt and held her in place. Scowling at his interference, she was tempted to lie. His face had a pinkish hue from her ministrations, however, it did not diminish his masculine beauty. Staring into his mischievous gray eyes, she studied the fine outer rim of dark blue almost eclipsed by the restless sea of gray. He was a handsome devil and she silently cursed him for it!

Without thinking, she absently caressed the line of his jaw. Maccus's smile widened at the affectionate gesture. "Am I still dashing?" he teased, recalling her earlier comment.

"Not in the least," she replied, jerking her traitorous hand away from his face. She had to move away from him before she started babbling.

"You tempt me to prove you wrong," he said, cheered by her growing agitation. "Then again, maybe that was your intention all along."

"No. No. No! I forbid it." He had that look in his eye again. The last time he stared at her so hungrily he—

A swift tug and she fell neatly into his lap. Before she could recover, his mouth was covering hers. The smell of bergamot from the shaving paste filled her nostrils while his agile tongue slipped between her teeth and stroked hers. Fayre moaned. She tried to pretend it was in anguish, even though his hand on her rib cage had her breasts swelling in painful anticipation of his touch. Leaning closer, she kissed him back with unexpected fervency. Her response surprised her as much as it did him. Maccus slid his hand approvingly up and down the length of her corset. She liked the taste of him. Tangling her tongue with his, she wondered if a person could become intoxicated by the essence of a kiss.

Sanity reared its practical head when he tickled her ankle.

Fayre tore her mouth away from his. "What are we doing? Hobbs could return at any moment."

"Hobbs will not bother us until we summon him," Maccus said, kissing her nose. "Besides, he likes you. Knowing him, he would have tried to steal a kiss from you if I had not had the good sense to claim you first."

He moved in to kiss her again. She refused to be diverted. "The devil you say! You and I have a bargain. Nothing *more*."

M accus was tired of hearing Fayre spouting words that had *no* within them. Taking advantage of the position the emphasis had produced on her lips, Maccus swallowed the rest of her protest and kissed her relentlessly until she whimpered. He had a preference for her lower lip, he decided. The soft fullness begged to be nibbled and suckled and he was content to indulge himself.

The mask of a gentleman was fragile, and the lady in his arms had the tendency of ruining his good intentions. Their first kiss, which had left him still aroused hours after her departure, had had Maccus questioning his wisdom in seducing her. The afternoon Fayre had entered the restaurant to meet her mother, she had, at first glance, seemed like a delightful diversion for the tedious necessity of his goals for London. When he had been apprised of her unfortunate circumstances with Standish, Maccus quickly realized her connections in polite society tempted him as much as her haunting beauty. In his arrogance, he had thought a deepened intimacy would give him a measure of control over the fiery stubborn vixen. It had never occurred to him that by touching her he was surrendering a part of himself to her. The notion had rattled him. He had deliberately kept a polite distance since he had lost control of their kiss in the drawing room.

Maccus had concentrated on the business aspects of their new friendship. It was not all one-sided. He had begun honoring his part of the bargain by sowing the seeds of discord that would eventually lead to Standish's downfall. Everything was progressing according to plan.

There were a few details beyond his influence that he found troublesome. His half brother was a perfect example of one factor.

Trevor was still out there somewhere searching for him. The boy was bringing ill fortune. Maccus could taste it on the air. If he had any sense he would hunt down Trevor and gain control over the situation.

Control.

The woman in his arms bit his lip, reminding him of what he lacked at least where she was concerned. Already his manhood was turgid, pressing against her rounded buttocks. Fayre was a stimulating handful of passion and vulnerability. Maccus slid his hand lightly over her calf and around to her knee. He really should heed her advice and hold to their bargain, he thought, nipping her chin with his teeth. On the other hand, he was a man who preferred risky ventures. His instincts whispered to him that dallying with Lady Fayre might be his most ticklish personal undertaking of all.

Fayre giggled and smacked him on the shoulder. "Cease your nonsense at once and put me down."

For a man in jeopardy, he was prepared to enjoy himself to the fullest. "Why should I?" He moved his hand higher, fingering her embroidered garter. "You like my . . . nonsense." Maccus nuzzled her neck.

She squirmed, fighting his sensual onslaught. "Maybe so." Fayre hissed when his exploration exploited a particularly sensitive nerve. "Nevertheless, you cannot go through life indulging every whim."

Maccus felt her body become rigid in his arms. She was probably thinking of her grand debacle with Standish. That sort of thinking was a terrible aphrodisiac. He preferred having her pliant and giggling.

"Denying yourself is closing yourself to new experiences. That is not my definition of living." To prove his point Maccus walked his fingers up her inner thigh.

Fayre clasped her hand over the one he had under her skirt. "The experience you are offering is older than Methuselah, Mr. Brawley," she said wryly.

"And here I thought you a staunch supporter of tradition," Maccus said, fastening his mouth on hers, kissing her deeply, reminding them both that they forgot about fighting each other when they focused on more pleasant matters. He eased his hand higher, needing to touch the heart of her.

The shock of his bold caress almost had them both seeing shooting stars. Startled, Fayre gasped and bucked, sending her hard head into his forehead. The burst of pain above his left eye left him dazed. "I knew you were a dangerous woman," he groaned, resting his injured head on her shoulder.

"It is your fault," she muttered, too dazed to notice his hand was nestled firmly between her thighs. "Oh, my head. I probably will have a bruise from your thick skull. What do you have rattling around in your head? Grapeshot?"

"Well, my jewel, at least we will match," Maccus said, his good humor returning as the pain eased. "Here, now, let me kiss it and fix it up right." He pressed a gentle kiss over the reddening mark on her forehead.

"Kisses are not healing."

She sounded so cross, Maccus grinned. "Mine are." He kissed her eyelids, her pert little nose, and rubbed his freshly shaven cheek against hers before hovering over her mouth.

"Arrogant, fiendishly scheming—*umph!*"

Maccus cut off her tirade with another heated kiss. He laughed against her lips when Fayre tried to sink her teeth into his tongue. She squirmed to evade his clever fingers, but her attempts were in vain.

"What is this?" he asked, his fingers parting the downy nest of hair between her legs and skimming her womanly cleft.

Fayre's expression was a mixture of panic and burgeoning arousal. "Hobbs . . . someone will come," she said, her voice strained.

"Hmm." Maccus delved deeper and the heart of her was like discovering a secret fjord. Despite her protestations, Fayre desired his touch. The realization made his cock pulse with his life's blood. He ached to free his rigid member from his breeches and plunge deeply into her welcoming depths.

"Maccus." She whispered his name against his cheek, her breath washing over his heated flesh.

If she had been any other woman, he would have opened his breeches, pushed her skirts up, and wrapped her long legs around him. He had succeeded in arousing her to the point that Fayre might have allowed him to take her hastily in the kitchen. It was later, when the passion had cooled, that shame and anger would surface. If he handled her clumsily now, he might never get to touch her again. In his present uncomfortable state, the notion was unbearable.

"Hush. I built the ache in you, I can ease it." He cupped the back of her head and tugged her closer for another lingering kiss. "Just close your eyes, sweet Fayre." His fingers stroked her womanly cleft. The slippery wetness of her desire was an invitation he could not resist. Maccus pushed his finger into her narrow channel. Its yielding softness made him want to howl in delight. He ground her bottom against his cock silently, demanding satisfaction, even though he would not ask her to be so reckless.

"I was a virgin when Standish—" Fayre blushed at the confession, which was ironic considering where his hand was. "He was my first lover," she said forging onward. "And it was only just that one time."

She looked so miserable after making her confession, he took pity on her. They had managed to ruin the pretty arrangement of her hair. Maccus used his other hand to push the loose strands back from her face. "Do you think I'm bothered that Standish was your lover? I'm not." It was a tiny lie. It was not her lack of virginity that offended him, it was Standish. Maccus burned with fury when he thought of the nobleman's callous treatment of Fayre.

She shook her head, though he could see she was pleased by his words. "I just thought it was important for you to understand that despite what people are saying about me—what I did with Standish—I am just not very experienced in the matters of passion."

It was clear to him that she was as innocent as a lamb and he felt like a savage for seducing her. No one had ever inspired him to feel so conflicted. One minute he was fighting to control his blinding lust and the next he wanted to protect her even from himself. It was damned confusing. He slowly withdrew his hand nestled between her legs.

Fayre placed her hand on top of his, halting his withdrawal. "Should I not be doing something? You promised to ease my ache, what about yours? Show me what to do."

Understanding lightened his expression. "Nay, Fayre," he said, when her hand brushed the buttons on his breeches. "There are different ways of pleasuring. Let me show you." Maccus kissed her fiercely, feeling damned noble about his decision. "Open for me. I won't hurt you."

She stared directly at him, her unspoken doubt clearly visible in those bottomless green depths. After a brief hesitation, she shifted, parting her legs. Maccus groaned. He was hard as flint rock and her little movements were ruthlessly undermining his good intentions.

"Close your eyes and concentrate on my touch," he said, slipping his fingers into her once again. The muscles of his stomach contracted in anticipation. "I'm inside you, Fayre. How deep can you take me?" He answered his own question by showing her how deeply he could stroke her.

The pace he set was slow and very thorough. Maccus devoured her with his mouth, his tongue mimicking the actions of his thrusting fingers. Every time he plunged into her his thumb pressed against her clitoris and teased the small nubbin of flesh in a circular motion. Fayre made a small sound of surprise and widened her legs further.

"You like it?"

She purred in his ear. "I do." Her arm around his neck tightened when he increased the pace.

" 'Tis only the beginning," he rasped. The friction of her bottom rubbing against his swollen cock was bringing him closer and closer to his own orgasm. The desire to be inside her was so intense he thought he might die if he was denied.

"Maccus—wait!" She dug her fingers into his shoulders.

Fayre did not seem to recognize the stirrings that would culminate in the ultimate pleasure a man could give his lover. Had Standish been so inept and selfish that he had not bedded her properly? The possibility made Maccus more determined than ever that Fayre discover her first womanly pleasure in his arms.

"Look at me," he demanded, ruthlessly driving them both higher and higher. Her green gaze locked on his as if he were the refuge in the wild passionate storm they had created. Fayre cried out and Maccus smashed his mouth against hers. He tasted blood, not caring if it was his or hers.

At the first pulse of her climax, she blindly bucked her hips against his hand, prolonging the sweet release. The combination of her musky scent clinging to him and her breathy cries were too much for Maccus. Snatching his hand from its warm berth, he shoved his hand into his breeches. Cradling her with one arm, Maccus's fingers, still damp with her essence, curled around his cock. He made a small choking sound and his forehead collapsed on her shoulder as his own orgasm claimed him.

Fayre stroked Maccus's damp hair, watching him prop his free arm on his thigh and suck in air as if he had been running. He looked at her and grinned ruefully. "I knew you were a dangerous lady. Christ, I think my heart stopped for a few seconds."

She expected embarrassment to seep in, dampening the calm she was feeling. The man had been caressing her intimately just minutes earlier. How had the simple act of shaving him transformed into a hedonistic display in the kitchen? Anyone could have walked in, for heaven's sake! Instead of slinking away in shame like a good woman, she surprised both of them by smiling.

"Does shaving always inspire you in this manner?" she asked.

"No. Just you, my lovely Fayre." Moving slowly, he shifted her off his left leg and onto the stool. Since he was bent over he smoothed down her skirts. "I'm crippled." He groaned and placed his hand on his lower back as he straightened. "In all my life, I have never pleasured a woman and myself on a stool. You have broadened my mind to the creative possibilities."

Fayre stood, noticing that her limbs were sore, too. She raised her brows skeptically. "Possibilities to do what? What we did has me questioning both our sound judgment. Good Lord, what if Hobbs had decided to return?"

Maccus was undisturbed by the notion. "I pay Hobbs a respectable salary and he obeys my commands. So far, it's been an agreeable bargain."

Fayre tried not to flinch when he said *bargain,* but he noticed anyway. There were not many things that escaped his notice, she guessed.

"I did not plan this," he said with such sincerity she had to believe him. "Still, I'd like to think that if there had been any risk of someone discovering us I would have stopped before matters moved beyond our control."

Thinking of everything he had done to her in the kitchen, she resisted the urge to cross her eyes at him in exasperation. Instead, she asked, "At what point was too far?"

Maccus cupped her chin to force her to meet his gaze and smiled. She felt the warmth of it all the way to her toes. "When you told me that I looked dashing with my unfashionable moustache," he replied.

8

Othilia, Lady Hipgrave, preened in front of her dressing mirror. Her attention was not on her reflection for she already knew she was beautiful, but rather on the man watching her. She had learned years ago that men enjoyed observing the mysterious rituals women performed as they prepared for a lover. Not that she ever permitted any of her lovers to see her before she had enhanced her natural beauty. A lady was allowed her secrets. Besides, she doubted any man wanted to glimpse his lady with puffy eyes or the imprint of the blanket still fresh on her face.

"Come to bed," Lord Standish pleaded, sitting on the

bed. He had removed his shoes and stockings in anticipation of their frenzied lovemaking.

She glimpsed his bare feet and sighed. The man was handsome, passable in bed, but always in a hurry. He did not understand the excitement of prolonging the moment. She once had a lover who took over an hour to undress her; each step of the unveiling was savored. How she missed the Duke of Solitea in her bed. He was a lover without parallel. The thought of him preferring Lady Talemon over her was beyond her comprehension. Othilia picked up a tiny pot and dabbed her finger within its contents. She dabbed the lip salve on her lower lip and smeared it with a practiced stroke. Pursing her lips, she admired the results.

For a lady of eight and twenty, she was holding up remarkably well, although her blond hair had darkened with age and now was streaked with chestnut and gold. Unbound, it was still an impressive bounty. If she were to be critical, she thought her eyes, an unremarkable blue, were too small for her face. In her youth, a traveling performer had introduced her to the art of cosmetics and had taught her to improve where nature had been stingy. The end result staring back at her pleased her like any artist viewing his work of art.

"I prefer talking rather than going to bed, Thatcher," Othilia said sulkily.

He reached for his cravat and tore at the stylish knot in a manner that would make his valet weep at his carelessness. "Compromise. We talk in bed."

It was her fault, really. She had spoiled him. Most of their planning regarding Solitea's meek daughter had occurred while he was rutting on top of her. Even an intelligent man was extremely cooperative when his brains were knocking between his hairy legs.

It was how she had convinced the reclusive Lord Hipgrave into marrying her, although he was forty years her senior. The old man dreamed of planting his heir in her fertile belly and she had let him climb on top of her enough times to tantalize him with the possibility. While her husband rusticated in the country awaiting her return, she was supposed to be recovering from a miscarriage. In truth, she had not been pregnant, nor did she ever intend to be. The lie served its purpose. Lord Hipgrave could keep his dreams of immortality and she had London and her lord's money to enjoy.

As for Standish, she did not consider him a clever man. He simply adored bedding women. If she indulged his whims, he would agree to her demands.

Othilia glanced over her shoulder and sniffed in disdain. "I prefer sitting. What of our plans, Thatcher? I have not seen Lady Fayre since that night at the theater. I must confess, the dear child did not look well. Her face had an appalling green cast to it. Do you think she is breeding?" The notion of Standish's seed bloating the young woman's figure like a plump pumpkin gave her almost as much pleasure as bedding the lady's former lover. Impregnating Solitea's daughter had never been part of the original plan. After all, she harbored no malice toward the chit. In hindsight, however, Othilia wondered if she had been hasty in snatching Standish away from Lady Fayre. If she convinced him to return to the broken-hearted creature, perhaps this time he could console her until she swelled with Standish's bastard. She could just imagine the duke's outrage when facing the choice of burying his only daughter in the country or marrying her off to her heartless seducer.

"No lady has ever caught my seed in her womb,"

Standish said, working on the buttons of his shirt. "I only had that one time with Fayre before she caught us together."

She cringed, disliking his whining tone and pathetic excuses. A weak man had impotent seed, Othilia concluded idly, dismissing the plan altogether. "Never mind, love. Lady Fayre is too inflexible in her thinking to appreciate a man like you," she said, subtly shifting her position to admire the way her thin chemise revealed teasing glimpses of her nipples. "It was her upbringing, I wager, though how a lustful man like the duke raised such a little puritan is beyond me."

"Fayre is not prudish. The time I spent in her company, I found that she possesses a taste for adventure like the rest of her high-spirited family. Since she is an unmarried female, the family has tried to shelter her. Not unusual, really. Solitea was likely preparing her for an advantageous marriage to benefit the family. With her beauty, I would have done the same."

Othilia bared her teeth in a parody of a smile. It had worried her that Standish might become smitten with Solitea's daughter. To discourage a change of heart, she had kept her lover tangled in her sensual thrall, binding him solely to her. A shy virgin never stood a chance of besting her. Still, she could not tolerate listening to Standish defend the lady and praise her beauty.

She rose from her cushioned bench and straightened her spine. Her breasts were high and firm, and good posture accentuated them. Strolling up to him, she noted with smugness that Standish's attention centered on her nipples.

"Why is Lady Fayre still in London? You should be stalking her, Thatcher. Every time she looks across a ballroom or a theater box, she should see your taunting smile and everyone else should be talking about the wicked things that sweet innocent allowed you to do to her."

Standish tried to grab her breast, but Othilia spun out of reach. Giving up, he said, "She and the family are brazening it out. I think she is pretending the liaison never happened and many are believing her."

By Jove, did she have to do all the thinking? Changing tactics, she returned to him and knelt before him. "Then you and I shall have to be more convincing," she said, glancing up at him slyly through her thick lashes. "Provoke her. If she has any of her sire's temperament at all, you should be able to prod her into a public confrontation. When we are finished with her, she will gladly pack her trunks and quit London in disgrace."

Othilia expertly opened his breeches and pulled out the length of shirt he had tucked into it. She boldly cupped his testicles. "You need to spend less time in the gaming hells," she said, kissing the head of his cock.

"Just as well," he said raggedly. "God-awful luck at the tables these past few nights."

"All you have to do is follow my instruction and I can guarantee that your luck will experience a surge," she promised, taking his rigid length into her mouth. Othilia took little pleasure in the act, but Standish needed a reminder of who was in charge.

Maccus stood next to Yemant and surveyed the room filled with the genteel and aristocratic. Fayre had insisted that they join her and her friend Miss Mableward for the evening concert. He could have listed at least six other activities he would have rather been doing with the Lady Fayre at his side. Still, she was honoring his request that she introduce him to her world.

"There she is," Yemant murmured, and from his elated expression Maccus did not know if the viscount was referring to Fayre or Miss Mableward.

Both ladies wore white dresses this evening. Maccus could not discern many differences between the dresses except that Fayre's had slashed sleeves and a square bosom and Miss Mableward's was rounded in the front and was trimmed with silver cord and tassels.

"Good evening, Lord Yemant," Fayre said brightly, her green eyes sparkling and rivaling the diamond necklace gracing her throat. "Mr. Brawley. You do remember my friend Miss Mableward?"

"Indeed," Maccus said, taking her hand and bowing over it gallantly. The gesture earned a thoughtful frown from Yemant. "It is always a pleasure to share an evening with two beautiful ladies."

"I have been looking forward to this concert with high anticipation," Miss Mableward said, moving closer to the viscount. "My lord, have you had the privilege of hearing our guest soloist, Miss Maria Kidd?"

"No, I confess my obligations until rather recently have denied me the pleasure," Lord Yemant admitted humbly.

Forgetting herself, Miss Mableward touched Yemant on the arm in her excitement and then hastily withdrew her hand. In an effort to recover, she rambled on, "Oh, then I am pleased you have joined us. I have been told Miss Kidd is originally from Salisbury."

Maccus was not interested in learning Miss Kidd's family history. While he was wondering how he could separate Fayre from her chatty friend, Lord Yemant fortu-itously intervened.

"Perhaps, Miss Mableward, with your permission, we could sit together so you may share your insights regard-ing this evening's concert." Yemant's valet seemed to have tied the poor man's cravat too tightly. His face red-dened at the slightest provocation and his expression seemed pained. "I am woefully ignorant and would wel-come your kind guidance."

"Oh . . . oh." Miss Mableward glanced at Fayre for her approval of the arrangement. Maccus was prepared to support Yemant if Fayre refused, but to his relief Fayre nodded. Jubilant, Miss Mableward turned back to the vis-count. "My lord, I would love to sit beside you. If you prefer, we could select our seats now and begin our discus-sion?"

"Run along, Yemant," Maccus said, noticing the vis-count was conflicted in doing what was proper versus fol-lowing his desire. Miss Mableward was clearly the one the man desired. "I will remain with Lady Fayre."

"I am in your debt, sir," Yemant said, happy with his fate. "We will reserve a pair of chairs in your name beside ours." He bowed respectfully and directed Miss Mable-ward toward the seating.

Fayre did not seem perturbed that her friends had abandoned her. In fact, her expression was rather smug. Despite what had occurred in his kitchen several days earlier, Maccus was not so arrogant as to believe she was pleased to be alone in his company.

"Trying your hand at matchmaking?"

His question had her glancing at him. "A wasted effort, I think, since they are doing well on their own."

She accepted his offered arm without hesitation.

"Walking is a sound idea. The concert is lengthy and those chairs look uncomfortable."

The concert room was large, although a bit stuffy. It could hold a crowd of three hundred. Guiding Fayre through the small groups of people awaiting the commencement of the concert, Maccus estimated the audience was exceeding the capacity.

Fayre opened her fan. "This room would be improved with larger windows."

"Did you want to join your friend and Yemant?" Maccus asked, wondering if there would be any chairs available to them. The notion of standing for hours was unappealing. He was tempted to whisk Fayre away from the crowds as he had the night she had been ambushed by Lady Hipgrave and her friends.

"No. Lord Yemant promised to reserve our seats. He will not fail us," she said, slowing as they approached one of the windows.

Maccus noticed immediately that something was amiss. Two women close to Fayre's age were standing in front of the open window fanning themselves. A gentleman who appeared as bored as Maccus felt stood between them. All three stopped talking when they recognized Fayre. A sly speculation crept into the gentleman's gaze that had Maccus bristling.

"Good evening, Miss Sheaf, Miss Piggot, and Mr. Farelle," Fayre greeted everyone politely. "Have you been introduced to Mr. Brawley?" She made the proper introductions after hearing everyone's quick denials.

Miss Sheaf peered at him through her spectacles. "So Mr. Brawley, are you new to London?" She was a plump blonde who spoke with a slight lisp.

The subtle cut that he was an outsider did not disturb

Maccus. Some resistance was expected. "Now, Miss Sheaf, is any Englishman *new* to London?" he asked, giving her a calculated smile, an outpour of charm. His efforts earned a reprimanding squeeze of Fayre's fingers into his arm. She obviously did not approve of him being charming.

Mr. Farelle chuckled and tapped his walking stick against his right shoe. The action must have been habitual because the inside of his shoe was scuffed. "Well said, Brawley." He might have been addressing Maccus, but he seemed fascinated by Fayre. Too fascinated. Maccus guessed his age somewhere in his early thirties. His hair was black and cropped short. He was just the sort of gentleman he imagined hovered near Fayre, vying for her smile and composing sonnets in dedication of her beauty.

Maccus already despised him.

Miss Sheaf bestowed on both men a look of aggrieved forbearance. "Forgive my impudence, Mr. Brawley. You are new to our little circle and I was curious about how you met Lady Fayre."

The nosy Miss Sheaf with her barely veiled insinuations was starting to annoy Maccus. He was thinking of a polite way he could tell her to go to the devil when Fayre replied, "Mr. Brawley is Lord Yemant's friend. He made the introductions."

"Oh," Miss Sheaf said, her eyes widening, eclipsing her spectacles. "How interesting. And here I thought you just arrived in town, Lady Fayre?"

Miss Piggot, silent until now, tittered behind her fan. She was the tallest lady present, with frizzy dark brown hair and large front teeth that reminded him of a beaver. Maccus's gray eyes narrowed, wondering what the woman found so humorous about the question and why Miss Sheaf looked smug.

Maccus stared down at Fayre, concerned. Her grip on his arm felt like a vise.

"No—" Fayre began to explain.

"Don't be a ninny, Hattie!" Miss Piggot scolded. "We saw her at—at—oh my, where were we last week?"

"Was it the countess's levee? Or was it the park?" Miss Sheaf asked, turning to her friend for confirmation.

"Neither, my dear Miss Sheaf," Mr. Farelle interjected, never taking his gaze off Fayre. Maccus could have sworn the man had not blinked once during the entire discourse. "It was the night we attended the theater."

"Oh yes, you are correct, Mr. Farelle." Miss Piggot pivoted to address Fayre. "We visited your box, but you had already departed. Your brother said that you had been feeling ill."

"Nothing serious. A slight headache," Fayre explained. She was squeezing his arm, but Maccus was not certain she was signaling him or just agitated.

"A pity," Miss Sheaf lamented. "We had hoped to catch up on the latest news with you."

A very telling silence descended on the group. The two ladies exchanged glances, while Mr. Farelle's rapt attention bordered on insulting. Maccus was ready to seize the man's walking stick and rap him on the head with it. The threesome had obviously heard the gossip. Maccus was startled anyone would confront her so boldly.

Fayre met each of their curious gazes, while she fanned herself. "What news? I fear the months away from London have been tedious, Miss Sheaf. I cannot recall a single anecdote I wish to relate."

To any of you was her unspoken comment.

Maccus was proud of Fayre. She stared the three of them down, daring them to call her a liar. For all her fancy speech and airs, she had pluck. It was one of the first things he noticed about her and he admired her for it. Stepping closer, he said, "Lady Fayre, I believe Lord Yemant and Miss Mableward are anticipating our return." If he was the reason she was suffering their calculated scrutiny, the least he could do was rescue her.

Fayre squeezed his arm approvingly. "Yes, we have tarried too long." She curtsied, prompting the others to follow her example. "I bid you all good evening."

Maccus bowed, leading Fayre away from the trio before he introduced them to his rougher facets. He sensed she would not approve and he did not want to humiliate her by drawing attention to them.

"First Lord Standish, and now Mr. Brawley," Miss Sheaf murmured behind them. "Lady Fayre claims many new friends this season."

The muscles tensing under her fingers were her first indication that Maccus had heard Miss Sheaf's spiteful remark. Fayre shifted her gaze from his arm to his face. She was startled by the luminous hatred she saw in his gray eyes. He slowed their pace and she could tell by the way his muscles rippled under her hand that he was poised for battle.

"Leave it alone, Maccus," she begged. "I know she is a horrid, petty creature. She deserves whatever you are thinking, I agree. Nevertheless, a scene will add credence to her words."

He finally looked at her. His handsome face was a rigid mask of belligerence. If she had not been grasping his arm, she would have taken a step back from all that smoldering fury he was trying to keep banked.

"Why should Miss Sheaf have all the fun?" he mused, and gently removed her hand from his arm. He strode off to confront Miss Sheaf.

"Damn you, Maccus Brawley," she mumbled under her breath and started after him. What was he planning to do? Challenge Miss Sheaf to a duel?

Fayre blinked in disbelief as she caught up with Maccus. The barely controllable rage she had glimpsed on his visage was replaced by a roguish grin.

Maccus bowed over Miss Sheaf's extended hand with exaggerated flourish. "Will you honor me, sweet lady, by walking the length of the room?"

Even the wary Miss Sheaf discovered it was difficult to resist Maccus when he focused all his attention on what he wanted. "Oh—why—I suppose," she said, casting an indecisive glance at Fayre.

The poor woman was probably trying to convince herself that she and Maccus had been too far away to hear her cutting remark. It was too late to prevent Maccus from carrying out his plans, so Fayre kept her expression impassive, leaving Miss Sheaf to her fate. In the end, the lady chose to believe the sincerity of his smile.

Fayre, Miss Piggot, and Mr. Farelle watched Maccus lead the fluttering Miss Sheaf away. She bit her lip, wondering if there was time to get Lord Yemant. There was likely to be a scene and she preferred not to be in the middle of this particular one.

"Rather peculiar turn of events," Miss Piggot huffed, fanning her face furiously, irritated that Mr. Brawley had chosen her friend over her.

"Unexpected," Fayre murmured, craning her head to the left to get a better view of Maccus. What was he saying to Miss Sheaf? From her limited perspective nothing seemed out of the ordinary. The pair seemed to be cordial as they strolled together.

Mr. Farelle tapped his walking stick against the silver buckle of his shoe, distracting Fayre from her vigil. "Miss Piggot," he said cordially. "It has just occurred to me that we have been remiss in reserving our seats. Why do you not oversee the task while Lady Fayre and I await Miss Sheaf's return?" He bowed solicitously to his companion. "That is, if you do not mind, Miss Piggot."

The lady was noticeably reluctant to leave the man she viewed as a potential suitor alone with Fayre. Miss Piggot evidently viewed Mr. Farelle's decision to remain in the company of an amoral seductress as imprudent. "Very well," the lady said, sounding unhappy. Nevertheless, the notion of refusing Mr. Farelle and risking his disapproval was not a consideration. "I shall have a footman reserve you a chair next to mine." She curtsied and stared pointedly at Fayre before she disappeared behind a large group of people.

Good grief, Miss Piggot was actually warning her to keep away from Mr. Farelle! Fayre was acquainted with both of these ladies. She had played cards with Miss Piggot and Miss Sheaf on numerous occasions last season. Miss Piggot's affections for Mr. Farelle had been apparent even then. Even if she had had feelings for the gentleman, Fayre would have not acted on them because she had honor. Miss Piggot and Miss Sheaf had completely dismissed Fayre's integrity out of hand. The injustice of it all made her want to scream!

"I consider it propitious that we have these few minutes alone. Permit me to extend my apologies for Miss Piggot and Miss Sheaf," Mr. Farelle began, his gaze weighted with remorse. "This awkward business with Standish has the *ton* agog and it is natural your friends are upset."

"Not half as upset as I am, Mr. Farelle, since there is nothing between Lord Standish and myself, awkward or otherwise," she said, praying for serenity.

Needing some reassurance that Maccus was not throttling Miss Sheaf, Fayre searched for the couple again. She spotted them across the room. They had stopped and seemed immersed in a private dialogue.

"Of course you are not at fault, Lady Fayre," Mr. Farelle said staunchly, his absolute conviction forcing her to return her attention to him. "You are so young."

"Other ladies of eighteen have already married and birthed their first child, sir," Fayre said, not caring to blame her foolishness over Standish on her tender age.

Mr. Farelle nodded solemnly. "True. Nonetheless, young enough to believe the tripe the lovelorn poets spout forth."

Fayre was about to protest, if not for her youth, then in defense of the poets Mr. Farelle unfairly attacked. But then she recalled the wonderful sonnets Lord Standish had composed for her, praising her eyes, her lips, even her hair. The man had a noteworthy talent with words. She inwardly cringed at the unguarded thought. Seeing the trap for what it was, Fayre closed her mouth.

"I am not here to criticize, unlike Miss Piggot and Miss Sheaf." Without her permission, he took up her hand and kissed it reverently. "I wanted you to know, my lady, that I understand. The first time we are smitten by Cupid's impish arrow, we see all things through love's eyes. We are blind to all flaws, deaf to all warnings."

"Very poetic. Have you ever considered dabbling in poetry?" Fayre asked, ignoring Mr. Farelle for a few minutes. She located Miss Sheaf by the back of her hideous dress. The person who assured the lady she needed all that lace should have been flogged. Several small groups of people walked by before she caught sight of Maccus. In those brief flashes, he was smiling. Well, that was heartening, she thought. What terrible things could he be doing to Miss Sheaf in a room full of witnesses with a smile on his face?

Fayre thought of the wicked things he did to her in his kitchen with servants within earshot. She bit her lip and worried.

"No one would have to know, naturally," Mr. Farelle added, unaware he had lost her.

Since she had no inkling what the man was going on about, she baldly asked, "Are confidences necessary?"

He laughed heartily and shook his head. "The arrogance of youth," he said, shaking his head. Fayre knew him to be thirty-two. Yet he spoke to her as if he were eighty-two and she were two.

"I do not see the problem," she said, very confused.

"My dear girl, I would have thought your unpleasant circumstances with Standish would have taught you a thing or two," he mildly scolded. "Discretion is key. Our shared interests and acquaintances will provide us ample opportunities for us to be seen together. Now, never fear, we will use such moments to slip away."

The fact that she had plotted similar plans with Lord Standish made her feel physically ill. "Are you asking me to be your betrothed, Mr. Farelle?"

She had managed to startle him. He tapped his walking stick and reflected on her question. "Marriage, eh? It might be something for consideration later." He tightened his grasp and only then did she realize belatedly that he had never freed her hand. "We are like-minded on this. Let us not taint our alliance with fathers, lawyers, and clergy. I am fully prepared to indulge your fantasies and carnal appetites, my lady. In this, maturity and youth merge as one. Unlike Standish, I can offer you my constancy."

Later, Fayre would claim madness. For now, she was enraged. "No man vows fidelity to his mistress, you—you pinhead!"

Without thinking, she yanked his walking stick out of his limp hand and struck him smartly on the foot. He yelped and hopped away from her. Feigning sympathy, she waved away the offered assistance of several kind people and followed him long enough to press the walking stick back into his hand. Mr. Farelle was going to need it this evening.

Immensely satisfied that she had discouraged Mr. Farelle from his youthful pursuits, she left him to find Maccus. With any luck, he and Miss Sheaf had reached an understanding and the scene she feared he would cause on her behalf had been avoided.

She nearly collided with Maccus.

"Where are you running off to?" he demanded.

"To find you." It was then she noticed he was alone. "Where is Miss Sheaf?" Fayre searched behind him but his companion was nowhere to be seen.

Maccus took her arm and they walked in the direction where their friends were seated. "Miss Sheaf decided to retire early. The poor lady, it appears, has an unruly constitution. She begged me to extend to you her earnest apologies."

From the corner of her eye, Fayre saw that Mr. Farelle was leaning heavily on his walking stick. Maccus had observed him, too. The man was moving slowly, favoring his right foot. As he noticed their regard, his pained expression altered to utter loathing.

"What the devil is wrong with Farelle?"

Fayre tried to look innocent. Maccus had already run off Miss Sheaf for her unkind words. What would he do to Mr. Farelle for wanting Fayre for his mistress? She was not fond of Mr. Farelle, but she preferred her evening did not end in bloodshed. Shrugging, she said, "Someone must have given him purpose for that walking stick."

Miss Mableward had been correct about the soloist, Miss Kidd, Maccus decided an hour later as he listened to the soprano sing "Caro Mio Bene." She had a voice that indeed rivaled the angels. Fayre sat serenely beside him, although he sensed she had questions about his private conversation with Miss Sheaf. He had been brooding about his brief discourse with the lady and Fayre must have sensed his foul mood. She occasionally glanced discreetly at him, but had said nothing.

Thirty minutes later, when Miss Kidd was accepting the audience's accolades with a regal curtsy, Maccus was still debating about how much he should reveal to Fayre. An intermission was called. Like Maccus, the majority of the audience was weary of sitting. The chairs around them became vacant as many people flocked around the bemused Miss Kidd to congratulate her on her performance.

Lord Yemant approached him with Miss Mableward protectively at his side. The size of the audience had prevented the viscount from procuring them chairs next to theirs, however they had been seated in the same row.

"A marvelous performance by Miss Kidd, do you

agree?" Yemant said enthusiastically. "We hope to say a few words to Miss Kidd. Would you care to join us?"

Fayre stared at the throng of people surrounding the soloist and wrinkled her nose in distaste. "I am content to remain here." Maccus was about to decline the viscount's offer, too, but Fayre held up a silencing hand. "Mr. Brawley, please do not allow my refusal to dictate your decision. I understand you prefer addressing all of your new acquaintances directly."

Yemant frowned at him, probably wondering what Maccus had said to stir Fayre's ire. Her coolness was uncharacteristic, because Miss Mableward gaped at her.

"I can forgo meeting Miss Kidd if you like—" her friend offered, suddenly feeling guilty she had abandoned Fayre to Maccus.

Fayre's features softened at Miss Mableward's selflessness. "No, you go on with Lord Yemant. I do not need coddling."

"I disagree," Maccus said, earning him a glower from Fayre. "Do not fret about your friend, Miss Mableward. I am feeling indulgent this evening and Lady Fayre is too well mannered to refuse my kindness."

She pounced on him the minute Lord Yemant and Miss Mableward had disappeared from view. "Kindness? Ha!" Fayre accepted his hand and rose from the chair. "You do nothing unless it suits your purposes. Now tell me the truth, for all sorts of ideas have been circling in my head until I am crazed. What happened to Miss Sheaf?"

Her suspicions chafed at his already raw temper. "You witnessed what transpired. The lady and I chatted." In exasperation he nudged her affectionately. "What did you expect, Fayre? That I would discreetly throttle the rude woman and hide her body behind the drapery?"

"I do not know," she confessed, her green eyes clouding with uncertainty. "You seemed so angry. It was highly unlikely you pulled her aside to discuss the weather."

"We never got around to the pleasantries," Maccus said, guiding her through the maze of chairs and out into an open area. "For the most part, Miss Sheaf raptly listened." He did not add that the discreet counterpressure he had applied to the lady's littlest finger had assured her silence and compliance. Maccus was not proud of his actions. Nevertheless, the vindictive twit, when she realized why he had pulled her aside, had not been above causing a scene to further humiliate Fayre. He had ruthlessly and effectively dissuaded her of the notion.

"Hmm." Fayre whirled around, stepping in front of him. "Are you certain we are speaking of the same lady? I have spent countless hours in the lady's company to know the only voice she enjoys listening to is her own."

"Perhaps I overwhelmed her with my boundless charm," he countered, admiring the dainty lace decorating the edge of her hand-painted fan. "I can recall an afternoon when you were equally overwhelmed."

The coloring in her cheeks revealed to Maccus that Fayre knew exactly to which afternoon he was referring. Each night he went to his bed alone, he thought about the way her lashes fluttered closed when he had touched her intimately, the smell of her hair, the soft, broken cries she made as he unlocked the passion within her. The hunger for her left him aching and restless.

"What an appallingly uncouth remark to make publicly, Mr. Brawley," she finally said, snapping her fan shut and moving away from him. "I pray you did not relate such comparisons to Miss Sheaf."

Not caring to be dismissed so easily, even by her,

Maccus stalked after her. She gasped when he grabbed her and backed her against the nearest wall. "Do you really want to know the details of my chat with Miss Sheaf?"

"I refuse to permit you to intimidate me," she said, matching his low, menacing tone. Her green eyes glinted like cut glass.

"Why not?" he fired back, crowding her. "It is rather effective in silencing mouthy little snipes who feel superior by glaring at all and sundry from their lofty perch."

The accusation enraged her. "Take it back. I have done no such thing!"

Maccus scowled down at her, knowing he was being unfair. It was not her fault that an accident of birth had granted her everything he craved and was denied for so long. "Not recently," he gruffly conceded. "Or as overtly as the Miss Sheafs of the world. Still, you see me as an aberration in your life, someone to use as you see fit and toss when something better comes your way."

"Oh, let us not forget you were the one who approached me with your notorious bargain." She stopped glaring at him and pasted on an angelic smile for the man and woman walking past. They nodded and smiled back, but Maccus's ominous presence kept them from approaching. "Despite my current predicament, do not think me a fool, Mr. Brawley. You are intelligent, handsome, and have acquired a respectable fortune. There are countless ladies who would have welcomed your courtship, and yet it was I you sought—not with a respectable offer of courtship, but a *bargain*." She spat out the word as if it were something vile. "Who is using whom?"

Fayre ducked under his arm blocking her way. Maccus reached out, still staggered and humbled by her praise of the man she thought him to be. He wondered how she

would view him if she learned of the past he had so carefully buried. Unable to let her walk away believing he was
a villain, he said, "I told Miss Sheaf—" He stopped and
corrected himself. "No, actually I threatened her to cease
spreading gossip about you or face my retribution. I called
her a few unsavory names you might have found upsetting."

Fayre's lips twitched. "Do not be so certain."

Maccus thought about some of the cruel observations
Miss Sheaf had made regarding his unsavory nature and
discovered in his frustration he had unjustly blamed
Fayre for them. Uncomfortable, he said, "Well, she does
not think well of either one of us."

Fayre fidgeted with one of the white ribbons on her reticule. Her mood was introspective and Maccus wished
that she would speak her thoughts aloud. "Though I appreciate your public defense of my honor, sir, I expect Miss
Sheaf will be rather vocal about your ill treatment. She
likely ran straight to the magistrate with her complaint."

"I doubt it." Maccus looked away. "Not everyone who
meets me sees an intelligent, handsome, wealthy gentleman," he said, deliberately using her own description.

"What do they see?"

His expression hardened, and his gray eyes were bleak.
"A ruthless bastard. A man you never cross more than
once."

"Oh," she said a little breathlessly.

Maccus tipped her chin up and held her gaze. She was
so beautiful, she reminded him of how unworthy he was
to be near her. "I did not lie to you about Miss Sheaf offering an apology. She will not trouble you again."

9

That night, Maccus dreamed of pain and darkness. A cold blackness swallowed him whole. He could not see or hear. Opening his mouth, he realized he could not breathe. The muscles in his face and throat strained as he tried to draw air into his lungs. The air around him rippled and he was pitched forward. Maccus felt the stinging slap of icy water as he went under. He tasted salt and knew he was drowning in the sea. Kicking, he blindly swam for what he thought was the surface, his lungs burning, starving for fresh air. He cleared the surface choking. Confused, Maccus gaped at the smoke and what seemed like hundreds of fires floating around him. A wave crashed over his head, pushing him toward the shore. His body was racked with unbearable pain and his eyes stung from all the smoke. He crawled the last fifty yards until he had reached the beach.

What had happened? An explosion?

Maccus rolled onto his back and wiped his eyes. He stared in dazed horror at the burning wreckage washing up on the shore. And there were dead bodies. Staggering to his feet, he glanced around in all directions. The seawater he had swallowed lurched in his stomach. He held on to his knees and vomited until he felt hollow. There were at least thirty dead bodies floating in the shallow water and dozens more on the beach. Straightening, he noticed his hearing was returning with his sight. He was not the only survivor of the explosion. Farther down the beach he could hear the discharging pistols and fighting.

Someone had betrayed them.

Maccus did not know how long he stood there shaking with the dead surrounding him, dazed from his injuries and the freezing water. He had not noticed the sound of riders approaching or flinched when one of the horses reared in front of him, its hooves dancing so close to his face he felt a breeze.

"By damn, you are a tough bastard," one of the riders said in awe. Maccus squinted dully at the lanterns they were carrying, but he could not identify the men. They had covered their faces with black cloth. "Good thing we checked. Got more lives than a cat, I say."

"Not for long," another man observed grimly. "He looks like he'll be dead before dawn."

"You're right." The man whose horse had reared in front of Maccus aimed a pistol at his chest and fired.

Maccus clutched his chest and lunged upright with a

snarl on his lips. Hobbs shrieked, nearly dropping the candle he held in front of his face into the bedding.

"Y'all right?"

"Put the candle down on a table before you ignite us both," Maccus growled, his nightmare too fresh for him to be civil. "What are you doing prowling about?"

The manservant, still shaken by his master's violent greeting, placed the candle on the table beside the bed. "I come to wake you. You have a visitor."

"Now?" Maccus asked, absently rubbing the scar on his chest. He could not recall the last time he had been haunted by that particular nightmare or when it had seemed so real. "What is the hour?"

"One in the morning. I told him to go away, but he insists on staying. Says he's your brother," Hobbs said, handing him a bundle of clothes. "Brother or not, you cannot receive visitors arse bared."

Swinging his legs off the side of the bed, Maccus worked a leg into his trousers. "Trevor is here?"

"How many brothers do you have?" Hobbs snapped, still irritated by his fright.

One. It meant his past was catching up to him.

Maccus trailed after Hobbs, still unsettled by his nightmare. He had been seventeen, and a smuggler by profession for ten years, when the masked man on the horse had coolly taken aim and fired his pistol into Maccus. If the men who had ambushed him and his men that October night had been custom officers, they would have subdued and arrested them. These men had destroyed their boats, burned the tackle, and slaughtered every man they caught. He had his suspicions, but he could never prove who had betrayed his whereabouts or the identity of the man who had tried to kill him.

"Can't just leave a man to his bed," Hobbs grumbled, shuffling toward the kitchen. "Callers at all hours of the night. Do I complain?" He cocked his ear in Maccus's direction, but he answered his own question. "No. And there ye were thrashing about the bed like a drowning man." He pushed open the door and Maccus followed him down the narrow hall to the kitchen. "I, a faithful servant, tries to shake ye and what do I get for me trouble? Snarling, and ye ambush me."

Trevor stood at their approach. Maccus had expected to see the boy he had known. Instead a young man of twenty-one stood in his stead. Hobbs had decided the lad needed feeding, because his brother had a chunk of bread in his hand and a tankard of beer in the other. There was also a wedge of cheese and a plate with two apples laid out on the table. "Ambush? What ambush?" he asked, his mouth stuffed with bread.

Maccus waited until Hobbs had returned to his bed before he started questioning his brother. He sat patiently, watching Trevor devour his cold supper like a half-starved wolf.

Trevor stopped chewing when he noticed his brother's unwavering regard. Swallowing a mouthful of food, he grimaced and reached for the tankard next to his plate. "What? Do I have a crooked ear or something?" his brother asked, gulping the beer.

Despite having different mothers, he and Trevor favored their father's dark good looks. Six years younger than Maccus, Trevor had black hair, familiarly thick and straight, that hung loosely just above his shoulders. There were differences, too. His face was narrower, his chin more prominent and shadowed with several days' growth of a beard. A thin white scar Maccus did not remember seeing hooked like a backward *c* from the corner of Trevor's right eye and over his cheekbone. His clothes were dusty and well worn. Briefly, Maccus wondered where his brother had been residing while he had been in London. His eyes were not gray, but hazel, the color and shape he had gotten from his mother, although his lacked the hopelessness Maccus had more than once glimpsed in his father's second wife.

"It has been five years," Maccus said simply. "You have added some length and muscle since we last saw each other."

"Hard work," Trevor said, slamming down his tankard.

"Honest work?"

His brother wiped his mouth with the back of his hand and glanced about him as if noticing his surroundings for the first time. "You have changed, too, Mac."

"How did you find me?" he asked, trying to ignore his connection to the man sitting across the hardwood table from him.

Maccus did not remember his own mother. She had escaped Seamus Brawley's drunken tyranny when he had been barely two years old. If she had tried to take her son with her, Maccus never knew. His father never spoke of her. Other women came after her. Whores, mostly, because Seamus was too hard on a decent woman. Some of them had been kind and had stayed around long enough to cook a few meals for the motherless boy before his father's temper and fists discouraged them from returning.

How Seamus had convinced Miss Sarah McAdams, the seventeen-year-old daughter of a weaver from the borough of Glossop, to marry him was a mystery. His father was a handsome man, and when he sobered, he had a pleasant manner about him that attracted the ladies. Perhaps he had heard Miss McAdams had a respectable dowry and set about courting her. Or maybe he had carelessly seduced her and the child growing in her belly had prompted her father's hasty consent.

Regardless how it happened, Sarah had brought to her marriage a dowry of one thousand pounds. For a few years, they lived a quiet life. Trevor's arrival seemed to settle the restlessness in Seamus, and Sarah treated Maccus as if he were her own son. Their peaceful life slowly eroded when Seamus resumed smuggling once the dowry was gone and he started drinking heavily again. Strangers started pounding on their front door at all hours of the night. Soon they were evicted from their home. The happiness Maccus had seen in Sarah's hazel eyes dulled as healing bruises marred her pale face and poverty whittled her slender body, weakening it. Sarah Brawley perished from influenza the year Trevor turned eleven.

With his mother gone, there was no one to stand between his younger brother and Seamus's drunken tirades. By then, Maccus, now seventeen, was deeply ensnared in the violent, secretive world of smuggling. By late October, he and his men would be ambushed. Hours later, and barely alive, his unconscious body would be discovered on the beach at dawn with a lead ball festering in his chest.

"It took some doing," Trevor said, bringing Maccus back to the present. "If I had aimed a little higher I might have found you sooner."

"Did he send you?"

"Christ, do you think me so low?" Trevor demanded, appearing hurt. "You made your feelings for Seamus clear ten years back when you accused him of attempted murder."

"Wrong. He succeeded, Trev. Fifty men lost their lives that night on the beach," Maccus said flatly, the old pain and anger of what had occurred resurfacing, his nightmare and his brother's appearance exacerbating an old wound.

"Seamus denies having anything to do with that ambush," his brother argued, still loyally defending their father. "Every man knows he is risking his neck when he takes up smuggling. You were luckier than most. You survived and were clever enough to cut your losses." Trevor got up from the table, his keen brain calculating the value of the house and its contents. "Moved on to better schemes, I'd say."

"You stood by the old man ten years ago when I confronted him with my accusations," Maccus said wearily. "You even followed in his footsteps five years ago. I won't waste my breath trying to convince you."

"Those steps were yours as well, Mac," Trevor shot back, startling Maccus. "You were one of the best. Even Seamus would agree. You had the brains for the planning, the muscle and meanness to carry it out. You never got squeamish about violence. Hell, you even knew when to walk away from it before you lost a limb or dangled from a noose."

Maccus heard the awe in his brother's voice and thought of all those dead bodies surrounding him on the beach, the acrid smell of gunpowder and the metallic taste of his own blood. "I took up smuggling because I was a smuggler's son. I did what I had to do to keep from starving and to avoid Seamus's fists, though I often failed at that," he said, thinking of the countless beatings he endured. "I quit because I had made some money and an abundance of enemies. I knew sooner or later I was going to kill a man, likely my own father, and discovered I was squeamish after all." He glowered at Trevor. "Don't admire me, lad."

Trevor's lip curled in derision. "I haven't been a lad for some time." He crossed his arms in contemplation, weighing Maccus with a level stare. "I'm on my own. Seamus and I went our separate ways shortly after I saw you last. Me and my men have been working the southern waters thereabout."

Maccus noticed his brother did not reveal exactly where he was conducting his operations. He had finally learned to keep his damn mouth shut. "Does Seamus have anything to do with the reason why you have been turning London upside down looking for me?"

His brother scratched at the scar on his face. "Well, I figured I owed you for what you did for me when I got in that spot of trouble five years back."

It had been Cabot Dossett who had alerted Maccus to Trevor's whereabouts in Deptford and the three months' imprisonment the sixteen-year-old was facing. Seamus had been a seaman as a young man, and had decided to revisit his old profession by taking up river pirating.

According to Trevor, the pair had disguised themselves as watermen so they could approach the anchored brigs and barges unnoticed. They had minor success pilfering clothes and watches so Seamus grew bolder. Armed with chisels and a chopper, they had planned to remove the copper from the bottom of vessels. Loud knocking had been heard and two constables had been summoned to investigate. The officers had apprehended Trevor and Seamus and confiscated a large quantity of copper from their boat.

Both had been sitting in the gaol awaiting trial when Dossett had contacted Maccus. With the assistance of a reputable lawyer, and several persuasive testimonies of character, Trevor had been released. Seamus had not escaped so easily as a result of his prior scrapes with the law. He was sentenced to four months for his crime.

"You did not deserve to rot in a gaol for Seamus's mischief," Maccus said, rising from his seat at the table. "Besides, if my interference freed you from Seamus, then it was worth it."

He had visited his father at the gaol. The old man had cursed Maccus for abandoning him and stealing away his son. Age and his drinking had slowed Seamus, and he saw his sixteen-year-old son as a tool to gain him the wealth he deserved. Trevor had stayed with Maccus in the cheap rooms he had rented in the neighborhood of Haymarket. This arrangement had lasted for four months. Maccus arrived home one day to learn he had been robbed and Trevor was missing.

"I thought he kidnapped you," Maccus confided. "For weeks, I searched the streets for signs of your whereabouts."

Trevor's eyes widened, obviously stunned that his brother had tried to find him. Idly, he admired one of the copper pots hanging overhead. "Nay, I went willingly. Figured I owed him and all that."

"How many times did Seamus say to you those same words? And how long did you believe him?"

His brother laughed. "Several times a day, I recall. It took me a month to figure out that I was going to end up in that gaol you spared me from if Seamus and I didn't part ways."

"You could have returned to Haymarket?"

"Aye, I could have," Trevor agreed so readily, they both smiled. "No offense, but you were pulling at me one way and Seamus the other; I figured I needed to find my own path."

"And did you find it?"

Trevor stifled a yawn. "Oh, I've stumbled, gotten lost a time or two. Name me a man who hasn't. I'm building something for myself. Eventually, I will find my way." He looked knowingly at Maccus. "Looks like you found yours."

Maccus thought of Fayre and their bargain. "I'm still working on it." His eyes narrowed as his brother yawned again. "Where are you staying?"

His brother shrugged. "Moving about mostly, since I did not know where you had gone. I almost gave up, thinking if I could not find you then Seamus never would."

"Yet you did."

"Aye, and if I did, then Seamus will. He tracked me to Cornwall and tried causing some trouble for me with the locals," Trevor said, his face darkening. "He's following the coast searching for you. Sooner or later, he'll come to London as I have."

Maccus scrubbed his face with his hand. He did not need Trevor to predict Seamus's reaction to the new life he was building here. Their father was a selfish, cantankerous man. What he could not claim for himself he usually destroyed. Maccus was not willing to let Seamus jeopardize the legitimate life he had meticulously spent years building for himself.

"Let him come."

It was foolhardy to dare something evil to enter one's life. Since Trevor had appeared at his door several days earlier, Maccus had thought about how he purposefully had been separating himself from his old life as a smuggler. There had been a transitional period, certainly, when he could have swayed either way. Still, his path was set now and there was no going back.

Maccus entered his house. No one appeared to greet him. He shook off the slight good-naturedly, following the snippets of conversation and laughter he heard. They were in the drawing room, he realized. One of the speakers was Trevor, while the other one was—

"*Fayre,*" he growled, and watched her eyes go round at his harsh tone. She was sitting primly in his drawing room, acting as his hostess in his absence. "What are you doing here?" Maccus glared at his brother, who held up his hands in a surrendering gesture.

She stood, perplexed and wary of his anger. "I told you that I would be coming this afternoon. Did you forget?"

Maccus could feel the rage rising within him. He wanted to strike at something. Someone. Seeing Fayre and Trevor together merged his two worlds and it was something he vowed would never happen.

"Trevor, leave us."

His brother did not understand what was wrong. He glanced at Fayre, clearly worried about leaving her alone. "Mac, we were just talking. That's all."

The fact that Trevor thought Maccus was capable of committing violence against Fayre enraged him further. He was not his father! "I have never hit a woman, but I cannot say the same about a man. Leave."

Trevor tipped his hat at Fayre. "A pleasure, my lady." He slipped out the door and likely out of the house until Maccus calmed down.

Fayre frowned, wary of him. "You did not mention having a brother."

Her comment sounded like a subtle reprimand and Maccus was not in the mood to be lectured. "No, I didn't. What were you talking about?"

She shrugged. "Many things. Travel. London. He asked about my family. Why? Is it important?"

Maccus knew he was being unreasonable. He could not get a grip on his temper. Seeing her in the same room with Trevor made Maccus feel violated. Lady Fayre had been given a piece of his past that he had not been willing to share, and with each additional piece of information she gathered, she would learn about the ugly history he had tried to forget.

He slammed his fist against the door. Fayre flinched at the thundering sound. "Keep away from my brother."

Her mouth tightened at his arrogant command. "Fine. I will respect your wishes, Mr. Brawley. May I leave?"

Since he had nothing to say, Maccus opened the door.

Fayre paused at the threshold. "All I was doing with your brother was chatting with him. He was keeping me company until your arrival. I found him respectful and charming, unlike someone else I could mention." She was trembling, but it was not from fear. "I cannot fathom why you think to protect your brother from me. Or maybe I can. You fat-pated man, what did you think I planned to do to young Trevor? Seduce him on the sofa?" She stomped off in a high dudgeon, hurt and angry by his behavior.

Maccus grasped the door and rested his head against his hand.

Fayre was correct.

He was a fat-pated man.

10

The duchess burst into the morning room with the fanfare one expected at the royal court. Fayre glanced up to see her father's two apricot-colored mastiffs bound in after her mother. Separating, the dogs moved about on opposite sides of the room with their muzzles to the floor, sniffing out carelessly dropped tidbits from the table. The housekeeper, butler, and her mother's personal maid followed in their wake, each vying for their mistress's attention.

"Good morning, Mama," Fayre sat, bussing her mother's cheek as she passed by. "Late evening?"

"Evidently so. I do not recall sleeping in my bed," the duchess said, allowing the butler to help her into her chair. She might not have slept in her bed, but she had visited her bedchamber long enough to change her attire. She wore a demure peach morning pelisse decorated with a double row of ruffles across the bosom and the cuff of the long sleeves. Her hair, a darker variation of Fayre's, was stuffed under a lace cap.

"Curdey," the duchess addressed the butler. "Be a kind man and bring me something delicate for my stomach." She closed her eyes and blindly gestured for her maid to approach. The young girl gently placed a dampened cloth over the duchess's closed eyes.

"Ah, Hilaire, you are an angel," her mother murmured, sighing. "Bless you."

"Your Grace," the housekeeper said, stepping forward. "Cook and I have prepared this week's menu, with your—"

"Impossible, Mrs. Virly." Her mother grimaced under her maid's vigorous massage of her shoulders. "My eyes are taxed and need a respite. I vow I shall not read a single letter before two o'clock."

Fayre sipped her hot tea to conceal her smile. Somehow her mother managed to turn even the mundane into a small drama. There were days when the intensity of each conflict was wearing, but Fayre adored her mother too much to fuss. "Leave the menus with me, Mrs. Virly. I shall look them over and discuss any changes with you later."

"Very good, my lady." The housekeeper dipped into an abbreviated curtsy and hurried off to her next task.

"You are such a good daughter," the duchess said, lifting the damp cloth from her eyes at the sound of Curdey's return.

The butler placed a plate with two toasted halves of a

split French roll in front of her. The centers had been hollowed out and an egg had been baked within each one. Accepting a smaller plate from the footman assisting him, the butler squeezed the bitter juice of a Seville orange over the eggs.

"Thank you, Curdey. An excellent choice for this arduous morning," her mother said, her spirits reviving. "Have Cook prepare two more for our guests." She dismissed the butler and her maid with an elegant swish of her hand.

Listening to the servants' departure, Fayre stared inquiringly at her mother. "We have guests?"

"Just a few friends who shared last evening's festivities."

The footman opened the door and two gentlemen entered, still wearing their evening attire. The fatigue vanished from the duchess's face as she beckoned her companions to join them.

"Lord Hawxby . . . Lord Crescett, please come in. After all that rich fare we suffered through last evening, I thought you both would prefer something light. Cook is preparing something special and it shall arrive momentarily."

Fayre was speechless at her mother's audacity. She had heard the rumors long before she had arrived in London. Lord Crescett was her mother's lover. At thirty-seven, the earl had the sort of looks her mother favored in a man. He was fair in coloring, a blond with hair that was prone to curl so he kept it cut short. This emphasized the size of his ears, but even Fayre found the manner in which they stuck out endearing.

Lord Hawxby was younger, later twenties, perhaps. He was taller than Lord Crescett and his lean, muscled body reflected his preference for the outdoors. Also blond, his long hair was tied in a queue. Noticing her regard, he grinned at Fayre, displaying his perfect, straight teeth for inspection. Good heavens, Fayre mused, was her father aware the duchess was collecting her earls in pairs these days?

M accus paused outside the bank and pulled out his pocket watch. Checking the time, he realized he was running late for his first afternoon appointment. It was uncharacteristic of him, he mused, crossing Thread-needle Street and entering the north entrance of the Exchange. Before Fayre had entered his life, he had dedicated most of the day to business. Lately, he had deliberately been shortening his business hours and postponing meetings in anticipation of Fayre's arrival.

He never knew what to expect when Hobbs announced her. Her instructional choices seemed whimsical rather than a set course of action. She might talk of fashion one afternoon and give him lessons in basic French the next. He discovered Fayre had benefited from her unique upbringing. Not only was she versed in the gentle arts all young ladies were accomplished in, but her eccentric parents whether by accident or design had encouraged her inquisitive mind, giving her an education that had rivaled that of her brother. She spoke both French and Italian fluently and was proficient in Latin and Greek. She was an avid reader but preferred practical applications of her knowledge so she spent many afternoons attending demonstrations and lectures in the sciences, mathematics, politics, and history.

In comparison, Maccus's education was woefully lacking. His rough and violent upbringing had not included tutors and public schools. When his father had married the gently reared Sarah McAdams, she had been appalled by her new son's ignorance and set about correcting Seamus's oversight by instructing Maccus herself.

By the time Sarah had succumbed to influenza, Maccus could read, write, and tally numbers. She had tantalized him with the possibility that he could rise above Seamus's underworld of thievery and violence. Sarah had given him a priceless gift, one she had never lived long enough to see take hold. Maccus had tried to repay her kindness by protecting her son from Seamus's bullying influence. However, he could not set much of an example since he was steeped to his ears in the murky business of smuggling himself. Once his mother was gone, the eleven-year-old Trevor never stood a chance of defying Seamus.

Maccus glanced up, and was mildly surprised he had reached his destination. His lips formed into a faint smile as he took in the activity of the Exchange. The energy enamating around him always managed to lift his spirits.

Within the piazza, merchants from all over the world assembled daily. It was here their business affairs were negotiated and goods were converted to gold. Maccus never tired of viewing the lively bustle within the Exchange. The air was different here, filled with exotic scents, and different languages overwhelmed his ears. Even in times of conflict, it was a place where politics could be put aside for a few hours and the commonweal of all mankind was debated. Once a visitor, Maccus had found a legitimate place in this international emporium.

"Mr. Brawley!"

Maccus turned toward the stairs, which led to the gallery. As late as the early seventeen hundreds the gallery had been used by shopkeepers. Now offices occupied the upper level. Mr. Kennith Hodge, a robust man of fifty, was a stockbroker who kept an office on the lower level. He lifted his hand in greeting and ascended to meet him partway. The high color in the man's cheeks indicated he had trekked the length of all four sides of the gallery in search of Maccus.

His companion leaned heavily against the stair railing for support as he caught his breath. "There you are, sir! Good day. I thought I had mixed up our meeting day with another."

"My apologies, Mr. Hodge. I was detained at the bank longer than I had anticipated," Maccus explained. He gestured upward. "Shall we move on to Lloyd's?"

The other man nodded. "Yes, indeed. Wait until you hear my good news, sir."

"I look forward to it, Mr. Hodge."

Good news from his stockbroker usually implied that their recent venture had been profitable. Maccus clapped the man on the back as they climbed the stairs together. He wondered if there would be time afterward to visit one of the jewelers on Bond Street. Feeling celebratory, he was of a mind to share some of his new wealth. Besides, a gift would ease his guilt over his unwarranted reaction to seeing Fayre talking to his brother. What lady could hold a grudge against a man willing to buy her expensive trinkets?

"Your sufferance does you credit," Lord Hawxby observed over her shoulder, distracting Fayre from the milliner's window display.

Meeting his gaze in the reflection of the window glass, Fayre hastily switched her regard back to the straw bonnet she had been previously admiring. She could not say what was more vexing at the moment, the earl's presumptuous reference to the scandal or her mother's insistence that the gentlemen join them on their afternoon of shopping. "What an odd thing to say, my lord. It is both praise and insult. How economic of you."

The earl's brows shot up in surprise, but he chuckled, appreciating her quick riposte. "My lady, in my defense and my new respect for your sharp wit, I humbly beg you to accept my words as the unqualified praise I intended."

"Praise for exactly what?" she asked, not hiding her suspicion.

He ticked off his reasons with his fingers. "For bearing Crescett and myself, for disturbing your morning repast, for the duchess and her assumptions." Fayre glanced away from the shop window and gaped at the gentleman in disbelief. She saw nothing but sincerity in his expression. Her parents' circle of friends were a rowdy, thoughtless group who rarely apologized for anything. As for the gentlemen in her mother's life, Fayre tried to distance herself from them, because forming a connection with any of her mother's former lovers was unthinkable.

Lord Hawxby continued, too polite to acknowledge his companion's incredulous stare. "Our presence created an awkward situation for you, and the duchess, well, she can be too outspoken in her comments."

The earl was referring to her mother's earlier comments in the morning room. In her defense, Fayre had not been prepared to share her breakfast with the duchess's lovers. She had heard about Crescett, but Hawxby, too? Foreseeing the inevitable brawl and scandal that would occur if the duke had presented himself that particular morning for breakfast, Fayre could not keep silent. When the gentlemen were engaged in a lively debate about the outcome of a horse race they had attended, Fayre confronted her mother.

"*You go too far, Mama,*" Fayre whispered to the duchess.

"*I am too weary for riddles, my child,*" her mother said, transferring the dampened cloth she had used for her eyes to her nape. "*What is upsetting you?*"

"*Lord Crescett and Lord Hawxby.*" Fayre brought her napkin to her mouth to conceal her side of the conversation. "*Why did you bring them here? What will Papa do if he discovers them?*"

Perplexed, her mother asked, "*Why would the duke do anything? I suppose he might take them down to the cellar.*"

Fayre did not bother concealing her horror as she imagined her father ordering Curdey to bury the earls' bodies in the cellar. "*Why are you doing this? This cordial tableau you have orchestrated is outrageous, even by our family's standards. If you desire Papa's attention, there must be another way to rouse his violent passions!*"

"*Daughter, you are practically babbling. What is so troubling about Crescett and Hawxby joining us for breakfast? We had planned to go shopping later. I see no reason why the gentlemen could not provide us escort.*"

"*Why? Have you taken leave of your senses, Mama?*" Fayre demanded, her voice rising with her exasperation. "*Sitting here at the table with both your lovers is a hullabaloo even the duke will not be able to overlook!*"

The conversation at the end of the table ceased as the two gentlemen stared at Fayre with varying degrees of astonishment and amusement.

The duchess had had enough of her daughter's hysteria.

"Lovers? Why would I possibly desire two? I brought Hawxby home for you!"

Fayre had been mortified by the duchess's admission. Too stunned to speak a single word, she had to admit that both gentlemen had recovered quickly and had attempted to smooth over the awkwardness brought about by the women's conversation with the recounting of their host's antics from the previous evening.

Now, returning Lord Hawxby's regard, Fayre said, "My lord, I am undeserving of any praise. In truth, I owe both you and Lord Crescett an apology for my accusations."

"Why? For speaking the truth? Crescett and the duchess are lovers." He nodded at the building of the silk mercer where the earl and her mother were selecting fabric for the new evening dress she fancied. "They are hardly being discreet. Nor do you owe me an apology, my lady. The duchess is a lovely, desirable woman. If I did not favor the interest of her daughter exceedingly, I might have been tempted to seduce Her Grace away from Crescett."

Flabbergasted, Fayre held up a hand in a protective gesture. "Lord Hawxby, you have never spoken—I was not aware."

The earl curled his hand tenderly around her extended one and lowered it between them. "I know. You saw no one but Lord Standish." At her alarmed expression, he murmured soothingly in an attempt to calm her, "Despite the duchess's optimistic expectations, I understand that your heart is conflicted. One day, it is my hope when your sorrow fades that you will consider—"

"Providence," Maccus said, his voice infused with false cheerfulness. "When shopping, a lady's astute opinion is always an asset."

Fayre whirled around to confront Maccus. Forgetting she had a gentleman attached to her hand, she jerked the man forward. "Oh, I do beg your pardon," she said, freeing her hand. "Mr. Brawley. Good afternoon, sir."

She hurriedly dispensed with the introductions since Lord Hawxby did not seemed happy about Maccus's presence, either.

"I thought you were attending Cadell's lecture on astrology this afternoon," Maccus said, revealing rather smugly an intimacy with Fayre he was certain irritated the besotted gentleman.

"It was astronomy," she corrected crisply, her tone hinting at her displeasure with him. "My plans were altered when the duchess had a whim for shopping. We—" She stopped speaking, and stared helplessly at the silk mercer's building across the street. "Mama prefers shopping with an entourage."

Lord Hawxby patted Fayre's shoulder encouragingly, earning him a murderous glare from Maccus. The pair was obviously sharing secrets. "So Mr. Brawley, you mentioned that you needed a lady's opinion," the man prompted.

"Aye. I was in the mood to celebrate. Earlier, I had learned a risky venture I was anticipating had yielded a sizable profit," Maccus said, not taking his gaze off Fayre's expressive face.

She was genuinely pleased for his good fortune. He was glad that she was not still angry with him. "Congratulations, Mr. Brawley," Fayre said softly.

"Nicely done, Mr. Brawley. What type of business are you in?"

Maccus noted the hint of derision in Lord Hawxby's question. Anyone *in trade* was not part of the earl's world. Or Fayre's. "The very risky, very profitable sort, Lord Hawxby."

A flurry of activity across the street distracted the earl before he could form a proper retort to Maccus's arrogant statement. Fayre, also noticing the small group exiting the shop, carefully stepped away from both gentlemen, putting a respectable distance between them.

Maccus recognized the lady in the center of the approaching whirlwind as the Duchess of Solitea. Spotting her daughter, the older woman charged across the street, heedless of the horses and carriages on the street. Two footmen, each carrying a small mountain of wrapped packages, and a fashionably dressed gentleman darted after their reckless companion.

"Fayre, my girl, there you are. I sorely needed your counsel inside for I could not choose between four exquisite bolts of fabric the proprietor had presented, and Crescett was no help," the duchess lamented, casting a wilting stare at her male companion.

"Why decide when you could purchase all?" Lord Crescett said, seeming bored with the argument. "The duke can afford to indulge you."

"Of course, but that is not the point, my darling man," the duchess said, exasperated. To Fayre, she said, "The colors flatter both our complexions so when the fabric arrives at the house you must choose two for yourself. The prospect of having new dresses made should brighten your gloomy disposition."

Maccus deduced there was some underlying friction between mother and daughter. It explained why Fayre had not attended the duchess in the shop and her reluctance for Maccus to encounter the lady.

"As always, you are generous, Mama," Fayre said

politely, stepping forward to kiss her mother on the cheek.

The duchess glanced speculatively from Lord Hawxby to Maccus. "And what are you doing with my daughter, Hawxby?"

"Nothing, Your Grace," the earl replied, earning Maccus's reluctant respect for shielding Fayre from her gregarious mother.

The duchess fluttered her lashes flirtatiously. "Then you disappoint me, my lord. And you, sir." The older woman's gaze honed in on Maccus keenly. Her transparent interest in him had Maccus wondering if Lord Crescett provided Her Grace other services besides gallant escort. "Who are you to my daughter?"

Anxious about Maccus's unpredictable response, Fayre said, "Mama, this is Mr. Brawley, an acquaintance of Lord Yemant's."

Maccus bowed. "And a humble admirer of your daughter."

Poor, brave Fayre, he thought as he watched her clear green eyes betray her distress about her mother's unabashed curiosity. Like all dutiful daughters, her attempts at subterfuge faltered in the presence of her mother.

"A lady can never have too many admirers," the duchess said blithely. "Do you not agree, Mr. Brawley?"

"I was taught never to *dis*agree," Maccus countered, kissing the older woman's hand, "with a beautiful lady." Both Lord Crescett and Fayre sulked at his flirtatious gesture.

The lady trilled with laughter. "Oh, I do like you, Mr. Brawley." Her Grace took his arm, adding him to her little group. "What good fortune has brought you to us?"

"The handsome increase of my own," Maccus quipped

and was rewarded with a playful squeeze on his arm by the duchess. He risked a brief glance at Fayre. She was looking everywhere but in his direction, following at their heels with Lord Hawxby and Lord Crescett on each side like stylish buttresses. "The news has prompted me to buy an indulgence for a good friend."

"Of which you no doubt have many," Her Grace interjected, her calculated flattery finding its mark in spite of Maccus's resolve not to be charmed. It was not surprising the duchess attracted the interest of gentlemen half her age. Her beauty and practiced sauciness were a potent combination. If Fayre ever decided to emulate her mother, she would be a formidable rival.

"Now you flatter me, Your Grace."

The duchess tossed a glance over her shoulder at her too silent daughter. "Fayre, my girl, why did you not present Mr. Brawley to me sooner? Is he merely being polite or is he always this modest?"

Fayre brushed imaginary lint off her sleeve. "I have discovered that Mr. Brawley is exceptionally amendable to all occasions."

Maccus winced at her frosty tone. At some point, he had made a grave miscalculation with Fayre. He found this bewildering because he had not only resisted throttling the earl, he had been endearingly polite to her mother. Had he not been the one aggrieved when he came upon her and Hawxby holding hands? Now the scoundrel, Lord Hawxby, was sneering at him, pleased by what he perceived as Maccus's bungling of the situation, and Fayre was not speaking to him.

The Duchess of Solitea beamed at him and refused to release his arm. Lord Crescett had finally noticed his lover's rapt fascination with Maccus and had lost his bored expression. The man, frankly, looked murderous. As Fayre had predicted, Maccus was amendable. Later, when he escaped his mad companions, the gift he sought to purchase would be used to placate instead of celebrate.

II

Dangling her legs over the armrest of her father's favorite chair in the library, Fayre was grateful it was evening. It had been an awful day. She should have cried off when her mother had suggested an afternoon of shopping with the earls. Then she would not have witnessed the doting affection of her mother's lover, no Lord Hawxby offering his admiration from afar and no Maccus Brawley.

The afternoon had been trying. Once she had disentangled her mother from Mr. Brawley's arm, Fayre had to sit beside Lord Hawxby in the carriage while both of them pretended not to listen to Lord Crescett's jealous tantrum regarding the duchess's outrageous conduct toward Mr. Brawley.

Fayre had bid adieu to all three of them, leaving her mother to smooth the ripples of discontent. Her own plans for the afternoon had been ruined. She had missed Mr. Cadell's lecture on astronomy, and after watching Mr. Brawley flirt with her mother in public, she had lost all interest in honoring her part of the bargain that day. Fayre had retired to her room, pleading a headache.

Hours later, her mother had sent her maid with a note inviting Fayre to attend the theater and a late supper with her, but she politely refused. She was not quite up to appeasing her mother's curiosity about Mr. Brawley. Sometime during her nap, her father had returned to the house, changed into his evening clothes, and departed again.

Fayre was alone. Most of the staff had been dismissed for the evening, and the remaining servants were either relaxing in the workroom or sleeping. Stoic about her self-imposed isolation, she considered reading a book or tackling the pile of correspondence she had been neglecting lately.

Fifteen minutes passed and Fayre was still considering her options. There was something to be said for being lazy, she decided, stretching out her right leg. She pointed her toe and admired her slipper. Frowning, she noticed several of the beads missing. They were her favorite pair! It was another indication what an abysmal day it had been.

Rolling her head so her cheek rested on the armrest, Fayre realized there was a man standing in the doorway watching her. Shrieking in fright, she scrambled out of her awkward pose in the chair and rolled onto the floor.

Maccus crouched down on the floor next to her. He stroked his chin as if contemplating her inelegant sprawl.

Fayre blew the strands of hair out of her eyes and glared at him. Blast the man, his shoulders were shaking! "If you laugh I vow you will regret it."

It took him a minute, but he fought to keep his expression somber. "I have often wondered what a lady did in her leisure. What exactly were you doing? Counting your toes?"

With the promise of violence in her eyes, Fayre launched herself at Maccus. "Your life is forfeited!"

Laughing heartily at her vehement oath, he caught her against his chest and collapsed on his back. "Enough, Fayre," he said, when she pummeled his chest with her fists. "I yield!"

Fayre ceased her assault as she noticed their compromising position on the floor of her father's library. Maccus was on his back laughing like a Bedlamite and she was astride him. Climbing off him, she backed up until she was sitting in the chair again.

"You took three years off my life, Maccus Brawley!" she said, placing her hand over her pounding heart. "What are you doing prowling about the house?"

Maccus sat up and pulled his knees up to his chest. "I realize it is a bit late for callers, but I knocked. No one answered so I went around back to the servants' entrance. One of your maids was stepping out with her man, and just happened to reveal that you were alone inside sulking."

Fayre's head snapped up indignantly. "No one told you such a thing." The man was being deliberately provoking. She had not mentioned what had occurred to anyone.

Maccus gave her an incredulous look since she should have understood the inner workings of household gossip better than he. "I regret I confessed all, my jewel. I told the couple that like all young lovers, we had had a row.

Naturally, they were sympathetic. You barely touched your supper and Cook was concerned."

She sputtered; the audacity of this man was beyond her realm. Oh, the lies he told! "How did you know I—"

"Fayre . . . Fayre, it is amazing what information can be bought for a few coins."

"You bribed your way in?"

In the spirit of his tale, Maccus rolled forward on his knees and took her hand. "I told them that I was repentant for my part and was willing to beg your forgiveness. The maid was in favor of the romantic gesture. The servants are very fond of you, Fayre. Neither one of them thought too much of Standish, you know," he confided, his eyes twinkling. "They wished me luck before they dashed off."

How her family would be thrilled to learn that the servants opened the door to anyone who had a sad tale and a few coins to spare. "If the duchess learns of this, your confidants will get sacked for your mischief."

Maccus wiggled his brows at her. "Then we will not tell your mother, now will we?" He jumped to his feet and held out his hand. "Come along."

Fayre slipped her hand into his and was unceremoniously hauled up. "What are you doing here?" He tugged her a few steps. "Where are we going?"

His swarthy skin darkened and his eyes smoldered in banked fury as he recalled why he had been forced to seek her out. "You did not come by the house this afternoon."

Still not pleased by his contribution to her awful afternoon, Fayre clutched at one of the balusters at the bottom of the staircase he seemed intent on dragging her up. "Was I supposed to? I do not recall the stipulation in your infamous bargain that I am required to call upon your residence daily. Besides, I might have come across your brother." She held tight, refusing to budge another step. "God forbid, I dare engage poor Trevor in a civil conversation."

He refused to dignify her taunt with a rebuttal or an apology, it was not surprising Fayre would point out that he had acted like a horse's arse about her meeting Trevor. Even his brother was avoiding him these days. He had disappeared shortly after Maccus had discovered them laughing and sharing confidences in the drawing room. Trevor probably planned to stay in hiding until Maccus's temper cooled. Glaring at Fayre, he sensed that day was not in the near future. "You know damn well I was expecting you," he said thunderously. "Firstly, because we had talked about it the previous day, and secondly, because you have a habit of reserving your Wednesdays for our visits."

Fayre could not refute his logic, which doubly vexed her. "My plans changed. Mama wanted to go shopping. I do not know why you are acting surly, we met up anyway, just not at your house."

"We haven't time for your tantrum. Let go of the bannister," Maccus growled warningly.

"Not until you tell me what this is all about."

"Very well, we'll talk." Without hesitating, Maccus severed her hold on the railing and tossed her over his shoulder. "Later." He marched upstairs with her pounding on his back.

Even with Fayre squirming in an attempt to unbalance him, Maccus bounded up the stairs without a break in his stride. Dossett had provided him with the basic layout of the Soliteas' town house so he was able to take his reluctant captive directly to her bedchamber with little effort.

Kicking open her door, he carried her across the room and dumped her on the bed.

"Dress for the evening," he ordered tersely, hoping to avoid arguing with her. He strode over to the window and closed the curtains.

With her hands at her sides, Fayre kneaded the soft bedding, most likely wishing Maccus's neck were in her grasp. "I have decided to remain in this evening."

"Oh, aye, I saw what a grand time you were having, humming softly to yourself and playing with your toes." He returned to her side and dodged the pillow she threw at him.

"For the last time, I was not playing with my toes!"

Fayre was clearly still mortified that he had glimpsed her in an unguarded moment. The servants Maccus had spoken with had not told him what Fayre had been doing; however, he had imagined her working on something refined like embroidering handkerchiefs or playing the harpsichord. The hoyden lounging sideways on an oversized chair with her legs exposed had been a revelation. He doubted few had ever seen her so relaxed and indulging in some private silliness.

"I'm not leaving you here to mope around the house like a persecuted ghost," he said curtly, deciding anger might encourage her quicker than sympathy. "Call your maid."

"I sent her away since I am not leaving the house this evening," she replied, petulant.

"Fine. Have it your way." He reached for her, but Fayre scrambled backward across the bed. Maccus crawled after her, grabbed her ankle and dragged her under him. The battle was fierce and lasted mere seconds. His long legs pinned her down, preventing her from kicking him.

He shackled her wrists and slammed them into the bedding above her head. "I have been thinking about kissing you since that day in the kitchen."

Maccus did not want to hear the denials her temper would prompt. Lowering his head, he firmly latched his lips on hers. He had expected her to fight him. Since she was no match against his strength, Fayre chose to remain passive. He grinned at the futility. The lady liked him, even if she was rather cross with him. With the tip of his tongue, Maccus laved her upper lip in a feathering motion. She tilted her head and laughed as his tongue teased her lower lip.

"It tickles, you rogue!"

Loosening his hold on her wrists, he stared down at her hungrily. "I wonder where else you are ticklish?" He leaned to the side and licked the delicate edging of her left ear.

She tensed and sucked in her breath. "You are not that irresistible," she said, trying to sound fierce.

"Or here?" Maccus pushed her head back with his thumb and kissed way down her throat, lingering at the bountiful exposed swells of her breasts. As he inhaled the sweet spice of her flesh, his cock filled and lengthened in his breeches. He had nurtured fantasies about Fayre's breasts. The teasing glimpses her dresses had offered made him feel predatory. His hands descended, covering the flesh denied him by her corset and dress as his teeth lightly bit the beckoning swell of her left breast.

"Y-you wanted me to dress? You win. Get off me and I will put on a dress," Fayre said, her voice strained by the onslaught of his ravenous mouth.

Maccus grimaced, stilling his tender exploration. It had not been his objective this evening to seduce Fayre in her own bed. He had put his hands on her because he had anticipated her decision. If given the choices of remaining in bed with him or leaving the house, she would choose the safest course. It was truly a pity. The simple act of lying against her soft body and fondling her breasts had left him painfully aroused.

Maccus rolled off her and rested on his side. Morosely, he adjusted his swollen cock to a more comfortable angle. Fayre climbed off the bed and assiduously began searching for an appropriate dress for their evening out. "I could make you change your mind," he said silkily.

"Probably," Fayre said, shaking out the dress in her hands and examining it for flaws. Satisfied, she carefully laid it across her arm and held his persuasive gaze. "I risk a part of myself confessing this, Maccus, but I feel something when you look at me . . . when you touch me." Her recollection of writhing in his arms as she found her pleasure was vivid in her eloquent gaze. "But I learned a harsh lesson about wanting. The having is not always pleasurable and the consequences are far-reaching."

"Fayre, I would not—"

"No! No! No!" she said, cutting off his hasty vow. "I am not asking for promises." Calming a bit, she smoothed out the fabric in her arms. "Nor would I believe you if you uttered them."

Her lips trembled. The lust Maccus was feeling doused when he saw the pain in her eyes. Putting his own needs aside, he came off the bed and put his arm around her. She accepted his comfort by resting her cheek against his chest. The feelings she was igniting within him were making him edgy and unpredictable. If Standish had entered the room in this instant, Maccus would have gladly slain him in front of her.

• • • •

Fayre looked expectantly at him as she settled into his coach. At his signal, the coachman barked out his command to the horses and their journey began. "Well, Mr. Brawley, you should be pleased with yourself. You succeeded in doing what my own family could not; you persuaded me to change my mind."

Maccus expelled an exaggerated sigh. "If that were true, we might have spent the rest of the evening frolicking naked on your bed."

She muffled her gasp with her hand, wondering if she would ever be immune to his forthright manner. "Good lord, not even a Carlisle would be so daring." She could just imagine how her father would react if he had arrived home and discovered a man in his daughter's bed.

Nonetheless, she had been tempted, Fayre admitted silently, shifting so her face was completely submerged in shadow. Maccus was too confident regarding his influence over her. Each time he touched her, she found herself willingly surrendering pieces of herself, pieces she could not afford to lose.

"So, sir, you have gone to a great deal of difficulty to bundle me off into your coach. Will you now tell me our destination? And what is in this sack?" She nudged the canvas sack with her foot.

Maccus had refused to tell her where they were going so she had been uncertain about her attire. With her maid, Amelie, out of the house, Fayre chose a dress that required little assistance. She had selected a dress of blue silk gauze over a white satin slip. An ornate panel the width of her hand composed of tiny beads of coral and sequins decorated the front from bosom to feet. White satin rosettes and beaded bows trimmed the short sleeves. With the exception of requiring Maccus to unfasten the dress she had on and tying the tapes of its replacement, Fayre had been able to change her attire with most of her modesty intact.

"So you are curious about the contents of the sack?"

She had noticed the sack immediately upon entering the coach. The longer he ignored its existence, the more her curiosity had increased. Her thoughts kept flitting back to earlier in the day when she and Lord Hawxby had encountered him. Maccus had mentioned several times during their outing that he had hoped to purchase a gift for a certain lady. Although he had not selected anything in her presence, Fayre wondered if he had bought something for her after they had parted ways. She playfully kicked him in the shin. "You assured me your choice of amusement is preferable to counting my toes. Now I am not so certain."

"Impudent wench!" He unwound the string securing the bag. Watching her face, he removed a black domino.

"A masquerade?"

"Aye. An adventure that maintains respectability if not our anonymity." He pulled a half mask out of the sack the same color as the domino and held it up to his face. "The night we attended the concert I sat there wishing we had instead attended a masquerade. After meeting Miss Sheaf and her friends I was certain of it."

Recalling her harsh rebuff of Mr. Farelle's unflattering proposal, Fayre was positive the trio had regretted encountering them, as well. "I assume you have a matching garment in there for me."

Maccus reached into the sack and retrieved a smaller, loose-fitting cloak of dark blue. Her half mask had been adorned with sprays of white plumes on each side, designed to conceal more of the lady's face. "How lovely," she said, holding up her mask and smiling. "Is anyone joining us on our adventure?"

"Who did you have in mind? Lord Hawxby?" Maccus removed his mask and tossed it on the seat.

Fayre scowled at him through her mask. Disgusted that he wanted to talk about their afternoon, she lowered hers until it rested on her lap. "Jealous?" she asked pleasantly.

"Immeasurably," he fired back. "How many gentlemen are trying to seduce you?"

"Dozens. Legions," she claimed dramatically. "A lurid scandal in my past and voilà, every gentleman I meet wants to be my new lover. I should have ruined myself last season. Think of the merriment I have missed!"

Not in the mood to be toyed with, particularly on the subject of her fictional lovers, Maccus studied his hand. "Like what? The firm swat on your backside I am tempted to deliver?"

"You may try, sir," she said smoothly, somewhat convinced he was teasing. "Though Lord Hawxby is hardly worth the retribution you will face if you succeed."

The tension in Maccus seemed to melt with her admission. "You and Hawxby seemed to be rather thick when I encountered you both. The man was holding your hand."

"The only thing thick is your impenetrable skull, Maccus Brawley. The duchess spent almost two hours clinging to you like a cocklebur, which I should warn you has not endeared you to her current lover, Lord Crescett. Does that mean you hope to replace the earl in her bed?" Fayre asked, not thrilled at the thought of her mother and Maccus together.

"Her Grace was not interested—" Maccus paused, recalling her actions and praise. "Crescett has nothing to fear. Your mother is a beautiful, vibrant creature. However,

I dislike sharing what belongs to me, so a married lady
has little appeal."

Fayre sighed softly at the earnestness of Maccus's
statement. She turned her face toward the small window
of the coach. He had spoken so little about his past, but
she had deduced it had been filled with strife. Any effort
to engage him into revealing details about his life had
been met either with silence or an abrupt change of topic.

Still, she believed she was beginning to understand him.
The harsh past he refused to acknowledge ruled him. Ac-
quiring wealth was only part of his goal and now seemed
secondary. He needed acceptance by the one group of
people certain to rebuff him for his humble beginnings.
This was why Maccus had sought her out even though she
seemed a dubious instrument. Fayre could provide him
with the introductions he needed to find a suitable bride
whose noble birth and position in society would obliterate
his past and legitimize his place so that his heirs rightfully
belonged. She imagined he was seeking a paragon, someone virtuous without a scandal in her past. The lady Fayre
had once been before Lady Hipgrave's revenge.

"Long silences, especially from you, concern me."

"If it was so simple to torment you, I would have remained silent often," she teased, trying not to dwell on the
fact that she had lost more than her virginity to Standish.

"Fayre, there is another reason why your mother could
never lure me into her bed." In the dim interior, she felt the
strength of his gaze on her. "I desire the lady's daughter."

Maccus had promised her an adventure. Partaking in
a masquerade at Vauxhall seemed the appropriate
amusement for a daring lady. Fayre had heartily approved

of his choice. Once the coach had reached their destination, they had donned their dominos and half masks and boarded the ferry, which would take them to the pleasure garden. During the ferry ride to Vauxhall, Fayre had confessed that she had never visited the pleasure garden in the evening because her father had previously considered her too young for the wild gaiety the nocturnal diversion offered.

As he followed her up the stairs, her body literally quaked with anticipation for them to reach the rotunda where an evening of music and dancing awaited them. The ferry had been crowded with other masked revelers so Maccus considered them relatively safe from thieves. As they made their way down the walk, Fayre softly murmured her appreciation for hundreds of colored lamps suspended from the tree boughs. Their impressive multitude reminded him of faerie torches.

They heard the music from the orchestra long before the walk widened into an open area. Fayre grinned up at him as she glimpsed the lit rotunda. The orchestra was playing a country dance. The mask she was wearing could not conceal her pleasure. "Oh, Maccus, there is something magical about the garden at night!"

Maccus stroked one of the feathers on her mask and resisted the urge to kiss her. He had already frightened her with his earlier confession of his desire for her and he did not want to ruin their evening together. "If there is magic, Fayre, you brought it with you, for I am enchanted." Without waiting for her reply, he took her hand. Together, they dashed forward into the mob and joined the other dancers.

12

The giddiness Fayre felt had nothing to do with the weak wine she had sipped at Vauxhall and everything to do with the gentleman beside her in the coach. Maccus had given her an adventure she would never forget.

"Are you still angry with me for kidnapping you this evening?" he asked, turning his head and pressing a kiss into her hair.

After spending hours with Maccus dancing and enjoying the music and people around them, Fayre did not think it strange to settle down beside him in the coach and rest her head on his shoulder.

"I was never angry," she said. "Nor did you kidnap me. I just changed my mind, that is all." He still wore his domino and the cloak covered her like a blanket as she nuzzled closer.

Maccus snorted at her outrageous lie. "Ha! You were vexed with me this afternoon when I caught you flattering Hawxby."

"I was not flattering—no, I refuse to argue with you on such a lovely night. Besides, I was vexed with Mama, not you." So what if the effortless familiarity between him and the duchess had provoked her temper? She was not planning on mentioning it.

Maccus lazily brought her hand to his lips and kissed each knuckle. "Will your family worry if they discover that you have left the house?"

"No. Everyone has been keeping late hours. I doubt anyone will notice my absence, but if someone asks, our butler knows I altered my plans." She had sought out Curdey before she had left the house. While her family might not pay much attention to her whereabouts, she knew the butler and her maid would notice her absence.

"I want you to return to the house with me," Maccus said suddenly.

Fayre sat up and looked at him in surprise. "I do not think that would be wise." She thought of his hands caressing her, his mouth at her breast, and knew that with a little gentle persuasion he could change her mind.

After a few charged minutes had elapsed, he said, "I agree. Thank goodness one of us is sensible."

"Yes, is it not?" she asked, not feeling very celebratory or sensible.

Neither spoke the rest of the journey. The coach halted in front of her town house and Fayre straightened. Maccus had given her a wonderful adventure and she intended to be gracious.

She untied the front strings of her domino. Removing the cloak, she folded it and placed the bundle on the empty bench across from them. "I may not have acted accordingly; all the same, I am happy that you received good news on your investments."

Maccus smiled at her and the sweetness of it tugged at her heart. "I knew how you felt this afternoon, Fayre. Your joy was there for me to see. It was there in your gaze, those striking green eyes so expressive. Or maybe I have learned to look deeper than most people."

The coachman opened the door and Fayre shifted away from him. She was already missing his warmth. Maccus caught her wrist before she could disembark from the coach. "I was fortunate to have the honor of your company, Lady Fayre. Good night."

Aware of the coachman's presence behind her, Fayre pulled her hand gently out of his grasp. "Good night, Mr. Brawley."

The house was dark when she entered it, indicating that the rest of her family was still out. She slipped quietly upstairs and headed for her bedchamber. Her parents tended to rouse the servants when they returned from their evening, but Fayre was content to see to her own needs.

Crossing to her dressing table, she lit a single candle. She glanced at her reflection and saw the sadness in her expression. Absently peeling off her gloves, she pondered their parting. Maccus had not kissed her farewell. It should not have bothered her.

Yet it did.

Discarding her gloves on the table, she started to move away, but noticed a slim, flat case. It was the sort of case

Fayre retreated into the house and Maccus followed after her, closing the door behind him. The stillness within the house was palpable.

"This way," she whispered. She took his hand and they ascended the staircase shrouded in darkness.

Maccus wondered belatedly if Fayre was expecting him to gather her up into his arms as he had earlier, and carry her up the stairs. He swiftly dismissed the notion. The stairway had been lit when he had swept her up in such a romantic fashion. The darkness and his rising need to claim her would likely cause him to fall and break both their necks.

She guided him down the corridor and halted in front of the door to her bedchamber. "Too risky," he murmured against her ear, though he loathed denying himself the pleasure of claiming her completely.

"No one ever checks on me," she said, reaching behind her and opening the door. "We will not be disturbed."

He briefly wondered as he entered her bedchamber how many young women had spoken similar assurances to their lover only later to face an enraged father or husband. Fayre smiled shyly at him and Maccus felt his blood heat. Having such a beauty as Fayre in his arms was worth the risk of a bullet. She reached behind him and turned the key in the lock. The candle burning on her dressing table drew him closer to the light.

Fayre joined him at the table. Opening her palm, she traced the floral design with her fingertip. "It is a splendid piece, Maccus." Even in the dim light, the diamonds twinkled merrily as she admired the brooch. "I shall always treasure it."

His gray eyes gleamed like the diamonds in her hand. He

was pleased that she favored his gift. "It seemed like something you might wear. Besides, I noticed your fondness for sparklers."

She held the brooch to her bosom, exposing the back to see how it attached. Maccus moved behind her and covered her hand with his, stilling her movements. "You will have to wear it for me another night."

He took the brooch from her loose grasp and gently placed it in the jewelry case. The implication that she would not be wearing her dress for long was a gauntlet he had tossed before her.

Fayre whirled around and faced him. Holding his gaze, she slowly pulled the light blue gauze over her head and dropped it. The white satin under-dress slip she wore underneath required assistance so she presented him her back. Maccus's hands, to his surprise, were not steady as he removed the pins securing the panel at the back and revealed the tapes concealed within. Uncertain about what to do with the pins, he placed them in the case with the brooch. Two quick tugs and the knots securing the tapes came undone.

She had insisted that he turn his face away earlier as she dressed for the masquerade. Now in the candlelight she bravely slid the short sleeves down over each arm and shoved the under-dress over her hips. Maccus held out his hand and she stepped away from the billowy mound of fabric.

"How fortunate you are not wearing a corset," he said, grateful he did not have to contend with the lacings. Fayre had not been wearing the constricting undergarment when he had arrived and the dress she had selected for their evening had not required one. She reached around and untied the drawstrings of her petticoat. It fell away, and now she wore only her chemise and stockings.

Uncertain of her next step, she crossed her arms over her bosom and then uncrossed them. "I have not had much experience in this intrigue, sir," she said, unfastening the remaining buttons he had neglected on his coat. She grasped one side and walked behind him, freeing his arm from one side of his coat and then the other. In his eagerness to touch her, he began undoing the buttons on his waistcoat before she had completed the circle around him. Fayre dropped his coat on top of her dress, and his waistcoat, cravat, and shirt quickly followed.

Maccus tensed, waiting for Fayre to notice the numerous scars marring his body. His life had been rough and his body bore evidence of violence.

Her hand fluttered up to her lips as she gasped. "Dear God, you have been shot!"

"Not recently," he quipped, hoping to make her smile. When the horror in her expression did not fade he tried to ease her fears. "I know it looks hideous, but it happened years ago. I swear it no longer hurts."

As she made an unintelligible soothing sound, her fingers gently stroked the ridged, cratered scar three inches below and slightly to the right of his left pap. "Oh, how you must have suffered. Who did this to you? Was it a duel?"

He shook his head, finding humor in her outrage. Fayre thought in terms of her world, where the violence was civilized and had rules. "No, it was an unsuccessful attempt at murder. You can understand why I prefer not to dwell on it. If it makes you ill to look on the scar, I can put on my shirt." Maccus crouched down to retrieve his shirt.

He should have left it on for her sake. The women he had bedded in the past were not the sort to be shocked by violence or the marks it left on a man.

"No. Stop," she said, ripping the shirt from his hand and throwing it down. "It is *horrible*."

He closed his eyes, not waiting to listen to her excuses about why they should not lie down on her bed.

Fayre sat down on the small bench in front of her dressing table and stared at him in naked misery. "Horrible that someone deliberately shot you. Horrible that you were in agony and almost died. And you think a scar marking your survival will *sicken me*?" she asked, aghast at his absurd assumption.

Before he could guess her intent, Fayre leaned forward and pressed her lips to his scar. Extremely moved by her sweet gesture to ease the pain of an old wound, he said gruffly, "Fayre, you do not have to prove anything to me. No lady wants to kiss ruined flesh."

"I want to." Placing a restraining hand on his hip, she licked his flesh as if tasting it. The muscles in his abdomen rippled beneath her mouth and his engorged cock craved her delicate ministrations, too.

"Fayre, you are killing me," Maccus said, his voice shaking.

His arousal was prominent and inches from her face. Fayre bit her lip in indecision. He vowed he would throw himself under the first coach that came his way if she refused him. He flinched when she reached over and unfastened the fall on his breeches. Freed, his cock spilled into her hands. She glanced down at his arousal, bewildered. Although no longer a virgin, Fayre was still an innocent in the ways of lovemaking. He stopped breathing for a few seconds as she lightly petted him.

Gently releasing him, she said, "Come to bed, Maccus."

F ayre walked away from Maccus and climbed onto her bed. From the size of his manhood, she doubted he would decline her request. Belatedly, she wondered if she should bring the candle closer to the bed.

"Wait. Don't burrow into the bedding. I want to see you," Maccus said, removing his breeches before he joined her on the bed.

She let her legs dangle off the side of the bed. Perhaps it was silly, but she assumed gentlemen treated lovemaking in a similar fashion. Standish had not been interested in watching her undress as Maccus had. Lord Standish had left her alone in the bedchamber, allowing her time to strip down to her chemise. She had awaited his return under the covers.

"You act differently than Lord Standish," she said without thinking, and winced.

"God, I hope so," he said vigorously. "The man is a cold bastard. Nor would the outcome be favorable for you, my jewel, if I turned out to be his twin."

Not particularly perturbed by her comparing him to Standish or the fact that he was standing naked in front of her, he slipped his hand under her knee-length chemise and untied her garters. He took his time at the task, giving each calf a lingering caress as he removed her stockings.

The hungry look he gave her had her toes curling in reaction. "Now the chemise."

"You want me completely naked?" she squeaked, and edged away from him.

"Aye. Why would I want to cheat myself out of seeing all your natural beauty?" As he took a deep breath, a look of understanding flashed in his gray eyes. "Oh, I see. Standish again. The man is not only a bastard, but an inept one, too." He grasped the hem of her chemise and pulled it over her head. Fayre was tempted to cover herself, but his gaze was everywhere. "No woman should look so perfect to a man."

Maccus was staring at her so avidly she half expected him to pounce. It was undignified of her, but her gaze kept lowering to his groin. The male form was so alien in comparison to hers. From a crisp mat of coarse hair, the erect length of his manhood jutted forth aggressively. The size of him was staggering to her innocent eyes and her enthusiasm waned at the thought of him inside her.

"Will it hurt?" she asked, her gaze unerringly shifting to what concerned her.

Maccus sat on the bed beside her. He casually began plucking out the remaining pins in her hair that her undressing had not dislodged. Her long, cinnamon-colored hair tumbled down her back, providing her with a modicum of covering. "Did I hurt you that day in the kitchen?"

Her face flamed at the reminder. She could not believe she was sitting beside him naked and having such an intimate conversation with him. What was it about Maccus Brawley that seduced her into forgetting the rules and risking her reputation on a man who was reluctant to speak of his past? "Well, no. But you did not—that is, it was your hand," she finished lamely, unwilling to continue their brazen dialogue.

"There was some pain your first time because of your maidenhead. Now that that has passed I can promise that all you will feel is pleasure." He lifted her chin and kissed her lightly. "We will fit perfectly. Let me show you."

Again he surprised her by lying on his back and hauling her down beside him. The position did nothing to diminish her impression of his arousal. "Easy now, there is nothing to fear," he murmured. "There are ways for a lady to have control. I want you to straddle me."

"I beg your pardon?"

He grinned at her primness. "Like a horse, Lady Fayre. Consider me your fine steed."

"Since my horse is a gelding, sir," she said, giggling when he flinched instinctively, covering his manhood, "I doubt your analogy is appropriate."

"Need I remind you that I am still of the opinion that a few swats on your bare bottom will tame your sass?" Maccus rubbed her backside affectionately. Seizing her hips, he pulled her on top of him and positioned her so that she was sitting on his abdomen. "This is an admirable view."

His bland tone had her smiling. The view he was admiring was her breasts. "I see why this position is advantageous for you." She jerked slightly as the head of his manhood bumped against her bare bottom.

A feral light flared in Maccus's gray eyes. The playfulness had faded from his expression and was replaced with what had always been there beneath the surface. Hunger. Using his fingers to part the cleft between her legs, he slid the edge of his hand along the hidden crevasse, revealing what he had suspected. She wanted him, too.

"You can take me, Fayre. How much is up to you." Putting his hands on her hips, he lifted her up and settled her on his rigid manhood. Anticipating his penetration, her body welcomed him. Heat and the wetness of her own arousal surrounded the broad head of his manhood and he seemed to melt into her. Fayre blinked at the ease with which the fullness she had feared pressed deeper into her.

"That's it," Maccus said, his teeth clenched, fighting the urge to seize control. "Move back and forth. Let your body adjust."

Fayre nodded, taking his advice seriously. Taking more of him inside of her, she experimented. She shifted her hips and used her legs to restrain her movements. He had not lied when he promised she had control. This dominating position gave her the power to decide when to retreat or how deep she took him. Maccus was passive beneath her, although she could tell by his strained expression that it was a battle to permit her to explore her newfound power. It was delightful! She was not surprised that Lord Standish, the selfish twit, had not revealed this aspect of lovemaking.

"More, Fayre," Maccus pleaded. "You can take more of me." His hand curled around the back of her head and he pulled her down to him. Spearing his tongue into her mouth, his hips jerked against hers, his body demanding.

She met his thrust and something deep within her gave way as her sheath accepted him wholly. Fayre moaned softly. The fullness of him felt exquisite and made her ache for more. Breaking off the kiss, she concentrated on moving up and down on him, recalling the sensations she felt when his fingers had been inside her.

"Faster, love," he coaxed, his hands kneading her breasts. From time to time, his hands strayed to her hips for he could not resist showing her how a subtle shift in position or pace enhanced their pleasure.

So this was what lovemaking was, Fayre mused. She splayed her hands flat on his upper chest and slid them upward to curve around his shoulders. As she rocked against him, the slick glide of his manhood filled her completely. Instead of easing her relentless ache to possess more of him, the continual thrusting against her womb heightened the wild hunger crawling inside of her.

Maccus was also ensnared by the intoxicating cadence of their passion. His hands fastened onto her undulating hips when she quickened the tempo. Maccus went wild beneath her. He ground his pelvis against her in punctuated thrusts, craving the wet depths of her sheath.

A tingling sensation shimmered through Fayre. Her skin itched and she rubbed her breast against his hairy chest. Maccus growled, impatience and lust shattering his self-imposed chains of restraint. His fingers dug into her buttocks as he took control and drove her down on his manhood at a frenzied pace. The tingling returned on the right side of her face and spread down her neck. Like honey it flowed over her breasts and pooled in her abdomen.

"Share it with me, Fayre!" Bringing her right breast to his mouth, Maccus suckled her nipple fiercely as his hips ruthlessly plunged his manhood into her liquid heat.

Fayre did not understand his harsh command, but her body instinctively did. The viscous flow of honey ignited and a fireball of heat and flame burst through her. She threw her head back and squelched her scream into a thin cry as her body endured wave after wave of scorching pleasure.

As they were joined together, her passion engulfed Maccus and his face contorted, a man pushed past his endurance. Clutching her in tight desperation, he stabbed into her sheath deeply and held himself rigid. Choking on a wordless oath, he hugged her so tightly she could barely draw a breath. She felt the warmth of his seed fill her and she pressed against him, her body craving this union. The wetness of his orgasm triggered another small surge of pleasure. She moved down on him one final time and buried her face into his shoulder.

Fayre was thoroughly compromised. She had thought she was prepared to surrender herself to the carnal demands of passion. What she had not anticipated was that she had blindly handed over her heart, as well. Unbeknownst to her, she had fallen in love with Maccus Brawley.

If not for her breathlessness, Maccus might have suspected Fayre was asleep. With her face pressed into the curve of his shoulder, she had not stirred from her pose for several minutes. Their intensely wild coupling had left him feeling lazy and bemused. He wondered if Fayre was embarrassed by the uninhibited reactions they had wrung out of each other. If she was, she was going to have to get past it. What they had shared was unique, and he was not about to let her ignore it because it did not fit into her plans. Maccus intended to make love to her again—and often.

His hand sought the muscles at her nape and kneaded them gently. "If I had known how incredible this would be, I would have risked the servants and taken you on the kitchen floor that afternoon."

"If I had known, I might have let you," she murmured, her smile against his throat. Giving him a kiss, she pulled away so she could see his face.

Maccus assumed he looked well sated because that was how his body felt. In the past, he had taken pleasure in sinking himself into a willing woman's body, lost himself in the blinding throes of his release, and had liked his companions enough to linger in their beds. It was humbling to learn that he had never truly experienced passion before Fayre.

She carefully separated from him and crawled to the end of the bed to retrieve her chemise. Maccus grinned at the inviting view of her backside. He had wanted her first time with him to be tender. Fortunately, she would not allow it and for that he was extremely grateful. There were so many aspects of loving he had yet to show her, so many positions and ways to make her climax. He wanted to explore them all with her.

"What are you doing?"

She was sitting on her heels, searching the chemise in her hands for the opening to stick her head through. "Dressing. When my maid arrives in the morning and discovers me naked in my bed, she will certainly suspect mischief."

Her practical reasoning, though commendable, was not the romantic chatter one expected from a lover. "If we had retired to my house you could have stayed all night." Nipping her chemise out of her hands, he stuffed the garment behind his back. He impulsively contemplated bundling her off to his house.

"Give it back!" Fayre landed on him and he grunted, exaggerating the impact. She wiggled her hands under him, trying to retrieve her chemise. "Your house might have afforded us an hour or so more, however, remaining all night would be impossible," she said, snatching the chemise from him.

Maccus sat up and plumped the pillows behind him before he settled back down. "Why?" He reclaimed the chemise. Rolling the fabric into a ball, he flung it across the room.

An exasperated sound escaped her lips. "Why? Because there is such a thing as discretion. The servants in both our houses rise before dawn. If we are careless, someone will notice and there will be talk."

Maccus thought of how he had come to Fayre earlier in the library. He had been a stranger to the Soliteas' servants, yet they had willingly divulged information about Fayre and permitted him to enter for a meager sum. The Soliteas' staff was larger than his own and some were hired strictly for the season. Maccus was still not comfortable surrounding himself with strangers to tend his needs so the staff he hired was small, but they were loyal to him. It was one of the reasons why he paid his servants above the customary wage.

Fayre started to crawl off the bed and retrieve the chemise he had thrown. Unwilling to let her go, he grasped her wrist. "I do not regret our lovemaking. I suppose I should wring my hands and bemoan my uncertain fate," she said, mocking her troubles. "I cannot, Maccus. I refuse to feel shame for desiring you."

"A healthy outlook. Come closer and I will reward you," he coaxed, pulling her nearer until she surrendered and plopped down next to him on her side. In deference to her modesty, Maccus grabbed a section of the blanket and covered her to her hips. For selfish reasons he left her breasts exposed.

The look of sleepy contentment had disappeared with her growing agitation. "Being here with you jeopardizes the stance I have taken against Lord Standish and Lady Hipgrave. For now, not everyone believes Standish is telling the truth. There are many who hope he is because my family has made enemies over the years. Regardless, both sides are clamoring for details. I cannot bear to think what might occur if Standish found out that we are lovers."

If she continued to worry about Standish and what he might do, Fayre was likely to convince herself to end their affair before the night was over. Maccus was determined not to let that happen. "Fayre," he said, stroking her hair. "We can be discreet. Standish will not learn about us. Besides, I have taken steps to switch his focus elsewhere."

She looked positively gleeful at the prospect of Standish suffering. "What have you done?"

"I am not ready to share the details yet." He suspected she would find some aspects of his plan disagreeable. "And rest assured I have not forgotten about the countess. I am still working on a proper revenge for her."

Fayre frowned, unsatisfied by his response. "We are supposed to be working on this together."

"Some things need to be independent of the other. It would not do for you to publicly attack them. Let them think they got away with it."

She bit her lip, mulling over his advice. "Perhaps we should distance ourselves in public?"

Maccus understood her fears, but she was not going to escape so easily. They had a bargain and he intended to hold her to it. In an attempt to distract her, he rolled her on her back. "Later on, it might be advisable in order for my plan to work. But never," he said, kissing her chin, "ever in private." His hand caressed her stomach and slid down to the springy curls between her legs. Maccus rubbed the swollen nubbin hidden within her feminine cleft. Still sensitive from his love play, her hips jolted at his touch. His cock, which had never quite settled, jerked on his thigh. Pulsing with blood, the turgid flesh firmed and lengthened in readiness. Moisture coated his inquisitive hand as he probed the entrance of her channel. "Can you take me again?"

"I do not know."

Maccus did not have a doubt. Pushing away the blanket partially covering her, he parted her legs and positioned himself above her. "Let us see?"

He only meant to tease her, a nudge against her cleft to test her readiness. As he prodded his cock persuasively against her, Fayre lifted her hips and opened her legs wider for his entry. Her sheath, still damp from their lovemaking earlier, made his foray swift and complete.

Maccus held himself still, reveling in the sensation of her body cradling him. He wished they had the entire evening to explore each other's bodies, but propriety demanded that he leave her bed soon before her family discovered his presence. Even so, with dawn hours away Maccus could not resist remaining a little longer.

"So, my untamed lady, care to indulge in another adventure?"

Fayre responded by guiding his face to her breasts. Lost in the sorcery of their own creation, neither thought of his leaving again until the sky lightened, hinting that dawn had arrived.

13

One of the footmen from the Solitea household knocked on Maccus's front door the next morning. The servant handed a sealed note to Hobbs, explaining that he was to await Mr. Brawley's reply. Hobbs left the footman waiting in the front hall, while he sought out his employer in the library.

Maccus was seated at his desk when Hobbs entered the room. He shook his head in a puzzlement at his manservant's odd manner, unaware that the older man was imitating the footman's overly polite demeanor and stiff stance. Hobbs presented a silver salver with a note. Taking the note, Maccus rubbed his thumb across the Solitea seal. He had discovered last evening that Fayre had a bolder nature than he had ever imagined. However, sending one of her father's servants was akin to putting a public notice in the papers. He doubted she was that daring.

Breaking the seal, he noticed immediately that the note had come from the duchess. It read:

My darling young man,

I pray that you enjoyed our shopping expedition as much as I. In the spirit of continuing our new friendship, I would be thrilled if you joined me as my very special guest for Lady Dening's *fête champêtre* tomorrow afternoon at two o'clock. My daughter will be attending as well and if you will accompany us in our carriage, what a merry little group we will be. Do not disappoint me, Mr. Brawley!

                                                          Yrs,
                                                             S

The *S* for Solitea was bold and flamboyant, like the lady herself. Maccus smiled down at the note, wondering if Fayre was aware of her mother's invitation. She had not been pleased by the duchess's interest in him. Indeed, it appeared Lady Fayre Carlisle was feeling possessive of him. It was a flattering notion.

"So Mr. Brawley," Hobbs said, interrupting Maccus's woolgathering about Fayre. "What should I tell the fancy livery waiting out there in the front hall?"

Maccus gave Hobbs a sheepish grin. "Tell him that I would be honored to accept Her Grace's invitation. Also"—Maccus winked jauntily at his manservant as he sauntered to his desk—"I have another message that needs delivering to the household."

"You arrogant miscreant! What possessed you to use one of my father's servants to deliver your private message to me?" Fayre demanded several hours later as she had met up with him at the park.

Riding beside him on a gray with half-stocking on all four legs, she looked magnificent in her dark blue riding habit with a wispy white plume stylishly sticking out of her hat. Maccus was in good spirits, despite his companion's fuming over his high-handedness.

"Calm yourself, my lady. No one in the household noticed if your servant returned with two notes from me instead of one. Besides, the footman was well compensated for his efforts," he replied easily. "It seems he is rather good friends with that sweet maid who let me in the other night when you so deliciously seduced me." His dimples deepened at her growl of frustration. "You should be aware that several members of the staff are in favor of our courtship, so I would not fret over them ruining our friendship."

"Mr. Brawley, befriending everyone under my father's employ is not what I consider being discreet. The tips you will be paying out for their silence will make you a pauper within a sennight."

"I can afford it," he said blithely, enjoying her annoyance. In fairness, perhaps he should have acted more discreetly than to use one of her family's servants. However, being around Fayre always seemed to bring out the reckless side he did his best to stifle.

"Ah, yes, Mac Brawley, the notorious smuggler."

Maccus winced. Clearly Fayre and Trevor had discussed

more than weather that afternoon he had found them together in his drawing room. He had always warned her
that he had no interest in sharing his past with her. She
had been respectful of his wishes until now. Her lapse
was proof of her ire at his daring. In deference to privacy,
he had chosen one of the trails less favored by the *haut
monde* but there was still a certain amount of risk that
their conversation could be overheard. "My lady, I prefer
not having my name connected with that particular nefar-
ious and *illegal* occupation. My business dealings are respectable now."

"Investments, you said." She lifted her delicate brow
inquiringly.

"Profitable investments," he corrected. Early on when
he started dabbling at the Exchange, his focus had been
centered more on profit than honesty. It had come as a
surprise that his natural skills could be applied to legitimate ventures with rewarding results. "I would bribe your
father's entire household if it bought me another night in
your arms, Fayre."

Her eyes glowed with pleasure at his words. Fayre hastily glanced away and admired the scenery. "We should
not speak of it. Not here. Not ever." She tapped her riding
crop on her horse's rump, causing it to leap forward.

Maccus spurred his horse into a canter to catch up with
her. She was an excellent horsewoman. Her spine was
straight as a lance despite the jarring stride of the horse.
"We can't pretend it didn't happen."

Fayre glanced in his direction. "I never said I would. But
our friendship complicates things between us. It diverts us
from attaining your goal," she argued. "And mine." Her
gray, sensing her agitation, shook its head from side to side.

"Are we racing?" he mildly asked. She groaned and

signaled her horse to slow to a walk. "I have several goals. Which one are we concentrating on today?"

"Being a gentleman. If you recall, you asked for my assistance on the matter," she snapped. Her exasperation at his continued teasing was provoking her anger. Determined to ignore his playful manner, Fayre had chosen to dedicate herself to the business between them. "The duchess clearly likes you—"

"I'm a very likable person," he quipped, earning another icy stare from her. "This invitation to the Dening affair does not trouble you?"

"Why would I be troubled?" she replied, perplexed.

He was not fooled. "Yesterday afternoon, I could have sworn the duchess's adoration had incited a smidgeon of jealousy on your part."

"I was as jealous as you were of Lord Hawxby's attentions to me."

"Oh, so you were *that* jealous," he said, grinning when she swiped at him with her riding crop and had no chance of hitting him.

"Will you be serious, Mr. Brawley," she said sternly, a line formed above her brow. For the sake of propriety, she addressed him formally to prevent any accidental slips in public. "You desired my assistance to help you move about in polite society. My influence is abysmally limited in comparison to my mother's. With her stamp of approval"—Fayre fluttered her lashes at him, her face cast with a sardonic expression—"and the duchess was obviously impressed with your inexhaustible charm, you will draw the interest of many members of the *ton*. You will soon have your pick from the multitude of unmarried ladies who will worship your face almost as passionately as your annual income."

"That sounds rather mercenary," he grumbled, thinking she did not have to sound so enthused about marrying him off to some unknown miss. Fayre was probably celebrating her liberation from their bargain. "And a very cynical view."

"Perhaps because I was raised in this world you crave and understand its nature. I am the Duke of Solitea's only daughter," she said indifferently. "I could look like an old hag and fortune hunters would still trip over themselves to vie for my hand in marriage."

Maccus had seen how the gentlemen of the *ton* reacted to Fayre. They buzzed around her like faithful, irritating drones, filling her glass of punch while they filled her ears with flattery. She was eighteen years old and had already been abused. He could not condemn her for her cynical outlook. "Well, my lovely Fayre, no one would ever mistake you for a hag. I have seen your potent effect on the gentlemen with whom you associate, myself included, and you can't convince me the gentleman who marries you will have done so solely for your family connections and dowry."

"I have yet to encounter such a gentleman. When I do, we can celebrate at Gunter's," she teased, but the humor of her inflection did not gleam in her eyes.

"And this is the fate you have been polishing me for?"

"You selected your course long before we ever met, sir." She craned her neck and squinted at something ahead of them. "It is my task to help you achieve it, and with my mother's help—" Something caught her interest. "Egad, could this day get worse? I should have burned your note unread the moment the footman delivered it."

Two riders were approaching them. From their attire,

Maccus deduced one of them was a woman. "Friend or foe?"

Fayre shot him a look of disbelief. "You can judge for yourself. Lord Standish and Lady Hipgrave are also enjoying an afternoon ride." She tightened the reins in her hand inadvertently and her gray whinnied. "I swear they are stalking me. Of late, I cannot go anywhere and not glimpse the countess's patronizing face."

Her distress slid beneath his skin and constricted his pumping heart. "You are not alone."

"In this, I am," was her inaudible reply.

Fayre fought down the urge to strike the haunches of her horse and gallop off before the couple joined them. She wanted to yell at Maccus. Blame him for giving them an excuse to taunt her. Nevertheless, her current predicament was her fault. When Maccus's note arrived, her initial reaction had been joy. The night they had shared together had surpassed all her expectations. The pleasure he had built and coaxed from her body had revealed that Lord Standish might have breached her maidenhead, but he had left her a virgin. It was Maccus who had truly been her first lover.

"Good afternoon, Lady Fayre," Lord Standish said, his gaze lingering on her with misplaced affection. The simpleton was smiling at her as if he had done nothing wrong!

Fayre was tempted to ride on without acknowledging the couple. Instead she signaled the gray to halt beside Maccus's bay. She refused to give them further excuse to gossip about her. "Good afternoon, my lord. Lady Hipgrave."

The countess wore a crimson riding habit with gold

frog fasteners down the front. Begrudgingly, Fayre thought the other woman looked dazzling in the vivid color. "It is so wonderful to see you again, Lady Fayre. I was just confessing to Standish how bored I was. Seeing you has definitely improved my day."

"You are so kind to say so," Fayre said, trying not to gag on her false words. Their speculative glances at her companion prompted her to add, "Allow me to introduce a friend of my mother's, Mr. Maccus Brawley."

"I am your friend, too, my lady," Maccus reminded her.

Lady Hipgrave extended her hand out to him. "Oh, pray, will you be my friend, as well?"

Expertly, Maccus maneuvered his horse closer and clasped the countess's hand. "I enjoy making new friends."

"As do I," Lady Hipgrave purred, causing both Lord Standish and Fayre to scowl at their exchange. "Shall we ride together?"

"I fear we must refuse," Fayre said, infusing mock regret in her tone. "There is no one near us, so trying to provoke me into a confrontation would be a waste of your time, and spoil our lovely outing."

Lady Hipgrave glanced at Maccus. She was clearly surprised that Fayre would reveal her hostility for them so openly in front of a stranger. "You have been sharpening your claws, little cat," she said approvingly.

"Just remember that the next time you decide to confront me. You might get more than you bargained for, Countess." Fayre finally looked at Maccus. Although it was difficult to tell what he thought of their brief meeting, a tiny smile played on his lips. "Let us not tarry, Mr. Brawley. The duchess is expecting us," she lied, supplying a more palatable excuse to depart than fear.

"A pleasure to meet you, Mr. Brawley," Lady Hipgrave called out to him. "Next time, I pray it will not be so short."

Maccus did not try to soothe Fayre's tattered nerves with worthless praise. They rode in silence while she fought to compose herself. Fayre was grateful he had been with her. His presence had given her strength, and rerunning the encounter in her mind, she decided she had departed the victor of their spiteful banter.

"A charming couple," Maccus mused, probably hoping to get a reaction out of her. "I thought Lady Hipgrave's riding habit most striking."

Fayre had thought the same thing. Grimacing, she said, "The dress was hideous. The color was scaring off the birds."

Maccus said nothing, but she sensed his gray eyes were laughing at her. His next words confirmed her suspicions. "Come along, my lady. We mustn't be late for the duchess's tea."

H er Grace, the Duchess of Solitea embraced Maccus before he could settle down beside her. When he thought of duchesses in general, he imagined them as humorless, brittle creatures that rarely deigned to speak to anyone unless they were issuing orders. The duchess had surprised him. At forty-five, her vivacious nature and beauty, a variation of Fayre's, could dazzle a man and make him forget she was old enough to be his mother. Even Maccus could not resist her warm, casual manner. Staring at his companions, he was certain the drive to the Denings' *fête* would be highly entertaining. As promised, Fayre had joined them on their outing. He would have been disappointed if she had used her encounter with the countess as an excuse to avoid attending the gathering, and being alone with Her Grace might have been awkward. The older woman's lover, Lord Crescett, would have disapproved, not to mention her husband.

Maccus wondered if his presence had not prompted Lord Temmes's sudden decision to ride with them. He guessed the young man to be close to his brother Trevor's age. That was where the comparison ended. He embodied everything one expected of a gentleman born into wealth and privilege. The young marquess sat beside his sister with a slightly bored expression on his handsome face. Side by side, the siblings were a striking couple. Their connection was apparent in their coloring. What spared the young man from being too pretty was the line of his jaw and his eyes. Whenever Lord Temmes fixed his stare on Maccus, the latter found it akin to gazing into shards of green ice. Fayre's brother did not like him and was not being particularly polite about it.

"Fayre, my girl, are you not thrilled Mr. Brawley was able to join us on our adventure?" the duchess said, not caring for the silence of her companions.

Maccus sensed Fayre's private amusement at her mother's choice of words. He had promised her adventures, too. The light staining on her cheeks indicated she was probably reflecting on the adventure they had shared in her bed.

"Yes, Mama." To Maccus she said, "Lord and Lady Dening keep a residence just outside London. Their gatherings are very popular and can go on for days."

There seemed to be a warning in her statement, but Maccus could not fathom what was troubling her. Since it seemed polite to mention the missing member of the

Solitea family, he asked, "Will His Grace be attending the Denings' *fête*?"

He received an interesting tableau of reactions from the trio. The duchess's smile wobbled and she suddenly discovered something fascinating about the passing scenery. The hand Lord Temmes had braced against his cheek curled into a fist. His sullen expression darkened with blatant hostility. If Maccus had not realized his grave error in mentioning the duke, Fayre cleared it up for him by kicking him in the shin when her mother was not looking.

"His Grace had other pressing commitments," the duchess explained, and Maccus regretted dimming the vitality he always credited her with because of his innocent question.

"My father usually misses the Denings' *fête*," Fayre said, her green eyes seeking out her mother. Maccus read sympathy in her expression.

Her brother stirred from his brooding slouch. "Well, 'tis a fact Lord Dening does not miss our father," the marquess muttered.

Fayre gave her brother a quelling glance and rewarded his callous remark with a not so discreet jab with her pointy elbow. Maccus thought it was nice to see her picking on someone else for a change. For a merry trip to the countryside, the beginning of their adventure was starting off rather grimly.

"All right, explain to me why my question about your father has the duchess sitting there like a flower wilting in the sun and has your brother plotting my death?"

Maccus demanded to Fayre when they had stopped at an inn to rest the horses.

Fayre had not joined her mother and Tem inside the inn, telling them that she preferred to walk the yard and ease the stiffness in her limbs. She knew Maccus would not leave her unescorted. Tem should have objected, but he was too angry right now to be thinking clearly.

"No one blames you," she assured him, then paused. "Well, Tem does, but he was surly before we even arrived at your house."

They walked the boundary of the enclosure. Years of the ground being trampled by people, equipage, and horses had prevented anything but a compact mix of dirt and dung to exist there. Crowded near the wooden posts of the decaying fence that wrapped around the inn and the outer buildings, wild grasses and a few stray flowers flourished.

"This is family business so if you repeat what I am about to tell you, Tem will try to give you a scar to match the one on your chest," she said, wanting him to understand that the subject was painful for her family.

"Your brother does not need any encouragement. For some reason he despises me," Maccus said, truly puzzled why anyone would not like him.

"He probably recognizes you for what you are," she said, shrugging. Fayre was not overly concerned that Tem was planning to ambush him. Her brother had the sense not to murder Maccus in front of the duchess.

"And what is that?" he asked. There was an edge to his husky voice. Great. She had managed to insult him.

She motioned helplessly with her hands. "A scoundrel. A seducer of innocents."

Fayre uttered her insults so blandly, he barked with

laughter. "My jewel, I am wounded," he mocked, grabbing his chest.

"Oh, and a liar, too," she added, after his feigned chest pains had reminded her of that particular flaw. "Even so, you do not have anything to fear from him. Tem is just posturing because the Solitea women are fond of you. If he had met you without the family interference, you might have grown to be best friends."

Maccus glanced back at the inn. He shook his head. "I disagree."

"No, truly. How could he condemn you? Tem is a scoundrel, too. With the Solitea curse on his head, there was no incentive for him to behave, I fear."

"There is no such thing as a curse," Maccus said flatly.

He did not believe her. She supposed that to an outsider, it did sound peculiar. "I confess I have not researched the origin of the curse to confirm it. Still, the Carlisle family for generations has believed in its existence."

Maccus cut her off and grasped her upper arms. "Fayre, if you don't want to tell me why your mother was upset by a simple question, then very well, don't tell me. You don't have to make up another tale to distract me."

Exasperated, she pushed aside his arms and kept walking. "Fine. Forget about the curse." Perhaps there was no curse. Her father seemed to have escaped it. And Tem, well, he was young and very wicked. She had always thought it prudent not to be too attached to him. "About my father—"

His handsome face creased in concern. "Fayre, if it is too upsetting for you—"

She shook her head. "This does not have anything to do with me. No, really. Like Tem, I am just an unwilling spectator."

Maccus knew better, but he could not seem to resist putting his arm around her and cuddling her for a moment. "Of what, love?"

"The Carlisles and the Denings have a history," she said, carefully picking her words. "I cannot think of a clever way of saying it. My father and Lady Dening were lovers." She saw his expression and waved away his opinion of her big confession. "I know what you are going to say. My father has taken many mistresses and everyone in the *ton* knows he is not particularly fussy if they are married or not. My mother is tolerant in ways I could never be." She pouted, thinking about Lord Standish.

He tickled her underneath her chin, reminding her of his presence. "But there was something different about Lady Dening?"

Fayre nodded, feeling wretched. "Papa fell in love with her. This occurred years before my birth. Tem was a few months old and Mama was still recovering her strength from the difficult birth. I cannot give you specific details on how they came together or why Lady Dening had captured my father's heart when his other lovers had not."

"I assume Lord Dening discovered that he had been betrayed and ended the affair?"

She raised her hand and squinted against the bright sun. The warmth felt good on her face. "It was a little more complicated than that. My father planned to leave my mother and run off with Lady Dening. It never happened. Perhaps Lord Dening caught them or Lady Dening realized belatedly that she could not destroy two families."

Fayre took a breath. Naturally, she had been curious about what had transpired, but this was not a subject she could discuss with her family. "Lady Dening remained with her husband. Seven months later she was delivered of a son. He will be introduced to you as Lord Jerrett." She paused, allowing the words to sink in.

Maccus was quick. "The baby was sired by your father. Christ, what a coil!"

Fayre nodded, feeling relieved to have unburdened herself. She had not even known the secret had been weighing on her until she had shared it with Maccus. "Now you understand why my father does not attend Lord and Lady Dening's gatherings. I assume my parents and the Denings came to an understanding. Lord Dening accepted the baby as his own. Each year as far back as I can remember, my mother brings us to the *fêtes*. Everyone is friendly. And no one speaks of the past."

Fayre sensed that Maccus liked her mother. His face was harsh with anger on her mother's behalf for the distress the duke's carelessness had caused her. "Why does the duchess subject herself to facing a woman who must bring her pain when she looks upon her?"

"For the duke. She loves him. Despite their odd ways, their marriage works for them. These yearly visits give her an opportunity to visit with the son her husband will never be able to claim. I would not be surprised if she shares with my father the changes she notes in Lord Jerrett and the tales the Dening family relate to her about him."

"It seems cruel to drag you and your brother into this mess."

She placed her hand on his arm, wanting to soothe the tension rising within him. "I doubt she sees it that way, Maccus. Lord Jerrett is our half brother. Trevor is your half brother. He is your family. We will never be able to call the viscount brother. Nonetheless, it was important to my mother and father that we know him."

Maccus pressed a kiss to Fayre's forehead. "Fayre—"

"Get your hands off my sister!" Tem said coldly behind them.

14

"Mr. Brawley," Fayre said, her gaze never moving from her brother's seething face. "I appreciate your escort. Might I impose on you to get me some refreshments before we depart?"

Maccus hesitated, not pleased at leaving her to face her brother's wrath alone. "Fayre, I do not stand behind a woman," he said, his concern for her causing him to use her given name.

"Nor do I need a stubborn man to hide behind!" she angrily retorted. "Please. You can entertain the duchess while my brother has a tantrum."

Tem waited until Maccus had left the yard.

"What is going on between you and Brawley?" he demanded.

She had strolled the yard enough to long for the carriage. "Just making conversation," she said lightly.

Tem held her in place, when she would have walked away. "He laid his hands on you, Fayre. Called you by name."

"Such crimes!" she said, sneering. "You are doing the same thing and I have yet to hang you!"

Her brother, realizing he was getting nowhere with his sister by yelling at her, struggled to soften his approach with her. "The conversation you were having with him seemed . . . involved. What were you talking about?"

Fayre made a vague gesture with her hand. "Miscellaneous topics. He knew his question about Papa upset our mother, so he apologized." Or would have had Tem not interrupted them.

"You didn't tell him," Tem said incredulously. "Pray tell me you did not tell him the reason why our mother was saddened by his question."

"Fine. I will give you the words. I did not tell him." It was her rotten luck her brother could always see through her subterfuge.

"Damn it, Fayre!" he shouted at her, scaring two scrawny chickens that were pecking in the dirt nearby. "Who is this man to you that you would spill family secrets to him?"

"Oh, please, Tem, it is hardly a secret. There are those who knew Mama and Papa twenty-two years ago. People who were aware of Papa's affair with Lady Dening," she said, weary of the pretense. "And let us not forget Lord Jerrett himself. The gentleman may have Lady Dening's raven hair, but he has the Carlisle eyes. No one can look at him and deny he is our brother!"

"Half," her brother growled.

"All right. Half. Mr. Brawley is not dim-witted. He would have eventually put it all together himself like everyone else has." Fayre looked beseechingly at Tem. "Are you not tired of the pretense? The Denings and the Carlisles are the only people who claim not to know the truth."

Tem roughly pulled her into his embrace and hugged her. "Sister mine, you cannot change the rules just because you do not like the game."

Fayre sighed against him. "I know. We are merely the spectators. I would not say or do anything to harm either one of them."

She thought of her attempts to protect her father from Lady Hipgrave's revenge. Sometimes it was difficult for her to be a good daughter. Her father's habitual indiscretions had hurt too many people. Fayre felt trapped between loving a faithless man and feeling disloyal for seeing his flaws as weakness.

"What of Brawley?" Tem asked, speaking into her hair. "Do you trust him?"

Fayre pulled back so her brother could see the truth in her face. "Yes, I do."

Maccus saw the Earl of Dening and his lady in a different light now that Fayre had revealed one of her family's dark secrets. Lord Dening was a large, imposing gentleman with thinning brown hair and a bald spot at his crown. Maccus approximated the man's age to be in the early fifties. The thickness around his middle seemed like misplaced muscle rather than fat from overindulgence.

In contrast, Lady Dening was petite. Her bones looked so delicate it was a miracle she had not been crushed by her robust husband. The duchess had confided to Maccus on their drive to the Denings' that the countess had produced seven children in as many years. Only four had survived past infancy. Discreetly observing this tiny lady with silver laced through her black hair, Maccus thought the strength of a woman was greatly underestimated.

One would have never guessed that there had ever been animosity between the Carlisles and their hosts. The earl and countess had warmly embraced the Duchess of Solitea when the carriage had arrived at the lavish country house. The couple was equally affectionate with Lord Temmes and Fayre. The duchess introduced Maccus to the Denings and he sensed their unspoken curiosity about his connection to the family. The couple might have thought he was the duchess's lover initially; however, the older woman herself had put aside such speculation by recounting the tale of their shopping expedition, which included Fayre. Much to Fayre's consternation her mother had neatly shifted everyone's inquiring gazes on to her daughter.

Now that Maccus knew the truth, he had wanted to meet Fayre's half brother, Lord Jerrett. Lady Dening had explained with profound regret that the young viscount had been unable to return home in time for the *fête*. Her Grace expressed her disappointment, but the relief on her children's faces had not gone unnoticed by Maccus.

While Lady Dening escorted Fayre and her mother away so they could refresh themselves from their journey, he and Tem had joined Lord Dening on a brief tour of the estate. The estate was large enough that they would have had to take horses to view the land wholly. With the house filling up with guests that were now arriving hourly, the earl was content to show them the immense gardens at the back of the house. Beyond the gardens, a pleasant walk in the woods gave way to an unexpected open area. The grass had been cut low to the ground in a circular pattern, highlighting the earl's newest addition. He referred to it as a Gothic temple.

Tem scrutinized the exotic building. "It is not Gothic," he murmured, and Maccus had no clue if the marquess was addressing him or his host.

Maccus did not consider himself an expert on architecture, but he had to agree that Lord Dening's temple was not Gothic, though he recognized an influence. Since he was a guest he decided to keep his mouth shut.

The temple had been hewed from marble and the outline of the building was square. In between the massive columns that numbered two on each side, the architect had inset windows that reminded Maccus of a church with their high triangular points at the top and their horizontal bases. It was the architecture at the top of the temple that was perplexing. The roof bowed deeply at each corner while the ends flared out like a Turkish slipper. Lanterns adorned the ends. Metal railings framing the uppermost section of the odd roof were bent up toward the heavens at each of the corners. The design looked like a square that had turned inward.

"It's an exotic," Lord Dening explained with satisfaction to his bemused companions. "My wife and I chose elements of architecture that we liked and had the architect put it all together. The building is a mix of Gothic and Chinese ornament. At night when the lanterns are lit, I feel like I've left England and have traveled to some exotic locale."

Tem was unimpressed. Shaking his head, he walked away from what he considered a monstrosity and returned to the formal gardens he understood and appreciated. Lord Dening smiled at his temple, clearly pleased with the results.

Maccus stared at the building thoughtfully.

Exotic locale.

He grinned at his host. Maccus could appreciate Lord Dening's desire to escape his mundane world. He shifted his gaze thoughtfully to the temple, wondering if he could convince Fayre to join him on another adventure.

"What are you doing out here?" Fayre demanded later when she discovered Maccus in the gardens. The man was standing alone on one of the many walks with his arms clasped behind his back. There was a smug expression on his face that put her on alert as he surveyed the landscape. Maccus was definitely up to something. "You disappeared almost two hours ago. The duchess has been asking everyone for her *preux chevalier,*" she said, fluttering her lashes in exaggeration.

Maccus groaned. "Peerless knight? It sounds as though the duchess's spirits have been revived. Fayre, I beg you to save me from your mother's clutches."

The expression he gave her was so boyish; she could not resist grinning at his appeal. "Too late, Mr. Brawley. We have been ordered by the duchess to mingle with the other guests. I can already tell Mama loathes sharing you with anyone, but I have persuaded her to introduce you around to several respectable families, all of whom have young unmarried daughters."

He cupped her face tenderly. "Trying to get rid of me?"

The gesture always did queer things to her insides. If she did not know better, she could have sworn she had swallowed a few of the garden's butterflies. Her stomach certainly felt as if she had one or two fluttering about inside.

"Just honoring my side of the bargain, sir," Fayre said faintly. When he teased her in that manner, she often wondered if he was testing her dedication in helping him. For a man who spoke of building a life for himself with a respectable bride at his side, he seemed reluctant to actually seek this mysterious lady out. It was wishful thinking for her to assume he was enjoying her company too much to consider replacing her with another lady.

"Where are we going?" Maccus asked, following her lead.

"Lady Dening has several activities set up on the front lawn. Guests have the choice of simply watching or participating." Fayre fought the urge to sulk. "If Mama has her way, I shall be demonstrating my archery skills."

Maccus patted her shoulder in sympathy. "Are you dreadful and fear humiliating yourself?"

Her lips thinned at his insult. "Why, Mr. Brawley, thank you for your boundless confidence in my abilities. No, honestly, I am quite proficient with the bow. You see, when I was a child, I was very competitive. Whatever Tem did, I had to try. Fortunately, Papa was indulgent." She bit her lower lip in agitation.

"Well, something is vexing you." He studied her face intently as if he could find the answers he sought in her eyes. "Is your brother still angry about catching us alone back at the inn?"

Since her brother had calmed, she decided there was no point in explaining that Tem had been more furious about their topic of conversation than about any propriety breached. "No. Tem and I are fine." She hated telling him what was truly bothering her because she felt cowardly. "There might be a problem. From a window, I saw Lady Hipgrave alight from her carriage. There are many people strolling about to distract her. The house and its grounds are extensive, but I will only be able to elude her for a short time."

She was acting pathetic. She despised herself for letting the horrid woman tie her nerves into knots. Maccus could no longer stand it. Uncaring who saw them together, he hauled her into his arms. Fayre closed her eyes and reveled in the strength and warmth of his body.

"You are not alone," he promised, stroking the back of her head. "Lady Hipgrave is cunning. She will not approach you when your family is so close. Take heart in her instinct for self-preservation."

Fayre nodded. There was truth in what Maccus was saying, so she latched on to his assurances like a talisman.

"I told you the duchess's stamp of approval held sway," Fayre said, approaching him several hours later with a superior look on her face. "I noticed Miss Knight and Miss Greffis were quite taken with you. How does it feel to have every female you meet gaze adoringly into your gray eyes, hanging on every word you utter as if it were poetry?"

Maccus would not have minded if Fayre had sulked a bit, her pretty green eyes flashing with jealousy. If she had been upset that he had spent the past hour surrounded by four enthusiastic young ladies, she was concealing it remarkably well.

"How could you tell? Every time I sought you out, you

were either dancing or cornered by several ardent admirers," he replied, ignoring the edge in his inflection that did in fact sound appallingly like jealousy.

The afternoon *fête* had not wound down as daylight faded into twilight. The outdoor amusements of the afternoon were packed away and all the doors and windows of the house were flung open for an evening of music, dancing, and impromptu performances by many of the guests.

Before they had departed, Fayre had warned him to pack a small trunk for their journey. The request had seemed ludicrous for an afternoon outing, but trusting Fayre, he had complied. His trunk had been strapped to the back of a second carriage that had been laden with the Soliteas' trunks and the ladies' personal maids.

After enjoying the Denings' hospitality for most of the day, he now understood Fayre's earlier warning about the popularity of the couple's gatherings. Everyone was having such a wonderful time, no one went home. There were plenty of bedchambers to accommodate the guests; some who had traveled vast distances for the *fête*. The lateness of the hour had already encouraged many of the elderly revelers to retire so they would be alert for tomorrow's planned amusements.

"What did you expect me to do while you were surrounded by dewy-eyed devotees?" she asked sharply. "We agreed it was best that you circulate without me. With Lady Hipgrave prowling about, we want to discourage any impression there might be an intimate connection between us. There is no cause for alarm, you have the duchess's support."

"I'll have you know that your mother has taken a personal interest in seeing me married off." The older woman's determination was frightening. If none of the ladies he had encountered that afternoon and evening were appealing to him, Her Grace assured him that there were dozens more she could present.

Fayre looked away and shrugged casually. "My mother can be tenacious when she directs her energies toward a task. Rest assured you will be posting banns in the autumn with her backing you."

Maccus deliberately kept his face neutral. "Then I shall be in the awkward position of being indebted to both of the Solitea women."

Her smile was wistful. "The duchess would not have it any other way."

They listened in silence to the music and laughter floating on the evening air. They had strolled from the ballroom to the front hall. Maccus glanced down at Fayre. The bevy of flirtatious beauties the duchess had thrust at him for his approval faded from his mind as his gaze met her green eyes. If anyone had encountered them, they would have blushed at his keen regard.

Fayre was wearing an evening dress of sea green. The material was wispy and fluttered on the air when she moved. The dress had been distracting him all evening. It had been difficult for Maccus to prevent his hungry gaze from seeking her out as she leisurely mingled with the other guests. Her cinnamon tresses were curled and piled high on her head, and she wore an ivy and honeysuckle wreath like a crown. Maccus inhaled deeply, taking in her intoxicating essence. The intermingling of her womanly scent and the sweetness of honeysuckle was driving him insane with lust. He wanted to drag her into the nearest corner and devour her.

Unbeknownst to Fayre, Maccus had not spent all of his

time flirting with the ladies. Secretly, he had been setting into motion his plan to whisk her away from the festivities. He suspected she might try to thwart him since she seemed as dedicated as her mother to marry him off. Maccus shook his head. While he appreciated everything she had done for him, Fayre did not have a clue as to what he truly wanted.

"You are wearing my brooch, Lady Fayre," he said, resisting the urge to nuzzle her delicate ear.

She touched the diamond floral spray she had pinned at the center of her bodice. The brooch twinkled at him, a subtle declaration of his claim on her. "It was a generous gift, Mr. Brawley."

Maccus leaned closer and whispered in her ear, "If you permit me, I would give you much more."

Fayre giggled at his exaggerated leer. "Behave." She playfully shoved him away from her.

He removed his pocket watch from his waistcoat pocket and checked the time. "Never." Maccus had purposely guided her away from the other guests. Since there was no one in sight, he decided to act on his plans. "It is time." He took her hand. Opening the front door, he pulled her outdoors.

She gaped at him as if he had grown a second head. "Time? Time for what?"

"Another adventure," he replied cryptically.

Maccus was up to mischief. She could not believe he was behaving so boldly when they had kept a respectful distance from each other for most of the day. He had not even asked her for a dance. He led her around to the back of the house and the Denings' gardens. There were torches positioned around the terrace for the guests. The rest of the gardens were shrouded in darkness.

He held up a long piece of fabric. "What do you intend to do with that swath?" Fayre asked.

"I told you. An adventure. Now cooperate," he ordered, spinning her around so her back was to him.

"And if I refuse?" She let her head fall back against his shoulder and fluttered her lashes flirtatiously at him.

Maccus growled in her ear, "A firm swat on your backside will be delivered." He gave her a light warning swat to show he was serious.

"Savage," she said, a smile on her lips. "What do you want me to do?"

He nipped her earlobe. "Close your eyes."

Fayre lifted her slender shoulders, expelling an exaggerated sigh. "Very well."

She closed her eyes. Immediately, he placed the swath of muslin over her eyes and tied it from behind. Fayre giggled at his muttered expletive and earned another swift slap on her buttocks. She knew what was frustrating him. The manner in which her hair was styled was making it difficult for Maccus to knot his muffle.

"Ready?" he murmured, kissing her cheek.

"Is this a game?" she asked, feeling the first stirrings of doubt and vulnerability. "It is not the one where you lead me into a room filled with people who silently laugh at me while I guess the identity of exotic items you have placed in my hands?"

Maccus laughed. "What an odd whim!" He gave her right breast an affectionate squeeze. "Not tonight, my jewel. I do not feel like sharing you with anyone else tonight."

The vulnerability she was feeling did not ease as he

guided her beyond the terrace and into the dark gardens. He must have picked up a lantern because his stride was surefooted in contrast to her hesitant one.

"You won't stumble," he said, coaxing her farther away from the house. She could smell the faint perfume of flowers and foliage. "You can trust me, Fayre."

"Is this the game?" she asked, ignoring his assurances.

Abruptly Maccus halted, forcing her to step into his embrace. He flicked a finger under her chin, tilting her face up. "In part," he said, being frustratingly vague.

She anticipated in that moment that he would kiss her. What she had not predicted was the ferocity of the claiming. Sinking his hands into the fabric of her skirts, he jerked her body tightly to his. She parted her lips to speak, but Maccus was not interested in words. He breached her lips with his tongue and worked his mouth over hers as if he could gain sustenance from a mere kiss. Fayre's head was spinning when Maccus just as swiftly ended the kiss. Grabbing her limp arm, he pulled her deeper into the darkness.

Minutes passed and the distance they had walked was befuddling her sense of direction. Without her sight, she was completely lost. She wondered if Maccus had circled them around the paths in a calculated effort to keep her from guessing their destination.

When he eventually halted, she was grateful. Her soft slippers were not designed for midnight walks in the gardens. "Almost there," he said, and she groaned in frustration.

She heard him set something down against stone. The lantern? A humiliating squeak burst from her lips as Maccus unexpectedly picked her up. She felt dizzy as her equilibrium shifted. He carried her up five steps, and even with the swath of cloth over her eyes, she could perceive their destination was brighter.

Maccus lowered her legs slowly until she could stand on her own. Fayre reached for the knot securing the cloth, but he grabbed her wrist to halt her actions. "Hmm, this is your notion of adventure? Fascinating." She paused and tried to figure out where she was. Stamping her foot, she realized the ground beneath her feet was solid. She sensed they were in some kind of building, but the wafting breeze and the symphony of insects indicated they were still outdoors.

"Did anyone ever tell you that you are a mouthy wench?" He let go of her wrists and moved to her right. She heard the rustling sound of fabric.

"I believe you are the only one who has made that particularly rude observation in my presence," she said, cocking her head. The soft impact of clothing being discarded silenced her.

Maccus moved behind her, brushing his chest against her back. "The walk was just the prelude. Consider this the beginning of our adventure." He reached around to the front of her dress and cupped her breasts. She was planning to murder him if anyone was witnessing his daring. A guttural sound of disapproval rumbled in his throat when she reached for the cloth covering her eyes. "Leave it in place."

"It is making me feel restless," she complained, knowing it was more complicated. The loss of control and the dependency on Maccus was heightening her trepidation. Blast him! The arrogant man knew it, too!

"Restlessness can be pleasurable," he murmured, tracing her spine with his fingernail.

His fingers continued their descent to the center of her

back and the silver wire hooks and eyes holding her dress together. Deftly, he unhooked the two at the top and the pair at her waist. Fayre shivered. After being confined in her corset all day, the night air felt cool in contrast to her skin. She jumped as Maccus's warm hand caressed her upper back. There was an inner drawstring, which he tugged sharply, pulling her flush against him. Even through the fabric of her dress and undergarments, she sensed his arousal.

"Pray tell me where we are?" she whispered, afraid her voice might draw someone's curiosity.

"Alone. I would kill any man if he saw you thus," he said, his voice sharpening with his conviction. Maccus widened the gap at the back of her dress and worked on the strings of her corset. Once he had finished, he peeled her sea-green satin and tissue dress down the length of her body along with her corset.

"Do you mean to strip me of all my garments?" Fayre asked, her voice high in alarm when he reached for the tapes on her petticoat.

"Everything, Fayre. Even your modesty," he said, twisting her face toward his and sealing his promise with a hot-blooded kiss.

Maccus knew the muffle was frightening Fayre. Standish's callous treatment had bruised her pride, and despite the night he had enjoyed making love to her in her bed, she was still wary of sharing herself. Maccus was not perturbed if she chose to keep other men at a distance, but he refused to let her deny him!

Fayre reminded him of a delicate butterfly. She fluttered about, enticing him with her grace and beauty until he was crazed, but alighted out of reach if he tried to cage her. He had kissed and stroked her until she was mindless with pleasure. Yet she could look him easily in the eye and talk of him marrying another woman. It was maddening! There was a part of her she denied him, when he craved all of her.

Perhaps this unrelenting lust to possess her was making him insane. The wild scheme he had concocted as a means to win her trust was highly atypical for him. More than once, he had tried to talk himself out of the erotic adventure he wanted to share with Fayre because he was worried about pushing her too quickly. Now that he had her alone and half naked in front of him, he was not about to let a little discomfort on both their sides deter him.

She licked her lips. "If you untie this muffle I could undress you."

He heard the question in her inflection. The idea of her removing his clothes and seeing the passion flare in her green gaze was tempting. His cock throbbed in response. Unbearably so. Maccus shook his head, forgetting momentarily that she could not see him.

"Not this time. I'm trying to show you something."

Fayre grimaced. "I cannot *see* anything with this cloth over my eyes," she grumbled.

"There are other ways of seeing." Her petticoat slithered to the floor. Maccus bent down and seized the hem of her chemise.

"Wait!"

The abrupt command echoed within the marble edifice. Fayre's breathing had quickened. He was certain it was not passion driving her heart to pound, but rather her fears. "Do not fear me. I will not hurt you." Sensing quickness was merciful, Maccus pulled her thin chemise over her head and tossed it on top of his discarded coat and shirt.

Wearing only his breeches, he knelt at her feet. Maccus took off one slipper and then the other. Gently, he untied the garters over her knees and removed her stockings. Standing in the middle of the room, awaiting his instruction Fayre reminded him of one of the marble statues he had seen at one of the museums she had insisted on visiting, depicting a nude Grecian goddess.

Fayre had a body worthy of worship. A man might sacrifice everything to claim such beauty. Still on his knees, Maccus curled his hands possessively around her calves. His fingers glided upward, exploring each sensual curve. Fayre made a faint sound.

"I love touching you," he murmured, and leaned forward to kiss the back of one of her knees. Unable to resist, he flicked his tongue along the crease.

Fayre shifted her stance. "That tickles. Is your intention to torment me?" She sucked in her breath as Maccus trailed kisses up her leg and nipped her left buttock.

"Yes," he said, turning her so that she faced him. Her neat triangle of down beckoned. The sweet womanly musk of her arousal was a honeyed lure. "But you are not alone in this." All his instincts were demanding that he push her onto her back and tear open his breeches. Maccus broke out into sweat, reliving how it felt when he nudged the head of his cock into her willing body. How the muscles of her moist sheath resisted his penetration slightly before giving way, allowing him to bury himself into her over and over.

"Maccus?"

Although he was still idly caressing her buttocks, the hesitancy in her voice made him realize he had been silent for too long. "Not yet," he replied, knowing she was anxious to remove the cloth from her eyes. "What you need is a distraction." Without giving her any hint to his intentions, Maccus slid his hand into the cleft between her legs.

He groaned as if in pain. "Already, your body awaits mine," he said, awed that she wanted him despite her fears. His fingers found the heart of her, and he pushed them deeply into her. Withdrawing his fingers, he used his dampened fingers to moisten and tease her clitoris. The nubbin of aroused flesh swelled beneath his fingers. Fayre arched against his hand, blindly widening her stance.

"I cannot take much more of this, Maccus," she pleaded. She threaded her hands into his hair, attempting to draw him in closer. "I need to feel you inside me."

Maccus's gray eyes darkened in response to her impassioned plea.

Placing a kiss on her stomach, he stood and unfastened his breeches. As he shoved them down, his cock strained in anticipation of the mating they both hungered for. Maccus kicked his leg free from his breeches and stepped around to face her.

"You are exquisite," he said, cupping her left breast. His thumb brushed over her nipple. The rosy flesh darkened and engorged with his caress. Her skin was flawless, its texture like warm silk.

"I cannot keep from trembling," Fayre said, trying to hold still.

Maccus's body thrummed with excitement. Bending his knees, he lowered his head and suckled her breast. His eyes were burning with lust when he stared up at her face. "As do I. This time, Fayre, it is not from fear."

❖ ❖ ❖

For the second time, Maccus picked her up. Her bare flesh rubbed against his hairy chest and Fayre realized he had removed his clothing as well. It was silly, but the insight calmed her. He swung her around and carried her several steps. Dizziness assailed her and she tightened her grip on his shoulders. He lowered her, and her back sank into soft bedding, something he had prepared on the floor.

"I want to see you," Fayre said, entreating him to cease his game. He had a beautiful body, an intriguing landscape of muscle that she wanted to explore.

"Later," he murmured, fondling her breasts.

She should have been mortified to have him touch her breasts so unreservedly or suckle her nipples. Standish had not touched her body in this leisurely manner, while Maccus seemed obsessed with exploring every dip and swell. Fayre supposed the swath of cloth over her eyes distanced her from what was happening. Yet Maccus would not permit her to lie passively on the bedding. His hands and mouth were everywhere, enticing her to share in his carnal adventure. She arched her back slightly when he bit the soft swell of her right breast.

"Do you like my hands on you, Fayre?" With his tongue he traced the curved bones of her ribs and worked his way down to her navel. She sensed his eyes were on her face, waiting for her response.

"Yes," she hissed, and wiggled as he stabbed the indentation with his tongue. Fayre felt the rigid length of his manhood brush against her leg. Maccus was fully aroused, and still he delayed in mounting her. He did not seem to feel the urgency she had assumed all males felt when a willing female was lying beneath them. His unpredictability was increasing the tension stealing into her limbs.

"And my mouth?" He moved lower and nibbled on each hipbone.

Were they having a conversation? She tried to concentrate, but the man was making it amazingly difficult. His teeth scraped the sensitive flesh just above the tuft of curly hair between her legs. Tingles spread like warm water across her abdomen and down her legs.

"W-what do you want?"

Maccus placed his hands on her thighs. His palms were so warm she thought his hands might scorch her. "To taste pleasure," he said, his hands sliding higher until his fingers found and parted her soft, womanly flesh.

Fayre tensed expecting Maccus to slip his fingers into her. She was not prepared for him to put his mouth on her. Her hands curled into fists. Shocked by the intimacy of such a kiss, she struck her fists fruitlessly against his shoulders. Maccus responded by spearing her with his tongue. From behind her eyelids, she saw a shower of falling stars.

"You—you must stop. Surely no man desires—" The strength of her voice faded as her words scattered like drying petals in a spring breeze. Maccus laved and teased the small nubbin hidden within her womanly cleft. "This!" she said, the word bursting out of her as pleasure coiled in her pelvis.

"Every place I stroke you, Fayre, you unfurl for me," Maccus said, pushing his fingers into her, proving her readiness for him. "Your generous response makes me a greedy man. I want to claim all of you."

Abruptly, he withdrew his fingers and surged up her body until his hot breath stirred against her cheek. "I can no longer deny myself," he said, his breathing labored.

The broad head of his manhood pressed insistently against her opening. Her wetness was a tepid, inviting spring and he plunged deeply into her. She gasped as he filled her completely and a guttural moan escaped his lips that Fayre took for relief. What had begun as teasing, gentle love play had given way to impatient fervor. His musky heat rolled off him like waves and their bodies grew slick with perspiration as Maccus rocked himself relentlessly into her.

Lost in the mindless pleasure of her body, he whispered no pretty love words to soothe her as Standish had, nor did she require them. Fayre threaded her fingers through his long, black hair, drawing him closer for a kiss. Maccus clamped his mouth roughly over hers. She could faintly taste her own essence on his lips. There was an unspoken urgency driving him and the finesse she usually attributed to his kisses had abandoned him.

Maccus released her lips and trailed kisses along her jaw. "Do you feel me, Fayre?" he whispered huskily in her ear. He slowed his pace, thrusting and retreating so that she felt the emptiness of his withdrawal. "So deep." He emphasized his words by filling her again. Each exquisite thrust forced her to take him fully and vibrated through her entire body.

"Yes," she said, aching with the need he was building within her that only he could assuage. She felt as if she were losing control of her body. Every inch of her skin was sensitive, yearning for his caress. She raised her hips, meeting each thrust, silently demanding that he give her more of himself. "Maccus, please."

Fayre no longer cared about the cloth covering her eyes. Her other senses had compensated for the loss of her sight. She could smell Maccus's scent on her flesh and the combined essences of their lovemaking. It was a ripe, earthy musk that was more tantalizing than any perfume she had ever worn.

She slid her hands down his back oiled with sweat and curved her hand over the muscled roundness of his buttocks. Fayre loved the feel of his body pressing down on hers. There was something reassuring about his weight. The coarse, black hair on his chest was creating a delicious friction against her nipples. Her breasts felt heavy and swollen. Sensing her unspoken desire, Maccus lowered his head and lavished his attention on each breast.

He made a throaty rumble of appreciation in his throat. She had always enjoyed listening to Maccus. He had a deep, sensual voice that could be lazy with amused indulgence or sharp with controlled fury. When he made love, his voice was huskier. He was very vocal about his pleasures, and he seemed to enjoy everything about her body.

Fayre was beginning to adore everything about him, too.

"That's it," Maccus said, when a faint mewling sound erupted from her lips. "Open yourself to me."

The spiraling tension building within her was coalescing in her stomach. She clutched him tightly, blindly seeking a release to the chaos he had ignited in her. Maccus knew what she was craving and he hammered frantically into her, heightening the wildness in both of them. Fayre dug her nails into his back and arched her spine to its breaking point. As she cried out, a whirlpool of pleasure spun outward, buffeting her body with brilliant, feathery whips of light. The ripples it created seemed to go on forever. Maccus must have sensed them, too. The muscles beneath her fingers jumped and he tensed. Latching on to her right breast and then urgently switching to her left, he fiercely suckled to prolong her pleasure. He buried his manhood deeply into her, and she heard the high-pitched keen of his own surrender. Seconds later, she felt the hot, rhythmic pulse of his seed against her womb.

Resting his cheek on Fayre's soft breast, Maccus opened his eyes and willed his breathing to return to its normal rate. His heartbeat, or perhaps it was hers, was pounding in his ear. Still buried deep within her, Maccus was feeling too relaxed to move.

"Do you intend to keep my eyes covered the entire evening?" Fayre asked lazily, no longer fearful of the vulnerability he had induced by blindfolding her.

"Nay, love, I believe we can do away with it." He hooked his thumbs underneath the cloth and peeled it over her head.

Fayre blinked and squinted as her eyes adjusted to the light. Maccus knew the second she recognized where he had taken her. She would have sat up if his weight were not still pinning her in place.

"You brought me here," she said in disbelief. "We made love in Lord Dening's exotic temple?"

Nestled in her warm sheath, his cock had not lost its rigidity despite his extraordinary release. Seeing the humor of the situation, Maccus said, "Somehow it seems appropriate."

Rising on his elbows, he realized he loathed pulling out from her, as if the action would break the enchantment of the evening. He did not want their time together to end. What he had shared with her had meant something to him.

There had been other women before Fayre. All of them had been casual flirtations, where once his physical needs had been satisfied, he had withdrawn, and his attention returned to the goals he had set for his future. He had never wanted to linger after the passion had burned itself out, nor had he ever yearned to start anew so soon.

"I cannot believe you brought me here," Fayre huffed, and then a look of horror doused her contentment. "Pray tell me that no one knows."

"Only our guard—"

"What?" she shrieked so loudly that he winced.

"Hush, love," he entreated, holding her in place when she tried to wiggle away from under him. "I did not want to bed you and have you think I was Standish all over again. I noticed immediately that no one could see the temple from the house because of the thick copse of trees. Dening had not lit the garden torches so I was not worried about the guests, but there was still the risk of being caught by one of the servants. While you were visiting with Lady Dening I found an ally and paid the servant well for his discretion."

"Bribing the servants again," she said through clenched teeth.

Tipping was highly effective, so he was not about to give it up just because Fayre did not approve. "While we were eating supper, the man brought in the bedding and lit the lanterns in anticipation of our arrival." Maccus did not add that they were not the first couple to use the Denings' exotic temple for their romantic liaison.

Fayre still looked uncomfortable. "Is your man close?" she asked, her voice an anxious whisper.

Maccus laughed and the marble walls echoed his mirth. "The servant watches the house, Fayre, not us. We are safe from prying eyes, trust me."

Some of the fear in her expression eased. "Strangely, I do."

Her hesitant confession touched him deeply. He understood better than anyone how difficult it had been for her to allow him to make love to her in a setting that reminded her of Standish's calculated deflowering.

Fayre's eyes widened as his cock twitched within her. "I thought you had—" She was too shy to complete her thought.

His face creased with his mischievous grin. Christ, she made him feel good. "I did. It appears I can again."

"Truly?"

Maccus surged and retreated, proving he was capable. "With you." He kissed a red mark he had put on her breast with his teeth. "The wanting never ends, Fayre."

She glanced away.

Maccus fought down his resentment. He wondered if Standish had said something similar to her before he cruelly broke her heart. Not wanting to dwell on the bastard or her love for him, Maccus surprised her by rolling them both so that she was the one on top.

He flexed his arousal within her, demonstrating the pleasurable course. Pinching her left nipple playfully, Maccus was already looking forward to this delectable view. "You know what to do. Ride, my lady."

"Will you tell me about it?" Fayre asked sleepily in his arms an hour later.

After their vigorous lovemaking, she had snuggled her back against his chest and together they had dozed. They could not remain there all night, but Maccus was feeling too sated to disturb the quiet contentment they shared.

"Tell you what, you insatiable witch?" Maccus nipped her shoulder teasingly. "I have praised you from your head to your toes and the wonderful places between. I doubt I left out any adjective on how much I adore your body."

She wiggled her backside against him to torment him. He growled and his hand curved around her breast possessively. It should have been impossible for his cock to stir, desiring her so soon, but Lady Fayre Carlisle was a bewitching enchantress.

"Not about *that*," she said, turning her face so she could glance back at him. "I meant about the scars on your chest. I noticed that you have some on your back, too."

He had had other lovers who had been curious about the marks on his body. Maccus usually brushed their questions aside and then distracted them by giving them something more interesting to concentrate on. His first instinct was to do the same for Fayre. At his hesitation, she rolled toward him. She rested her cheek on his arm and gazed somberly at him.

"I told you that I had a rough past," he said gruffly, needing to warn her again.

She brushed the loose hair from his cheek. "I had already guessed as much. The scars on your chest and back only confirm it."

"I can't tell you much about my mother. Seamus never spoke of her," he began, sifting through his memories and trying to decide how much to tell her.

"Seamus?" she prompted.

"Seamus Brawley, my father. He was a sailor then. Considering the type of women he usually consorted with when I was a child, I assumed my mother was just another whore he had visited and had gotten with child."

"But he raised you," she said insistently.

"Aye. Seamus said that he gave up the sea for me. Oh, I don't know, it could have been true, though he was a selfish man, prone to drink, and with the drinking came violence."

The tender expression in her gaze sharpened in horror. "He beat you?"

"When the drink was ruling his brain, and that was more often than not, Seamus did not know how to touch anyone with anything but his fists unless it was a strap of leather."

Fayre pressed her fingers to each faded scar within her reach. She closed her eyes as a disturbing thought occurred to her. "The marks on your back. He did those, too?"

Maccus softly chuckled, easing her back down when she would have sat up. "Calm down, love. It happened long ago."

"He flogged his own son?" she said, her voice rising in anger at a man she had never met. "How old?"

"Fayre," he said, humbled by her concern. "I've had so many beatings I could not tell you which one left the scars you see." Her eyes welled up with tears. "Aw, don't cry for me. You are making my heart ache. Look, it doesn't matter anymore."

"He had no right to hit you," she said fiercely.

Fayre was such a sheltered innocent. Maccus doubted he had fared worse than any of the other boys who lived in the decaying borough. "I hated him for it but never thought he didn't have the right to lay his hands on me. Later, when he married Sarah McAdams and she bore Trevor, my father seemed to settle down into his life. Sadly, it didn't last. Seamus went back to smuggling, for the money was good, but with it came the drinking and whoring. Sarah died when I was seventeen, a shell of the sweet, loving woman she had been. My father managed to ruin her, just like everything else he touched," Maccus said with a trace of bitterness.

Fayre nuzzled her face into his arm. "You loved her."

"Aye. I suppose I did," he said, realizing he had never dwelled on his feelings for her. "For a time, she was the closest I ever had to a mother."

She traced the jagged edge of the scar made by the bullet. Maccus tensed under her gentle caresses, sensing the question she had held back. "You are wondering about how I got shot."

"I realize it must be painful to think about it. If you prefer not discussing it, I would understand," she assured him hastily.

Maccus covered her fingers caressing his scar with his hand. "The day in the park when you called me Mac Brawley, the smuggler, I assume Trevor told you bits and pieces of my past."

Fayre sighed. Since he had never mentioned her taunt after their encounter with Lady Hipgrave and Lord Standish, she had believed he had forgotten the incident. "Some."

He was certain his anger at seeing her and Trevor together encouraged her silence. "You must have chewed a hole in your tongue to keep from asking the dozens of questions that must have been whirling around in that inquisitive brain of yours."

She calmly studied his face, trying to understand the unexpected humor she saw there. "Hundreds. Though better my tongue than you deciding what portion of my anatomy to take a bite out of. Maccus, you have made it clear from the beginning that any questions about your past were unwelcome."

He had demanded her trust. It was a matter of fairness that he give her the same courtesy. "I mentioned that my father was a smuggler. A son tends to be pulled along into his father's business. I was six when I joined my father on my first run."

"You were a smuggler at such a young age?" She looked incredulously at him.

He shrugged. "A decent one, too, as I grew older. I turned out to have a natural talent for it and moved up quickly in the ranks." He thought about Seamus's jealous tantrums and his accusations that Maccus was using his influence to keep his father down. "After making a sizable profit, I decided the money wasn't worth my neck and retired when I was seventeen."

Something in his inflection must have tipped her off that there was more to the tale. "No. It was more than that. That was when you were shot, was it not? Someone shot you because you were a smuggler."

It was more complicated than that. He suspected she would not like the truth so he hedged, giving her pieces of what had happened on Carew Strand. "The crew I was leading was ambushed. My memory is foggy in parts, but I recall feeling the concussions of several explosions and fiery debris floating all around me in the water. Bodies were everywhere, lying broken and bleeding. I was muddled from the explosion so I did not immediately notice there were riders on the beach checking for survivors. Anyone who was not able to run from them perished by pistol or by the thrust of a sword."

Her green eyes reflected the light of the flickering candles around them and the horror she felt from his sketchy description of the events that night. "These men just shot you and left you for dead?"

Maccus stroked the curve of her hip, soothing her. "I was lucky they thought I was dead. I doubt I could have survived a sword in my gut. As it was, the blood loss and ensuing infection almost finished me off."

"Were they ever punished, these men who attacked you?"

He threaded his hand through his hair in annoyance. It was prickly business sorting through the truth and various versions of the tale to satisfy her curiosity. "Three men were arrested months later. Fifty men had died on that beach and justice was done. They hanged for their crimes." Maccus abruptly sat up. Heedless of his nudity, he reached for her chemise. "We should get back to the house. Although we've been careful, someone might notice our absence if we linger here further."

Fayre accepted her chemise from him and sat up. "I did not intend to upset you, Maccus."

"I'm not upset, my jewel," he said, gathering up their scattered clothes. "I just rarely dwell on it. For a time I was plagued with nightmares." Fayre made a small sympathetic noise. "It was my guilt over what had happened, my chance to rewrite history and save the men who had perished. Punish the men who had ruthlessly murdered men for their own ambition."

Bewildered, she placed her hand on his arm. "But you said that the men were arrested and hanged for their crimes."

Cursing his slight slip, Maccus cupped her face with

his palm. "I did, didn't I?" He fastened his mouth over hers, savoring the taste of her. Drawing back, he said, "This is one of the reasons why I avoid talking about Carew Strand. It pulls me into a brooding mood about things I cannot change."

"You are a good man, Maccus Brawley," she said, her eyes glistening in the candlelight like bottomless green pools. He had allowed her close enough to see the scars on his body and the shadows in his eyes. Instead of being revolted, she wanted to heal him.

A shallow dimple appeared as his lips curled up into a grin. He tried to ease the somberness in her eyes by teasing her. "Ah, pretty Fayre, if this is your impish way to flatter me into lying down with you on the bedding, I must resist."

His aroused body contradicted his words. Maccus did not attempt to conceal his interest. He liked the way she devoured him with her hungry eyes.

Catching on, Fayre let her chemise slip to the floor. Sauntering over to him, she slowly lowered her gaze to his straining cock. "So you are resisting?" Her lashes fluttered up at him and he flinched under the potency of her gaze.

"For your sake," he said, shuddering as she slid her body painstakingly down his until she was on her knees.

"Then I should return the favor." Fayre brushed the underside of his cock with her moist tongue.

Maccus's eyes crossed in pleasure as her sweet, untutored mouth engulfed the swollen head of his cock and surged to take more of him. He had never imagined Fayre wanting to love him thusly. The act had seemed too daring for a gently reared lady, but now that she had her mouth on him, he thought he might die if she stopped.

"An hour," he gasped. Any practical thought of returning to the main house before they were discovered missing faded with her delicate ministrations. Her nimble tongue was stealing his strength. "Just an hour, or two." Maccus let Fayre have her way just this once.

15

Maccus stealthily entered the bedchamber his host had assigned to him, though for most of the night it had gone unappreciated. After their lovemaking, it had been difficult to resist the urge to tuck Fayre into her bed himself, but they had tarried at the temple too long. At the edge of the garden, they had tenderly kissed one last time and then gone their separate ways. He had heard muffled laughter somewhere deep in the house, so some of the guests were still enjoying Lord Dening's brandy and embellished tales. Still, no one had seen him reenter the house nor did he encounter anyone on the journey back to his bedchamber. Maccus could hope Fayre had been as fortunate.

He untied his cravat. Exposing the collar of his shirt, he realized he had forgotten in his haste to fasten the buttons. Tying the frustrating knot had been a complete waste of time, but it had seemed sensible to be fully dressed if by chance someone had glimpsed him. Maccus lifted one of the limp ends of the cravat, dismayed. It was hopelessly wrinkled from his careless handling. Unwinding it from his neck, he tossed it on a chair.

A knock at the door stilled his hands. With a narrowing gaze, he approached the door. The hour was too late for visitors. He could not fathom who could be visiting except for Fayre. If she had defied him by ignoring his order to return to her room, Maccus was planning on definitely spanking her backside. Being with her was making him act outlandishly. Since he could not claim her publicly, the creative maneuverings he had employed so they could have intimate time alone together were beyond reckless. He was becoming obsessed with her, and she was not helping matters by inciting him whenever she was within his proximity.

Maccus opened the door, preparing to lecture the mischievous girl. The lady waiting for him on the other side was a surprise, and not a pleasurable one. "Lady Hipgrave. Are you lost?"

"No, Mr. Brawley." She was still attired in the evening dress he had noticed her wearing at supper. Her blue-eyed gaze slid slyly away from his puzzled expression to the empty, immaculate bed. "I was about to ask you the same question. Might I come in? The corridor is chilly."

He blocked her attempt to enter by bracing his arm

against the doorframe. "I hate to be discourteous, my lady. However, the hour is late and you are most definitely married."

The countess's effervescent laughter had him itching to check the outer corridor for witnesses. "My beautiful man, how amazingly provincial of you. I realize you have not been long in our society, but I can assure you that Lord Hipgrave does not care what I do or whom I do it with as long as I am discreet."

She spoke as if instructing him, but her smile betrayed the insult. Maccus kept his face expressionless. The countess possessed a striking beauty. Everything about her, from her walk, the dresses she wore, and the manner in which she spoke, was designed for one goal. Seduction. From what he had learned about her, she wielded it like a weapon.

Like a fly wiggling on the beautiful, intricate strings of a spider's web, the man in this lady's clutches was doomed and he did not even know it.

Maccus saw the countess clearly and knew exactly what she was capable of. "Your husband is a generous man. Regretfully, I am not, so I will bid you good night."

"Why the haste, Mr. Brawley? Does being alone with me seem daunting or just too tempting?" She moved close so he could feel the heat of her body.

After spending the night loving Fayre, Maccus thought that having another woman so near felt like a betrayal. Feigning amusement, he said, "You have been playing with boys for too long, Countess. I have all the right instincts. I've just learned to control them."

She glanced up at him, wide-eyed and appealing. "I look forward to the moment when we can judge your impressive instincts. Regrettably, my only desire is to talk to you."

"In the morning, perhaps," he said, dismissing her.

"Not even if our discussion revolves around Lady Fayre Carlisle?" Her smile was triumphant when he let his arm drop to his side. "I do so adore a reasonable man."

Fayre was relieved to return to London. After giving orders to her maid, Amelie, regarding her belongings, she greeted the butler. "How are you, Curdey? Is that leg of yours giving you any trouble?" A touch of rheumatism was settling into the servant's right leg. She had noticed before their departure that he had been favoring the leg.

"You are kind to ask, my lady. Cook brewed me one of her special elixirs and it has eased the discomfort somewhat," Curdey replied.

She pursed her lips, wondering how much whiskey had gone into the making of this miracle elixir. "The duchess will be in shortly after she bids farewell to Lord Temmes." Actually, when she disembarked from the carriage, her mother and Tem were arguing. "Has my father returned?"

"Yes, my lady," the butler said, surprising her. Whether it had been intentional on some level, she had not spent much time in her father's company since he had learned of her debacle with Lord Standish. "His Grace has been in the library for most of the afternoon."

"Thank you, Curdey. You might want to check on my mother." Perhaps he could rescue Tem from the duchess's quarrelsome farewell.

Fayre crossed the hall, not really certain of the reason for the conflict between Tem and their mother. She had been too busy puzzling out Maccus's silence. Encountering him in the morning room the next morning, she had expected to see a glimpse of the man with whom she had spent hours the previous night writhing on the makeshift bedding in untamed and ravenous passion. Instead Maccus had been preoccupied and for some reason he avoided her curious gaze. His politeness was painful when she thought of all the things he had done to her body.

They had only remained at the Denings' for a day and a half. If Lord Jerrett had been present, the duchess would have insisted that they remain for at the very minimum four days so she could have had a proper visit after the majority of the guests had departed.

She knocked on the library door. At her father's booming command to enter, she opened the door. "Do I not know you, sir? You seem strangely familiar," Fayre teased from the threshold.

"My lovely Fayre," he said, rising and opening his arms out for her embrace. She ran straight into his arms. The duke chuckled, amused by her fierce hug. "When did you return?"

"Just moments ago," she admitted, pulling back so he could sit down at his desk. Fayre selected one of the nearby chairs.

"Hmm. And your mother?" he asked, scowling as he shuffled through the papers he had been reading when she had entered.

"Sitting in the carriage. She and Tem, uh, had a difference of opinion on some trifle," she said, choosing to be diplomatic about the altercation.

The duke was not fooled by her choice of words. Raising his brows at her, he said, "Fighting like two half-starved mongrels over a piece of meat, are they?"

Fayre covered her mouth with her hands and laughed. "Papa, what do you think Mama would say if she heard you comparing her to a half-starved mongrel?"

Her father winked at her. "Why don't we keep that comparison to ourselves, shall we?" Satisfied with the organization of his paperwork, he set it aside. "Did you enjoy your visit with the Lord and Lady Dening? I had anticipated your staying longer."

She stretched out her legs and pointed her toes to ease the ache in her legs from hours of inactivity in the carriage. "Who could not? The Denings' *fête* was marvelous as usual. We only left early because Mama had invited a guest to join us in our carriage. I assumed she did not want to impose on Mr. Brawley by staying longer."

Her father did not overtly react to her announcement that a gentleman had traveled with them. "Who is this Mr. Brawley?" he asked, expressing only mild curiosity.

"A friend of Lord Yemant's. I was introduced— Oh, never mind," she said, not wanting her explanation to end with the mention of the shopping excursion with Lord Crescett. "Suffice to say, Mama took a liking to him when she learned Mr. Brawley was seeking a bride among the eligible ladies of the *ton*. You know how Mama can be when she has been given a worthwhile task. I doubt a single unmarried lady visiting the Denings escaped her regard."

The duke chuckled, knowing firsthand how persistent his wife could be. "I'll warrant the duchess will have Mr. Brawley betrothed by the end of the season."

Fayre smiled, too, but her merriment was superficial. "I predicted autumn." When Maccus chose his perfect lady, their friendship would end. Even if he were interested in continuing the physical aspects of their relationship after he married, she would reject his generous offer. Fayre never intended to be a married gentleman's mistress.

"Well, I am pleased you agreed to go to the *fête* with

your mother. After this Standish business, I wondered if you planned to hide in the house all season."

"I have gone out, Papa," she said, resenting his insinuation that she had been cowering in her bedchamber. "You just have not been interested in attending the functions that I have. It is enough to make me wonder if you are avoiding being seen with me!"

Fayre knew she was being spiteful and unfair. Her father was not acting any differently than he had done any other season. This season it was the widow Lady Talemon who distracted her father. The year before that it was Lady Hipgrave and so it went, on and on, countless beautiful faces her father turned to for affection and comfort while he forgot he had a family for a while.

Her mother had turned to Lord Crescett this season. There had been other men. Fayre closed her eyes, disgusted at herself for the rising anger at her parents. They were not the ones acting out of character. She was the one who had changed. Her little world had been shaken up because she had taken the chance on the wrong man to love.

She was not sure if she should curse her fate or be grateful. The mistake had brought Maccus into her life, but he had his own dreams. The glimpses he had given her of his life before he had arrived in London were horrifying. She would not act like spiteful Lady Hipgrave, who could not forgive her lover for choosing another. Fayre would not stand in Maccus's way. She reflected again on his silence. Perhaps the end was closer than she had imagined for them and he did not know how to tell her.

The duke's brows came together, forming a V. "What is this nonsense about, my girl?"

He pivoted his chair away from his desk and invited

her to come closer. Fayre jumped out of her chair and went around the desk to her waiting father. She climbed onto his lap as she had when she was a small child and laid her cheek on his shoulder.

The duke wrapped his arms around her. "Is this about Standish? Did someone say something hurtful?"

"Papa, sometimes it is so awful. Lord Standish and Lady Hipgrave seem to be everywhere I go." Her sinuses burned with suppressed tears. "I cannot seem to escape my foolishness."

The hand stroking her head paused in mid-action. "Othilia has taken up with Standish?" her father said, amazed by the news.

Fayre grimaced. Apparently, the duke was so smitten with his current mistress that he had not been keeping up with the latest gossip. Fayre stifled a sigh. She would have preferred that he remained unaware of his former mistress's connection to Standish. Regrettably, there were too many people in town who could provide him the information if he bothered to make the inquiries. Perhaps it was best if she were the one who told him.

"Lord Hipgrave is not in London. Lord Standish has been providing her escort," she said lamely. He was also providing other services she had no desire to contemplate.

"Hipgrave abhors town life," the duke said, dismissing her inadequate excuse for explaining Standish's presence. "Othilia could not have married a man more opposite in disposition. I cannot believe their match is a happy one."

Her father did not sound jealous of the lady's husband or new companion. The countess had underestimated her influence on the duke. "I do not believe Lady Hipgrave has ever experienced that particular feeling. I have found her a very unpleasant woman," she said carefully.

His chest lifted as he sighed. "I agree, my girl. Has that bastard Standish been goading her to be cruel to you?"

It is the countess who is goading Lord Standish, she thought. "Not precisely," she hedged. *Are you planning to tell me about your past with Lady Hipgrave, Papa? She despises you so much that she plotted your daughter's ruination to hurt you.*

Her parents did not openly discuss their infidelities, so it came as no surprise that the duke did not offer any explanation of why the countess had private reasons for hating his daughter.

"Othilia is a difficult, troubled woman," her father said, not revealing any insight into the lady's amoral character that Fayre might use to her advantage. "If she says anything to you that is untoward, I want you to tell me immediately."

"I will, Papa," she quietly lied, unable to unburden herself with the secret she had kept since the night she had followed Lord Standish down to the Mewes' gallery.

He patted her affectionately on the shoulder. "I wish I could do something about that scoundrel Standish. I had words with Pennefeather regarding his son—"

Fayre sat up straight and gazed at her father with a stricken expression. "You spoke to the marquess? Papa, how could you? I told you that I would not have Lord Standish as husband even if you stripped him bare, tied him up with a golden bow, and stuck a diamond the size of your fist in his mouth!" Once she would not have married him because of pride, now she simply did not want him.

"Calm down," the duke said, snickering at the image her humorous words conjured. "I realized months ago that you would not have him. Nor is he worthy of you. I just could not stand silent because you wanted to pretend away his cruelty. Pennefeather has been displeased with his second son for some time now. He plans to cut Standish's purse strings in hopes of curtailing his son's wild behavior."

Her father glanced at her expectantly, hoping she was pleased with Standish's punishment. Fayre was not. "Papa, Lord Pennefeather has been vowing to cut his son's purse strings for years. As far as I can tell, the marquess has never carried out his threat."

It was a pity, really. Standish would have been quite miserable if he had been forced to spend his evenings contemplating his financial woes instead of frittering his nights away gambling and seducing young innocents.

The duke reluctantly nodded in agreement. "I expect Pennefeather still has hopes of you and Standish making a match. Nothing would silence the gossips quicker than marriage—"

She pressed her cheek to her father's weathered one. "No. I could never marry him. Not even to silence the gossips."

"Stubborn chit. You will not let me challenge the bastard, and you will not consider marrying him. What else can a father do, I ask?"

"Nothing." Standish would pay for his betrayal. She would see to it with or without Maccus's assistance. Fayre hugged her father tightly. "I love you, Papa."

He patted her awkwardly. "I love you, my lovely Fayre. Do not worry. We will think of something else if Pennefeather does not carry out his promise to cut Standish's funds."

There was no doubt in Fayre's mind that Standish would suffer for his sins, one way or another.

M accus's viewpoint was analogous to the Duke of Solitea's as he observed Standish at the gaming tables. His brother, Trevor, had joined him at Moirai's Lust, and they had discreetly watched the man lose heavily for the past three hours.

His thoughts kept drifting back to Fayre. They had parted awkwardly and he was to blame. He had sensed her gaze settling on him countless times during their drive back to town. He heard her unspoken plea, *What have I done?* The note he planned for Hobbs to deliver would only add to her confusion. Maccus tightened his fist, which was braced against the underside of his chin. He had never meant to hurt her, but everything had happened so quickly. Maccus knew he had to seize his chance.

"What are we doing here, Mac?" Trevor demanded. He imbibed the fresh beer the barmaid had placed in front of him. Maccus was pretending to sip from his first. "It seems like a fine establishment for a man to relax with his cronies, but there is no sign of Seamus here. Shouldn't we move on?"

Xavier had told Maccus earlier that he had made a small fortune off Standish's stupidity. His friend was almost feeling guilty for taking the man's money, or was until Maccus had explained why this particular man could not enjoy his spoils. The losses had not slowed Standish down. Instead of quitting, he had increased his wagers and his recklessness.

Maccus spared his bored brother an impatient glance. "Seamus is not my only quarry." He had waited patiently for this night, and according to Xavier, it was time to make his move.

Trevor turned his head, his gaze scanning the table of gentlemen Maccus was watching so attentively. "Which one?"

"Green waistcoat," he murmured. "I can smell his desperation from here. Can you?"

When Maccus had returned to his town house after the Denings' *fête,* Trevor had been waiting for him. His brother reminded him of a stray cat who disappeared for days at a time, only to return when he had gotten hungry.

"Yeah, I suppose," Trevor replied, lacking conviction. "Why are you hunting this man? What did he do to you?"

Maccus picked up his beer and sipped it. He had not revealed anything about his bargain with Fayre or why she needed his help. It was a shame, but he could not bring himself to trust Trevor with Fayre's secrets.

"Nothing."

His brother gaped incredulously at him. "Nothing? The man has done nothing and you are doing what? Intimidating him with your glare?"

He silenced his brother with the highly effective stare he had just mocked. "I did not say he had done nothing; just that he had done nothing to me." There was a difference.

Trevor snorted. "What do you plan to do?"

Maccus set down his beer. His eyes gleamed with anticipation. "Ruin him." The woman he had been waiting for glanced in their direction. He motioned for her to approach.

The alluring brunette took her time wending her way to their table. Neither man protested because whether she was coming or going, the view was worth watching.

"Good evening, handsome," she purred in a voice that reminded Maccus of smoke. "Moirai's Lust always appreciates your patronage."

Maccus gave her a lazy grin. "You must bedevil Xavier."

While Trevor ogled the woman's breasts, she leaned down and whispered in Maccus's ear, "Every chance I get." She straightened and smiled at Trevor. "Who is this?"

"Forget it. You would eat him alive," Maccus said, goading his brother to slam his hand on the table.

"Now Mac, if the lady wants to eat me alive that's my business," Trevor argued.

"No. You don't want the trouble Xavier will deliver," Maccus countered, focusing his attention back on the woman. "I need a favor."

"Anything," she purred, making every man within hearing distance envious.

"Not that kind of favor. I need an introduction to the man over there," Maccus said, nodding to Lord Standish.

Nine days later, Fayre approached Maccus's house with trepidation. Something had happened at the Denings' *fête*. Something after their lovemaking in the temple. Maccus had delivered two notes the day after they had returned to London. The first was addressed to the duchess, thanking her for inviting him to the Denings' *fête*. The second was addressed to her. Fayre had slipped into her bedchamber to read the note in private. She had expected an apology for his odd mood that morning or love words praising her beauty. With anticipation pounding in her breast, she had opened his note. In his distinctive script he had thanked her for her kindness, but released her of her obligation of visiting him at his house. He had explained that his business prospects had been neglected so all his afternoons were committed.

All?

Maccus was lying.

He had thanked her for her kindness. *Kindness*. What had she done to deserve such an uninspiring compliment? She preferred his temper to this polite indifference. His actions reminded her too much of Standish.

In a pique over his note, she had neither responded nor tried to visit him. Fayre assumed her silence would force him to seek her out. Maccus never knocked on their door.

Two days later, Fayre had overheard her mother telling the duke about meeting Maccus at the theater. She had first spotted him in Miss Greffis's box, and he had remained by the lady's side for more than thirty minutes. The duchess had been heartened by the news. Fayre had been devastated.

The following afternoon, she had attended the Spraggs' card party. She had forced herself to go because she refused to sulk over another undeserving gentleman. Her heart leaped to her throat when Maccus joined the gathering. Noticing her regard, he inclined his head slightly. Fayre had turned away, confused. She could no longer tell if he was being polite or mocking her. To her relief, he had never approached her. Discreetly, she observed him chatting with Miss Knight and several of the lady's friends.

On the fifth day, her mother inadvertently provoked her to take action by telling Fayre an amusing tale over breakfast about her previous night that involved Maccus, Lady Glasse, and the marchioness's terrier. The man had gone too far. Fayre had slapped down her napkin and stalked out of the room. Two hours later, she presented herself at Maccus's door. His manservant had greeted her warmly, but told her that Mr. Brawley was not there. She had returned to her house deflated. Maccus had abandoned her and she could not fathom why.

It had taken her four days to work up the courage to try again. Fayre had not bothered with protocol by sending her footman to the door. Hobbs opened the door immediately. Perhaps he had been watching her from one of the windows.

"Why, Lady Fayre Carlisle, aren't you looking pretty this afternoon," the manservant greeted her.

"Good day to you, Hobbs. Is Maccus at home?" she asked, already wishing she had ordered the coachman to drive on without stopping.

The older man's face fell at her question. He gave the interior of the house a swift glance before looking at her. Her smile faded at his grim expression. "The master is not at home. He has been spending a lot of his time out these days."

Fayre wet her lips to ease the sudden dryness. "I know. Well, thank you, Hobbs. You have been a gentleman." She turned to walk away.

"I know Brawley will be upset he missed you," Hobbs said, trying to cheer her up.

"No, Hobbs, he will not." She tried to smile at the manservant. "Tell Mac—no, tell Mr. Brawley I will not intrude upon his privacy again."

Hobbs stood stiffly in the doorway, watching Lady Fayre's carriage drive off. "Did you hear what she said?" His angry tone was disrespectful and the manservant did not care.

Maccus stepped out of the shadowed interior into the light entering through the open doorway. His gray eyes were bleak. "Aye, I heard."

16

Fayre despised Maccus Brawley.

The same question circled within her head. How could a man show her such overwhelming tenderness, have passed the night with her, worshiping her body so thoroughly with his own, and then, akin to slamming a door, the next day and the ones thereafter, act as if they were strangers? There was a hideous answer to her question that she had not been willing to face until tonight.

Maccus had used her. He had treated her like a whore and she had been so dazzled by him that she had reveled in it. She brought her hand up to her mouth, feeling sick.

His rejection was so much worse than Lord Standish's, she thought as she paced her bedchamber. By God, why had she fallen in love with him!

If she ever spoke to him again, she could not trust herself to be civil. A soft knock at her door brought her head up. Vivid streaks of tears marred her face. Her parents were out enjoying their evening apart from each other. It was most likely Amelie. She had shooed the maid out of the room before Amelie had finished preparing Fayre for bed.

"You may retire, Amelie," she croaked, choking on her grief. "I finished taking down my hair and have brushed it." Fayre picked up her brush as proof that she was not lying.

Ignoring Fayre's order, the maid opened the door. Alas, she had been mistaken. It was not Amelie, but Maccus Brawley standing in the door.

His presence in her bedchamber callously ripped her already battered heart into pieces. "Bribing the servants again, Mr. Brawley? At this rate, my father will have to sack the entire household." Remembering the tears on her cheeks, she used her fingers to briskly scrub them off.

Maccus did not gloat. His hands parted in a surrendering gesture. "I thought you might be vexed. I tried, but I could not stay away."

It did not matter that he had touched and kissed every inch of her body. He was not going to witness her tears. "Get out!"

When he did not move, she threw the hairbrush at his head. In her fury, her aim was off and it struck him in the shoulder. Maccus did not bother trying to evade the blow.

"The days we have been apart have been endless," he confessed, the hint of shadow around his eyes indicating that his nights had been as restless as hers. He walked into her bedchamber. "I often dream of our last night together in the temple." He closed the door.

"Liar!" she screamed at him. Covering her mouth, she doubled over in agony.

Maccus rushed to her side at her obvious distress. The moment he touched her, she straightened and attacked. Her hand cracked him hard across his face. She never got another opportunity to land a blow. Roughly, he grabbed both her wrists to prevent Fayre from hitting him again. The fury that had been raging in her fed her strength. She twisted and kicked, fighting him for her release.

"Damn you, enough!" he bellowed at her.

Maccus forcibly dragged her across the room to her bed. She fought him in earnest. For a few desperate seconds, she feared he planned on taking her against her will. They landed on the bed. Fayre squirmed from underneath him, but his weight effectively had pinned her body.

"Settle down," he snarled in her face. "I don't want to hurt you."

Her face was inches from his. "Too late. You already have!" she yelled back, straining against him. "And I hate you for it."

Maccus's harsh features went white at her words. "Fayre, you don't mean it."

She was pleased her admission had hurt him. "I do, you heartless, conniving scoundrel. Get off me! If you are looking for an eager, warm body you will have to look elsewhere. No longer will I be your whore!"

Shock flared in his gray eyes, and then fierce denial. Seeming to shake off his stunned expression, Maccus surprised her by releasing her arms. He climbed off her and backed away, giving her the space she had demanded.

Staring blindly out her window, he said, "You are not a whore. I never thought of you as one when—when we were together." His voice wavered, hinting at the sincerity of his confession.

Fayre sat up, refusing to comfort him. He had caused the strife between them. "You used me, Maccus. When you tired of me, you tossed me aside. You even had Hobbs to lie and tell me that you were not home." His expression betrayed him, confirming her suspicions. "Perhaps we have different definitions for what a whore is."

Maccus made a horizontal cutting motion with his right hand. "Damn it, stop calling yourself a whore!" He inhaled, striving to control his temper. "You will probably not believe me, but I care about you. What we shared means something to me."

Fayre slumped in defeat. "You are correct." She hopped off her bed and walked over to retrieve the hair-brush she had thrown at him. "I do not believe you." She caught a glimpse of herself in the mirror and winced. The tears had ravaged her face and Maccus's rough handling had tangled her long hair. She looked dreadful. Unable to stand it, she returned to the bed, sat down and began brushing her hair.

"You don't have to speak. I just want you to listen," he ordered. Taking her silence as consent, he continued. "I know this is my fault. I've bungled things. Badly. I've known since the afternoon I glimpsed your face at the Spraggs' card party. You looked so hurt, but I had already started on this path. There is no going back."

He paced back and forth in front of the window. "No." Maccus shook his head at the inner dialogue he must have been having with himself. "*We* started this. Fayre, we agreed to pretend that we barely knew each other. We were already acting in that manner at the Denings'. That a time would come when it was important that Standish and the countess believed there was no serious connection between us."

Fayre had to concede that everything he had said was true. She worked the brush through her hair. "Well, since you have been seen in the company of every young unmarried lady in the *ton,* even I am convinced that *I* do not know you."

Maccus muttered a few creative curses that had Fayre lifting her brows. He closed his eyes and pressed his fingers to his eyelids. "If you are upset about ladies, blame the duchess. The lady is determined to marry me off thanks to you."

"What did I do?" she whined.

He jabbed a pointed finger in her direction. "You were the ninny that told her I was seeking a bride."

"You are," she argued.

His eyes blazed in amazement that she would be so provoking. "Not this bloody minute!"

Maccus crouched down on his haunches and stared at her. "Look, I know I hurt you by staying away. I thought a clean cut would be kinder. Fayre, I was wrong. I am bleeding inside. You are in my thoughts each day. Every time I see you in public, the pain in your eyes bludgeons me. Perhaps it was cowardly of me not to discuss in advance with you my decision to distance myself from you. In my defense all I can say is that I am a man, not accustomed to explaining myself. Nor am I comfortable confiding in you now."

"If this is an apology, Maccus, it is a wretched one." Fayre brought her chin up defiantly when he straightened suddenly.

"Your face is so expressive, my jewel. Whether you love or hate, everyone who observes you knows your true feelings," he explained, frustrated that he could not breach her anger. "For my ruse, it seemed better that you hated me."

Ruse? Was he referring to their bargain? His explanation only confused her more. Still fighting him, she said, "Congratulations, you succeeded brilliantly."

"I might have, but I cannot stand it. Fayre, I love you," he said, bracing for her rejection.

How could he say those precious words to her now? "Damn you, sir. You never play fairly!" She placed the hairbrush on the bed.

Encouraged that she had not hurled the brush at his head again, Maccus moved closer. "I once told you that I was a ruthless bastard. I didn't lie to you then, and I'm not lying to you when I tell you that I love you."

"Stop saying those words," Fayre begged, her resolve weakening. She loved him so much that she wanted to believe he was telling her the truth. "You are so skilled at deception. I am so confused, Maccus. How do I know this, too, is not a lie?"

"You have to trust me." His gray eyes pierced hers, demanding that she believe in him.

Fayre touched her brow. She had a headache. If it had been his plan to twist all her emotions into a confusing muddle, it had worked. "I have to think about what you have told me."

Maccus was unmistakably disappointed that he had not acquired her trust. She had no sympathy for him. He deserved to suffer the uncertainty along with her. "You said that my feelings are transparent. Are you not risking your plan by revealing the truth to me?"

"Aye." His face softened and he reached out to caress her cheek. Fayre backed away, not ready to forgive him for everything yet. "All right. I deserved that. I won't touch you." He nodded, trying to accept that he had a far journey back into her good graces. "It's best that I don't reveal all the details at this point. As it is, I'm risking much telling you what I have, but I can't stand the discord between us."

Exasperated, she crossed her eyes at him. "You have not told me anything."

Maccus walked to the door and opened it. Faint dimples appeared on his cheeks as he grinned. "Aye, I have. I revealed the most important detail that I've kept hidden. I love you."

Fayre thanked her dance partner and bid him farewell. Reluctant to be dismissed, he followed her while offering her everything from his heart to a glass of lemonade. Smiling, she politely refused all the gentleman's offers. There was only one man's attentions she desired and he was off courting other ladies of the *ton*.

She was acting like a shrew, but she could not stop herself. After Maccus had slipped into her bedchamber four nights earlier, she could not decide if he had told her the truth or was so diabolical that breaking her heart was not enough to satisfy him. He had to destroy her spirit, as well.

Where was Maccus?

Fayre had not spoken to him since that night. Her mother still mentioned seeing him at various functions so his private declaration had not altered his pursuit for a bride. Maccus had begged her to trust him. She was trying, but it was difficult.

Yesterday he had sent her a note, demanding that she attend this evening's ball. Fayre had already planned on going, but his insistence had made her reluctant. Why was her presence so important? She assumed that he wanted to talk with her. Still, he had remained elusive to her and she was too wary of him to act daringly.

Feeling slightly deflated, Fayre acknowledged that Maccus did not need her advice or connections anymore. The duchess's stamp of approval and his dark, handsome looks assured that each day numerous invitations arrived at his door. Although it had always been part of their mutual plan, it had been more difficult than she had ever imagined watching him flirt and dance with the dozens of ladies who flocked around him vying for an introduction.

"Lady Fayre," Lord Yemant greeted her, when she walked by him, too lost in her thoughts to notice him.

"Good evening, my lord," she said, flustered by her inattentiveness. "I was wondering." She stepped closer and lowered her voice. "Have you by chance seen Mr. Brawley?"

The viscount frowned thoughtfully. "I noticed him speaking with Miss Knight near the doors leading to the gardens. What has the rogue done? Forgotten that he had asked you for a dance?"

Seizing his excuse for her own, she replied, "I fear he has. Perhaps he is too enamored with Miss Knight to recall his earlier promise."

She had also seen Maccus chatting with the shy eighteen-year-old. A match with Miss Knight would have been viewed as a favorable one. She was pretty, well mannered, and brought a dowry of ten thousand pounds to the gentleman who married her. If Maccus were privately making a list of prospective brides, Fayre would have added the young woman to it.

"Enamored or not, Maccus is too fond of you to offer offense."

She was startled by his observation. "His arrogance is insufferable at times, but we have learned to tolerate each other's company."

Lord Yemant raised one brow, skeptical of her bland opinion. Needing to smooth over his friend's carelessness with her feelings, he confessed, "Truly, these gatherings are hellish on us unmarried gents. The mothers hoping to barter their daughters are bold and creative in their scheming. I predict one of these fiendish creatures has cornered him and he cannot dream up a polite lie to escape. It happens practically every time I dare show my face. Small wonder most gentlemen prefer the safety of their clubs."

The viscount was indeed a fine prize for an ambitious mother or lady. Fayre was sympathetic to his plight. "I am certain Miss Mableward appreciates your bravery."

His handsome face brightened at her friend's name. "Ah, yes. I believe she does. Encountering her at these affairs has always made the evenings bearable." Recalling his manners, he added, "As does your presence, my lady. If Brawley cannot be found, I would be honored to take his place."

"You are very generous, Lord Yemant," she said, believing he would be the perfect husband for Callie. "However, I have tired of dancing. I think I will check the gardens for Mr. Brawley. If Miss Knight's mother does indeed have him cornered, he will be in my debt for my assistance."

Couples enjoyed the gardens for reasons other than its beauty or the fresh air. Suddenly concerned that Fayre might stumble on Maccus in a compromising position, Lord Yemant said, "If you like, I could accompany you."

"There is no need to trouble yourself. I will just take a peek outdoors. If I cannot find him, then I will leave it to him to seek me out."

She curtsied and inclined her head. Rising, she headed for the double doors that led to the garden. Fayre tried to blot out the pity she noted in Lord Yemant's gaze. She could tell he regretted mentioning that he had seen Maccus near the gardens with Miss Knight. If Maccus and Miss Knight had slipped outdoors, there was a chance what she might glimpse would be distressing.

Fayre wished she could have assured the viscount that she was strong; she would not collapse if Maccus indeed were pursuing Miss Knight or any of the other ladies to whom he had been introduced. Fayre loved him and she refused to feel regret over it. She had always known she was not what he sought in a bride.

Many of the guests lingered close to the door, appreciating the cool air after dancing. Fayre did not see Maccus or Miss Knight so she walked farther away from the house. Lanterns were lit throughout the grounds and the gravel paths provided the more adventurous solitary views of the garden. She did not believe Maccus was out there in the shadows seducing Miss Knight with his clever flattery and intoxicating caresses.

Sincerely, she did not.

Her faith in him did not prevent her from walking the east side of the gardens and then moving deeper toward the back. There were fewer lanterns in this area. Shivering in the night air, she began to be more concerned about the dangers of wandering too far from the house and the other guests than Maccus's disappearance with Miss Knight.

Masculine voices halted her retreat. Peering into the shadows, she walked past an unlit lantern and down a path she had avoided earlier.

"What did you tell the chit?"

Fayre froze, recognizing Lord Standish's voice. She slipped off the path and hid behind a small tree. He had been drinking heavily. She could tell because he had a tendency to be wearing on the ears when he was deep in his cups. The other man replied, but she could not hear more than a low incomprehensible murmur. Treading off the gravel path was treacherous, but she could not risk coming face-to-face with Lord Standish and his companion.

"Fair of face but too meek, in my opinion. Some prefer that sort," Lord Standish said disapprovingly.

Fayre used his ranting to guide her slowly closer to him. Her hand brushed against the dense barrier of a tall hedge. It reminded her of a wall. A faint light burned through it in places so she began searching for the entrance to what she perceived was part of a maze.

A few minutes later the mystery of the wall was solved. A shaft of light drew her to the back. What she was touching was not the wall of a maze, but rather an enclosure for a small Gothic ruin. Fayre peered through a substantial gap where a portion of the hedge had died and withered. Someone had placed a lantern on a base of a broken column. Another lantern was set on the ground several yards away from her position. Crouching down to get more comfortable, she almost screamed when a man stopped in front of her. His back was to her, but she recognized him to be Lord Standish.

"We expected you earlier. Was there a problem?" he demanded of a new arrival. For now all she had was a spectacular view of the gentleman's backside and not much else.

"Not precisely." The sound of Lady Hipgrave's sensual drawl slid into Fayre like a rusty dull knife. "Just enjoying the amusements," the countess said cryptically.

Standish moved away from Fayre to fawn over his mistress. His departure allowed Fayre to glimpse her nemesis. As usual, the lady chose to stand where the light was the most flattering to her curvaceous figure. She wore a white sarcenet dress with a robe of violet crepe. Her dark golden blond tresses were swept up and supported by a long crepe handkerchief.

The countess extended her hand out in a graceful motion. It was not Standish she was addressing but his companion. Craning her head for a better view, Fayre lost her balance and landed on the soft ground when Maccus stepped into the light. He clasped the countess's extended hand and bowed over it courteously.

"Regardless of the delay, I always look forward to our intimate encounters, my lady," Maccus said, his gray eyes devouring his companion.

From her hiding place, Fayre shook her head in denial. Maccus had deliberately gained introductions to both Lord Standish and Lady Hipgrave so he could study her enemies. Not once had he mentioned to her that he met with the countess on other occasions.

"As do I, sir," Lady Hipgrave said, her tone insinuating there was more than superficial civility to their meetings. "I noticed you earlier in the ballroom flirting with Miss Knight. A passable choice for a gentleman in your position."

"Too tame, I say," Lord Standish interjected. "Once

you plant your heir in her, you'll be wanting to spend your nights with a more lively bit of muslin."

"I was just speaking to the lady," Maccus replied mildly.

"I have to agree with Standish," Lady Hipgrave said, sitting down on what remained of a collapsed wall. Miss Knight is a representation of the insipid fare the London season churns up for the marriage mart. There is nothing wrong in selecting the girl as a potential bride, if you prefer a dutiful, uncomplicated creature."

"I would think such a lady ideal as a wife?"

"For some, I grant you," the countess conceded. "You, however, are a gentleman who would never be satisfied with such an ordinary miss. Time in your company has revealed to me an ambitious gentleman whose appetites are distinctive and vigorous. Heed me when I tell you that marrying someone who is your inferior creates a tragic marriage."

Fayre clasped and unclasped her hand over her heart. Lady Hipgrave was probably thinking of her own marriage to Lord Hipgrave. The earl was rarely seen in London, but she recalled her father had mentioned Lord Hipgrave's reclusiveness. He had chosen to marry a lady who was his opposite in all respects. Fayre did not understand why Maccus had joined the pair for a nocturnal meeting, but she could not shake a sense of foreboding of the outcome.

"Unless she is worth seventy thousand pounds annually," Lord Standish quipped, laughing vigorously at his own wit.

Lady Hipgrave glanced at him and smiled. "Yes. Money overlooks many unflattering flaws. Do you not agree, Mr. Brawley?"

Maccus shrugged dispassionately. "Wealth provides

ample compensation. It opens closed doors, buys loyalty and respect before it is earned, and noble ladies who once would have deemed me beneath them beg for a place at my side."

Standish took a flask from his pocket and sipped. Gesticulating with it, he said, "And in your bed, I wager."

Maccus fixed his potent gaze on the man. "Besides other places."

Fayre felt her insides congeal. Was he referring to the night they made love at the temple? She had told Maccus once that she feared Lord Standish and Lady Hipgrave would find out about them. Had he betrayed her by revealing her secrets to her enemies?

Lady Hipgrave rose and placed a presuming hand on his coat sleeve. "Well, Mr. Brawley, with your wealth and the proper friends, I predict you can aspire higher than the Miss Knights of the world."

Maccus stared down at her hand. "With your help?"

"Oh, I sense our alliance will be a rewarding experience," the countess assured him, gazing up at him with liquid blue eyes. "Lady Fayre Carlisle is just the first of many collaborations I envision."

"Simpering little bitch," Lord Standish muttered to himself. "Gullible, too. Does she suspect anything?"

"I can be remarkably convincing when properly motivated," Maccus said confidently. The ruthless ambition Fayre had always feared ruled him hardened his face into a cynical mask. "Solitea's daughter is mine. She trusts me completely."

Fayre lightly touched the brooch Maccus had given her. Each word he uttered condemned him, slashing at her so deeply she was numb from the pain.

"Then this is a time for celebration. Standish, if you

please." The man handed his flask to the countess. "A toast in your honor, Mr. Brawley . . . and to you, Lord Standish, for your sacrifice and cunning." She tossed back the brandy in the flask with flourish. Handing the flask to Maccus, she stepped into Standish's arms.

Maccus stared at the flask in his hand while Lady Hipgrave and Lord Standish kissed. Fayre knew he shunned strong spirits because of the unyielding influence it had over his father. She had never seen him drink anything stronger than beer. Lady Hipgrave pulled back from Lord Standish and stared expectantly at Maccus. With a devilish grin, Maccus swallowed a healthy portion of the brandy.

Approvingly, the countess moved from Standish's embrace into Maccus's. "Lady Fayre should thank me for sharing two of my favorite friends with her," she said, offering her mouth up. Maccus accepted her unspoken invitation.

They were still locked together in a passionate embrace, when Fayre backed away silently, the image of Maccus eagerly kissing Lady Hipgrave burning tauntingly in her brain as she slowly made her way back to the gaiety inside the house.

After his sojourn in the dimly lit gardens, the light in the ballroom seemed harsh. Maccus squinted against the light of the glittering chandeliers as he stalked through the crowd. The music and the laughter around him contrasted greatly with the sanctimonious intimate gathering in which he had just participated.

His disposition volatile, he pushed his way through daring anyone to challenge him. They were all meek as sheep, he thought contemptuously as everyone gave way.

This was the world he had coveted, and he did not belong. Maccus was halfway across the room before he realized he was searching for Fayre. He had seen her earlier when he had arrived, so he knew she had acquiesced to meeting him in public. His desire to see her this evening was putting his plans at risk. Nevertheless, he could not resist, though he had yet to approach her. There were rules of propriety to be followed and for her sake he had tried to play the complicated game that made no sense to him.

When enough time had elapsed, he had intended to seek her out, but Miss Knight had waylaid him. Afterward he had private obligations that needed tending. Now that he was unfettered, she was nowhere to be found. Confound the lady for not staying put!

Spotting Fayre's friend Miss Mableward, he changed directions in pursuit of the lady. Not surprisingly, Yemant was close at her heels. The viscount was so besotted it was amazing he did not injure himself with his single-mindedness.

Pleasure lit up Miss Mableward's face as she recognized him. She dipped into a brief curtsy. "Good evening, Mr. Brawley."

"It might be if I could locate Lady Fayre," Maccus said, striving for patience. "Have you seen her?"

"When I spoke to her, she was searching for you," Yemant offered helpfully. "The lady was rather upset that you had forgotten your promise to dance with her. Did she ever find you in the gardens?"

His gaze sharpened on the viscount. Maccus took a menacing step forward. "She was in the gardens?"

Yemant looked apologetic. "Forgive me, Brawley. I might have made a hash of things. I let it slip out that I had seen you and Miss Knight together near the doors to the gardens. When we parted, she was wandering off toward the doors. When Lady Fayre did not return, I assumed she had found you."

Maccus forced himself to remain calm. Fayre might have strolled in the gardens; however, the place where he had met Lord Standish and Lady Hipgrave was far from the house and they had extinguished numerous lanterns to discourage the other guests from interrupting.

He appealed to Miss Mableward. "Have you seen her?"

Bewildered by the tension radiating off him, she stammered, "N-no. I regret I cannot offer more."

Maccus abruptly nodded. Bidding the couple farewell, he planned to search the entire house for Fayre, starting with the ballroom. She was somewhere close and the edginess strangling him would not ease until he found her.

"What are you doing out here?"

Fayre accepted her cloak from the footman she had engaged and took her time adjusting it before answering Maccus. Fortifying herself, she met his stern gaze.

"Do not be obtuse, Mr. Brawley. I am leaving."

"Leaving? Why?" he demanded, crowding her.

Fayre edged away from him. After she had left the gardens, she had sought an empty room to collect herself. Although it was difficult, she prided herself on not shedding one tear for the worthless villain. She was stronger than Lord Standish, Lady Hipgrave, and Mr. Brawley had ever guessed.

She glanced at him coolly. "Why? This is not the only ball I planned to attend. I promised Mama I would make an appearance at the Hakewells'."

Lowering his voice, Maccus said, "Then I shall join

you. You know the duchess will applaud my impudence."

Fayre almost smiled. His nerve would indeed amuse her mother. It was a pity he had turned out to be such a black-hearted scoundrel. Not looking at him, she said in a clipped manner, "I would rather you refrained. You have worked diligently to establish yourself in polite society and you are much admired. Bravo, sir." She started to leave but he caught a portion of her cloak.

"If this is about Miss Knight," he began, his gray eyes pleading for her forgiveness.

Fayre tugged the fabric free from his grasp. "Rest assured, Mr. Brawley. This is not about Miss Knight." She walked into the night without glancing back.

Sheer pride kept her from breaking down as she settled into the interior of the coach. It was only when the coachman shut the door to the coach that Fayre let her posture slump. The finality of the thwack proclaimed the ending of her ties to Maccus Brawley. She was grateful. The ending of their relationship had been lurking on the distant horizon. She had been aware of that fact even before she had become Maccus's lover.

It was a relief the agonizing wait was over. Before the lies, she had been prepared not to blame him for moving on without her. The life he had been born to had almost killed him. Instead of being repulsed by the life he had led before his move to London, she had been astounded by his strength. His struggle to better himself had inspired her and she had genuinely wanted to help him succeed even if she lost him.

Conversely, losing Maccus to Lady Hipgrave was a duplicity she had not anticipated. How they all must have laughed at her while she gave herself wholly to Maccus. Twice betrayed by the gentlemen she had loved. Her father had been right all along. She had indeed become a cautionary tale for every silly miss who dared to love a rogue.

The coach rolled forward, distancing her from the man whose ruthless ambition had made a debacle of her life. Fayre covered her face and sobbed into her hands. All she could see was Maccus smiling charmingly at the countess, Maccus greedily kissing her. How could she have been so wrong about him? She felt so shattered, she did not know if she would ever recover from the pain.

Something large hit the door from the outside. Flinching away, Fayre screamed. While the coach was still moving, someone flung the door open. Maccus's head popped through the opening.

"Stop the coach!" he bellowed, the dark fury of his gaze never leaving hers.

"Please halt the coach," she croaked, her voice ruined by her tears. She was about to repeat her command, but refrained as she felt the coach slowing.

Maccus climbed into the compartment. His large body filled the interior of the coach, intimidating her with his size and rage. With precise, controlled movements he sat in the seat across from her. Studying her face broodingly, he reached into the inner pocket of his coat, retrieved a handkerchief and offered it to her.

Fayre accepted the handkerchief and dabbed at the wetness on her cheeks. Unwilling to give the soggy linen back to him, she stuffed it into her reticule. His presence had effectively doused her sudden bout of tears, for which she was grateful. She did not want to feed his self-love by showing him how devastated his betrayal had left her.

"Did you really believe we were finished back there?" Maccus said quietly.

After his violent entrance, she had expected him to shout accusations at her. It would have given her an outlet for her own pent-up anger. She was uncertain how to handle him when he was being reasonable. "Yes. I am weary, Maccus. There is a ballroom filled with ladies waiting to be dazzled by your looks and your flattery. Why do you not return to them?"

"You're jealous," he said, and her spine stiffened at the accusation. "You have no plan of seeking out the duchess. You are leaving because something upset you this evening."

She gazed at him with mocking admiration. "Amazing. You intend to play this out to the end."

"Play what out, Fayre?" he asked, cocking his head questioningly.

She rubbed her temple; her agitation was giving her a headache. The lying villain was staring at her as if she were behaving irrationally. Then again, Maccus was not aware that she had seen the three of them together. She wondered how long he was supposed to continue his charade before delivering the coup de grâce.

Frustrated by her silence, Maccus said impatiently, "I spoke to Yemant. I know he told you about Miss Knight. You looked for us in the gardens."

Had the viscount been privileged to Maccus's confidences? Fayre immediately dismissed the likelihood. He seemed to be an honorable gentleman. All the same, she no longer trusted her judgment regarding men. She did trust her friend Callie and doubted any gentleman she admired would align himself with vipers. "Is Lord Yemant blaming himself for his careless tongue? It would be so like him, since he is an *honest* gentleman," she said, unable to lessen her biting inflection. "You must not blame him. Like everyone else in the room, I too witnessed your intimate conversation with the lady."

Maccus seemed relieved by her confession. Lifting an inquisitive brow, he asked, "And you looked for me in the gardens?"

"Did Lord Yemant mention that I did?" she countered slyly. Crossing her arms, she waited for his next move.

"Answer me, Fayre. Did you go into the gardens?"

"Yes." She saw no reason to deny it.

Maccus nodded, drawing his own conclusions. "And you did not find me and thought the worst?"

He had the nerve to act disappointed in *her*! If Fayre had been a man, she would have physically thrown him out of the coach. Instead she used the only weapon she wielded with finesse. "Do you blame me, sir? I have experienced firsthand your predilection for shadowed encounters."

Her insult pricked his temper, and the fury she knew was simmering within him boiled over. Edgily, he slapped his thigh. "I knew jealousy ruled your displeasure! Perhaps I should allow you to suffer, but I cannot. I was not with Miss Knight." He scowled, his stony features daring her to disprove his claim.

"No?"

There were subtly annoying ways to call a man a liar, and Maccus sensed he was being goaded. "No. Miss Knight and I parted ways in the ballroom. I did go out into the gardens, but I was alone."

Fayre supposed it was partially true. There was a point he was alone in the garden. "It is odd that I did not encounter you then. What were you doing out there?"

She leaned forward, desperately willing him to tell her

the truth. If she had misunderstood what she overheard, this was Maccus's opportunity to confess about his meeting with Lord Standish and Lady Hipgrave.

Maccus removed his hat and smoothed back stray hairs. Glancing away, he said, "Escaping mostly. I was coming to you when Miss Knight approached me. She was pressing me to ride with her in the park tomorrow afternoon. The young lady was very persistent. Afterward, I went outside to clear my head."

Tell the truth, she silently pleaded. "Nothing more?"

His expression became roguish. He started to take her hand, but she carefully moved out of reach. "Without you in my arms, what possible reason would I have for lingering in a dark garden?"

Fayre laughed, trying to fight back the tears that brightened her gaze. "Oh, I could think of one or two amusements. Let me think . . . hmm." She pretended to ponder her choices. "Oh, I do not know. Counting stars? Or listening for the sweet call of a nightingale? No?" she asked, watching his gray eyes narrowing at her false joviality. "Or mayhap you were out there meeting Lord Standish and your mistress in secret so you could praise one another for making a fool out of me!"

Despite his dark coloring, Maccus paled. "Fayre!"

She was likely to murder him if he tried to placate her with lies. "I saw you laughing with them. Lady Hipgrave mentioned other intimate meetings so I know this one was not the first. And I saw you kiss her!"

He flinched at her increasing hysteria. When he tried to take her into his arms, she shoved him away. "Permit me to explain."

No. No. No. She was not going to listen to him. She had listened to him before and look where it had gotten her. He was a skilled liar. "Explain what, Maccus? In your quest for beating the *ton* at their own game did you decide Lady Hipgrave was a stronger ally than I? The woman who has conspired for months to hurt my father and ruin me? How extraordinarily cold-blooded of you, sir. Did you approach her with this vile scheme or did the countess present you with a tantalizing offer you could not turn down?"

The muscle in his jaw ticked. His gray eyes were enigmatic when he said, "You are in no mood to listen to reason."

She sneered at him. "I am in no mood to listen to your *deceit,* Mr. Brawley! Get out of my coach or I will summon the coachman to remove you by force."

He seemed unimpressed with her threat. Nevertheless, to her immeasurable relief, he climbed out of the compartment. In the doorway, Maccus sullenly stared at her. "Fayre, we cannot part like this."

She made a surrendering gesticulation with her hands. "Fine. You want me to be reasonable. I will leave you with some parting advice. Never attend a ball with both your mistresses in attendance. It is bad form. I suppose I could not expect a man who was born from the union of a violent, drunken sailor and a dockside whore to understand the subtle nuances of civility." Fayre tore the brooch he had given her from her bodice and threw it at his head. Maccus snatched it from the air before it struck his face. "Keep it. Your gifts mean nothing to me. And you even less."

Shouting at the coachman to drive on, Fayre closed the door.

17

Maccus stormed into his town house, the slamming door heralding his arrival. At this late hour, no one came to greet him. Nor did he expect anyone. Hobbs and the rest of the staff had retired to their beds. Lighting a candle, he headed for the drawing room and shoved the door open. Moving about the room, he lit candles until he was surrounded by light.

In his mind, he could see Fayre standing beside him in the middle of the room as she demonstrated the steps of a country dance for him. Her green eyes had been animated with laughter as she called the dance steps aloud.

Removing his hat, Maccus tossed it on the sofa. In quick succession his gloves and frock coat joined his discarded hat. Collapsing into the nearest chair, he scrubbed his face wearily.

Fayre hated him.

It was for the best. Had he not set out to drive her away? He dug two fingers into his waistcoat pocket and retrieved the brooch he had bought for her. The diamonds glittered as he tilted the piece, examining the elegant floral design. When he had given it to Fayre, she had been so overwhelmed by his kindness her eyes had been moist with tears of joy. This evening the tears he glimpsed had been bitter when she flung his gift back at him. Rejecting his gift.

Rejecting him.

Christ, what a coil, he thought. He should have told her about the meeting with the countess and Standish. In hindsight, he could see that although Fayre believed he had betrayed her, she had been silently willing him to confess his sins. She might have even forgiven him.

Not likely.

Fayre had seen him kissing Lady Hipgrave. She thought he had met with her enemy in secret, believed he and the countess had become lovers while they plotted against her.

Forgive him?

Never.

He had committed the ultimate betrayal from Fayre's point of view. Maccus stared down at the diamonds. They would always remind him of her tears. Stuffing the brooch back into his watch pocket, he stood. She was the strongest female he knew and he had broken her with his actions, his silence.

Love had been so rare in his life it had taken him some time to recognize it. However, it had been there for him to see in her clear green gaze, embracing him each time he made love to her. He had almost convinced himself that he could accept everything she silently offered. Or had, until the countess knocked brazenly on his door at the Denings'. Their private chat had forced him to alter his plans without Fayre's knowledge. The encounter also reminded him that the past was difficult to ignore. Had he not spent years trying to forget his own? Trevor had warned him that their father was searching for him. Maccus had to face the truth that he would never be rid of his father, or of the danger and violence that clung to him like a second skin.

Striding to a small cart, Maccus picked up the decanter of brandy he kept for his guests. He never drank strong spirits. A part of him had always feared that drinking would release the raging beast that moved just beneath his civilized veneer, a version of his father, but something worse. Turning the cut crystal in his hands, he thought the amber liquid looked inviting. The temptation to imbibe and ease his guilt over Fayre whispered softly to him. No one would think badly of him if he had one drink or emptied the decanter.

"Your gifts mean nothing to me. And you even less."

Maccus took the brandy and shattered the decanter against the nearest wall. A mournful roar erupted from him. He had lost Fayre and he knew he deserved his bleak fate. Kicking over the cart, he picked up a chair and splintered it over the back of the sofa.

Charging the chimneypiece, his hands swept across the mantel and glass and porcelain shattered as the various knickknacks struck the floor. This room had been a symbol of his wealth and elevated status, yet it meant nothing to him. Maccus noticed his reflection in the mirror and he did not recognize the feral man staring back at him.

Seizing a wood carving of a horse from another table, he heaved it across the room at the gilt mirror. The surface fractured on impact into a large cobweb pattern obliterating his reflection. The sculpture and several glass daggers fell to the floor.

Swaying slightly, Maccus surveyed the damage he had wreaked to the room. He lifted his hand to wipe the sweat from his forehead and noticed he was bleeding from several deep scratches. As much as he longed to, he would not pursue Fayre and force her to listen to his explanations. It was best that she thought him worse than Standish. Beauty was too fragile to last long in his care.

Fayre longed for Arianrod. The solitude and splendor of the land was soothing, a harsh contrast to town life. If leaving London had not seemed so cowardly, she would have packed her belongings that night. Her mother had warned her that her choice to brazen the scandal out was a precarious one, especially with Lord Standish and Lady Hipgrave whispering in the gossips' ears. In her arrogance, she had thought she could beat them at their own game.

She had never anticipated meeting Maccus or the part he would eventually play in her life.

When had his deception begun? He had studied her before approaching her, that much she had guessed. Was he already working for Lady Hipgrave when he contrived an introduction at the park or had his treachery occurred later? She had been too upset to press him for the answers he seemed so reluctant to give. Not that it signified anything. There had been no future for Maccus and her. The private hopes she had woven in his arms about them had been a chimera.

There was a shout and the coach lurched as the horses veered to the right. Fayre peered out the window into the darkness. The coach was slowing down. What was the man doing? They had not reached the town house. She heard the coachman speak to someone. Had Maccus returned? Or worse, had brigands forced her coachman to halt?

For the second time that evening, the door was unexpectedly flung open. Fayre jolted, her hands fluttered to her throat in fear. It took mere seconds for her brain to recognize the masculine face grinning at her. Her fingers curled into claws as she lunged at the intruder.

M accus sensed he was not alone. Whirling around he saw Trevor in the doorway, his shrewd gaze assessing the damage done to the drawing room and the man who had caused it.

His half brother whistled softly in astonishment as he entered the room. "If you were not pleased with the fancy frippery, Mac, you could have ordered Hobbs to remove it." Trevor noted the smudges of blood on Maccus's left sleeve and the cuts on his hands. Wisely, he said nothing.

"I thought you had left," Maccus said inanely, feeling ashamed that his brother was glimpsing a side of his nature he had thought suppressed.

"Did. Now I'm back." Trevor righted the only chair Maccus had been unable to splinter into kindling because of the thick upholstery and sat down. "I brought news about Seamus."

His eyes sharpened on his brother at the mention of their father. "You've seen him?"

"And shared words. He wants to meet with you, Mac."

Maccus kicked aside a large broken vase with the side of his foot as he made his way to the chimneypiece. Resting his fist on the empty mantel, he stared into the cold hearth. "Where?"

"Where else?" Trevor countered, his face grim. "I found him at a tavern named the Bronze Scarab. Seamus said to tell you to come at once, else he will come to you."

"You told him?" Maccus asked, his eyes hot and accusing.

Trevor looked away. "He has ways of getting things out of a man. It matters little. You know he would have eventually found out anyway."

Maccus swore vehemently. He kneaded the knotted muscles at the back of his neck. Seamus had a hold on his half brother that Maccus had never been able to break. Whether it was a sense of misguided loyalty or fear that motivated Trevor to side with their father, Maccus did not know or at the moment care. He had cruelly, albeit unintentionally, hurt Fayre this evening with his half-truths. Even if she could find it in her heart to forgive him, he did not want her tainted by his family. Once Seamus learned about the life his eldest son had built for himself, nothing short of murder would keep him from claiming his stake. In his present mood, Maccus was feeling accommodating.

"Oh, another thing, Mac," Trevor said, pulling his brother from his menacing thoughts. "Seamus was almost sober when I saw him. I cannot promise you will find him in the same condition if you delay."

♦ ♦ ♦

Fayre struck her brother in the chest. "Confound it, Tem! I almost had heart failure. I thought the coach was being attacked."

Her brother caught her fist and hauled her into a crushing embrace. "I have missed you as well, sister," he said, slightly slurring his words. "I saw the Solitea crest and thought to bid good evening to my kin."

"You are as drunk as an emperor," she groaned, shaking off his embrace and falling back into her seat.

"Beg to differ. You aim too high. Drunk as a duke is more fitting," Tem said, chuckling at his joke. He climbed in after her. Misjudging the height of the step, he pitched forward face-first into Fayre's lap. Recovering quickly, he crawled in the rest of the way and plopped down beside her. "There, much better, don't you think?"

The coachman managed to startle her by sticking his head through the door. "Forgive me, my lady, for frightening you. I thought it best to stop when I saw Lord Temmes. I've tethered his horse to the back of the coach."

"You did the right thing, John." Tem laid his head on her shoulder, wringing a sigh of resignation from her lips. "Drive us to his residence. He can sleep off the brandy there in peace."

"Very good, my lady." Having his orders, the coachman shut the door.

Fayre removed Tem's hat and threw it on the seat. Affectionately, she stroked his hair. "You are indebted to me, my brother, and I shall hold you to it."

"How so?" he murmured, stirring slightly but not opening his eyes. She had thought him asleep.

"My kindness in delivering you to your own residence

instead of just going home. This will spare you the lecture Mama would most assuredly deliver if she learned you tried to fulfill the Solitea curse by falling off your horse."

Tem snorted loudly in her ear. "Already been done. If I must die young, I want to be original about it."

Fayre wrinkled her nose, appreciating her brother's odd humor. "How sensible of you."

"Thought so," he said sleepily, snuggling closer. "What are you doing about town by yourself?"

She rolled her eyes at the reprimand she detected in his question. "You are in no position to scold me, my lord. Besides, I have ended my evening, early I might add, and was heading home when you halted the coach."

"You've been crying."

"How would you know? You cannot keep your eyes open."

Tem proved her wrong by lifting his head and opening his eyes. His green gaze was bloodshot, but he was not as foxed as she had assumed. Satisfied he had made his point, he closed his eyes and settled back down against her.

"What upset you? Has that bastard Standish been bothering you?" he demanded. "Never should have listened to you. If you had let me challenge him, we would have all been spared his annoying presence."

Fayre's lips parted in surprise at her brother's matter-of-fact offer to kill. She despised Lord Standish, but she could not be responsible for his death or making her brother her tormentor's executioner. "No. I am not upset over Lord Standish. At least not in the manner you infer, anyway." She closed her eyes, too. In the darkness, it was easier to speak about her failings. "Oh, Tem, I keep making a muddle of my life. I should have listened to the duchess and gone abroad this season."

He grunted. "Run away? Not like you to give up when things get sticky."

"No, you are right. It does not sound like me, does it?"

"Tell me," he invited her.

"Why should I? You will not even recall our conversation when you awaken."

"Fayre," Tem growled threateningly.

She had started this. Now her brother would not relent until he had heard her grand confession. "Fine. You want to know what I believe? I do think the Carlisles are cursed. What is it about us, Tem, that we cannot find love? Or is it that we find too many? Oh, in the end we make good matches, which increases our wealth and position in society. We breed the next generation to carry on the family's recklessness. What about love, fidelity, honor? Why am I so unlovable, Tem?" she asked, her voice breaking with emotion.

Her brother did not respond. Fayre was convinced he had slept through her outburst when he quietly asked, "You are not speaking of Standish, are you?"

He would certainly challenge Lord Standish to a duel if she agreed. "No. There was someone else. A gentleman I thought was my friend. I—I discovered this evening that he has been lying to me."

"And does this man have a name? Is it Maccus Brawley?"

She was no longer fooled by his casual tone. As he lay slumped against her, Fayre could feel the tension gathering in his body. "No. It is someone else, a name I have no desire to share with you."

"Fayre—" he groaned, knowing that she was lying to him.

"No, Tem. He is not worth your anger or my tears,"

she said, her sadness silencing his scathing retort. "That is what I am telling myself. Mayhap tomorrow I will believe it."

The Bronze Scarab was just the sort of tavern that appealed to his father. Close to the docks, it attracted fishermen, sailors, laborers, coalwhippers, and sellers of small wares. If a man knew whom to approach, information flowed as freely as the spirits.

Maccus had been sitting by himself in the tavern for an hour. There had been no sign of Seamus. Idly, he rolled his beer pot between his two palms, discreetly studying the faces of the people who entered the tavern. He had ordered Trevor to remain at the house. His brother's loyalties were divided and Maccus could not rule out Seamus using Trevor to manipulate him.

Where was his father?

He assumed Seamus had availed himself of one of the prostitutes while he awaited his son. Maccus hunched his shoulders; his expression and posture were uninviting. Sitting in a dingy tavern all night was not likely to improve his ill temper. If Seamus did not arrive within another hour, Maccus was leaving.

Fayre closed the front door and rested against it. She was pleased to be home. With the coachman's assistance, she had walked her brother to the door. She kissed him farewell, abandoning him to the care of his manservant. At first, she had worried her confession had prompted his need for revenge, something she had not desired. The thought of Tem and Maccus facing each other on a common at dawn was horrifying. Fortunately, the brandy her brother had imbibed had dulled his wits and temper. Tem had naturally expressed concern over her upset, but he was too foxed to act on his violent impulses. With luck, by the time he awoke, what she had told him would have been forgotten.

She was devious enough to feign ignorance if he pressed her. At least she had not mentioned Maccus Brawley by name. Fayre unfastened the clasp at her throat and shrugged off her cloak. Climbing the stairs, she felt strongly enticed by the notion of burrowing into her bedding and shutting out the world. After she had slept away the fatigue weighing on her, she would consider what should be done about Maccus.

Fayre hesitated at the door of her bedchamber. A shaft of pain stole her breath at the thought of his name, of what he had done.

"You will not let them break you," she whispered furiously. "Never give them the satisfaction."

"Spirited words," a man observed, causing Fayre to whirl around and confront him. A man she had never seen before was standing behind her in the shadows. "And beautiful. I like that in a wench. You and I are about to become friendly."

The man stepped closer and walked through a shaft of moonlight. Fayre stared at the pistol in his hand.

Maccus charged into his house for the second time. This time his fury was directed at his father instead of himself. He had wasted two hours waiting for his father and the man had not the decency to appear.

"Trevor!"

He began shoving doors open as he passed, but his call was met with silence. Maccus was getting damned tired of his brother's unexplained disappearances. Prepared to reprimand Trevor for Seamus's absence, he marched into the drawing room and was taken aback by the changes. His attack on the drawing room had not escaped the notice of the servants or maybe Trevor had alerted them. Regardless, in his absence, someone had made an effort to clean up the debris. The furniture he had damaged had been removed and the bits of glass and porcelain had been swept up. Even the mirror he had smashed had been taken away.

"Sir," Hobbs addressed him from the entry. If he had an opinion about what had occurred earlier in the drawing room, the servant was keeping silent about it for once. Maccus had always admired the older man's backbone. The rest of the staff had probably scurried off to their beds after they had cleaned up the room, leaving Hobbs to face Maccus's wrath alone.

"Where is my brother?" Maccus demanded.

"He left shortly after your departure," the servant said, confirming Maccus's suspicions that his outburst in the drawing room had awakened the entire household. "Your brother left this note for ye. He said that he forgot to give it to you earlier."

Maccus snatched the folded paper secured with a wafer bearing his personal seal. Tearing it open, he read the brief message. The paper was crushed as his hand tightened into a fist. Forgot to give him the note? Not bloody likely. He knew where his father had gone. His traitorous brother had told Seamus about Fayre.

18

There is no need to fear me, little lady," Fayre's uninvited guest said, cagily peering in all directions to make certain they were alone. "I've only come to chat with ye."

Eyeing the pistol, Fayre was not convinced the man was harmless. He looked to be about her father's age, she guessed. What had once been dark hair had silvered and now hung in a greasy tangle to his shoulders. He might have been handsome in his youth, but time had not been kind. There was a puffy aspect to his cheeks and a bulbous nose that hinted the man worshiped the bottle. Permanent wrinkles were carved around his eyes and forehead.

Fayre doubted the deep lines were the result of a humorous outlook on his difficult life. His suit was tattered and poorly made. There was even a fairly large hole in his right stocking.

"We don't want to disturb the rest of the house," the man said pleasantly, acting as if he were not aiming a pistol at her. "We could talk in there."

Fayre's stomach roiled at the thought of being shut up in her bedchamber with this man. It was more than his offensive smell that caused her to rebel at his suggestion. She feared the private room and her bed would give him ideas even Fayre did not want to contemplate. Attempting to flatter him with proper respect, she said, "You must forgive me, but a lady's bedchamber is not the proper setting to entertain her guests."

The man scratched his head, shaking it. "Can't say I agree. Some of my best recollections took place in one."

If she dashed for the stairs, he would have a clear shot at her back. Still, she would rather die than have him touch her. Ignoring her screaming instincts to flee, she took a cautious step toward him. "Since my family is out and unable to greet you properly, why do we not retire to the drawing room or perhaps the library? My father stores a most excellent brandy there."

The man's dull light blue eyes brightened at the suggestion of the duke's brandy. "The library sounds cozy."

Pouring brandy into her unwelcome guest was probably risky, but Fayre was too grateful he was not insisting that they enter her bedchamber. Besides, if her parents returned or one of the servants became curious about the activity in the library, she had increased her chances for escape.

Fayre led the way. Upon entering the library, she lit

as many candles as she could. Their radiance was soothing to her raw nerves and created a beacon to her whereabouts. "Much better," she said, cheerful. "Would you
care to serve yourself or shall I do the honors?"

The man used the pistol to wave her away. Fayre deftly
moved away and chose her father's favorite chair. Tilting
her head, she watched him pour a generous glass of
brandy with his free hand. For a housebreaker, he was a
strange fellow. Why had he gone to her bedchamber? It
was almost as if he had been waiting for her.

"Forgive my impertinence, sir, but have we met?" she
asked, waiting until he had sampled the brandy. Perhaps
if she got him drunk it would work in her favor. There
were plenty of items she could bash him on the head with
if given the opportunity.

"Us? No, miss," he said, winking at her. "Guess we
failed to introduce ourselves proper like. I'm Seamus,
Seamus Brawley."

Speechless, her lips parted. "Maccus and Trevor are
your sons?" Her evening was taking a strange twist she
had not expected, especially after her unpleasant confrontation with his eldest son.

"Fine boys, both. Strong. Handsome. They take after
their old man, not the mewling bitches who whelped
them," he said, grimacing as if the brandy had soured in
his mouth.

Fayre fidgeted with the tips of her gloves, uncertain
how to respond to his remark. "We never spoke of family,
Mr. Brawley. As it happens, I only met Trevor once." She
did not mention that Maccus had been furious about their
accidental meeting. At the time, she had been hurt by his
peculiar reaction, as if his connection to her had been

something to hide. Now she wondered if it was not his relationship with her that he was concealing, but rather he was hiding *her* from his family.

"Trev has nothing but praises for ye, miss. If Mac wasn't so partial to you, I think the boy would keep you for hisself," Mr. Brawley confided. He sat down on the wide armrest of one of the other chairs, his blue eyes admiring her just above his glass of brandy.

Now that she knew of their connection, she could pick out bits and pieces of Maccus and Trevor in their sire. She was certain Maccus would not be pleased by her casual observation. "Your son was just being kind," she murmured, curious as to what had prompted his nocturnal visit. Thus far, if she did not count the pistol or the fact he had broken into her house, Mr. Brawley had not threatened her. She stared at the pistol resting on his thigh and bit her lower lip nervously. Not exactly.

"'Tis my eldest you favor." He swallowed the rest of his brandy, and rose to pour himself another. Clasping the glass, he aimed his finger at her. "Enough, I wager, that Mac has seen the insides of that bedchamber you were unwilling to show me."

Fayre swallowed the indignation welling up within her. He turned his back to her partially while he filled his glass. Perhaps he really did not view her as a threat. Despite his age, he had the strength to subdue her attack, even if she managed to take him off guard. "I doubt this conversation would please your son, Mr. Brawley."

"I am never pleased when Seamus is around," Maccus snarled, stalking after his father.

◆ ◆ ◆

"**M**accus!" Fayre jumped to her feet, looking thrilled to see the man she had sworn hours earlier meant nothing to her.

His stern gaze lingered on her long enough to see she was uninjured and then honed in on his father. "We were supposed to meet at the Bronze Scarab, Seamus. What are you doing here?"

The pistol waved wildly as he gestured with his hands. "Don't blame Trev. He was just honoring his father. I needed a small ruse to keep ye occupied while I visited with yer lady."

If his father was expecting him to behave himself in front of Fayre, he was about to be disappointed. Undaunted by the pistol, Maccus lunged at Seamus, his hands finding a hold around the older man's neck. In the distance he could hear Fayre screaming at him, but he would deal with her after he had taken care of his father. Seamus's face quickly turned the color of ripe cherries as he struggled to breathe. Maccus slammed him against the wall, rattling the serving tray beside them that held decanters and glasses.

"Drop the pistol," Maccus growled, and slammed him again against the wall.

"Maccus, please, you are killing him!" Fayre exclaimed, tugging on his arm.

Trevor suddenly appeared. "Mac!" His brother charged at him. "Christ, man, have you gone mad?" He wrapped his arm around Maccus's throat and tried to pull him away from Seamus.

He realized his brother must have been watching the house to warn Seamus of Maccus's arrival. Maccus sneered back at his brother, who had betrayed him. "No!

But you must be, telling him about Fayre. What did you think he would do once he got her alone? Serenade her?"

Trevor sent Fayre an apologetic look. "He doesn't plan to do anything with her. He was just curious and wanted to meet her."

Seamus's face was altering from red to a fascinating purple. The pistol slipped from his hand, followed by the glass of brandy. Maccus kicked the pistol away with his foot. Spinning crazily, it skidded across the floor and disappeared under an escritoire. His father's hands scratched at Maccus's hands, feebly attempting to pry his fingers loose.

They must have been quite a comical sight with Maccus doing his damnedest to strangle his father, and Fayre and Trevor trying to stop him. His cravat helped impede his brother's hold, but Maccus was beginning to see swirling dots of lights in front of him. "Bull. My God, Trevor, we might not have been raised like royal princes but even you must know breaking into a house at midnight with a pistol in hand is not considered a social call!" Pinkish spittle had formed in the corners of Seamus's mouth. "Give me one reason why I should not snap his neck and rid myself of this bastard."

"How about they will bloody well hang you for it!" Trevor shouted back and pulled harder.

"Please, Maccus, stop. He did not hurt me. You can let him go," Fayre begged. "D-do not kill him."

Her plea ended with her sobbing. Maccus finally looked away from his father's strained features and stared at her. When he had come upon them, she had been sitting calmly and chatting with his father, ignoring the pistol Seamus had used to gain her compliance. It was Maccus who had managed to terrify her with his violent need to protect her. Ashamed, he loosened his grip and

Seamus fell to the floor, flopping about and gasping for air. Trevor released his hold on Maccus and crouched down next to their father.

"Hush. Don't cry," Maccus crooned, stroking the hand she still had clutching his arm. He desperately wanted to hold her, but feared she would fight him if he tried. "Trevor delivered a note written by my father. In it, Seamus boasted that he had you. Maybe I did go a little mad. When he is drinking, he is prone to lash out; not even the people he has affection for are spared. I couldn't bear for him to hurt you, Fayre."

Fayre shook her head, her tearful gaze focused on Seamus. "I do not know what he intended when he broke in, Maccus, but all he did was talk."

"What did you have planned for her, Seamus?" Maccus demanded. The urge to throttle his father for his part in scaring Fayre was rising in him like a wild beast. Maccus pushed Trevor away from Seamus and hauled the older man to his feet. "Is this one of your grand schemes? Did you think to hold her for ransom?"

Seamus held his hand to his throat and coughed. "When did ye become so cynical, Mac? Can't a man be curious about the lady his eldest son is planning to marry?"

Taking pity on his undeserving father, Fayre poured another glass of brandy and handed it to him. "Mr. Brawley, you are mistaken about my relationship with Maccus. I merely acted as an advisor and provided a few introductions. There is nothing serious between us. Your son has no aspiration to marry me."

Agitated by her slapdash explanation of their relationship, Maccus snapped his teeth together in response. He supposed he should be thankful she had omitted from this version her belief that he had conspired with her enemies.

"Fayre, love, I fear I must disagree on a point or two," Maccus said, his expression warning her to keep silent. "But I prefer to hash out our differences in private." He returned his attention to his father. "And as for you, the only thing you care about is how you can turn a profit."

Seamus's laughter came out like a hoarse wheeze. "Old age has made me sentimental."

"Not likely. With you, there is always an angle. What did you hope to gain this evening? Were you hoping to barter Fayre's safety for my cooperation?" Maccus saw the answer he was searching for in Seamus's crafty gaze and cursed. "You knew I'd hand-deliver you to the devil myself if you came near me."

"Ain't that the truth?" Seamus replied, his color improving with each passing minute. "I needed your help, Mac. I have an associate who is letting me in on a deal of his; an honest one, not like those in the past. All we need is a backer, with your brains and—"

He had heard his father make this pitch countless times. "No."

"I figured you'd spit on the deal for spite," Seamus crossly muttered. Sensing Fayre was the one who could influence Maccus, he appealed to her for help. "You look like a sweet girl, miss. If you could ease the burden life has placed on your father's weary shoulders, would you not help him?"

Anger imploded like a bubble within Maccus. He personally knew how much Fayre would sacrifice to protect her father. Stepping between them to shelter her from Seamus's prying questions, he said, "Fayre cannot help you, old man. Leave her alone."

Nothing would be settled with Fayre present. She did not understand how twisted his life had been with Seamus, or how ruthlessly the two men dealt with each other. It was not a side of himself he was proud of or had wanted to reveal to her. Gently, Maccus placed his hands on her shoulders, turning so his back was facing his family. Lowering his voice, he said, "There is no reason why you should be a part of this mess, Fayre. Why don't you go up to your bedchamber and lie down?"

Her green eyes, wide and anxious, searched his face. "What are you planning to do?"

"Damn it, Fayre! This business does not concern you," he yelled, his grip pinching her flesh.

He could practically see the sparks flare between them as his outburst touched off her own temper. "Fine. If it is none of my business, then why do you not remove yourselves to the street? There, if you desire, you can pummel your father senseless without my interference." She waved him off dismissively. "Go, begone."

Maccus hesitated. Although he had Seamus and Trevor to contend with, he wanted to remain and talk things out with her. Earlier she had ordered him out of her life and he had been prepared to accept her dictate. Now that Seamus's impulsive scheme had brought them together, he loathed letting her out of his sight. If he respected her wishes and left, he feared he would never have another chance to atone for his actions.

"If I leave, will you open the door for me on my return? Pride aside, I owe you an explanation about this evening. You were right about some things, wrong about others. We need to sort through them together." Maccus cocked his head back at his curious family. "Without spectators."

Fayre bowed her head in contemplation. "I suppose it would be best if we discussed our differences in private," she conceded stiffly.

Forgetting himself, Maccus bent to kiss her on th
mouth. Fayre stopped him by pressing her fingers to hi
lips. "Listening does not automatically imply forgiving
Mr. Brawley," she firmly reminded him.

Fayre slipped out of his slack embrace. Walking ove
to the escritoire, she crouched down and retrieved the pis
tol. All three men stared at her in disbelief as she exam
ined the pistol. Her experience with firearms was reveale
in her expert handling of the weapon. Satisfied with wha
she had discovered, she tossed the pistol to Maccus, star
tling him by her sudden carelessness.

"It was not primed," she explained, though relief wa
clearly visible on her pale face. "You might want to re
member that, when you *discuss* this business with you
father."

They followed her to the front door. Maccus kept a
firm grip on Seamus because he expected his father to
flee at first opportunity. He stopped at the threshold and
stared hard at Fayre. "Your word that you will see me?"

"My word, Mr. Brawley," she said, smiling slyly at him

"What did ye do to rile the wee faerie queen?"
Bracing his foot against the opposite seat to
bar the door from his passengers, Maccus scowled at his
father. There was a certain irony hearing the hard, griz-
zled sailor spout poetic descriptions about a lady. In op-
position to his brother's wishes, Maccus had bound
Seamus's hands with a length of rope during their journey. He was half tempted to take the old man to the docks
and hand him over to a press gang.

"Who says it was I who upset her? You were the one who broke into her house and stuck a pistol in her back," Maccus said, aware that Fayre could hardly view him in a kind light after Seamus's unsettling mischief. "If she changes her mind and decides to press charges, I will feel obliged to deliver you up to the magistrate personally."

Trevor stirred in protest. "Lady Fayre is kindhearted. If she thought to prosecute, she would have summoned the watch. It is you who want to see Seamus shackled in irons or dangling from the hangman's noose."

"Aye. The best part is I won't have to do a thing but watch and rejoice." Maccus pointed his finger at his brother. "You, you traitor, secured her fate by revealing to our greedy father the lady's connection to me. It is best you keep silent."

"Do not be so harsh on the lad, Mac. He tried to protect ye. But, alas, ye know how persuasive I can be," Seamus said. The swelling and bruising at his throat was visible in the dim light of the compartment of the coach.

Trevor stared out the small window into the darkness. He did not acknowledge or deny his father's explanation. Maccus had been convinced when Trevor had first arrived at the house that his brother had severed all ties with Seamus. It had cut him deeply to see them united together while he stood alone, the enemy. Maccus leaned his head back against the seat and studied his brother through hooded eyes.

"What does he have on you?" Maccus asked quietly.

His brother choked on a burst of laughter and shook his head. "Leave it be, Mac. It's my business alone. Suffice to say, I've not lived a sainted life. Some days you wallow in the sinning, other days are spent paying for them."

Maccus knew whatever Seamus held over Trevor to obtain his support had to be significant. Since Fayre was waiting for him, he would have to put off the confrontation with his brother until later. Moreover, as long as Seamus was close, Maccus doubted nothing short of a beating would encourage Trevor to confess.

"What shall I do with you, old man?" Maccus mused.

Seamus raised his hands bound together at the wrists and gestured at him. "I'd rather talk about ye and the faerie queen. What are ye doing dallying with a duke's daughter? Have ye taken up seducing innocents or have ye been funding yer fancy life by whoring yerself out to noble ladies?"

The urge to finish what he had started in the Duke of Solitea's library flickered within him, just as Seamus had wanted. From the corner of his eye, he noticed his brother tensing, preparing for Maccus's attack. Purposely, he slumped down, forcing his body to relax under his father's malicious stare.

Maccus idly traced one of the seams lining the inner compartment. "Thinking of putting yourself up on the auction block? You're a little long in the tooth to attract the young ones, and the stale foulness emanating from your unwashed body will discourage the widows and spinsters."

Amused, Seamus wheezed; his throat was too damaged by his son's throttling to laugh properly. "Wearing silk has softened ye, Mac. Another time, ye would have done more than hurled insults at me."

The corner of Maccus's mouth lifted slightly. "Perhaps time has taught me something you never could quite grasp. I'll leave the beating of helpless children, wives, and old men to you, Seamus."

His silent regard must have disconcerted Seamus, prompting him to say, "Trev was right when he said that I meant no harm to the lady."

Maccus scratched the underside of his jaw, marveling at his father's sudden switch in tactics. "That I have no doubt. If you had harmed her it would have been your corpse I would have dragged out of her house."

Seamus brought his coat sleeve up and endured a brief fit of coughing. "Ye have gone and fallen in love with yer fancy pigeon, haven't ye?" He seemed disappointed by the prospect.

Maccus had not expected to fall in love with Lady Fayre Carlisle.

Right now, she was berating herself for being duped and smothering any affection she held in her heart for him.

He was not lulled into complacency by the tiny advantage that she had preferred him to his father. After she had seen him kiss Lady Hipgrave, he would never convince her that his feelings for her were genuine.

"My dealings with Lady Fayre Carlisle are not your concern. What should concern you is what will happen if I learn that you or Trevor have approached her or any members of her family. The family is off limits to your schemes, Seamus."

"Bah!" his father baldly scoffed at the threat. "That little miss might have worn down the edges of yer hard heart, Mac, but from the looks she was giving ye, I'd wager she'll stick a blade in it and twist it fer good measure. What happened? Did she catch ye tickling another plump pigeon that caught yer roving eye?"

The fine muscles in his jaw ticked in agitation.

Seamus pounded his thigh with his bound hands. He

nudged Trevor with his shoulder. "See, Trev? It sticks in Mac's gullet that the face he sees in the shaving mirror each morning is mine. Yer me, my boy, incarnate."

"I am nothing like you," Maccus snarled, knowing he had stared at his reflection and thought the same thing.

"Nay, yer worse," Seamus thundered back at him. "Ye shirk away from drink and whoring, dress yerself up in a fashionable suit, take on airs, and think just because ye don't strike the weak and the stupid ye are better than me. Ye use your wits like I used my fists, but yer still deep down the rabid mongrel chained in a stable yard. Yer only fooling yerself if ye think the people around ye cannot be hurt by yer ambition."

Maccus could picture Fayre's face in his mind. She had tried to hide it from him, but he could see the misery burning in her green eyes as she ordered him out of her coach.

"If you are offering fatherly advice, don't waste your breath," Maccus said grimly. "I want nothing from you except for your absence." He leaned forward. "And I shall have it."

"Ye've been tickling fancy pigeons too long to be any real threat," his father said and spat on the floor in defiance.

"Oh, I have on occasion dedicated myself to other efforts. Like hunting down the men responsible for the massacre at Carew Strand," Maccus said casually, his shrewd gaze never leaving his father's face.

"Carew Strand?" Seamus tasted the words and judged them bitter. "Why are ye poking into sad matters better left alone?"

"I'm not. Or haven't in some time. I have always had my suspicions as to who ambushed me and my crew that night on the beach, though it took a few years to prove it."

Trevor finally looked away from the window and stared at his brother. "Prove what? The case was solved long ago. I was still a boy when you were shot, but even I heard the news of the arrests. The son of the local magistrate was one of three men who were eventually captured and charged with the murders."

Maccus nodded slowly. "The authorities assumed Nisbet Riply had aspired to seize control and profit from the local smuggling ring running right under his father's nose. To assert his right to rule, he had plotted a deadly ambush on one of the night runs. The attack would provide him with the opportunity to kill anyone who might oppose him and put fear in the locals, gaining their allegiance."

"Past history, Mac," Seamus muttered, twisting his hands to test the strength of the rope binding his wrists. "Ye can't avenge yerself on men already dead."

The ropes would hold his father, but Maccus did not underestimate the old man's desire to escape. "True. Riply shocked everyone by not waiting for his trial. He hanged himself in his cell. Two weeks later, his cohorts were pronounced guilty for their part and joined him in hell."

Giving up on his attempts to loosen the coils of rope around his wrists, Seamus made a surrendering motion with his hands. "So ye had yer justice. I don't see what this tale has to do with me?"

His father's innocent posturing didn't fool Maccus. "No? I think you do. I had a friend of mine do some investigating on my behalf and he turned up a few witnesses who told a slightly different tale."

"The men were innocent?" Trevor asked, shifting his gaze from his father to Maccus. Both men stared at each other, a silent battle of wills.

"Oh, the men were deserving of their fate. The authorities just didn't know there was a fourth conspirator who had escaped them."

A sound of disbelief rumbled in Seamus's throat. "Ye can't believe everything ye hear late at night in a tavern when men are cast away on a sea of hell-broth and crank."

"Several years ago, when I spoke to the witnesses, I deemed they were credible. Do you know what they told me?" Maccus arched his back to ease his stiffness. He had stuffed the unloaded pistol into the front waist of his breeches and now the barrel jabbed him unmercifully in his hip. Removing it, he laid the side of the pistol on his thigh. Seamus glanced down apprehensively at the weapon. "It seems that Nisbet Riply was a nineteen-year-old who had felt his own ambitions had been stifled by his rigid father's influence. A born braggart with a fondness for violence, the young man sadly lacked the brains to think his schemes through, and his recklessness had caused his magistrate father all sorts of trouble."

"Sounds like the lad was destined to strangle on the hemp," his father interjected.

"Most likely, since he surrounded himself with unsavory companions who listened to him boast about his grand plans for riches and adventure as long as he paid the publican to refill their cups. The witness I spoke with revealed that one day a new companion had joined the young man and his drunken companions. This one was older, canny, and he whispered in Riply's ear, telling him how he could achieve the riches he craved as well as the dark pleasure of violence. This man had connections to the smugglers, you see, and with Nisbet Riply's help he saw a way to line his pockets with gold without risking his own neck."

"This is a Banbury tale. Ye don't have any proof, Mac."

Trevor paled. He gaped at his father in horror. "How could you have betrayed your own blood? You would have known Mac was down there on the beach, when they detonated the explosives and rode through to finish off the wounded."

It pleased Maccus that his brother was finally seeing that Seamus spared no one when it came to getting what he wanted. He could only hope Trevor would one day sever his ties and avoid their father before he ended up facedown and bleeding to death from a bullet fired by the old man's pistol. "I have enough evidence to take to Nisbet Riply's father. The magistrate might have been a rigid man, but he loved his son. He never believed his son was responsible for the massacre on Carew Strand. There was even a rumor that Riply had hanged himself after speaking with a close friend who had visited the gaol to offer comfort. What do you think a grieving father might do if handed evidence that another man had convinced his gullible son to commit unforgivable acts of violence? A devilish character who walked away from his wickedness unscathed, unpunished?"

His father's eyes gleamed at him, hinting at the obsessive madman within. "If ye had such proof, ye would have used it against me years ago."

Maccus rubbed his brow wearily. Seamus would never understand why Maccus had not used the evidence he had collected to convict his father. The man had certainly not deserved his son's mercy. Loyalty and compassion were beyond his comprehension. "You should have left me alone, Seamus. You had your chance to kill me and bungled it. Another man would have cut his losses, but I knew your greed would lure you back one day."

"Are we making a bargain, son?" Seamus leaned forward, anticipating his reprieve.

Maccus pounded on the trap door above his head and ordered the coachman to halt the coach. He reached behind his back and retrieved a knife he had concealed there. "Aye." Maccus grabbed his father's bound wrists and sawed through the ropes. "A simple one. Stay out of my life, and the lives of my friends." Once the coach halted, he opened the door. "You're free. How long you remain that way is your choice."

Trevor climbed out first. "I suppose I'll be leaving, too."

It was not what Maccus wanted, but as long as his brother sided with Seamus, it was prudent to keep his distance. Still, he could not prevent himself from offering, "Is there anything I can do to help you?"

His brother shook his head. "Nay, but it means something to me that you bothered to ask." Maccus tossed him the unloaded pistol.

"Then I wish you well, brother." Maccus watched Seamus climb out of the coach. He kept the knife in his hand, just in case his father was daring enough to attack him. "And another thing, Seamus. Later, when you have had a few drinks to relax and begin to feel cocky about evening the score between us, just remember that all I have to do is cast suspicion in your direction." Reading the older man's expression correctly, he added, "Killing me will not save you. My solicitor has orders in the event of an untimely demise to send certain letters out on my behalf. The magistrate in Carew Strand will see to it that you are brought to justice."

Seamus chuckled, accepting that his eldest son had outmaneuvered him. He leaned heavily against the door of the coach. "Yer a cunning bastard, Maccus Brawley. Is that why the faerie queen despises ye?"

"Drive on," Maccus ordered the coachman.

Over the rumbling of the wheels of the jouncing coach, he heard Seamus shout out, "Ye should have perished on that beach. 'Tis the damnedest luck ye have!"

19

Fayre had given her word that Maccus could return to her once he had come to terms with his father.

Of course, she had lied.

Sticking her chin up defiantly, she sat on the bottom step of the grand staircase and listened as Maccus pounded at the door. He was determined, she conceded. She had listened to his persistent knocking for fifteen minutes.

Curdey, their butler, came shuffling into the hall with a lamp in his hand. Still dressed in his nightclothes, he was so preoccupied with a yawn that he did not immediately notice Fayre.

"My lady, is there something amiss?" the servant asked, his gaze drifting to the door. "Who is calling at this hour?"

"A very tenacious gentleman. I do not think we should let him in," she said, glowering at the door.

Thump. Thump. Thump.

The door shuddered with each impact but it would take more than anger to breach solid hardwood.

"I should say so, my lady," the butler muttered, cautiously approaching the door. "His Grace will be most displeased when he learns of this young gentleman's conduct."

"Then perhaps we should not tell him, Curdey." Of all the things Maccus had done to her under the veil of night, waking the household was the least of his crimes. "We can handle the matter ourselves."

Fayre stood. Now that the butler was beside her, she was feeling braver. "You might as well answer the door. Something tells me he will not go away until he sees me."

The butler peered anxiously at her. "I have a pistol in my room. Do you think I should fetch it?"

Even though the pistol the elder Mr. Brawley had brandished had not been loaded, Maccus had not been aware of it when he attacked his father. Fayre had a vision of Curdey gasping for life-giving air under Maccus's capable hands.

"In his present mood, I do not think we could discourage Mr. Brawley with a cannon," she confessed. "Open the door."

The butler opened the door. The evening had not been

pleasant for either one of them, and Fayre's defiance had ignited Maccus's fury. Despite his informal attire, Curdey managed to convey his disdain for their unwelcome visitor. "Off with you, sir. What has possessed you to disturb the household at this late hour?"

Maccus looked past the servant's shoulder and noticed Fayre standing on the stairs. "Fayre. I told you that I would return. You gave your word!"

Fayre met his seething rage unflinchingly. "As did you, sir. I suppose that makes us both liars," she said coldly. Addressing the butler, she ordered, "Close the door, Curdey."

The servant was only too eager to comply with her request and slammed the door on the enraged stranger. "My lady, should I wake one of the footmen and send him for the watch?"

Maccus had resumed pounding on the door; this time she could hear him shouting her name. Fayre pressed her fist to her stomach. She could hear the underlying pain beneath the anger in his voice, but she refused to be moved by it.

"Go back to bed, Curdey. Mr. Brawley will soon realize his efforts are futile and return home," she said, not entirely convinced she spoke the truth.

The butler winced at the harsh pounding. "If you say so, my lady."

"And Curdey," Fayre said, delaying his retreat. "I think it best that we do not mention Mr. Brawley's visit to my family." He nodded reluctantly before departing for his room. Nor was Fayre planning on mentioning the prior incident with the entire Brawley clan in her father's library.

Fayre was halfway up the staircase when the front door splintered open. Maccus limped across the threshold, his gray eyes searching the hall for her. She must have made a soft sound of distress, because his gaze shot up and locked onto hers.

"Maccus. No," she said, knowing she had provoked him too far. Snatching up the front panel of her skirt to prevent herself from tripping, Fayre dashed up the stairs.

Fayre was no match for Maccus. Taking the steps two at a time, he quickly overtook her before she had reached the top of the stairs. Tossing her over his shoulder, he smacked her on the bottom when she squirmed.

"Hold still," Maccus said, slowly descending the stairs. "I am not feeling playful."

"Nor I, Maccus Brawley. If I were a man, I would show you just how serious I can be!" she spat out, and tugged hard on his queue.

"See here," the butler said, meeting them at the bottom of the staircase. In all his years of employment with the Carlisle family, he had never encountered this particular situation and was uncertain how to proceed. "I must insist that you put my lady down, sir."

"I will not harm her, old man." Maccus moved around the frightened servant toward the drawing room. "The lady gave me her word that we would talk this evening and she is too principled to refuse me." He patted her backside. "Is that not so, my lady?"

He dumped her on the sofa and immediately turned to confront the butler. The man scurried back, unconvinced the man was harmless. "Tell him, Fayre. Your servant fears for your virtue, mayhap your life. You are too kind to permit him to suffer needlessly."

"Curdey," Fayre said, rising from the sofa and joining Maccus. He sent her a swift glance, hoping she was not preparing to bash him on the skull with whatever was handy. "Mr. Brawley is selfish, condescending, and boorish, but he does speak the truth. I did give him my word that I would receive him this evening, regardless of the hour. Pray return to the comfort of your bed. I will not be harmed."

"My lady, what about the door?" the man whined. "The damage will not escape His Grace's notice."

Fayre glared at Maccus, viewing the entire predicament as his fault. "You will pay for the repairs." Her expression warned him that he had better heed her command. Softening her features for the servant's benefit, she said, "Curdey, awaken a few men and have them secure the door for the night. We will worry about fixing it in the morning."

Her smile slipped when the butler closed the door.

"Will he obey your orders or should I worry that he ran off to fetch a constable?" Maccus asked, twisting the key in its lock to deter any further interruptions. As an afterthought, he removed the key from the keyhole and dropped it into the inner pocket of his coat.

"Curdey has served the Carlisles faithfully for decades. However, your destructive entry may lead him to believe my orders were coerced." She raised her right brow, silently acknowledging that she indeed felt bullied. "So if I were you, I would speak quickly."

He was not going to allow her to provoke him. Given Fayre's current annoyance at him, the notion of having him locked away in a gaol was probably tempting. "If I am guilty of anything, Fayre, it is my negligence of explaining myself fully. I let you drive off thinking I am a villain."

She scratched at a speck on her spotless sleeve. "Do not concern yourself, Maccus. I had already thought you a villain long before I was seated in my coach."

There was no other way to get through her brittle, prim façade except with the truth. "I assume you are referring to that business you witnessed in the gardens?"

"Business," she said, pacing in agitation. "That business was you betraying me with the two people who have spent weeks inventing new ways to hurt me," she said, her green eyes hot with misery. "And you helped them. Perhaps you had been helping them all along."

"What you saw was deceiving."

"Oh, then I did not see you kiss Lady Hipgrave?" she mocked, causing him to wince. "No, Maccus, for the first time since I met you my vision is sharp. It was you who deceived me."

"Not intentionally. Damn it, I was trying to protect you!"

"If you dare try to tell me that you were kissing that harpy on my behalf, I swear I will ask for Curdey's pistol and shoot you myself."

Maccus felt as if he had a stomach full of hostile bees stinging his insides. His throat was thick with desperation. "Listen to me. We spoke of this, late at night, as we lay in each other's arms."

"Something that I will always regret."

Fayre was hurt and striking out blindly. He absorbed her barbed comments unflinchingly. "Think, Fayre. I warned you that a time would come when we would have to distance ourselves publicly. I also told you that there were parts of my plan that you would not find pleasing. I had to take certain unpleasant steps in order to win Standish's trust."

"You must have succeeded brilliantly since he was willing to share his mistress with you."

"I never bedded the countess."

"Of course not. She was trying to swallow your tongue because she was hungry."

"I did not say the lady did not want to fuck me, Fayre," Maccus said bluntly. He was tired of her poking at him. "The countess has a healthy appetite for men. If I had been a different man I might have taken what she offered." As it was, she had been getting suspicious of his lack of interest in her persistent invitations. Standish had been willing to share her. The only reason he had kissed her was to let her believe he was susceptible to her wiles.

"How was befriending my enemies supposed to help me?" Fayre asked in bewilderment.

"I was an outsider. The choices I made were ruthless and perhaps unforgivable in your eyes, but I did what was necessary to help you."

"Ah, yes, for the bargain."

"No. For you, just you, Fayre." At her skeptical glance, he added, "All right, in the beginning it was for the bargain we struck. I saw an opportunity to use your anger to my advantage and I took it. It was later, when you let down your guard and let me know the woman hidden underneath the lady, that it became as important to me as it was for you to help you gain your revenge against Standish and the countess."

She was not moved by his confession. "Forgive me, sir, if I find your affection for me difficult to believe."

Someone tried to open the door and discovered it was locked. There was a distinct authoritative knock. "Open the door."

"Papa!"

Maccus grabbed her arm before she could step away from him.

"What are you doing? That is my father on the other side," she said, struggling to free her arm. "Unlike your father, mine does not march around waving pistols at everyone. Give me the key so I can let him in." She held out her hand expectantly.

"No."

Fayre flounced around in a huff because she was not getting her way. Crossing her arms, she asked, "Speaking of your father, what did you do with him? Pummel him senseless? Throw him in the Thames?"

"Neither. I took your advice and let him go." He was privately amused that she could change from furious to pleased to being furious at him again within seconds.

"Fayre, my girl, are you all right? The rogue has not hurt you, has he?" The duke sounded worried.

She moved as close to the door as Maccus would allow. "I am unharmed. Mr. Brawley has a peculiar sense of humor. He does not mean to scare anyone."

"Curdey said the man kicked down the front door and carried you off over his shoulder like a savage. Do you call that amusing?" the duke demanded.

"It sounds like an odd courtship to me!" Maccus shouted at the door.

"What?" Her father pounded the door with his fists and tried the latch again. "You, there . . . Brawley, release my daughter at once or I will have you in front of the magistrate before sunrise!"

Fayre punched him in the shoulder to gain his attention. "Are you mad? With my father's support, you will be clapped in irons and transported out of the country. And that is if you are lucky."

"Fayre," Maccus pleaded, needing her to listen to him. "We have so little time. I need you to put aside your resentment and jealousy, and judge—"

Her eyes flared wide at his accusation. "I am not jealous. No. I am disgusted. Disgusted I ever—"

"Standish is ruined," Maccus said, speaking over her diatribe. "With my help, he started losing heavily at one of his favorite gaming hells. I approached him, pretending to be his friend, and covered some of his losses to win his trust."

The duke was not leaving his only daughter in the hands of a potential criminal. Maccus and Fayre heard him call for a kcy to open the door.

"Once he trusted me, I was in a position to slip him false information about certain ventures I have invested in. It is not common knowledge but Standish has borrowed deeply from several unsavory moneylenders. Unless his father rescues him from his creditors, and Standish has already confessed to me that his father won't, I predict the gentleman will be leaving the country on an extended tour."

"How do I know that you are telling the truth?"

"Someone has alerted Standish's creditors about his financial difficulties." Earlier in the afternoon, Maccus had personally called on the shops the viscount frequented and had incidentally revealed to the proprietors Lord Standish's dire circumstances. "I doubt he will remain in London once the vultures descend on his house."

Fayre started when her father slammed his fist against the door in frustration. There was a loud argument going on about a missing key.

Maccus dragged her farther away from the door and pushed her down on the sofa. He knelt down in front of her. "Once I got to know you, I wanted to kill Standish for the cruel games, Fayre. However, death would have been merciful. So I sentenced him to the same fate he had intended for you, but which you were too strong to accept quietly. Banishment from the world in which he thought he reigned."

Fayre was finally listening to him. When her father shouted her name, she said, "Papa, I am not Mr. Brawley's hostage. We are merely having a private conversation. I will be out shortly."

The duke did not take being dismissed by his daughter lightly. He called for the servants to break down the locked door.

"And Lady Hipgrave?" Fayre asked, challenging him to prove his innocence when she had seen with her own eyes his unfaithfulness. "What fate awaits her besides befuddlement from your kisses?"

He grinned, absurdly thrilled by her admission. "My kisses befuddle you, my lady?"

Trapped by her own words, she gnashed her teeth and rose, moving away from him. "Evading my question with one of your own is a clever stratagem for not answering the one put forth." She picked up a figurine from the table and studied it. Even from a distance, he saw that it was a griffin carved from ivory.

Maccus straightened his knees and sat in one of the nearby chairs. He watched her warily, hoping she was not planning to throw it at his head. "I am not dodging your question, Fayre," he said tersely, glaring at the distracting activity going on beyond the door. "Lady Hipgrave was not as easy to fool as Standish. A clever lady, she had noticed the undercurrents between us. When she confronted me at the Denings' *fête*, I had to make her believe the only side I was on was my own. Naturally, she could not resist luring me to hers."

"Naturally," Fayre echoed sarcastically.

"Your face is about as green as your eyes, love. You are thinking with your heart. Lady Hipgrave does not possess one, so you need to think like she would. What would she do if she were convinced you had a lover?"

Fayre did not hesitate with her response. "Use the knowledge to her advantage."

"Aye. You have been denying your relationship to Standish, which was becoming a problem since many people sided with you. But if she could prove there was another gentleman sharing your bed—" Maccus did not finish his thought, wanting Fayre to reach the conclusion on her own.

She set the figurine down on the table. "Then I unintentionally support her claims. Good grief, I am such a goose!" she exclaimed in disgust.

"Not on that point anyway." Taking a chance, he got up from the chair and came up behind her. "The countess would have revealed our affair because she was not going to allow you to escape unscathed from her sordid game. When I admitted I had my own immoral purposes to seduce you, Lady Hipgrave saw my, ah, delicate position in your bed as a means to her own ends. I convinced her to wait, promising the delay benefited both her and me. She agreed. However, she is not a patient woman."

"She wanted you for herself."

"Aye, she wanted me in her bed. Unlike you, she was not roused by love or even lust." Uncomfortable with his insight regarding her feelings toward him, she tried to turn away. Maccus trapped her against the table with his body.

There was so little time left before a small army broke down the door. "The countess prefers bartering her body in exchange for her lover's compliance. The fools. She is counting on the man being so stirred and captivated by her that he will do everything and anything to please her."

A spark of hope was kindled in Fayre's green gaze. "You never bedded her?"

Something heavy banged into the door, cracking the wood on impact. The door exploded open on the second attempt. Two footmen staggered into the drawing room and collapsed in a heap on the floor. The Duke of Solitea stepped over them and headed toward his daughter and Maccus. The older man did not look as if he were grateful his daughter was safe; he looked bloody furious.

"Papa, wait! I told you Mr. Brawley and I were just talking!" Fayre screamed when her father swung his fist wildly at Maccus's jaw.

Maccus ducked low, avoiding the blow. He seized Fayre's hand and hauled her along as he ran for the door. As he passed the footmen, he shoved one man into the other, knocking them off their feet again. They dashed past a small crowd of curious servants and across the front hall.

"Maccus," she panted, the excitement making her breathless. "Where are we going?"

He pushed her into the music room and closed the door. Maccus scanned the room, searching for something he could use to barricade the door. Near the window was a marble statue displayed on a pedestal. It was the full figure of a nude woman in a classical pose clutching a length of drapery to protect her modesty.

Fayre, noticing his regard, said, "Oh no, do not even consider moving that pedestal. Papa paid a king's ransom for that Helen of Troy. I sometimes think he places more value on that chunk of marble than his flesh and blood."

Maccus surrendered gracefully, deciding the harpsichord was closer. He grabbed one side and dragged the stringed keyboard instrument in front of the door. Nodding in satisfaction at the barricaded door, he figured he had bought himself a few more minutes with Fayre.

Fayre looked somewhat ill. "You cannot simply move a musical instrument as if it were a table or a chair. The harpsichord is a delicate—"

He waved her argument away with his hand. "Your father can add any damage my moving has done to my repair bill. Though in all fairness, I shouldn't have to pay for the damages his staff might cause when they break down this door."

There was a distinct thud at the door. His barricade would not hold for long. Maccus glanced at Fayre. She was poised at one end of the sofa, looking expectantly at him. Striding to her, he continued the discussion they had started in the drawing room.

"No, I did not bed the lady. After being with you, my jewel, all ladies pale in comparison." He anticipated her next question. "Aye, I kissed her, and kissed her well, for it had to be convincing. Lady Hipgrave had to believe I was following her dictates even if she had yet to lure me into her bed. I found no pleasure in it, though I would have kissed her again if it spared you the anguish she had planned for you. How long are you going to punish me for trying to protect you?"

The door burst open partway and struck the harpsichord. A disharmony of chords vibrated within its case. The duke howled in outrage that his men had struck the expensive instrument.

Fayre flinched as the door continued to batter the side of the harpsichord. "Maccus, I am not punishing you."

"Really? You tossed my brooch at my face and ordered me out of your coach. What do you call that?"

"Being sensible!" she shouted back. "After Lord Standish, I never thought I could trust another gentleman." Fayre stood up and gestured broadly with her hands. "And then you convince Lord Yemant to introduce us. My life has not been the same since you entered it. I am not the same person."

The footmen shoved the harpsichord aside and charged Maccus. The duke looked mournfully at his damaged instrument before training his fuming gaze on the man responsible.

"Hold, sir," His Grace ordered, withdrawing his cutlass from its scabbard and tossing the sheath aside.

Maccus ignored the older man's command. He had too much to lose if he was captured now. Punching one of the footmen and dodging the lunge of the second, he grabbed Fayre's wrist and pulled her toward the door.

"Not again," she muttered, mildly exasperated by Maccus's determination to drag her from room to room. Her father sliced the air with his cutlass as they passed. Fayre shrieked as his blade barely missed her and was buried deep into the gilded case of the harpsichord.

This insanity had to end. Her father had almost beheaded her in his attempt to halt their escape. Maccus weaved them through the growing crowd of spectators— made up of servants—and down the corridor. Fayre was certain she had heard one of the grooms placing a wager with the cook on the outcome. Maccus bundled her into the library and turned the key. Crossing her arms, she watched him build a barricade with a large desk and several upholstered chairs.

"Enough, Maccus. Between your antics and my father's we shall not have a single usable door," she said, frustrated by his stubbornness. "Let us end this now."

"No!" he said, adding another chair to the growing tangle of furniture. "I won't let you cut me out of your life, Fayre. I love you. You love me."

She expected arrogance from him, but his confidence regarding her own feelings was galling. "You sound awfully sure of yourself, Mr. Brawley."

He curtly nodded. When he approached her, she expected him to haul her into his arms and kiss her senseless, demonstrating the passion between them. Instead, he walked by her and selected another chair. "I am. You wanted to murder me for kissing Lady Hipgrave."

It was unwise of him to mention the countess. Her hands curled at her sides. "On the contrary, I wanted to murder Lady Hipgrave. You, on the other hand, I wanted to maim."

Maccus hesitated at his task of fortifying his barricade. "Only a woman in love contemplates violence for a minor transgression."

She suspected he was deliberately provoking her. Still, she could not refrain from replying to his taunt. "It was a major transgression. One I still might maim you for."

Setting the chair down, he came after her. "Marry me, Fayre."

She stumbled back, distancing herself from him and his unexpected proposal. "W-what? No, you do not want to marry me."

"I don't?" He studied her through his lowered lashes. "There is an enraged father beyond the door preparing to separate my head from my body at first opportunity. Why would I risk my life?"

Her mind was blank. "Pride?"

He lightly caressed her face. "I risk everything because without you I have nothing."

"You exaggerate, sir," she protested, backing away. "You may have a fondness for me, enjoy our lovemaking, but I am not the woman you seek to marry."

There was a flash of pain in his gray eyes. "You still do not trust me."

It troubled her to see that she had hurt him. Maccus did not understand that she had to protect herself. She had fought her feelings for him for so long because they bared her soul and gave him the power to shatter her. "It is not about trust. Maccus, despite your attempts to keep your past hidden, I have come to understand you. You are arrogant, ruthless, and ambitious."

He sighed resignedly. "They are not very noble qualities."

"I disagree." She took up his hand and frowned, noticing the bloodied nicks and scratches. "You needed strength to escape the shackles of a dark dangerous past I cannot even begin to fathom. I can admire that part of you."

His gaze felt like a caress as it moved over her face. "I will never be completely free of my past, Fayre, though God knows I've tried. My father and brother will always remind me that the life I have built for myself here is an illusion."

Fayre placed light kisses on his superficial wounds. "It is not an illusion, Maccus. You became the man you desired to be. You have found a place in the polite world; have earned respect and admiration from your new friends. Within you I have discovered more compassion and honor than could ever be found in a dozen Lord Standishes. You just have to learn to reconcile that Mac the smuggler also resides in you."

Maccus's fingers tightened around her hand. "Is that why you won't marry me? You can't accept my less than noble past?"

"No. Your past does not trouble me," she replied truthfully.

"Then it is my family that you can't bear."

Hours earlier she had stood almost in the exact spot while his father waved a pistol in her direction. She was certain he was harmless. At least he had threatened her with an unloaded weapon. "I like Trevor just fine. He is young and needs someone other than your father to guide him. As for Seamus—"

Maccus pulled her up against him. Staring keenly into her eyes, he asked, "Will you have me as husband if I promise to keep them out of your way?"

"An admirable promise." She grinned at the sudden heated pounding at the door. "Though not very practical. Family has a way of intruding on one's life, usually uninvited."

He did not think her observation was humorous. "What can I say to convince you? I love you, Fayre."

Her heart flared to life beneath her breast at his words. It hurt to know she did not deserve them. She released his hand. "Please, now you are being cruel."

He circled around her and refused to allow her to walk away from him. From them. "I am being cruel by telling you that I love you?"

Maccus would not be satisfied until she spoke her fears aloud. "Yes, because I know I am not the lady you desire."

His temper blazed at her confession. "What nonsense is this? Not desire you? My lady, I have made love to you so many times my cock hardens just at the thought of you." As he rubbed his hands up and down her arms, his face softened. "I love everything about you; your eyes glazed with passion, the sweetness of your smile; even your tenacity when the odds are against you as they are now. Marry me."

She felt her resolve weakening. In defense she blurted out, "What about your perfect paragon, your virtuous lady, the one without a scandalous past? The one you saw sitting primly at your table and bearing your heirs? The wife you desired and have been discreetly seeking within the *ton*?"

Understanding lightened the harsh lines in his face, filling his gaze with hope. "Fayre, my love, you are everything I hoped for in a wife."

"I have a past."

"As do I," he reminded her softly. "We belong together. Marry me." He dug into his watch pocket and revealed the brooch he had given her. "On this brooch, I make a promise to you, Lady Fayre Carlisle. No man will ever love his lady as much as I do. Marry me, and make me the richest man in England." Maccus pinned the brooch onto the bodice of her dress.

Fayre stared up at his handsome face in wonder. He loved her. Not for her family or their influence, but just her. Even now, she saw the fear and strain in his expression because he expected her to reject him.

An ax broke through the paned window. Withdrawing, the head of the ax reappeared and knocked away bits of wood and jagged glass shards. Maccus instinctively placed himself in front of Fayre and the window. The Duke of Solitea was armed like a brigand with a cutlass in one hand and a loaded pistol in the other.

Keeping the pistol aimed at Maccus, her father stepped through the opening. "I have had enough of this idiocy. Stand down, sir."

Fayre had faced too many pistols for one evening. Moving in front of Maccus, she ignored his quiet, urgent order for her to remain behind him. "Papa, you cannot shoot Mr. Brawley."

His Grace snorted at her imperial request. "I disagree. If you move to the side, I can adjust my aim."

Maccus kept trying to move around her, but she held her position between the two men she loved. Undeterred, Fayre glanced sorrowfully at her father. "He has ruined me, Papa. I have to marry him."

The duke roared and in his shock inadvertently discharged the pistol. Fortunately, his aim was a little wide. The bullet missed Fayre and Maccus but put a sizable hole in the door. That was the fourth one destroyed that evening.

20

Sitting in her dressing room, Othilia read the missive that had arrived that morning from her husband, Lord Hipgrave. The earl was demanding that she return to the country immediately. It was the third such command she had received from him in the past fortnight.

"At the zenith of the season? The man is not only old, he is insane," she scoffed, tearing the paper in half and tossing the pieces into the hearth. Othilia sat down at her writing table.

She had not replied to his previous letters, and she sensed his increasing impatience. It was prudent to respond to this particular letter. Picking up her pen, she pondered what excuse she could offer her husband that would persuade him to allow her to remain in town. After all, she was having too much fun in London to leave, especially now that she had Maccus Brawley within her grasp.

Mr. Brawley was an unparalleled specimen of manhood. She adored his eyes. He had an intense manner of looking that had her toes curling within her slippers. The man made even Lord Standish, who had always been beautiful and virile in her opinion, seem effeminate in comparison. At first glance, Othilia had desired them to be lovers. However, she had refrained from acting impulsively. Maccus Brawley was his own master. He was not one to be led by his desires, nor would he permit a mere woman to rule over him. Handling him had taken delicacy and with relish she anticipated the day desire would overrule his instinctive caution and they became lovers.

Othilia stared at the blank paper on the desk and sighed. She could hardly explain to her husband that she was awaiting the lovemaking of another man. Perhaps she should write that she was still indisposed due to the complications of the miscarriage she had told Lord Hipgrave she had suffered. The internal workings of the female body were a mystery to most gentlemen. Since he abhorred speaking of delicate matters, if she worded her letter cleverly the earl would readily agree that she should continue her recuperation in London.

Then she could dedicate the rest of the season to Maccus Brawley. Soon he planned to cruelly end his brief dalliance with the Carlisle chit. Othilia was certain the grief and gossip about two ill-fated love affairs would send Lady Fayre Carlisle into seclusion at her precious Arianrod. The Duke of Solitea would have to face that his daughter had played the whore for his ex-mistress's lovers. Othilia planned to spread the dreadful news throughout the *ton* with Mr. Brawley at her side.

Later, when they were alone in her bed, Othilia intended to lavish her appreciation on the man for his immeasurable assistance in her revenge against the duke. Naturally, she would give up Lord Standish. As lovely as the man was, he was faithless and lacked the ambition she admired so in Maccus Brawley. Only last evening, she had overheard several gentlemen discussing Standish's abominable play at the gaming tables. It was only a matter of time before the Marquess of Pennyfeather cut his son's purse strings. An impoverished second son was positively unworthy of her attentions, she decided, mentally discarding her former lover without remorse. Her thoughts returned to Maccus Brawley. She wondered if he was a possessive lover? She squirmed in her seat just at the thought of him claiming her.

The blank page gleamed at her.

Tapping the pen against the inkwell, she grimaced. Lord Hipgrave would not be put off forever about begetting his heir on her. Othilia shuddered, recalling his last clumsy fumbling in her bed. She had actually praised him for his prowess, when in truth all she had wanted to do was be sick. If she gave him a son, then she would be free to indulge her whims far away from the old fool.

Othilia tilted her head in contemplation. Perhaps there was a way she could satisfy both her and Lord Hipgrave's desires. As she tucked her fist under her chin, her lips turned upward into a devious smile. What if she were already carrying Hipgrave's heir when she returned to him? Of course, she could not reveal her delicate condition until she had shared her husband's bed once or twice. It was positively wicked of her to consider birthing a changeling as the true Hipgrave heir. Though her husband deserved what he got for being so old and disagreeable. Othilia happened to know the perfect gentleman to sire the Hipgrave heir, too. Maccus Brawley was as ruthless as she was. She imagined if she confessed her daring plot to him, Mr. Brawley would enthusiastically dedicate himself to the task. The man had few weaknesses, but she had immediately sensed he was bothered by his own ignoble birth. The notion of his son being heir to an earldom would be a temptation few gentlemen could resist. Othilia placed her hand over her womb. Perhaps today she should seek out Mr. Brawley so they could begin their pleasurable alliance.

The door opened behind her. "I told you that I did not want to be disturbed," she snapped in irritation.

"Forgive me, madam. Lord Hipgrave said that he waits for no lady, especially his wife," her maid said, stepping aside for the earl's entry.

"Good morning, wife," her husband said gravely, looking about her dressing room. "I pray I have not disturbed you."

Othilia placed the pen in its holder and rose to greet her husband. She curtsied and kissed him boldly on the cheek. "My lord, this is unexpected. I just received a missive from you this morning and was preparing to reply." She gestured at the blank paper on her writing table.

The earl meandered about the room. "Then I have saved you the chore. I assume you were complying with my wishes and have alerted the staff to pack your belongings." He opened the door to her bedchamber and peered inside.

She suppressed a frisson of panic. Lord Hipgrave was acting suspiciously, as if he expected her not to be alone. "My lord, I have not recovered fully from the loss of our child. I had hoped to remain in London with your permission."

"It is with regret that I must refuse you, Othilia, though it pains me to deny you since you have suffered so for both our sakes."

She demurely lowered her gaze and sniffed. "I pray you will forgive me for my inadequacies, my husband."

"As I hope you will forgive me mine, dear wife. Someone reminded me that I have been remiss in my attentions to you. Cast in that harsh light, I have come to make amends."

The man lived in an uncivilized part of the country. There was not a soul within miles of the estate except for the servants. Had someone in town been corresponding with her husband? "Who has filled your head with falsehoods, my lord? You have been the kindest of husbands."

Leaning heavily on his walking stick, he waved away her protests. "It is considerate of you to spare my feelings. However, I am prepared to do my duty by you. I have already alerted your staff of our departure this afternoon."

He was taking her away from London, from the life she adored. "Afternoon," she echoed weakly.

Lord Hipgrave's somber features were resolute. "Once we have returned home, I shall summon the finest physician to examine you. A month of rest should heal the residual ills plaguing you. With the physician's blessing on your good health I shall return to your bed, dear wife, and endeavor to fill your arms with the children I had promised you on the day we wed."

Othilia wanted to stamp her foot in indignation. She did not want to retire in the country with an old goat of a husband. If he was planning to give her a month to improve her health, why could she not remain in London? She opened her mouth to propose such an option. Something in his level gaze prevented the words from escaping. Lord Hipgrave was staring at her, not with the blind adoration he had always given her, but with cold derision. Somehow he knew that she had taken lovers while in town. He was keeping her under a physician's watchful eye for a month to insure that she was not with child before he began filling her womb with his own.

A lump formed in her throat. "My lord, if I may explain—"

Her husband patted her cheek. "There is nothing to explain or apologize for. I blame myself for your careless ways, Othilia. A babe in your arms and a quiet life in the country will keep you out of mischief."

Genuine tears blurred her eyes. Her earl planned to keep her locked in a gilded cage for the rest of her life. Whoever had warned her husband of her faithlessness had been ruthlessly thorough in their revenge. Her life was ruined. Othilia could not help but wonder if Lady Fayre Carlisle had finally gained the revenge she had promised months earlier at Mewe Manor.

Maccus stood in the middle of the Duke of Solitea's conservatory contemplating his fate. He had slept little since Fayre had announced to her father that Maccus had ruined her. The duke had taken the announcement better than most, Maccus supposed. Instead of shooting his daughter's seducer, he murdered yet another door. The notion that his daughter had narrowly missed his blade and the shot he had fired had subdued His Grace's temper swifter than any explanation either he or Fayre could have offered in their defense.

Fayre came up behind him and covered his eyes with her hands. "What are you doing out here alone, sir?"

Maccus peeled her fingers away from his eyes and kissed them. "Is it not obvious? I am hiding from your family." He turned around to face her.

Fayre had probably gotten less sleep than he had. Regardless, she looked radiant in her morning dress of sprigged muslin. The duchess had returned shortly after Fayre's shocking announcement. He assumed her parents had taken turns attempting to talk her out of her decision to marry a commoner.

"You make them sound horrible, Maccus."

"Your father kept staring at me while we were all together in the breakfast room. He has a look that can put a man off eating."

"My mother adores you and has accepted the match. She cried for hours after you were settled in your bedchamber, but not once did she mention an extended tour abroad," Fayre confided, standing on her tiptoes to kiss him fully on the mouth. "Trust me. It is a very good sign."

"Your father is not pleased. I think he hopes I'll accidentally cut my throat whilst shaving, or get trampled by a team of horses."

Fayre laughed, her humor glistening like sunshine around him. "My father is harmless. However—" She sobered as a thought occurred to her. "You might want to avoid my brother until he has had some time to digest our good tidings."

After she had observed his meeting with her enemies, Maccus had feared he would never see her smile at him again. "Well, your proposal almost brought the house down around us," she said, recovering her mischievous grin. "Give him time and he will grow to love you as I have. Besides, I warned him that it would be best for the children if they were born on the right side of the blankets."

Maccus gaped at her, flabbergasted. "Fayre, are you trying to tell me something?" She suddenly looked fragile to him. Perhaps, he thought frantically, she should be sitting down.

"No." She batted her lashes coyly at him. "At least, I do not believe I am. Be that as it may, if you persist in continuing our nocturnal adventures, Mr. Brawley, children are the usual consequence."

She did not seem bothered by the notion at all. In fact, she was glancing at him in a flirtatious manner that always stirred his blood. "You do not mind bearing my children?"

Fayre fastened her lips to his. Lingering over the kiss, she wiped out any doubt he might have had. Drawing back, she said, "I forgot to mention a snippet of gossip Mama heard at the ball last evening. It appears Lord Standish has had a falling-out with his father. Something to do with his lavish spending and shoddy investments."

"Really?" Maccus murmured, feigning surprise.

Fayre nodded solemnly, also seeming astounded by the news. "Wagers are starting to appear in the betting books in many of the clubs around town on whether the Marquess of Pennefeather will rescue his son or if poor Lord Standish—and I do mean that in the literal sense— will be forced to leave the country."

She looked fiercely pleased by her old lover's fate. Maccus could not blame her, considering how indifferently he had treated her. "I also have heard some gossip," he said, cuddling her in a loose embrace.

"When did you have time to listen to gossip? Last night you were too busy flirting with Miss Knight"— Maccus groaned at the reminder—"having secret meetings with very bad people, rescuing me from your father and then dealing with him, fighting me, my father, and the house." She ticked off each incident on her fingers. "Did I forget anything?"

"You forgot the part where you agreed to marry me."

"Ah yes," she said, grinning up at him. "Definitely the highlight of the evening."

Maccus tweaked the tip of her nose. "That and not getting shot or stabbed." It was fortunate the duke wielded weapons as if he were nearsighted. "I did manage to hear some news that will please you."

She fidgeted with the folds of his cravat. "Oh?"

He thought of the anonymous letters he had had a messenger personally deliver to Lord Hipgrave. "Aye, my jewel. Someone whispered in my ear and told me that Lord Hipgrave will be collecting his countess soon. The gentleman longs for his heirs and they are not likely to be born if his lady spends her evenings cavorting with other gentlemen."

"The countess wanted to cavort specifically with you, Mr. Brawley," Fayre said tartly. The thought of Maccus and Lady Hipgrave together was something she still needed to recover from. "If the earl is clever, he will keep her pregnant for the next ten to fifteen years. I doubt I am the only one in the *ton* who will not miss the lady's conniving ways."

Maccus had promised to help Fayre revenge herself for Lady Hipgrave and Lord Standish's treachery. He had gone about it in his usual secretive manner, but Fayre seemed too pleased with the results to quarrel with him. In exchange for his help, she had promised to help him refine his rough ways and facilitate his entrée into polite society. She had kept her promise, and exceeded it by giving him more than he had dared to dream of. Fayre had given him love and a place in *her* world. He desired nothing else.

"About our bargain—" Maccus began. He lifted her high above his head and spun around, blurring the world and slowing it down for a moment. "Are you satisfied?"

Fayre raised her arms high, reaching for the rays of sunlight shimmering through the glass panes overhead. She trusted him wholeheartedly, knowing that he would not let her fall. "In your arms, Maccus. Always."